Beyond Fear

The Florida Wildlife Warriors
Book 3

Connie Mann

Praise for Connie Mann's
Romantic Suspense

"Heart-pounding excitement...left me sitting on the edge of my seat."—DEBBIE MACOMBER, *New York Times* bestselling author, for *Angel Falls*

"Charming, exciting, and thoughtful."—*Publishers Weekly* for *Beyond Risk*

"[Mann] has begun this series with a bang—lots of action, suspense, and twists and turns."—*Harlequin Junkie* for *Beyond Risk*

"An enthralling suspense that will keep you turning the pages."—*Long and Short Reviews* for *Beyond Risk*

Also by Connie Mann

The *Florida Wildlife Warriors* Series

Beyond Risk

Beyond Power

Beyond Fear

The *Safe Harbor* Series

Tangled Lies

Hidden Threat

Deadly Melody

Stand-Alone Titles

Angel Falls

Trapped!

For Lisa Blomdahl, who years ago invited an overwhelmed, exhausted new mom into her home more times than I can count. Over coffee and pastries, she offered the kind of love and encouragement that has lasted a lifetime. Thank you, Lisa, for loving me and my babies with such an open heart.

Chapter One

"That's it, ladies! Again. Left. Right. Left." Lisa Bass shouted encouragement to the seven sweaty women throwing air punches while they ran in place, their sneakers pounding the old gym floor. She picked up the pace, feeling the burn in her own legs.

The Wednesday night self-defense class she taught at the Forest Community Center had nothing to do with her job as a Florida Fish and Wildlife Conservation Commission officer and everything to do with helping women find their power. It was hands-down her favorite night of the week.

She should have cancelled tonight.

Exactly two years ago today she let her mama die.

Guilt pounded her like surf against a rocky shoreline, and the never-ending waves of regret nearly flattened her.

She rubbed the ache in her chest and forcibly shoved her guilt into a mental box to deal with later. She'd been accused of being cold and unfeeling, but the ability to compartmentalize and view things objectively made her a great cop. It was also the reason her mother had died alone. Helping these women avoid her mother's fate was the only thing she knew to do, the only way she could survive the guilt.

After a quick glance at their flushed faces, she jogged to the boom box and turned down the theme song from *Rocky*. "Don't stop, keep moving. Come on, ladies, you've got this."

Ranging in age from sixteen to fifty-something, most of her students had never done anything more strenuous than push a grocery buggy. Never mind fend off an attacker. "No collapsing on the floor. You're tougher than that."

She shook out her arms and jogged in place, ignoring the agonized moans and raspy pants because she knew magic happened in this close, windowless room, gaining power in fits and starts much like the lopsided, creaky ceiling fan overhead.

"I ain't gonna need no self-defense class, cause you gon' kill me right here," Charity muttered, but she didn't stop, didn't sink to the floor as she had the previous two classes.

Lisa stifled the urge to fist-bump the other woman and instead pulled out her best southern drawl. "Honey, we are juuust getting started!"

Charity rolled her eyes and laughed along with the rest of the class. Which told Lisa that two years after moving here from Los Angeles, she obviously still needed to work on her southern accent.

A glance at her watch sent a frisson of worry sliding up her spine. Shelley was running late, that's all. Just because she hadn't shown up for class, didn't mean something awful had happened. Lisa's LAPD-required counselor had warned her to stop catastrophizing everything.

Delilah Atwood stepped up beside her and quietly asked, "Is everything okay?" During a recent investigation, the feisty monkey researcher had not only impressed Lisa with her determination to protect her sixteen-year-old sister at all costs, Delilah had become more than an acquaintance. In time, she might even become a friend. She also happened to be fellow Fish and Wildlife Officer Josh Tanner's new fiancée.

Lisa wiped sweat out of her eyes with the corner of her tee shirt and debated how much to say. Apparently, her poker face needed as much work as her southern accent. "I'll be fine. Just a lot on my mind." She ignored Delilah's raised eyebrow and turned to smile at her class. "You ladies are doing great. Are you feeling more confident?"

Delilah glanced at her sister and then her mother, who remained a step apart, eyes averted. The older woman's overbearing, militia-leader husband and son had been arrested recently, and she was slowly finding her way. Just showing up here was a huge step. If only Lisa had been able to convince her own mother to—

Not now.

She smiled at two newcomers in their forties who fidgeted in the second row, looking as guilty as if they'd just robbed a bank. "Let's practice the self-defense move we learned last week, and then we'll add another, okay?" She had no doubt these two would turn the corner soon. Another week or two of classes, and they'd start standing up straighter and quit trying to be invisible.

"Patty, come help me demonstrate, will you?"

Compact and tough, Patty high-fived the hollow-eyed woman next to her, then sauntered onto the mat despite her pronounced limp, courtesy of her now-deceased loser of an ex-boyfriend. This wasn't the same woman who'd first slunk into class and hovered at the back of the room several months ago.

"Let's not get too cocky," Lisa cautioned.

Patty shrugged, smile wide. "When you've got it, you've got it." She propped her hands on her hips. "Bring it on, Fish."

When Lisa joined FWC's Ocala scrub squad two years ago, they'd instantly dubbed her "Fish" because of her last name, and it stuck. It wasn't the nickname she'd have chosen, but it beat "Bossy," as her LAPD Metro colleagues had dubbed her.

"Charity, why don't you show Patty how it's done?" She raised a brow and the other woman grinned as she swaggered onto the mat.

The two women circled each other while the rest of the class called encouragement from the sidelines.

When they circled each other a third time, Lisa barked, "Come on! Take control. If some lowlife corners you, they're not going to play Ring-Around-the-Rosie while you decide what to do."

At her strident tone, several of the women jumped and the room fell silent.

Lisa made eye contact with every woman there and motioned toward the mat, gentled her tone. "Your best chance to escape a bad situation is in those first few seconds, before the perp has time to think and plan. Don't wait. Use one of the moves we've been practicing and get the heck out of Dodge."

The two combatants eyed her for a moment, then Patty, the smaller, slighter, of the two swung her leg out, hooked her foot around Charity's ankle, swept the larger woman's feet out from under her, and took off running.

The class cheered. Stunned to find herself flat on her back, Charity shook her head as she accepted Delilah's help and slowly hefted her bulk to her feet. "Girl, you have got this down. Ain't nobody going to sneak up on you in a dark alley."

"Good thing we don't have any dark alleys out here then." Patty grinned as she walked back and bumped Charity's shoulder.

Lisa nodded approvingly to both women. "Nice job, both of you."

The other women applauded. Patty took a bow.

"Okay, ladies, take five. Hydrate and we'll get the next group on the mat." She had just taken a swig from her water bottle when Patty stepped up beside her.

"Shelley's not answering her phone."

Lisa's worry inched up another notch, but she pushed it down. "Did she say she was coming? Maybe Remy isn't feeling well." Shelley's eight-year-old was fragile, susceptible to every little bug that went around the elementary school. But it was the fact Shelley's husband had started acting weird lately that fueled her concern.

"She told me she'd be here, whether Brad liked it or not."

"That's not going to help," Lisa muttered, mind racing. She'd heard Brad was struggling with PTSD after his last tour in

Afghanistan and she worried he'd started using narcotics to deal with it, though Shelley insisted that wasn't the case. "Why don't you call her again?"

As Patty headed to her gym bag for her phone, they heard raised voices outside the Forest Community Center, what sounded like a man and woman arguing. Lisa called, "Stay here, everybody," and ran for the door.

"I'm coming with you." Patty was hot on her heels, Delilah right behind.

"Don't get between me and whatever is going on, understood?"

Both women nodded, and Lisa burst out the front door.

A kaleidoscope of images from her childhood tried to yank her back in time, but she shoved them aside. This wasn't her mother and one of her many "gentlemen friends." This was Shelley, and her husband, Brad Larsen, had blocked her aging little sedan with his shiny new pickup. The voices came from behind the truck, out of sight.

Lisa heard the demand in Brad's voice, the conciliatory tone of Shelley's, and...wait. Was that her own gran's voice? It sounded like her, but Lisa couldn't be sure. Was Gran teaching her quilting class tonight? She broke into a run and rounded the truck's hood, taking in the scene at a glance.

"Get lost. This is between me and my wife!" Brad shouted at Gran. As they faced off, Gran pushed Shelley behind her.

When Brad stepped toward Gran and reached into his sweatshirt pocket at the same time, Lisa didn't stop to think. She grabbed his forearm, spun him around and used his own momentum to flip him onto his back.

He skidded, cursing a blue streak as his shoulders hit the gravel parking lot. Before he could get his feet under him, Lisa rolled him facedown, yanked his arm up toward his shoulder blades, and leaned over him, her knee in his back. "FWC Officer. Keep your hands where I can see them."

He snarled and tried to buck her off. "Let me go. What are you doing?"

Lisa shifted her weight, dug her knee in deeper. "The more you fight, the worse this gets." She kept her voice calm, professional detachment firmly in place. She'd get mad later. She reached for the zip ties on her utility belt, only to realize she was in workout gear. No cuffs. And her weapon was locked in her vehicle.

Pounding feet sounded on the pavement behind her. "Larsen? Fish? What the hell is going on here?"

At the sound of Pete "Bulldog" Tanner's voice, Lisa bit back a sigh. Of course, he'd be here tonight, to see her unprepared. Josh's brother worked for the Marion County Sheriff's office and had recently been promoted to detective, which had bumped his know-it-all attitude from irritating to completely obnoxious.

Brad turned his head. "Get her off me, would you, Tanner? Since when can't a guy talk to his wife without some fish cop butting in? Or an old lady. Bunch of crap."

"You were not only yelling, you grabbed for my grandmother. And reached for a weapon."

"Weapon? What are you talking about? This?"

Before she could stop him, he shoved his free hand into his pocket and tossed out two pieces of paper. "They're movie tickets. Judas Priest. Let me up, for crying out loud."

Behind her, she heard Shelley gasp and Gran mutter something unflattering.

Pete's eyes flicked from her to Brad and back again. He scrubbed a hand over his face, muttered a curse. "Stay here while we sort this out, Brad." He inclined his head and walked several feet away, obviously expecting Lisa to follow.

Irritation spiked, but she stood and shot a glare at Brad. "Don't move." Then she stepped up beside Tanner. "Look, Bulldog— "

He interrupted, arms crossed over his chest. "What happened? Did he try to hit either of them?"

She didn't like being put on the defensive. "We heard the shouting all the way inside. You must have heard it on the basketball court, too, or you wouldn't have come running." She glanced at the cluster of sweaty boys hovering nearby, then replayed the scene in her mind. Honesty forced her to admit, "I didn't see Brad hit either of them. But he tried to grab Gran. And was reaching for what I thought was a weapon."

A cloud of Chanel Number 5 engulfed them a split second before Lisa's grandmother, Sunny Bass, marched up, her black biker boots crunching over the gravel. Eyes the same color as Lisa's blazed, her gray braid fairly vibrating with fury. "I had the situation well in hand, Officer Bass. I did not need you to come barging in."

Quilt fabric from the class she taught was tucked under one arm, and her other hand was fisted at the waist of her flowing skirt, her chest heaving under her peasant blouse. Despite the bohemian garb, she had the commanding presence of a four-star general. "Stay out of things that don't concern you."

Lisa leaned closer until they were nose to nose. "Your safety always concerns me. It's my job to barge in, if I think the situation warrants it. Family looks out for family. Isn't that what you've always said?"

Gran's eyes narrowed. "Too bad you didn't think your mother's safety or situation warranted your interference."

The barb dug deep. Lisa refused to flinch or look away as she absorbed the direct hit.

"Miz Bass, ma'am, what are you saying?" Pete asked.

Gran turned her back on Lisa and gave Pete her full attention. "I think those two," she waved a hand at Shelley and Brad, "have been through a rough patch, Brad especially, and they need our support, not official harassment." She swung on her heel and marched toward Shelley; Lisa's class had closed ranks around her.

Lisa let her go, sighed, then turned back to Pete. "Something's going on with Brad. Shelley says it's not drugs, but I'm not sure."

Pete considered, nodded. "Yeah, he's been squirrely lately, hasn't shown up for basketball night in about a month." Which, Lisa had learned via the grapevine, was a sacred ritual for his group of friends, who'd gone to high school together. "But that doesn't mean he assaulted his wife. Maybe take a minute next time to be sure of the situation before you dive in."

Okay, maybe she'd jumped to conclusions, but being chastised like she was a rookie cop chafed. Her chin came up. "I'd rather over-react now, than wait and wish I'd taken action." A mistake she would never, ever make again.

He studied her, expression unreadable. "Josh says you passed the lieutenant exam. If you want that promotion eventually, you'll have to control your impulses, think before you act."

At his lecturing tone, the only impulse she was controlling was the one to wipe that smug look off his face. Especially from leap-before-you-look Bulldog Tanner. Instead, she took a calming breath and walked over to where Shelley stood with the class and asked her to step away. Pete walked up beside them. "Can you tell Detective Tanner what happened?"

Shelley glanced at Brad, then sent Lisa a pleading look. "We were just arguing. Then we made up. Don't make this a big deal, okay? It's embarrassing."

Larsen's hands were clenched at his sides. "No law against buying movie tickets, is there?" He shot Shelley a warning look that made all the color drain out of her face.

"Bulldog! Look at my new elephant!" Eight-year-old Remy hopped out of Shelley's car and galloped across the parking lot.

"Remy!" Shelley started toward her daughter.

"Let me," Pete murmured as he intercepted the girl. "Hey, Squirt!" he scooped her up and swung her around. Remy's laughter rang out, a stark reminder of all that was good in the world. He settled her on his hip, even though she was too big for that, and Remy tucked her chin against his chest, totally content as she chattered about her stuffed elephant. Seeing them together, Lisa's heart softened several degrees toward the annoying detective. But then she remembered his condescending attitude.

"Remy, come here, honey." Shelley wouldn't meet Lisa's eyes as she said, "I need to get her home." Arm wrapped around her daughter, she started for her car. "I'll try to make it to class next week."

Gran laid a gentle hand on Shelley's arm. "Honey, why don't you let Remy spend the night with me? We haven't had a chance to bake cookies together in a while."

A twinge of longing slid through Lisa at the close relationship her gran had formed with Shelley, a local resident, when she barely acknowledged her own granddaughter. "You can't put that child on the back of your Harley," Lisa whispered to Gran.

Gran stiffened, eyes narrowing. "I wouldn't dream of it." She tilted her head toward the parking lot. "I was running late, so I brought the Caddy tonight." According to local gossip, Gran had accepted the Cadillac twenty years ago as payment for one of the racy boudoir paintings she did on commission.

As Gran put an arm around Shelley, the other woman's stiff shoulders relaxed. "Thank you, Sunny. You're so kind to me. Remy would love that."

Gran shot Lisa a look over her shoulder. "We women have to look out for each other." She turned her back again as she pulled Shelley in for a gentle hug.

Lisa's gut churned at another of Gran's endless reminders that Lisa hadn't done enough for Mama. Hadn't even tried, to Gran's mind.

Since she was right, Lisa couldn't argue. But the pain ran deep.

A quick glance at the parking lot showed everyone at the community center clustered outside watching the action. Not just her class and the boys from Pete's basketball team. The ladies from Gran's quilting class stood nearby, along with all the members of the county commission who'd no doubt – still and again -- been hotly debating the proposed safari rides at Dr. Castile's animal sanctuary.

She watched Tanner carefully settle Remy in Gran's caddy before he walked over to speak to his basketball team.

Lisa waited until Gran drove away, then stepped close to Shelley and said, "Why not go with them? Might be good to give Brad some space."

"Everything's fine. He's just had a lot on his mind. But thank you." Shelley swallowed hard, gaze darting to Brad.

Lisa wanted to force the other woman to go with her, but her hands were tied. "You have my number. If you need me, call. Day or night, okay? I mean it."

Watching the other woman drive away, her frustration built like a pressure cooker with no release valve.

What would Brad do once they were alone?

As he walked back toward FWC Officer Lisa Bass, Detective Pete Tanner realized two things. One, Fish was still vibrating with fury. And two, she had a body that curved in all the right places and made his mouth go dry. He was used to seeing her in no-nonsense khaki and a utility belt, not skin-tight workout clothes. He swallowed hard and reminded himself she was a colleague. Apparently, a hot colleague.

But she was also wound really tight, always sparring with him over something, assuming she knew best with her carefully thought out arguments. Just last month, Fish had spent considerable time at a Tanner family cookout debating the merits of ketchup over mustard on hot dogs.

Tonight though, she'd completely overreacted.

Or had she?

"Is Shelley okay?"

She shrugged. "For now."

He scrubbed the back of his neck again, cursed some more. "I'll keep an eye on him."

"Thank you, Detective Tanner. I'm sure that's a great comfort."

When she tried to brush past him toward the group of women clustered outside the building, he stopped her with a hand on her arm, unsure what to say.

She stared at him for a long moment. He dropped his hand and she walked away.

The disappointment in her expression gnawed at him as he walked over to Brad. "What the hell happened here, man?"

Indignation had Brad puffing out his chest, fists clenched. "Don't you start with me, Tanner. It was nothing. That fish cop just over-reacted."

Pete crossed his arms and waited. He'd known Brad since grade school. The man couldn't handle silence.

Brad glanced at him, huffed out a breath, then sighed. "Fine. I acted like an ass. This idiotic self-defense class Shelley's going to has me all worked up. She's got attitude all of a sudden and I'm afraid she's planning to take Remy and leave me." He swallowed. "I couldn't deal with it if that happened."

"It's more than that." They'd both served, but Brad had stayed in longer. He'd come back from his last tour different and seemed to be getting worse, not better. "You still seeing the shrink for PTSD?" Pete had fought his own demons, was still fighting them. He and their group of friends had talked about some of it while shooting hoops every month. "You've been skipping basketball night, too."

Brad wouldn't meet his eyes. "I've been busy."

"Doing what?"

"Back off, Tanner. Stay out of my business."

Pete studied him for a long moment, then leaned closer, aware of their audience. "I'm going to be watching you, Larsen. Very closely. You don't want to deal with your issues, that's your choice. But if I find out you've been mistreating Shelley, you'll answer to me. And if you touch Remy, there won't be a hole deep enough for you to hide in."

The threat hung in the air.

Brad's jaw clenched, but then he got himself under control and walked away. Pete watched him go, one hand on the badge at his waist. Memories of Afghanistan and Omar's family tried to intrude, but he shoved them away.

If he got this wrong, if he failed Shelley and Remy, he had no business wearing the detective shield he'd worked so hard to earn.

He turned and nodded to local veterinarian Martin Castile and the mayor, who stood apart from the rest of the commission members, watching as Lisa went back into the community center with the other women.

Pete herded the boys inside to finish basketball practice, but he couldn't concentrate.

Should he have handled things differently?

"Let's go." A beefy hand shook her shoulder.

Shelley's eyes popped open but she held herself perfectly still. Her back was to Brad, balanced on her side of the sagging mattress. She'd been awake for hours, listening to him mutter and throw things as he searched the house. His last tour in Afghanistan had changed him and he'd become a scary, angry man she didn't recognize. He wouldn't talk about what happened, with her or a counselor, so she couldn't figure out what triggered him. Instead, she'd learned to tiptoe around his temper. She calmly sat up in the dark room, heart racing, and tucked her long braid out of his reach. "What's up?"

"We're going frog gigging. Pack the cooler." Each word was deliberate and carefully enunciated, which meant he'd been drinking, heavily, while he ransacked their house.

Anxiety slid under her skin and she nodded past the bile rising in her throat. She'd once made the mistake of letting him know that the idea of spearing frogs with small, improvised pitchforks made her gag, so now he insisted on going whenever she ticked him off.

Which she'd clearly done earlier tonight.

She wouldn't risk commenting on the mess he'd made; she simply stepped over the broken glass and debris, making note of his bandaged hand. Twenty minutes later they were on the road in Brad's new truck – which he'd never explained how he'd paid for – their airboat on the trailer behind them. She glanced at Brad's hands where they gripped the steering wheel, the knuckles white as he muttered under his breath. He'd been acting more and more erratic. Secretive. Paranoid. Frustrated and angry. It felt different from the PTSD symptoms she'd researched online, but she couldn't figure out what was going on with him.

The small notebook she'd found filled with numbers and letters might explain some of it. But not all. Either way, something was very wrong. She had to figure out how to protect herself and Remy from whatever he'd gotten involved in. Thank God Remy was safely with Sunny tonight.

Once they reached the wooded lot his uncle owned at the lake, Brad launched the boat at the homemade ramp and then Shelley jumped into action, strapping the cooler in place, checking supplies while he parked the truck and trailer.

He stepped aboard and started the motor. She winced at the roar of the airplane engine and mentally apologized to all the lakefront residents trying to sleep at this hour of the morning.

Just as she prepared to step aboard, he hopped off and gripped her by the shoulders, fingers digging into her skin. Hard. She'd have bruises. "Where's the notebook? I know you took it. And don't lie to me. Tell me. Right. Now." He shook her with every word and spit hit her face. Shelley recoiled at the desperation burning from his eyes, the fury visible even in the moonlight reflecting off the lake.

She raised her chin, steeled herself. "I don't know what you're talking about."

His fist came out of nowhere and hit her square in the abdomen. She bent double and stumbled back, hand raised to block another blow.

"I warned you!" he shouted.

In that second, she read his intent and Lisa's oft-repeated words from their classes echoed in her mind. "Don't hesitate. Don't wait. Take action before your attacker does."

As he charged her, she raised her right leg and caught him under the chin with all the force she could muster. He grabbed her leg and pulled her down with him. He landed on his back with a sickening crack. She tumbled on top of him, then scrambled to her feet before he could come after her again.

Only he didn't.

Breath heaving, heart racing, she braced her hands on her thighs and studied him by the light of the moon. He wasn't moving. No moans, no curses. She stepped closer, but not too close. What if he was playing possum?

She tried to see if his chest was moving up and down, but she couldn't tell. She nudged him with her foot. He didn't stir.

Now what? Her heart pounded like a runaway train. Careful to stay out of his reach, she circled him, coming up behind where he lay. She sucked in a horrified gasp at the blood pooling under his head. A tree root stuck up from the sandy soil where he'd fallen.

Dear God, had she killed him?

She reached out with two fingers, poised to leap back if he tried to grab her. But he didn't move. Her hands shook as she set two fingers against the side of his throat, feeling for a pulse. Her own heart was racing so fast she couldn't tell if it was hers or his.

Panic tightened her chest and her eyes darted around the clearing, breath coming in heaving pants. What to do?

She had to get away. Grab Remy and keep her safe. Until tonight, she'd held onto the foolish hope that things would get better, that Brad would somehow turn back into the man he used to be. She'd started a contingency plan, but had been hoping she wouldn't need it.

A sound somewhere between a hysterical laugh and a sob escaped her throat as she ran back to the boat and turned it off. No more wishing and hoping. She had to be smart. She reached into the side pocket of the cooler and grabbed the notebook, raced back to the truck. Thankfully Brad had already positioned it to pull the boat out later, so she didn't have to turn the truck and boat trailer around. She wouldn't know how.

Her hands were shaking as she reached for her cell phone. She should call 911. What if he was merely unconscious? She had to get help.

Her fingers hovered over the phone, but she couldn't bring herself to dial. What if he was dead? She'd have to tell the truth and then she'd go to jail. Which would only be fair. Or maybe he was alive, but she'd still go to jail for it. No. She couldn't call 911. The consequences for Remy were too high. Her daughter would end up in foster care, doomed to the kind of horrible childhood Shelley had barely survived. She couldn't sentence Remy to that. No matter what. She couldn't.

She had to think.

Hands around the steering wheel in a white-knuckled grip, notebook tucked under the front seat, she turned onto the deserted country road, trying to keep the trailer on the asphalt. Headlights approached from the opposite direction and the driver flashed his brights in her face. "Sorry, sorry," she muttered, barely pulling the truck and trailer back into her lane in time.

She swiped at the tears that kept blinding her, trying to figure out what to do. Dear Sweet Jesus, she'd killed her husband.

Probably.

She was a horrible person. She'd loved Brad once, with all the passion an eighteen-year-old could love. But she wasn't that naïve girl anymore. He'd seen to that. She was a mother, and mothers had to protect their children.

Oh, God. I'm sorry Brad.

Shudders rippled through her and her teeth chattered. Her thoughts spun and tears streamed down her cheeks as she careened through the night.

Remy. She had to protect Remy.

No matter what.

She fumbled for her phone and dialed Sunny. She'd know what to do.

Chapter Two

Later that Night

Sunny Bass knew she'd needed a distraction today of all days, but tonight had been more than she'd bargained for. She unlaced her biker boots and stowed them in the hall closet, then padded to the kitchen and sank down in one of the aging wooden chairs she kept meaning to buy cushions for. Every muscle in her body ached, whether from worry or old age, she had no idea. The good news was that Shelley and Remy were safe and Shelley could quit worrying she'd killed her worthless husband. When Shelley had finally spilled what had been going on at home, Sunny wished Lisa *had* arrested him.

Sunny had driven out to the lake where Shelley and Brad had fought, prepared to call 911, but he was gone. That didn't mean he might not pop up somewhere like one of those terrifying jack-in-the-box toys, though.

She eyed the palm-sized leather bound notebook on her kitchen table like she would a coiled rattler. From what Shelley had said, whatever was going on with Brad centered on what was between these pages.

Lost in thought, she glanced at the calendar on the fridge and a sudden tide of grief hit her with enough force to bend her double. This is what she'd been trying to avoid all day. Without conscious thought, she slid her chair back and reached into the bottom cabinet for the bottle of Jack Daniel's. She stared at the glass in her clenched fist, having no memory of taking it out. Hand gripping the bottle, she forced herself to think. To act, instead of react. Still, the temptation to numb her senses, to avoid thinking for a while, tugged at her, hard.

If ever she had a reason to drink, this was it. She still couldn't quite wrap her head around the fact that Donna had been gone for two years already. Her daughter had always been so full of life. No one had argued when, at six years old, she decided everyone would now call her Dazzle. The name stuck, but over time, her dreams lost their glitter and reality became harder and harder for her to deal with. So she'd found other ways. Other people, who hurt her.

Sunny had let her daughter down and the regret almost choked her.

But Lisa had done worse. She'd abandoned her own mother completely and let Dazzle die alone.

That, Sunny couldn't forgive.

With gritted teeth, she put the glass back and shoved the bottle to the very back of the cabinet, ignoring the tremble in her hands. She should pour it out. But she didn't. She'd keep it for emergencies, she told herself.

Resolute, she filled the teapot and set it on the stove, flexing her fingers and forcing herself to take deep breaths. Even so, the itch to snatch the bottle out and pour it down her throat nearly overwhelmed her.

No. She would be strong. She couldn't help Dazzle—and oh, it hurt to admit that—but she could help Shelley. She grabbed the notebook, hurried into the living room and sat on the aging sofa.

She read the whole thing through, twice, and the picture that emerged had far-reaching implications. It had been written in some kind of code she hadn't completely deciphered. There were dates, and numbers she assumed were dollar amounts.

Were the groups of letters people's initials? Places? She thought names, but couldn't be sure.

What was Brad keeping track of, exactly? Her first thought was drugs. But she couldn't picture Brad being involved in that, no matter how he'd been acting lately. He loved Remy with his whole heart. He'd never endanger her by getting involved in something like this. Would he?

She should call Lisa. Even though Sunny had never had much use for the police, her granddaughter was a good cop. She would know what to do. But after the way Sunny behaved toward her earlier, she was loath to call her in the middle of the night.

Family looks out for family.

As she reached for the phone, the kettle whistled from the kitchen, startling her. Outside, a storm cell had blown in and wind whipped the trees, sending palm fronds clacking. Rain pounded on the roof, adding to the feeling of isolation.

She poured water over a tea bag and carried it back to the living room, set it on the coffee table.

She stepped to the window, standing off to the side and parting the curtain with one finger. No one would be out in this weather. But that didn't stop the prickling at the back of her neck that said she was being watched.

She'd been in too many sketchy situations in her lifetime to ignore that feeling.

"Don't be ridiculous," she muttered as she let the curtain fall and went back to the sofa. Her mind was playing tricks on her, that's all. As she sipped her tea, she studied the notebook again, tried to make sense of the neat rows.

She heard a thump at the side of the house and sprang to her feet. That wasn't from the storm.

Another thump. Someone was definitely out there. If it were Shelley, she would have come to the door. Or called first.

The only other possibility was Brad.

A chill slithered down her spine. She wasn't ready to give him the notebook until she understood exactly what he'd gotten involved in – and how that would affect Shelley and Remy.

Best to keep it safe. Just in case. But where?

On a sudden burst of inspiration, she hurried into the guest bedroom and snatched the stuffed elephant from the bed.

She heard footsteps on her porch, followed by pounding on the front door. She glanced at the clock on the nightstand. Three a.m. She kept a loaded shotgun by the kitchen door. She'd send him packing in short order.

But first, she yanked open the Velcro on the back of the stuffed animal and pulled out the voice box, then shoved the small notebook inside and closed the back, trying to stay calm and keep her wits about her.

The pounding came again, but this time it came from the back of the house.

The doorknob jangled and the glass rattled in the kitchen door.

Whoever stood outside was out of patience.

She raced toward the kitchen. She'd grab the shotgun, stop him, then call Lisa.

Halfway down the hall, she heard the door crash open.

Too late. She spun around and sped back the way she'd come to the breezeway door that led to her garage and studio. Her hands were shaking so hard she couldn't get the deadbolt open and the chain lock undone. A quick glance over her shoulder highlighted the shadow of a man in the darkened hallway, backlit by the living room lamp.

"Get out of here, Brad!"

His face remained in shadow but his build was all wrong.

Not Brad.

"Stop!" He stormed down the hall toward her, a knife clenched in his fist.

Sweet Jesus, help me.

One more try and she finally tore the door open. She launched herself through the doorway and out the breezeway and almost landed in a heap on the muddy ground.

Run. Don't stop. Don't look back.

Instantly soaked to the skin, she bolted across the open backyard, desperate to reach the tree line. Once she was under cover, she could lose him. Even in the dark, these woods were as familiar to her as her own house.

He crashed through the underbrush behind her. She darted left, then right, tried to leap over a fallen log and slid in her socks, landing hard in a puddle. Cursing her arthritis, she scrambled to her feet and circled around the shallow sinkhole she'd recently discovered.

His muffled curse and loud thump said he'd stumbled right into it.

It only bought her a few seconds, but she'd take what she could get.

Suddenly, the woods went silent. She paused behind a tree. Her chest heaved but she forced herself to take slow, quiet breaths. A wave of dizziness swept over her and she wished she'd thought to grab her heart pills. Where had he gone?

She leaned around the tree and scanned the area, listening for his footsteps.

Beyond the howling wind and pouring rain, she heard nothing.

Indecision kept her in place, poised to run again. But which way?

She hesitated only a moment, then gathered her strength and headed north, ever deeper into the forest.

A sound came from behind her, but she didn't stop. She just kept running.

Lisa woke with a jolt, heart thumping when she couldn't move her hands. Several moments of wild flailing ensued before she tossed the half-finished afghan to the floor, freeing her fingers. She huffed out a breath as she tried to slow her racing heart. The first streaks of dawn slipped around the living room curtains and a loud *meow*, followed by indignant tapping, sounded from the cat door in the kitchen.

She let out a long sigh and pushed to a sitting position. As her brain cells fired, last night's frustration came back with a vengeance. Bulldog's condescending attitude, Gran's well-aimed barbs, Shelley's refusal to trust her, Brad's snotty arrogance. But mostly, the guilt over her mother's death.

By the time she'd arrived home, she'd been spoiling for a fight, but given the anger was directed at herself, it was probably a good thing she'd been alone. When two texts to Shelley went unanswered, Lisa had driven by the Larsen place. All was dark and quiet, but her nagging worry continued, so she tried to burn off her frustration and guilt in her home gym. Had she really thought she'd sleep on the anniversary of her mother's death?

It was after four a.m. when she plopped down on the couch with her yarn and crochet hooks. She must have dozed off.

Now, another *meow*, more impatient tapping.

She dragged herself to her feet and careened off the archway in the living room. "Ouch." She rubbed her elbow as she stumbled into the tiny kitchen and squinted against the overhead light.

Meooooww. Tap, tap, tap.

With a yawn, she unlatched the little door. An orange tabby missing half an ear sauntered in, sat down in front of the empty food and water bowls and looked up with disdain.

Meow.

"Good morning to you, too."

Cat hissed as Lisa reached for the bowls and filled both. When she set them back down, Cat jumped back and eyed her warily, back arched.

"Really? Still? You're not even my cat." She started coffee, eyed the haughty feline. "I don't even like cats," she muttered.

The day she moved in, Cat had shown up demanding to be fed. Since she'd looked half dead at the time, how could Lisa refuse?

Mug in hand, she headed for the shower to get ready for work. When she returned to the kitchen, both bowls were empty and Cat was gone, the little door swinging to mark her exit. "You're welcome." She re-locked the cat door—no snakes or other slithery things were coming in while she was gone, thank you very much.

By nine a.m., temps were already in the upper 80s and predicted to go higher still. The Bimini top on her official eighteen-foot Sea Ark kept the sun off her as she patrolled the Ocklawaha River, but the humidity made her uniform stick to her skin like wet toilet paper. On days like this, she missed Southern California's dry heat.

After another call to Shelley went unanswered, she decided to check on her in person. As she spun the boat toward Tanner's Outpost, the radio clipped to her collar crackled. "Five-six-five-Ocala, this is dispatch."

"This is 565-Ocala. Go ahead."

"Someone just called in an airboat accident out on Chapel Lake and you're closest to that location."

Chapter Three

The familiar adrenaline kicked in as Lisa spun the boat around. "Do you have any more details?"

"Couple of kayakers said they found the boat crashed into a tree. No sign of anyone onboard or nearby. I asked them to wait until you got there."

Her pulse kicked up. "Ten-four. They give a location where they found the vessel? Registration number?"

"They said they launched at the boat ramp and headed left and had been paddling for about thirty minutes."

Lisa pictured the shallow lake in her mind. Most of it was more prairie than water, so it was popular with airboats, which could go where a regular boat couldn't. "I'm headed to Tanner's Outpost. I'll swap my Sea Ark for the airboat and head that way." Pete and Josh Tanner's family owned the Outpost, and they allowed FWC to store boats on their property.

"Let me know when you get there. Be careful, Fish," the dispatcher said.

"Always. Let me know if you hear anything else."

"Ten-four."

Her cell phone immediately buzzed with a call from the squad captain, which was unusual. FWC officers generally set their own schedules and reported to their lieutenant, in her case Hunter Boudreau, who in turn reported to the captain. "Good morning, sir."

"Morning, Fish. I heard the call and wanted to give you a heads up. I just tapped Josh for a Search and Rescue mission in Hillsborough County, so I'm switching things around. You'll take over as acting lieutenant until Hunter gets back from his honeymoon."

Lisa froze in surprise for a split-second, then excitement zinged through her. She fought the temptation to shout, "YES!" and punch her fist in the air. *Act calm. Professional.* She cleared her throat. "I, ah, thank you, sir."

Finally. It was temporary, but still. This was what she'd been working toward since she started with the Fish and Wildlife Commission. Her change from big-city cop to small town wildlife officer hadn't been without its share of adjustments, but she was ready for the next step. With Hunter's blessing, she'd taken and passed the lieutenant's exam and was awaiting her board interview. She wanted more responsibility. A leadership role. She knew she could do it, and do it well. She just hadn't expected the opportunity yet.

"I won't let you down, sir." As the words left her mouth, self-doubt slithered in like a well-camouflaged rattler. Would her single-mindedness get in the way, again? When she worked a case, she was all-in, no distractions. But that same laser focus was why she had put off calling Mama back – until it was too late. She took a slow, deep breath. She'd never make that mistake again. And if it meant she occasionally overreacted, as Pete had claimed, then so be it.

"I know you won't, Fish. Find that boater and keep me posted. And call me Ed. I'll text the rest of the squad so they'll know to expect orders from you." He chuckled. "You worked for LAPD Metro, for cripes sake. This job is a cakewalk."

She disagreed, though she'd never say that aloud. Things were different in a small town. Here, as an FWC officer, situations were dealt with up close, involving far more interpersonal interactions and shooting the breeze than she was remotely comfortable with. All that relational chit-chat was enough to make her break out in hives. And yet, she'd applied for the job and found she loved it. She taught a self-defense class. And was slowly making friends. This was her town now. These people were her responsibility. She could do this.

"You can count on me, sir, ah, Ed. I'll be in touch." She disconnected and started a mental checklist as she headed for Tanner's Outpost.

But first, she called Gran. It went right to voicemail, as usual, and she pictured Gran scowling at the answering machine. "Hi, Gran. Listen, I can't get hold of Shelley. I was just heading to her place when I caught a case." She paused. "I want to be sure she's all right. Is Remy still with you? I need you to humor me and call her, please. Let me know when you've talked to her, okay? Thanks."

It was a full forty-five minutes before Lisa pulled up to the ramp at Chapel Lake with the airboat in tow. Way out here, everything took longer. The remote county park consisted of a dirt parking area, a cracked concrete boat ramp, a porta potty, two rickety picnic tables and a bear-proof trash can. The kayakers who had called dispatch were nowhere to be seen.

Acutely aware of time ticking by, she quickly launched the airboat, but it took another twenty minutes before she found the vessel, wedged sideways between two trees about fifty yards from the banks.

"Hello? Anyone here? It's Officer Bass, Fish and Wildlife." In this part of the lake, the water was barely two feet deep, so she tied her boat to a tree, notified dispatch, and waded over, ever alert for water moccasins. She'd been told the venomous snakes weren't aggressive, but she had no desire to test that theory.

She kept calling as she studied the scene, but there was no response.

The two front seats had stopped the vessel's forward momentum, jamming it between the trees. Her stomach knotted when she spotted a ball cap wedged up against one of the tree trunks. There were three bright orange life jackets carefully stowed beneath the seats, two adult size, one for a child. *Oh, God. Why weren't they wearing them?*

She forced emotion down. First rule of investigating: Don't jump to conclusions.

When she found a cooler strapped to the boat, its jumbled interior filled with sandwiches, sodas, a juice box and beer, her anxiety rose further. The ice in the cooler had barely begun to melt, so the accident hadn't happened very long ago.

She did a quick search of the boat. Besides fishing gear, a colorful tote bag strapped under one of the seats contained towels, but no identification or driver's license, no car keys or cell phone. There were no registration numbers on the boat, either. Though that wasn't too unusual. Many of the locals didn't bother to register their vessels, claiming ignorance when questioned.

She cupped her hands around her mouth and called again. "Hello? Anyone here?"

Had whoever been on board just made too quick a turn, crashed the boat, and then walked out through the shallow water? Or maybe another boater picked them up? Either scenario would be ideal, but she had to make sure.

She kept calling as she checked in both directions, but found nothing to indicate anyone had passed this way recently.

Finally, she keyed her radio. "Dispatch, this is 565-Ocala. I found the airboat, but no sign of the boater or boaters. Three life jackets aboard, one for a child, but nothing to tell me who the boat belongs to. I'm going to do a circuit of the lake in case I missed them somewhere."

"Ten-four, 565-Ocala."

Most cops, Lisa included, didn't believe in coincidences. Just because Shelley had mentioned Brad owned an airboat didn't mean this was his.

Still, she called Byte, FWC's resident tech expert, and asked him to check if a boat was registered to Brad. If not, call the boat ramps and bait shops along State Road 40 and check if anyone had seen a family of three this morning. Next, she asked fellow officer Sanchez to grab another airboat. She gave him the GPS location of the crash site and asked him to dust for prints, see if they could possibly identify the owner that way. It was a long shot, but sometimes those paid off.

Then she called Shelley again. It went straight to voicemail.

Nothing from Gran.

The longer she was out here, the more her dread grew. She scanned the lake inch by inch with her binoculars, looking for a flash of clothing, a hat, anything, to lead her to the missing boaters. The memory of that child-size life jacket made her queasy.

Remy's face flashed in her mind, but she shoved the image away.

She was on the opposite side of the lake when Byte called back just before noon, voice grim. "No boat registered to Larsen, but Sanchez got some good prints off the boat and had me run them through the system. I just got a hit."

Chapter Four

Lisa's stomach cramped. "The boat is Larsen's?"

"Yeah."

Lisa took a steadying breath. "Call the sheriff's office, let them know, would you, Byte? Ask them to send a deputy to the Larsen residence. Make sure they didn't get a ride home and are eating lunch as we speak." She hoped and prayed it would be that simple, but her gut said otherwise.

"Will do."

She dialed her gran's landline again and got voicemail again. "Gran, I still can't reach Shelley and I'm worried. Brad's boat crashed last night and we can't find any of them. Remy's still with you, right? Call me as soon as you get this. Please," she added.

Her worry escalated when she called Shelley and got her voicemail yet again.

Several hours later, Lisa headed toward the boat ramp, worry buzzing under her skin like mosquitos at dusk. She was worn out from the midday heat, hungry, frustrated by the fruitless search and had a bladder threatening to burst.

When she stepped out of the outhouse, she studied the half dozen pickups in the parking area. It constantly amazed her how quickly word got out when there was an emergency. Folks had simply shown up with canoes, kayaks, and small jon boats, ready to help with the search. The fact that everyone knew your business in a small town was one of the worst things about living here. But on days like today, it was also one of the best.

Several Fish and Wildlife Commission trucks and boat trailers were parked to one side, as Sanchez and every available offer from the Ocala FWC Scrub Squad combed the lake. So far, they'd found no sign of the Larsens.

An unmarked sheriff's department vehicle pulled up and she steeled herself as Pete Tanner slid out and strode toward her. In a button-down shirt, sleeves rolled up on his forearms and a loosened tie, he looked like he belonged in a police promo video. She'd finally learned to ignore the way Bulldog's green patrol uniform molded to his muscled body. Now she'd have to learn to ignore his crisp, fresh-from-the-cleaners plainclothes uniform, too. It was most annoying.

He shoved a to-go cup from the Corner Café and a turkey sand-wich into her hands. "Figured you could use this."

She quirked a brow. "Why thanks, Tanner. I didn't know you cared."

He slid his wrap-around sunglasses up on his head and gave her a critical once-over. "You look like you've been keelhauled."

"Aw, Sugar, you say the sweetest things," she drawled, biting into the sandwich. His woodsy aftershave tempted her to move closer for an extra whiff so she stepped back, annoyed with herself, especially since she smelled like swamp mud. She clearly needed food. And caffeine, so she'd quit behaving like an idiot. "Thanks for lunch."

He propped his hands on his hips. "Have you found Larsen yet?"

"No. We haven't found Shelley or Remy, either." She raised a brow and saw him blanch. "Remy supposedly spent the night at my gran's, but I can't reach her. Which, by the way, isn't unusual. She hates talking on the phone and rarely remembers to take her cell with her. I'm hoping Brad and Shelley simply walked away. The water's only a few feet deep out there." She swallowed hard. "We've been moving the search farther out from the crash site, but it's like they just disappeared."

Pete stilled, then he said slowly, "Maybe that's what they want us to think."

She'd been too focused on finding them to even consider it. But he had a valid point. People disappeared in the Ocala National Forest every year, never to be heard from again. It was usually one person trying to start over, though. Not a whole family. Unfortunately, people died out here, too. "For what purpose, though? If they wanted to leave town, why stage a crash? Besides, Shelley would never leave without Remy."

Bulldog scrubbed a hand over the back of his neck, heaved out another sigh. "I would agree with you, but we have to consider all the possibilities."

"There is no 'we', Tanner. You know FWC takes lead in marine incidents." She kept her tone level, calm. She knew if she didn't set boundaries immediately, he would run right over her without even realizing it. When he opened his mouth to protest, she held up a hand. "Let's just deal with what we know. We can speculate – and fight over jurisdiction - later."

"Fair enough. Josh said he got pulled for Search and Rescue, and with Hunter still out of town, I know you're short staffed. My boss sent Marion County Sheriff's Office to assist." He pointed to the dive team, which had just arrived and was launching their boat. "Show me where you've already searched."

She wanted to bristle at his tone, but reminded herself he wasn't Bill. Her former LAPD partner—and the guy she'd foolishly fallen for—had manipulated and used her to hide his own agenda. By all accounts, Bulldog's agenda was the same as hers: find the Larsens.

In case she was wrong, she'd keep a close eye on him.

"I'll show you. Come with me." She walked over to greet the dive captain, then motioned Bulldog closer as she outlined a search grid.

She had her ear protectors in hand and was preparing to head out again when Casey Wells from the local paper sauntered over. He also carried a to-go cup from the Corner Café and Lisa scowled at Tanner when she saw it. Had Wells followed him here?

Behind Wells, Bulldog met her eyes and shrugged.

"Officer Bass," Wells said. "I hear you're acting lieutenant. Any news yet on our missing boaters?"

Lisa kept her expression carefully blank. How the man got his info so quickly never ceased to surprise her. But it was the gleam in his eyes that worried her. What did he know?

"There will be an official statement at a press conference later, but so far, no news." She crossed her arms over her chest. "How about you? Anyone call you with information?" Locals tended to call Wells directly, which bugged local law enforcement no end. Byte, and others, had tried without success to uncover his sources.

He shook his head, sipped his coffee. "Nothing yet, though I heard you identified the owner of the boat as Brad Larsen.

"I can't confirm anything at this time."

"Any signs of his wife or their daughter?"

"Again, nothing yet. News conference later. If you'll excuse me."

She turned to find Bulldog untying the lines on her boat. She stepped aboard, pulled on her life jacket and fired up the motor. When he joined her and reached for the second life jacket, she eyed him suspiciously. "What are you doing?" she yelled over the motor.

"What does it look like?" he shouted back. When he tightened the straps on the vest, she noticed he'd traded his shoulder holster for a utility belt similar to hers.

She pulled her FWC ball cap over her chin-length bob, tucked the ends in and pulled down the bill. It'd been drilled into her at the police academy that loose hair and ponytails were handles for a perp to grab. She'd never make it easy.

She slipped on her ear protectors, handed Bulldog the extra pair, and notified dispatch as she pulled away from the dock. The sun beat down on their heads and the huge airplane propeller whipped the water into chop. Bulldog sat in the seat beside her, too far into her personal space, but she wouldn't shift away. She eyed him over the top of her mirrored sunglasses as he handed her the coffee she'd set on the floor and continued sipping his own.

She couldn't get a clear read on him and it was making her squirrely. They both had a lot to prove and she knew he was extremely competitive. On the other hand, she couldn't dismiss the affection between him and Remy. Maybe the real problem was that she'd started noticing him as a man, not just an annoyance. She mentally rolled her eyes. She didn't have time for this nonsense. The only thing that mattered was searching their quadrant of the lake.

Binoculars in hand, they scanned every cove, bank and bush while more FWC and MSO officers canvassed the houses surrounding the thousand-acre lake, asking if anyone recognized the boat or had heard anything.

She thought they'd finally caught a break late afternoon when an older gentleman flagged them down from a rickety dock and asked what the commotion was all about. He claimed he'd heard an airboat making a racket about three a.m., five hours after things should have been quiet, mind you, and then just as he was drifting off to sleep, he heard what he thought was a tree falling.

Which might have been the crash. He had no other information. Disappointment swamped her as she thanked him and they kept going. It narrowed the timeline, but didn't provide any answers.

Where were they?

Pete eyed Fish's white-knuckled grip on the rudder stick and the way she scanned the lake like it was a ticking bomb. Her worry matched his own. Given the amount of food in the cooler—and the juice box— they were operating under the assumption that Shelley and Remy had been aboard the boat with Brad. Maybe Shelley had changed her mind about leaving Remy with Lisa's gran overnight. But if so, where had they gone? His department had sent an officer to Sunny's home and he reported that no one answered the knock on the door and the place appeared empty.

The water wasn't that deep at the crash site, but it dropped off in one direction and it was a good slog until you reached relatively solid ground in the other. Which was why Fish had another team searching the surrounding area on foot.

Pete shook his head. The whole thing felt really off, like they were missing something important. But he had no idea what.

He reached out a hand, ready to cup Fish's shoulder and tell her they'd find them, but pulled his hand back just in time. She'd think he'd lost his mind if he said or did something so stupid, so he gripped his coffee cup instead.

The need to shift away built inside Lisa. Bulldog was way too big and he was sitting much too close. But she could never let on that his presence bothered her. He'd jump all over any sign of weakness or discomfort. From the corner of her eye, she saw him open his mouth, then close it again, shaking his head. *Yeah, right back at you.* Knowing she wasn't the only one who was uncomfortable made her feel marginally better.

Up ahead, her attention caught on something in one of the many little coves along the lakeshore. She strained to get a better look. Not vegetation, but it didn't appear to be moving either. Grayish in color, it floated near the shore.

Bulldog yelled, "What do you see?"

She pointed off the starboard bow. "Not sure, but there's...something." She aimed the boat in that direction and pulled up alongside it, then cut the engine.

Her heart pounded in the sudden silence and she strained to see what was in the water. "Can you tell?"

He leaned over the port side, then glanced over his shoulder. "Not a person. Looks like trash."

Lisa's breath *whooshed* out as he used the boat hook to drag an empty plastic grocery sack aboard. Water had gotten inside and filled it so it looked like a person's back.

He pulled on gloves and inspected it, but it was exactly what it appeared to be: trash.

He bagged it anyway and they kept going.

Lisa's anxiety rose along with the late-afternoon temperature. "Come on, Brad, where are you?" she muttered.

The sun was getting lower in the sky when they rounded another sharp bend. "Hang on," Lisa shouted as she spun the wheel hard to port to avoid a huge tree that had fallen into the water. Pete rolled with the boat's motion, completely at ease.

As she maneuvered around the branches, he leaned forward intently, then grabbed the binoculars and pointed. "I see something."

She stopped the boat too quickly and it slid sideways. "Where?"

"Under the tree trunk."

Dread pooled in her gut as she turned the boat back in that direction.

Bulldog swept the binoculars back and forth, then stopped. "Crap." He leaned closer so she could hear him. "I think we found him."

She exhaled carefully. Some sixth sense had known it the moment she'd seen the flash of blue.

Bulldog grabbed one of the bow lines and when she got close enough, wrapped it around the trunk and secured it while she brought the stern alongside. He tied that off too, making sure their boat was secure before they did anything else.

She leaned over the side for a closer look and jumped when his hands came around her waist.

"Don't want you going in, too," he said.

She told her ridiculous heart rate to calm down and turned her attention to the task at hand. The body, presumably Brad's, was face down in the water, his back to them. The flash of blue was his tee shirt. Still, she stretched as far as she could to check for a pulse. "I can't feel anything, but let's get him in the boat and make sure."

Bulldog whipped out his cell phone and snapped a few pics before they set to work. Between the slippery tree trunk and branches that prevented access, the awkward angles, and the man's dead weight, they were both wet, sweating, and breathing hard by the time they maneuvered him aboard. It was clearly Brad Larsen and he was obviously beyond saving.

Lisa called dispatch and apprised them of the situation. "Have the medical examiner meet us at the boat ramp."

She let the dive commander know, too. "I need your team to keep looking. Work your way in this direction, since we still don't know if the victim was alone or if his family was with him." *Please God, don't let that be the case.* "I'll text you the coordinates."

Bulldog looked up from where he crouched beside the body. "It looks like he hit the back of his head. Maybe that knocked him out and he fell overboard and drowned."

"We're a ways from the crash site. There's no current in the lake. How'd he get over here?"

Bulldog stood and they studied the area around them. "Maybe a gator found him and dragged him over here and stashed him for later. But he broke loose and surfaced."

A shudder passed over her. "I hope you're wrong." She knew alligators did that with their prey, but doing it with a human was completely out of character. "Maybe he was flung from the airboat, hit a tree, and drowned."

"More likely, but still speculation," Bulldog agreed.

She covered Larsen's body with a silver emergency blanket before they untied the lines and headed back to the boat ramp.

He watched the activity from his kayak, ball cap pulled low, sunglasses shading his eyes, just a helpful local, part of the informal search team looking for the missing boaters. Damn, he hadn't expected them to find that idiot's body just yet. He'd counted on the gator he spotted nearby finishing him off.

Fury simmered under his skin. None of it had gone the way he'd planned.

He hadn't been able to find the "insurance" Larsen had boasted about either. Had the man been bluffing?

Not twenty yards away, that damn fish cop issued orders like a drill sergeant. He'd seen her do the same thing at the community center. Larsen had grumbled about how she kept an eye on Shelley, too, filling the woman's head with all kinds of nonsense.

The same way she had turned his girlfriend against him. She'd pay for that.

He paused as another thought occurred to him. What if Shelley had the so-called insurance? If she did, who better to give it to than her friend, the meddling FWC Officer?

The very last thing they needed right now was some determined fish cop asking questions, digging around making a nuisance of herself. Too much was riding on the big event. If he screwed up, becoming fish food would be a blessing.

But this could work in his favor. He'd keep an eye on her, get whatever evidence Larsen had supposedly collected, and then eliminate both her and Shelley.

It was genius. Two birds, one stone.

He stuck his paddle in the water, smiling as he headed back the way he'd come.

Chapter Five

It was almost sunset by the time they reached the boat ramp. Lisa turned her back on the small crowd and crouched beside Larsen's body once more. She pulled back the blanket and gave him another careful onceover.

No matter how hard she looked, though, nothing new jumped out at her, so she carefully covered him from prying eyes. Hopefully the medical examiner would find something they could use.

She stepped off the boat and almost collided with Casey Wells from the local paper.

"I take it that's our missing boater?" he asked.

Lisa crossed her arms and stepped sideways, blocking his view. "You know better than to ask that, Wells. Once an ID is made, we'll certainly notify next of kin first."

He had the grace to look chagrined. "Right. Of course, apologies." He looked at the body again, then back at her. "Brad Larsen doesn't do social media, I checked, but his friend Jason Holberg does. From a couple photos I found, Brad and his family enjoy being on the water. Do you know what the relationship is between Jason and Shelley?"

He waited a beat. "By the way, have you found mother and daughter yet? There was no one home when I went by their place."

Lisa blinked at the sly innuendo, determined not to react. Did Wells know something? If Brad suspected his friend of having the hots for his wife, that could definitely come into play. "If you have information that will help, let's hear it, Wells. Otherwise, let us do our jobs, and we'll let you know when we have something to report."

He shrugged like it didn't matter, but his eyes sharpened. "I just find it interesting, is all, that an apparently good swimmer drowned and the wife and daughter are missing."

She raised an eyebrow. "The medical examiner determines cause of death, last I checked. Not reporters spinning theories."

As he opened his mouth to respond, Bulldog stepped up behind them. "What are you doing here, Wells? You need to move behind the police line like everyone else."

Wells strolled back the way he'd come and Lisa narrowed her eyes at Bulldog. "I had him under control."

"Of course, you did." Then he raised a brow, grinned. "You're welcome."

She could never quite tell when he was being competitive and bossy or genuinely helpful. He knew it, too, dang him and his cheeky grin.

The newly hired county medical examiner arrived and Lisa greeted her. "Thanks for coming, Doc." In her fifties, Eleanor Ward had recently moved to the area from New York and still tended to move and work at the clipped pace common to city dwellers. Which Lisa hoped would work in their favor. Dr. Ward crouched down and did a visual examination, then shifted the body and pulled a wallet from the back pocket, slid a driver's license out. "Brad Larsen?"

"No question," Lisa said.

"Good enough." Dr. Ward peered at her over the top of her glasses. "You'll notify the family?"

Never anyone's favorite task, but Lisa nodded. "Yes, we'll take care of it.

As one of her assistants readied the body for transport, Dr. Ward assured Lisa she would get to the body as quickly as possible.

Lisa thanked her, then asked Byte to dig into Larsen's life and friends, including Holberg. She updated her captain and tried to contain the anxiety about Shelley and Remy that hummed under her skin. Were they still out in the lake somewhere?

After Larsen's body had been removed, she walked over to Bulldog, who'd been on his phone and typing away on his dash-mounted laptop. "I've got Byte digging into both Larsen's and Holberg's backgrounds. I still can't reach Shelley. Or my gran. I'm hoping she and Remy are out in the forest somewhere painting and didn't hear the deputy. Knowing Gran, she forgot her cell phone. But I'll head that way as soon as I can to find her and make sure Remy's with her."

She kept her tone even, unwilling to let him see the mental tug-of-war raging in her head. She was trying to balance Gran's need to live life on her terms against her own concern for her welfare, especially since Gran had Remy.

He rubbed the back of his neck. "Let's hope it's as simple as that. Better still if Shelley is with them, but in the meantime...Brad's parents moved to Arizona a while back, and there's one sister in California. I've left a message for the parents to call me."

Déjà vu hit like a bolt from the sky and Bill's words the day her mother died echoed in her mind. "Don't worry, Babe, you go do what you need to do. I'll take care of this." He'd taken care of it all right; he'd tried to destroy evidence.

Lisa yanked herself back to the present. "You do realize that's my job, right? This may be my first case as lieutenant, but it's a long way from my first day on the job, Detective." Obviously, no one looked forward to death notifications, but she would never shirk her responsibilities, especially on something this important.

He sighed. "I know. I also know FWC doesn't have to make as many notifications as the sheriff's office. Besides, I know the family."

"All the more reason to follow protocol." She kept her tone even, professional. She couldn't let her guard down or he would bulldoze right over her.

"Is it possible for you not to take offense at every single thing I do?"

"That'd be easier if you stopped trying to do my job."

A beat passed as they stared at each other. Then one side of his mouth kicked up in that lopsided grin, and Lisa found her own smile sneaking out.

"Touché, Officer Bass." Then he sobered. "For the record, I was trying to help. Let me know what you find out?" When she opened her mouth to protest, he added, "I'll do the same, of course." He sent her a quick grin, then headed for his car.

The man was going to make her crazy. But he also made her laugh at herself, even in the midst of a very troubling investigation. Which was saying something.

She was still biting back a grin when her phone buzzed. "Hey, Patty. Did you get hold of Shelley?"

"There's nobody here." Patty's breath hitched, like she was crying. "But-but, the place has been trashed, like there was a big fight. Broken lamps, shattered glass."

"Where are you?" she demanded, but she knew, even before Patty answered.

"Brad and Shelley's. After last night, I was worried about her and when I couldn't get her on the phone, Mama and I came out here. Shelley gave me a key a while back, as a precaution."

"What? You should have called me first."

"I figured you had your hands full with that missing boater. We both took our shotguns, just in case."

Oh, God. Just as Lisa opened her mouth to ask what she'd been thinking, Patty took another shuddering breath, then whispered. "I found blood."

Lisa drew in a sharp breath. "Are you both safe? Is there any sign that anyone is still there?" After Patty assured her the place was empty and she and Mama T were back in their vehicle, Lisa said, "Take a breath and walk me through it, okay?"

Her voice was calm, though her own fears for Shelley and Remy flapped around like angry birds. She shoved them into a box and locked it, just as she had when she was part of SWAT. She had to think clearly or she wouldn't be any good to anyone.

After Patty told her exactly what happened, Lisa instructed her to head home and said she would call her later. She didn't want her or Mama T to disturb any evidence or put themselves in danger if the perpetrator came back for some reason.

She hung up and saw Pete approaching.

"What happened?" he asked when he reached her, his face mirroring his concern.

"Patty hasn't been able to reach Shelley either, so she and Mama T went over there." She grimaced. "Armed with shotguns. Said the place was trashed. The deputy who went by there earlier never mentioned anything being disturbed. Casey Wells said he went by this morning, too. So, either someone was there after that, or you couldn't see the mess from outside the house."

"You should have told them not to go alone."

"Which I would have done had I known they were going. Give me a little credit here, Bulldog."

He huffed out a breath and stepped back. "Right. Sorry. How did they get in?"

"Shelley had given Patty a key. Besides the mess, Patty also found what looks like blood." Lisa worked to keep the emotion out of her voice, to keep the visions of her own mother's death at bay. Her focus had to stay on Shelley and Remy. "Do you know where Brad went after he left the community center last night?"

"He told me he was going to cool off and then head home. I need to get over there, take a look at the scene." He scanned the horizon. "It's too dark to search anymore tonight, so you might as well send everyone home. I'll head over to Larsen's place."

Lisa took a deep breath to get her irritation under control before she notified the dive team to call off the search for the night, though she hated to do it. But Bulldog was right; it was too dangerous to continue in the dark. Then she notified the rest of the FWC squad, instructing everyone to return at first light. She turned back to Bulldog. "As soon as I get the boat out of the water, I'll head to the Larsen place. I'll let you know what I find."

"With both Hunter and Josh out of town, now might not be the time to turn down help, Fish." He had his arms crossed, daring her to argue

"I hadn't realized that was an offer. I thought you'd simply invited yourself along to be annoying." She raised a brow. The Marion County Sheriff's Office and the Fish and Wildlife Commission often worked together, especially in a case like this. But he wasn't nicknamed Bulldog for nothing. And she still wasn't one hundred percent sure she could trust him.

"It was every bit an offer." There was that mischievous grin again.

Drat the man. First, he got her back up and then made her feel foolish for doing so. "Just don't get in my way."

He sent her a smart military salute. "Understood, Acting Lieutenant. I'll follow you there."

As Lisa drove farther and farther into the forest, first on pavement, then on one of the many dirt roads that crisscrossed the area, she gripped the steering wheel and fought the endless recriminations. She should have done more to insure Shelley and Remy were safe. Though Gran had Remy with her. She hoped.

But *woulda-shoulda-coulda* didn't matter now. They just had to find them.

Twenty minutes later, she pulled up in front of a little cabin that had seen better decades, Bulldog's unmarked car right behind her. Built of rough timber, the mountain-style building looked out of place in Florida. She pulled out her service weapon and held it down beside her leg as she walked towards the sagging front porch, eyes searching the area around the cabin for any sign of movement. Bulldog walked beside her, his weapon out as well.

"Shelley? Brad? This is Officer Bass, Fish and Wildlife. Detective Pete Tanner with the Sheriff's Office is here, too. We're just checking in, making sure you guys are okay."

They stepped onto the porch, but the empty feel of the place told her there was nobody there. She nudged the partially open front door with her foot. "Shelley? Remy?"

She and Pete exchanged a nod before they went inside. She went left and he went right, then they slowly walked through the place, clearing each of the rooms. It had indeed been trashed, as Patty had said. Broken lamps, overturned chairs, and a broken glass-topped coffee table littered the living room floor.

Once they'd checked under beds, in closets, and behind the shower curtain, they met back in the living room.

"This doesn't look like a search. This looks like somebody had a mad on." Lisa's stomach churned at the destruction.

"The blood Patty mentioned is in here," Pete said and she followed him to the kitchen. Broken dishes crunched under their feet. "It's not a lot, but— "

"Any amount is too much," she snapped, automatically reaching for the St. Michael medallion tucked under her uniform. Dazzle had given it to her when she graduated from the police academy, saying she expected the patron saint of law enforcement to keep her daughter safe. Lisa should have made her mother wear it. She took a fortifying breath, kissed it, and tucked it back out of sight.

They followed the small drops out the narrow kitchen door, down a set of rickety steps to the driveway.

The trail ended at the sagging carport, which stood empty.

"I'm guessing they left in Brad's truck, since it can tow the boat. But Shelley's car should be here." She pulled out her cell phone. "I'll add it to the BOLO. If we find either vehicle, hopefully we'll find Shelley. We also need a search warrant, ASAP."

She called dispatch and reported what they'd found, requested a search warrant, then called Sanchez and asked him to come process the scene once they had the warrant.

"I'll get a couple of our crime scene techs out here to help, too," Bulldog said.

"Thanks." She paused. "The more help the better." She ignored his raised eyebrow at her ready agreement, but they didn't have time for pettiness. She asked Byte to call the local hospitals again, see if anyone matching Shelley's or Remy's description had been brought in. "I need it as quickly as you can get it."

"Yes, ma'am."

"Thanks."

After she hung up, she glanced at Pete, who had called his people and now squatted near the drops of blood.

"Did you confront Brad the other night? Or did you just laugh off the whole situation, couple of women, overreacting?" The questions popped out before she could stop them.

He slowly rose to his full height and stood so close she had to tilt her chin up to meet his gaze. She didn't back up an inch, though fury shot from his eyes. "As a matter of fact, I told him if I found out he was mistreating Shelley, he'd answer to me. And if he hurt Remy, he'd never find a hole deep enough to hide in."

Heat raced over her skin as she realized she'd seriously misjudged him. Chagrined, she cleared her throat. "I bet that went over well."

"He said her going to your class freaked him out, got him worrying she was planning to leave him."

"So that made trying to force her not to come to class okay?"

"I didn't say that. He didn't say that, either."

Lisa took a deep breath. "Okay, what do we think happened here? Brad leaves the community center, not happy with Shelley. He comes home and, assuming the blood is hers, beats her up and forces her into his truck. Then what? They go for a boat ride in the middle of the night? That doesn't even make sense. If that's what happened, where's her car? And if Remy was with Gran, why were there kids juice boxes aboard?"

Pete paced away from the driveway and back. "I don't know. Maybe they keep the drinks in the cooler. We don't know whose blood it is, either. Could be one of them just had a bloody nose." When she snorted, he drawled, "Easy on the assumptions, Fish."

She ignored that as she studied the scene. "What if Shelley picked up Remy and they took off in her car and were never on the boat?"

"Also possible."

Impatience clawed at Lisa while they waited, but the warrant came through surprisingly quickly. They donned gloves and went back into the house. Lisa walked to a rickety desk wedged in a corner of the living room, drawers bulging with receipts, bills, junk mail, all shoved in willy-nilly. She rifled through everything, but found nothing that might help them locate mother and daughter.

Brad had been furious when Lisa intervened last night, and it made sense he would have directed all that anger at Shelley. She should have had Shelley spend the night at her place. Or with Remy at Gran's.

Woulda-shoulda-coulda.

She forced her attention past the obvious mess in the bedroom and searched through dresser drawers, the closet, surprised by what she didn't find. Usually, women kept boxes of mementos, baby photos of their kids, little keepsakes, but there was nothing like that here. Either Shelley didn't have any—or Brad had destroyed them.

There were no clues in Remy's tiny bedroom, either. It was neat as a pin, the faded quilt on the twin bed undisturbed. She hoped that meant Brad hadn't been in here. *Please, God.*

Lisa carefully checked the drawers, under the bed, and in the old trunk in the corner Remy used as a toy box, her pace fast but thorough. The longer the two were missing, the less likely they'd be found alive. Had they survived the crash only to drown trying to get back to shore? She squeezed her eyes shut.

"Find anything?" Pete asked from behind her.

She shook her head, but didn't turn, blinking back tears she wouldn't allow herself to shed. "Everything is here except Remy's stuffed elephant. All Remy's clothes. There's no sign Shelley packed anything."

He stepped around the bed. "Are you crying?"

Lisa snorted. "Like that ever helped anybody. I need to call— "

He stepped in front of her and tipped her chin up. "We're going to find them. We won't quit until we do."

Shock at the compassion in his brown eyes held her motionless for a heartbeat before she stepped away, cleared her throat. *Keep things professional.* "Of course, we'll find them."

A vehicle approached and they hurried toward the door, peeking through the curtains to see who it was. A late-model pickup barreled down the driveway and a thirty-something man leaped out almost before it came to a complete stop.

He ran up onto the porch and pounded on the door frame. "Shelley? You here?"

Lisa and Pete exchanged glances before Lisa stepped into the doorway, her weapon at her side. "Who are you?"

He was about Brad's age, only thinner and lanky, but clearly in a panic. "Who are you? Where's Shelley? I just heard Brad didn't show up for work."

"I'm Officer Bass, Fish and Wildlife. This is Detective Tanner, sheriff's office. Where does Brad work?"

"He's a driver for UPS. Makes deliveries all over town."

Lisa kept her tone even, merely curious. "Why would that make you rush over here? Are you a friend of the family?"

He paused, glanced away. "I'm Jason Holberg. I've known Shelley since high school. I heard what happened last night at the community center." He eyed Pete, who didn't respond. Then his eyes widened in horror as he registered the destruction beyond the open doorway. "What happened here?"

She and Bulldog exchanged glances. Lisa stepped closer to Jason, while Pete took up a post by the railing, letting her take the lead. Progress. She'd take it. "That's what we're trying to figure out. When was the last time you talked to Shelley?"

"Two days ago. I didn't get a chance to check in yesterday, but then today I heard..."

She waited, but he didn't say anything else. "How does Brad feel about your friendship with Shelley?"

Jason stiffened like she'd poked him with a stick. "Don't make it sound like there's something going on here that isn't. We're friends. No more. I don't like the way he's been acting lately, so I keep an eye on Shelley and Remy."

Which Lisa figured was man-speak for, "I have a thing for her and I don't want Brad to know."

"How has he been acting? Is he abusive to her or Remy?"

Jason propped his hands on his hips. "Shelley won't admit to anything, but I have my suspicions. Mostly, he's being unpredictable and that makes me nervous."

She and Pete exchanged another look. "Where does Brad launch his airboat?"

The question seemed to surprise him. "I'm not sure. I know he uses it to go fishing. Sometimes just joyriding. Why?"

"We found his airboat in Chapel Lake this morning, lunch in the cooler."

Jason paled and swallowed hard. "Were Shelley and Remy with him?"

"We are assuming they were, and are trying to find them." Lisa studied Jason, watching the wheels turn in his head. "Do you have any idea where Shelley might have gone if she didn't want to be found?"

Jason's eyes widened as her meaning sank in. "I have no idea." He shoved a hand through his hair, paced the porch. "They have to be okay," he muttered, almost to himself.

She hoped so too, with everything in her. She asked him for his contact info, then handed him her card. "If you hear from Shelley or you think of anything that might help us find her, call me. Day or night."

"Will you do the same for me? Let me know they're all right?"

When Lisa nodded, Jason walked back to his truck without another word, looking completely shaken.

"You think she and Remy walked away from the boat and took the opportunity to get out of town?" Pete asked.

"That's what I'm hoping."

"Dive team hasn't searched the whole lake yet," he reminded her.

She stifled a shudder. "I know. I'm hoping we find them before that's necessary."

"You know her better than I do. Would she have notified someone that she was okay?" he asked.

"Byte is looking into Brad's and Shelley's backgrounds, their social media accounts, looking for friends we can contact. Since I haven't heard from Gran, I'm going there next." She looked up as Sanchez and the MCSO techs arrived to process the scene. "I'm also going to follow up with Patty and Mama T, see if there's anything else they can tell me."

Pete read an incoming text, then tucked his phone away. "Call me if there's any news. I need to interview a witness on another case."

"Don't worry, we'll try to muddle along without you."

His mouth kicked up in that half-smile and he shook his head. But as he turned to go, he gave her shoulder a reassuring squeeze. An unexpected little shiver passed over her skin and she automatically shook it off.

Oh, no. There would be no shivering, unexpected or otherwise, around Bulldog. Sheesh. She climbed into her pickup and headed back into the forest.

She had far more important things to think about.

Chapter Six

Pete backed out of the driveway, still shaking his head. What was it about that woman? She challenged his thinking and annoyed him every single time he saw her. She also made him laugh with her cheeky comebacks and quick wit. But it was the tears she'd tried to hide that had undone him. He'd almost pulled her into his arms before his brain kicked in. Which would have been colossally stupid. To say nothing of completely unprofessional.

Focus, Tanner. The picture emerging of Brad didn't match what he'd observed and that gnawed at him and brought memories of Omar to mind. He'd completely misread him, too. The man had been terrified and trying to enlist Pete's help, and he'd missed all the signs until it was too late. He slammed a hand on the steering wheel. He was a detective. If his instincts about people were that unreliable, Fish had every right to distrust his opinion. Hell, it made him distrust his own.

What are the facts? There weren't many. Just possibilities to check out. Given the contents of the cooler, it made sense that the family had gone out on the boat together. But Shelley's car was missing and Remy supposedly spent the night with Sunny Bass. So where were they? And where was Larsen's truck and trailer?

Was Fish right? Had Shelley survived the crash and taken the opportunity to leave town with Remy? He hoped so, because the possibility that they were still out in the lake somewhere waiting for rescue made his heart hurt. The look on Remy's face as she'd chattered about her stuffed elephant hardened his resolve.

"I'll find you, honey. Stay safe."

He turned left at another forest road and looked up in surprise. A gold Lexus sat by the side of the road, trunk open, a guy by the left back tire jumping up and down on a tire iron, trying to loosen the lug nuts. He was wearing dress pants, a button-down shirt, and a tie.

Pete let dispatch know what he was doing, pulled in behind him, and left his headlights on as he climbed out of the car. He looked into the trunk as he approached, saw a centerfire rifle lying there. The man straightened, alarm crossing his features as Pete pulled out his badge. He rushed over and slammed the trunk shut.

Too late, pal. "How are you doing? I'm Detective Tanner, Marion County Sheriff's Office. Looks like the lug nuts are giving you some trouble."

The fifty-ish man tried to look calm. He pushed his thick glasses up on his nose and shook his head, sweat glistening on his bald spot. "Haven't changed a tire in decades. Can't get the dang lug nuts off."

Pete nodded. "If they tighten them by machine, nothing but a machine is going to get them off. Might want to call Triple-A."

"I'm kind of in a hurry, so I was trying to save time."

"I noticed you have a centerfire rifle in the trunk. Mind if I ask what you were doing with it?"

The man shrugged. "Wasn't doing anything. Just taking it home after a weekend with family."

Pete leaned closer, noticed a tuft of fur or hair protruding from the seam of the trunk lid.

The man's eyes darted around and Pete went on alert. If the guy planned to try something stupid, now would be the time. "Keep your hands where I can see them, sir." Then he snapped a picture of the trunk with his phone. "That looks like animal hair. Care to tell me where it came from?" Pete leaned closer, studied the strands.

"My wife took the cat to the vet recently." He shrugged. "Princess doesn't like the car carrier."

Uh, huh. "Please wait here, Sir." Pete kept his eyes on the man as he returned to his vehicle and ran the plates. Mr. Santiani had a Miami address, no outstanding warrants, no priors. No guns registered to him.

Pete stepped out of his car, and turned back to the man. "Unfortunately, Mr. Santiani, I'm going to have to confiscate that weapon."

The man's eyebrows shot almost to his receding hairline. "Seriously? Why?"

Pete kept his hands in reach of his weapon, alert. "Because you don't have a permit for it." He paused. "Florida Fish and Wildlife Commission will also be curious about the fur in your trunk."

Santiani chewed the inside of his cheek, then blurted, "I was hunting, okay? I got a deer. It wasn't a big deal."

"Deer season isn't until the fall." Pete narrowed his eyes. "But I'm guessing you know that. I'll need to call FWC and they'll issue you a citation. Can you tell me where you left the deer carcass? We'll make sure a needy family gets the meat."

Santiani pointed vaguely into the forest. "I really don't know. That way, I think." Then a speculative look came into his eyes. "How much would it take for you to forget all this?" He pulled out a wallet and Pete whistled at the number of hundreds he held out. "Will that do it?"

Pete sighed. "You just went from several citations to attempting to bribe an officer of the law, Mr. Santiani. I'm afraid you're going to be much later than you expected."

Santiani's jaw dropped open. "You're kidding, right? I'll double it, no problem. I just really need to get going. Come on, what's it going to take?"

Pete shook his head. The guy was clueless. He Mirandized him, loaded him up, and then took a sample of the fur for FWC.

But the entire drive into Ocala he wondered what an obviously wealthy Miami resident—given the size of the diamonds in both pinky rings—was doing in the Ocala National Forest, in a Lexus, with fur and a centerfire rifle, when it wasn't hunting season?

Lisa drove to Gran's, increasingly aware of just how isolated the place was. Her house sat in the middle of ten wooded acres in the Ocala National Forest just off a two-lane road. Lisa glimpsed the nearest neighbor's security light as she passed, but after that, nothing.

Without the ambient light of populated areas and with the tree canopy overhead, it was darker than dark. She flipped on her brights, surprising an armadillo who was scurrying across the cracked asphalt.

The twinge of anxiety she'd fought all day clamped down harder when Lisa pulled into the gravel drive and found the house dark, except for the yellow glow of the front porch light. She studied the scene a moment before she slipped out of her pickup. The blinds were closed, as was the overhead door on the detached garage. The light in the covered walkway connecting the two was not on.

She knocked on the front door. "Gran? You home? I need to talk to you."

No sounds came from inside. She stepped to the living room window, but couldn't see past the blinds. No light came from anywhere inside. "Gran?"

She dialed Gran's landline and heard it ringing from inside. Then she tried her cell. Same thing. *Dang it, why wouldn't she take her cell with her when she went somewhere?*

The front door was locked, so Lisa scanned the careful chaos of the flower bed and its well-placed rocks. "Got it," she muttered, picking up a fake rock and sliding open the false bottom. She plucked out the spare key Gran had kept there since Lisa was a little girl and unlocked the door. If Gran didn't like it, she could finally give her a key.

Lisa pulled her service weapon from its holster and kept it down next to her leg as she eased the door open, then flicked on her Maglite with her other hand. "Gran, it's me. I'm coming in."

A quick search confirmed the house was empty, no sign of either Gran or Remy, injured or otherwise, thank goodness. Relieved, she went back through and turned on the lights.

Where had they gone?

She started with the small guest room, surprised when she didn't see anything of Remy's. There should have been clothes, shoes, something. Lisa spotted the stuffed elephant on the bed. At first glance, she thought it was Remy's, but a closer look brought an old memory crashing back. This was her old toy, one she'd loved as a child. When Mama took them to California when Lisa was six, she'd left the elephant with Gran, her childish way of insuring they'd come back to Florida. They hadn't, but the fact Gran had kept it anyway made her breath hitch. She pressed its stomach to see if it would trumpet like when she was little. Sadly, it didn't, but just holding it made her smile.

She set it carefully back on the bed and went to Gran's home office next. An antiquated computer with a huge monitor sat on the desk. Several of the desk drawers were slightly open, but Lisa didn't know if that meant anything. Nothing seemed out of place.

Gran's bedroom was a study in contrasts. The bed was unmade, the flowered comforter half on the floor, ruffled throw pillows strewn about. In contrast, all her skirts and blouses hung neatly in the closet, her shoes lined up on the closet floor.

A quick scan of the kitchen and living room showed more partially opened drawers and disturbed pillows, but did that mean Gran wasn't a fastidious housekeeper or that someone had searched the place? It hurt her heart that she didn't know the answer, since she'd been inside only a handful of times. If someone had searched the house, what were they looking for?

She checked the key rack by the kitchen door before heading for the sub-divided two-car garage. No keys.

She crossed the breezeway. Gran's aging Caddy sat in its usual spot, but her Harley wasn't there. Had she simply gone for a drive? But where was Remy? She'd told Lisa last night she'd never put a child on the back of her Harley. Unless she made an exception? She could never predict what her gran would do.

Tears clogged her throat and she swallowed hard. Gran used to be her rock, her safe place, the one person she could always count on to love her unconditionally. California, and then Dazzle's death, had changed everything and she didn't know how to make things right.

Lisa went into the other side of the garage, which Gran had turned into her studio, hoping for some clue. Gran had installed large windows, though she did most of her painting outdoors, weather permitting. Canvasses were stacked against one wall, several others propped on easels, in various stages of progress. Lisa glanced at a finished one and blushed at the woman's seductive pose, nearly-naked state and Cheshire cat smile. She'd never be able to greet her at church again without remembering how she looked here.

Bypassing the table littered with jars and tubes of paint, she flipped through the stacked canvasses. Surprised, she pulled out a smaller one, barely eight by ten, showing Gran with Janet Phillips, wife of local horse farm owner Gene Phillips, their arms around each other, grinning over some private joke. She hadn't even realized they were friends, especially since the Phillips' were decades younger. But then, there was a lot about Gran's life she knew nothing about.

Lisa pulled out her cell phone, found the number online, and dialed. "Good evening, Mrs. Phillips. This is Lisa Bass, Sunny's granddaughter. I'm trying to reach my gran."

The other woman laughed. "Well good luck with that. Your gran prides herself on being unreachable – unless she wants to be reached. She never remembers to take her cell phone anywhere. Drives me crazy."

"I know," Lisa said. "I didn't know you two were friends until I saw a painting of the two of you."

"Oh, we've known each other for years. We met at the library and have served on lots of committees together."

"I've been trying to reach her all day. Her cell phone is here. So is her Caddy. But not her Harley. Any idea where I should check?"

She laughed. "Oh, then, she went for a drive. She'll be back sooner or later."

"It's pretty late to be on a Harley, isn't it?"

"Insomnia is one of the curses of getting older. Sunny says riding in the evening helps her sleep."

Lisa decided this was not the time to play things close to the vest. "You heard we found Brad Larsen's boat out in Chapel Lake today?"

"I did. I heard you found a body, too, and were still looking for Brad's wife and daughter. Did you find them?"

"Not yet. But Remy, their daughter, supposedly stayed with Gran last night."

"Oh, that's a relief. I'm glad she's safe. But what about her mother?"

"That's the thing. I can't find any evidence that Remy was here. And there's been no trace of Shelley, her mother."

She heard the woman's sharp intake of breath. "That doesn't make any sense."

"Not yet, no. I'm trying to figure out what's happened. Would Gran take a child for a ride on her Harley?"

A long pause. "I'd like to say absolutely not, but I can't. The one thing I've always known about your grandmother is that she does her own thing. I can totally see her wanting to give that child a thrill and heading off on the back roads with her."

Lisa sighed. She could, too. "Thanks for your help. Would you let me know when you hear from Sunny?"

"Of course. You do the same, you hear?"

Lisa went back outside and did a circuit of the backyard, but after the rain last night, there were no tracks, nothing to indicate Gran – or anyone else – had been anywhere near her house.

She pulled out her cell phone as she climbed into her truck. "Hey Byte, I need a quick favor."

"Okay. Official or unofficial?"

"Both." She filled him in on what she had – and hadn't—found at Gran's. "It's entirely possible Gran simply took Remy for a ride. But on the off chance something else is going on, will you check security cameras, see if she went through Ocala recently? But, ah, quietly. I don't want her to know if it turns out to be nothing."

Byte chuckled. "I hear you. Family is complicated. Your gran especially."

Her cell phone rang just as she thanked him and pulled out of the driveway.

"Office Bass."

"You need to get over here," Mama T said without preamble.

"Shelley told you Brad threatened her?" Lisa asked Patty. She kept her expression neutral, her fury hidden, as she sat on the sagging sofa in Mama T's tiny but immaculate living room. Mama T sat in her rocker, Patty in a matching one beside her, hands clasped in her lap.

Patty's eyes burned with fury. "He told her that she'd better not be thinking of leaving him, because that was never going to happen. The only way he'd ever let her go was if he was dead. Or she was."

A bone-deep chill slid over Lisa's skin, raising gooseflesh on her arms. "Do you know when he made this threat?"

Patty shook her head. "No. When she told me last week after class, she said she had it under control. She had a plan."

Lisa's chill went deeper. "Did she give you any specifics on what she meant by that?"

"No, though I tried to get her to spill."

Lisa stood, hugged both women. "If you hear from her, call me immediately, day or night."

Once back on the road, she sifted through the ugly possibilities. Had Brad made good on his threat, killing them to keep Shelley from leaving? What if he staged the crash, but then something went wrong and he died, too?

It would be a satisfying kind of justice. It was also complete speculation and she hoped and prayed she was wrong. But after years in law enforcement, people's cruelty to each other no longer shocked her, though she had to wall off her heart to survive. Remy had smashed down those careful barriers. Worry for the little wisp of a girl shredded Lisa's heart.

She wouldn't stop looking until she found them both, even if it meant dredging every pond, lake, river, and drainage ditch in the county.

After she'd turned off County Road 314 and onto a less-traveled two-lane highway, headlights appeared in her rearview mirror. She glanced at the speedometer and automatically calculated the speed of the other vehicle. Based on the headlight height, she'd guess a pickup, and at the speed he was going, he should pass her before the next curve, never mind the double yellow line.

Only he didn't. He slowed and kept a steady pace, just far enough back that she spotted him after every curve. A shiver of unease pricked her skin as another car passed the truck, and then passed her, too, while the pickup stayed behind her.

At the next curve, she found a dirt road and veered sharply onto it, then stopped and counted off the seconds. The pickup picked up speed as it raced by. She waited another couple of minutes, then pulled back onto the road and continued driving.

When she spotted what looked like the same truck barreling toward her from the opposite direction, she tried to get a glimpse of the driver, but between the dark of the forest and the tinted windows, she couldn't see a thing.

Just to be sure they didn't double back, she took a roundabout route home and pulled into her driveway a full thirty minutes later than she'd planned. Doubts plagued her. Were they really following her? Or was she imagining things?

She sat in her truck and surveyed her property. The vapor light over the freestanding garage lent a yellow glow to the area. The porch light was on, as was the lamp timer inside. All looked as it should, but she still glanced over her shoulder before she went inside.

As she flipped the light switch in the kitchen, something streaked by her feet. She yelped as she jumped back and smacked her elbow against the doorframe. "Ow. Geez you startled me."

Cat stood in the middle of the floor and glared. Then she hissed for good measure.

Lisa rolled her eyes. "Right back at you, fur ball."

Meow.

"Yeah, yeah." She set down food and water, then leaned against the counter. Cat eyed her suspiciously and when she realized Lisa wasn't leaving, she headed for the food bowl, sending haughty looks as she crunched.

Lisa laughed. "I love you, too."

She suddenly noticed the open latch on the cat door and froze. Weapon in hand, she started down the hall, feeling slightly ridiculous. There was no way someone could fit through that small opening.

But she knew she'd secured it before she left.

When she returned to the kitchen and found the bowls empty and the little door ajar, she locked it firmly before she went into her workout room and pulled on her boxing gloves.

As she punched the heavy bag, her brain wouldn't shut up. She ran through every possible scenario of what might have happened at Brad and Shelley's, the whole gamut of possibilities regarding the airboat crash, Gran's disappearing act, Remy's whereabouts, and still came up empty, without a single clue to point them in the right direction. She punched harder, again and again and again, until her legs gave out and she slid down to the floor.

Once she stood in the shower, her mind suddenly turned to the way Bulldog had reassured her earlier. What had that been about? She'd seen his gentle side with Remy, but it was disorienting to have it directed at her.

None of that mattered.

Feet tucked under her on her sofa, she jotted down on a yellow legal pad every thought related to the case, in no particular order. Sometimes, just looking at the puzzle pieces from a different angle helped her see the pattern she couldn't find before.

The picture was still fuzzy. She needed more information. A couple of clues. Something.

Until she got them, the investigation was at a dead end.

Chapter Seven

Lisa was back at Gran's before dawn the next morning, but nothing had changed. The note she'd left asking Gran to call her the minute she came home was still on the kitchen table. The Harley was still not in the garage.

As soon as the sky began to lighten, Lisa searched the yard and surrounding woods in ever-widening circles. But there were no footprints anywhere, at least no human ones. Deer and raccoon had been in the area, but that didn't help.

There was no evidence Gran or anyone else had been in her backyard recently.

She called Byte as she climbed into her truck.

"Morning, Fish. I was about to call you. I got nothing on the traffic cams in and around Ocala, but I know your gran likes the back roads, where there are no cameras."

"Thanks for checking. Any news from our tip line?"

"Nothing worth anything." He let out a huge yawn.

"When's the last time you slept?"

"I'm good. I don't need much."

"You didn't answer the question," Lisa chided. "Okay, put out a

BOLO for my Gran's Harley, then go get a few hours shut-eye. Otherwise you won't be any good to anyone."

"Are you sure?"

"BOLO, then sleep."

"Roger that.

If Gran was merely out on a joyride, she'd be ticked off about the BOLO. But she'd deal with it. Better that than something far worse.

She updated her captain and issued assignments to the other officers as she drove back toward Chapel Lake. It wasn't a road she traveled often. She came around a bend and almost ran into the back of a slow-moving semi. What was it doing way out here? Seeing the bobtail—the cab portion—of a long-haul trucker's rig in someone's front yard wasn't unusual. Seeing one pulling a fully loaded trailer on these narrow back roads, was.

There was a solid double yellow line along this stretch, so Lisa couldn't go around to see the driver or get a look at the name on the door. The driver certainly wasn't speeding, and the truck was in good shape. Still, it was odd.

She was tempted to follow and see where it went, but she had other priorities. Her brain kept conjuring worst-case scenarios involving Shelley and Remy, but she yanked it back on course. She could hear her first police captain, Jim Barrett, endlessly reminding her, "Don't assume facts not in evidence." Cops, like anyone else, could miss the obvious when they latched onto one theory too soon and started trying to fit evidence to a theory, instead of letting the theory grow out of the evidence.

She couldn't assume Shelley had taken Remy and left town after the crash, or that Gran was out for a joyride.

When she pulled up at the Chapel Lake boat ramp, she hooked up her airboat and backed the trailer down the ramp. Just as she climbed out of her truck to launch the boat, Bulldog appeared. "Go ahead. I'll get the truck."

Lisa stepped aboard and backed the boat off the trailer while he drove the truck up the ramp and tucked the trailer out of the way at the edge of the woods. Once he unhitched it from her truck, he walked back over.

"I could have done that, you know."

He grinned. "Of course, you could have. You do it all the time. But since I was already here, you didn't have to."

She propped her hands on her hips, all her defenses rising. Every time Bulldog appeared, some ridiculous internal trigger pinged and made her want to smile and flirt. Or at least be nice. Or even more terrifying, move closer to him. No, he was a cop and after Bill, she'd sworn off men in general and cops in particular. She had to keep him at a distance. "Why do you keep showing up and doing nice things? It's not like you and it's driving me nuts."

"I'm a nice guy."

She couldn't help it. A smile slipped out at his innocent expression. "Since when?"

He pantomimed getting struck in the chest. "You wound me."

"With that thick hide? Doubt it."

He eyed her for a moment. "Did you have breakfast?"

She shook her head. She'd been too focused on Gran this morning to think about it.

"You should eat. You get cranky when your blood sugar is low."

"What do you know about my blood sugar, Bulldog? And I'm not cranky. Geez, you make me sound like a toddler."

One corner of his mouth ticked up. "If the pacifier fits." Without another word, he walked back to his car and returned with a white sack from the Corner Café, which he thrust in her direction. "I picked up an extra egg, bacon, and cheese sandwich for you."

Her stomach chose that moment to let out an unladylike growl. At his smirk, she snatched the sandwich out of his hand. "Who are you and what have you done with Bulldog?"

"One and the same, Fish. One and the same. You're just getting a look at my friendlier side."

"I don't like it," she muttered around a mouthful of food. Manners forced her to add, "But thanks for breakfast."

He stepped closer, right into her personal space and her eyes widened, but she didn't back up. "What are you doing?"

"Do I make you nervous?"

He took another step, until the hands holding her breakfast almost brushed against his chest. She froze, her gaze locked on his, completely unnerved by the flare of attraction in his eyes. Or was she imagining it?

"You like me, Fish. Admit it."

It took far longer than she would have liked for her brain to kick back in. "Almost as much as I like ticks, Bulldog. Apparently, you're both hard to get rid of."

He laughed. "Eat."

When he stepped back, she finally remembered to breathe again. This was Bulldog, not only Josh, aka Hollywood's brother, but a cop who seemed to collect "badge bunnies" like dandruff. There was always a shiny new woman following him around, but they seemed to disappear as quickly as they arrived.

She decided just to ignore him until whatever weird thing was going on passed. Just like she'd steel herself against the little flip in her stomach whenever he sent her that crooked grin, too. Maybe the moon was in some goofy phase that was messing with everyone. She finished the sandwich and disposed of the trash, giving herself time to regain control.

"You find your gran?"

"Not yet. Byte put a BOLO out on her Harley. But she hasn't come home yet."

"You think she'd take Remy somewhere on the back of her bike?"

"I've been asking myself that same question since yesterday. I don't think so, at least not without a good reason."

"I spoke to Brad's parents. Since we can't find Shelley, his father agreed to ID the body via video conferencing."

Lisa blew out a breath. "That's not something any parent should ever have to do." Or a grown child, for that matter. Memories of her mother's still face flashed through her mind. She squeezed her eyes shut.

Her phone buzzed. "I thought you were going to get some sleep?"

She heard Byte stifle a yawn. "I'm about to, Lieutenant, but I thought you'd want to know I heard back from the Larsens' cell phone carrier. Neither phone has been used since two nights ago. But," he paused, "the last GPS location for both phones was near Chapel Lake."

Finally, something they could use. "Text me their numbers and the GPS locations. Then you're off the clock for at least four hours." When he started to protest, she said, "That's an order." She hung up and relayed the info to Bulldog.

Without a word, he hopped aboard and donned a life jacket and ear protection. Lisa automatically opened her mouth to protest, then thought better of it. Neither of them had time to argue. Besides, Brad had been his friend.

She kept one eye on her phone's GPS as she maneuvered the airboat, blocking out everything but the task at hand. The motor whipped up the water around them, and if not for the coordinates Byte sent, they'd never have found the makeshift ramp.

Hidden behind several cypress trees, it had escaped notice when they searched the lake before. The water was much deeper here, so she pulled up to the bank and Pete tied the boat to another tree. The flattened grass indicated someone had backed a trailer down recently.

"Looks like we figured out where Brad launched from."

"Maybe we'll get lucky and find his truck here, too," she said.

They slogged through the mud near shore, then followed the tire tracks inland, scanning for clues as they went.

She dialed Shelley's number, hoping to hear it ring nearby. After three rings, it went straight to voicemail.

After dialing Brad's cell with the same result, they walked until the tire tracks ended at a dirt road, then turned and headed back toward the lake. The fact that neither phone had moved from this location filled her with foreboding.

She called the head of the dive team.

"I was just about to call you, Officer Bass. We've almost finished combing the area between the crash site and the location of the body and we've found nothing."

Lisa let out a small sigh of relief. "Detective Tanner and I are on Chapel Lake at the last known location of both Brad's and Shelley's cell phones. I'll text you the GPS coordinates. Once you finish there, I need your guys to search this area. Thanks. We'll be here when you arrive."

"They may not be here, Fish," Pete said when she hung up and returned to the water's edge, peering into the murky water.

"That's what I'm hoping." She kept her eyes on the lake as she paced, considering and discarding possibilities, none of them good.

Once the dive boat arrived, the two-man team wasted no time getting into the water. As the minutes ticked by, Lisa decided standing around watching their air bubbles as they searched in a grid pattern was the worst kind of hell on earth.

Just when she thought the tension would snap her in two, the divers surfaced and climbed out of the water. "There's no sign of their phones or of them, but we can work our way back to where the other body was found, make sure we didn't miss them," the younger one said.

"Appreciate that."

The older man lowered his voice. "Given the timeline, you know we're thinking recovery, not rescue, right?"

She did, and the knowledge formed a knot in her stomach. "Yes, I know."

They stepped back into the water to continue the search, the dive boat slowly following. Lisa looked up to see Bulldog hurrying toward her.

"Just got a call on the BOLO about Brad's truck. Someone called in a dark pickup in a pond not too far from here."

Chapter Eight

The pond was located in a cow pasture not far from Chapel Lake. The narrow road made a sharp hook to the right there, and the truck had missed the curve, plowed through the thick hedges that lined the fence and ended up nose first in the pond, with only the truck roof and rear wheels of the trailer visible.

Lisa pulled up beside a rusty tractor and the elderly farmer leaning against it. The man pulled off a ball cap and swiped his arm over his forehead before replacing the cap.

"Afternoon, sir. I'm Lisa Bass, Fish and Wildlife." She held out her badge and then leaned forward to shake the man's hand.

"Al Dodge."

Bulldog walked up behind her and she introduced him as well.

"You made sure there was no one in the truck?"

He eyed them both. "I told 'em that when I called it in."

"Just making sure, sir. What time did you discover the truck?"

"Right before I called you." He pulled out a bandana, wiped the back of his neck. "Me and the missus were visiting her sister and just drove home this morning. We saw it when we pulled in. I checked to be sure it was empty, got Mother out of the car and then called you."

He shook his head. "Happens too often, somebody not paying attention—or drinking and driving--and lands right in my pond. At least this time, they got out."

"Have they not gotten out before?" Lisa asked quietly.

The man looked away. Swallowed. "Once. Years ago, now. Terrible thing. They were trapped and we weren't home when it happened. I found them."

"That had to be hard." Lisa waited several moments, then asked, "How long were you and your wife at her sister's, Mr. Dodge?"

"Just overnight. Don't like to leave the place longer than that." He hitched a shoulder. "Me and the wife both prefer sleeping in our own beds, too."

"I can sure understand that," Lisa said, just as the commission-contracted tow truck lumbered down the gravel drive.

Once he'd backed the truck around, the driver approached. "Howdy. They told me to get on out here and pull this combo out, quick-like. You Officer Bass?" When Lisa nodded, he asked, "Nobody in it, right?"

"Far as we know."

The man nodded and got to work, using an electric winch to slowly pull the trailer from the pond.

Despite his efficiency, the process seemed to take forever. Bulldog stood beside the wrecker, watching the proceedings while Lisa wiped at the sweat on her neck as she chatted with the farmer. Even after two years in Florida, she couldn't stop longing for California's lower humidity.

Mrs. Dodge cruised out of the trees on a golf cart and offered lemonade and cookies. By the time Lisa had eaten two, Bulldog, she noted, had polished off four.

The truck cleared the water, and Lisa thanked the woman and hurried over just as the driver opened the door and water gushed out of the cab. Lisa breathed a sigh of relief that no body came with it, despite what Mr. Dodge had said.

The windows were down, so whoever had been in the truck

should have been able to climb out. The question was, who had it been?

After the water drained out, Bulldog opened the passenger door and they studied the inside of the cab. "I ran the plate while you were chatting with Mr. Dodge. It's Brad's."

She raised an eyebrow. "Great minds and all that. I did the same."

He ignored that and eyed the soggy fast-food wrappers on the floor. "He sure wasn't a neat son-of-a-gun, was he?"

Lisa pulled on gloves.

"Not waiting for a warrant?" Bulldog asked, pulling a pair of gloves from his pocket and slipping them on.

She shook her head. "I can't wait around that long."

Their eyes met, held. Anything they found wouldn't be admissible in court, but that wasn't their primary concern here.

"Works for me." He walked around to the other side and started searching.

Lisa ran her hands between the bucket seats, then opened the rear doors and studied the back. She pulled a Barbie doll from under the front seat and ignored the pang it sent to her heart, then checked the side pockets and glove box, but didn't find anything useful.

Doll in one hand, she stepped away and tucked her flashlight in her utility belt. "We need to find out if anyone saw that truck go into the pond. If they did, they might be able to tell us who was driving."

Bulldog looked at her. "Doesn't make sense for Brad to launch his boat, then drive the trailer all the way back home—though he obviously didn't make it there—and then walk back to the boat. That's a couple miles from here."

"Agreed. Though it's not that far as the crow flies." Possibilities flipped through her mind. "What if she changed her mind about going, dropped him off, then crashed the truck, walked home and got her car?"

"Then she took off?" Bulldog chewed the inside of his cheek as he considered. "Possible. Explains the juice boxes in the cooler."

"But she'd never leave town without Remy."

"Right. So, did she pick her up from your Gran's and then disappear?"

"Maybe. But then why hasn't Gran come home?"

Bulldog studied her a moment. "You know your gran is fond of what she calls her walkabouts, right?"

"I know. Yes." She huffed out a frustrated breath. "Let's see if we can find anything that gives us more than speculation."

While she searched behind the rear seats, he climbed into the truck bed and studied the shiny metal toolbox fastened behind the cab. He crouched down and tugged on the padlock, surprised when it opened.

He slowly opened the lid and peered inside as water drained out. "Did Brad have some kind of side business that you know of?"

Lisa climbed up beside him. "Byte didn't mention anything besides his UPS delivery job, which Jason also mentioned. And Shelley's never said."

He reached past the assortment of hammers, screwdrivers and other tools and pulled out a suede packet tied with leather straps. He untied the knots and unrolled it, revealing a dozen sharp tools in varying lengths and sizes tucked neatly into separate compartments. The whole thing looked like something a surgeon might use.

"What is all that?"

He glanced at her before he slipped one out and looked closely at it. "I'm guessing taxidermy tools. Pretty high end, looks like."

Lisa fought a shiver of revulsion. She didn't hunt, and she had no issues with people who ate what they caught or shot. It was the senseless waste of trophy hunting that made her furious.

She leaned closer and Pete's familiar woodsy scent teased her nostrils. "Wait. Is that blood?" She pointed to a dark spot on the handle of one of the tools.

He nodded. "Probably. Wish I had my presumptive blood test kit with me."

"I'll get the lab to check, see if they can tell what kind it is."

They searched the rest of the truck, but nothing jumped out at them, though her cop brain could conjure all sorts of horrible scenarios where those wicked-sharp tools might be used. "If Brad did taxidermy, where'd he do it? You need a place to, ah, stretch out the hide and, uh, remove the insides, right? But there was nothing like that at his and Shelley's place."

Bulldog looked her over. "You okay there, Fish? You're looking a little green around the gills."

She breathed through her nose, jutted her chin up. "I'm fine." If she admitted the idea of butchering animals made her queasy, she'd never hear the end of it. She cleared her throat. "Where else would he do that?"

Before he could respond, Lisa's shoulder radio crackled. "This is 565-Ocala. Go ahead, Dispatch."

"We have a message for you from a Casey Wells. Said he might have some information on your deceased boater."

She and Pete exchanged looks as she pulled out pen and paper and jotted down the number. "Thanks, I'll call him." She hung up and turned to Bulldog, raised a brow. "Sounds like he's speculating again, though once he learned who the boat belonged to, it's not a stretch to think the deceased is Brad." She dialed the number. "Mr. Wells, it's Officer Bass with FWC. I got a message you had information?"

"I need to talk to you, right away. There are some things going on that I think relate to your case."

His urgent tone surprised her. "Why not toss out more speculation in the paper, like you usually do?"

He sighed. "I know you don't like me much, and that's fine, but I think there's something going on that might have caused Brad Larsen's death."

"What do you mean by caused? Where are you getting your information?"

"I don't know anything for sure. Yet. But I think it's very possible. Likely, even. These are not people you want to mess with."

Lisa rolled her eyes at the melodrama. "What people? What something? Just tell me what you know, Wells. I don't have time to guess."

"Not over the phone. Meet me at the Corner Café. One hour."

"No. Tell me now— "

He disconnected.

"What was that all about?"

Pete frowned as she relayed the conversation. "He's cocky and obnoxious and pushes the boundaries of what qualifies as journalism, but he also spends a lot of time digging into things."

"Agreed. I don't have much patience for his methods, but I am curious, especially since he sounded scared. I figured I'll swing by, see what he has to say."

"I'll go with you."

Lisa narrowed her eyes and studied him. "Why?"

"My boss wants me to keep him posted, as I said before. But mainly, I just can't resist your sparkling personality." He shot her that cocky grin.

"I think I can handle talking to a reporter without you tagging along. I'll be sure to keep you updated." Then she stopped as a thought occurred to her. "Did Hunter tell you to keep an eye on me or some such idiot macho-man thing?"

He wouldn't meet her eyes as he closed the lid on the toolbox. "He just asked me to offer assistance if needed."

"Oh, for crying out loud," she muttered as she hopped out of the truck. When she turned back to him, she propped her hands on her hips. "Newsflash, Bulldog. Trained officer. Former SWAT. No assistance needed."

Which was a total lie, but she couldn't let him know that. Her failure to act had cost Mama her life. She'd sworn she'd never make that mistake again. So, until Shelley, Remy and Gran turned up, she'd never quit looking for them. Ever.

He looked at her oddly. "We all need a hand sometimes, Fish. Just saying."

Lisa climbed into her vehicle and drove toward the café, unsettled by the way he'd looked at her, like he knew what was going on inside her head.

She whipped around a bend in the road, still annoyed that he was following. If she hadn't glanced into the surrounding trees at that exact moment, she would have missed the glint of sunlight on metal.

Chapter Nine

Pete pulled onto the road behind Fish, glad she couldn't see his idiotic grin. She was a study in contrasts that absolutely fascinated him. One minute she was standing toe-to-toe with him, her eyes shooting fire, and the next he caught a glimpse of vulnerability that grabbed him by the throat. He was still mulling her quick-silver mood changes when she whipped her truck into a U-turn in the middle of the road so fast he almost ran into her.

She pulled to the side of the narrow shoulder and hopped out almost before her vehicle came to a complete stop. He pulled up behind her and raced to catch up.

"I think it's Wells' car," she yelled over her shoulder.

Pete was right behind her as Lisa skidded to a stop by the driver's door and muttered, "Dear God."

The little sedan had crashed headfirst into a tree, the whole front end crumpled like tinfoil. The steering wheel was pushed up against Wells' chest, blood everywhere.

Pete bit back a curse as Lisa reached in and felt for a pulse, exhaling in relief when she found it. "He's alive."

Bulldog nodded and put his cell phone to his ear, requesting an ambulance at this location. Dispatch assured him she'd send EMS immediately, and would notify Florida Highway Patrol, as well, since FHP handled all traffic accidents in the county.

Pete studied the scene while Lisa ran back to her truck and grabbed her first aid kit, pulling on gloves as she hurried back. She poked her head through the open window. "Hey, Casey. Can you hear me? You've been in an accident, but help is on the way." As she spoke, she wiped his face, searching for the source of the blood. When she found the gash above his eye, she applied pressure and studied his still face. "Casey? Can you open your eyes? Let me know you can hear me, okay?"

He didn't twitch or move. Lisa met Bulldog's eyes, both aware things did not look good for Mr. Wells. Just extricating him from the car was going to be tricky, never mind concerns about internal injuries. Bulldog's admiration inched up several more notches as Lisa kept pressure on the wound and spoke to Wells as they waited, making sure he knew he wasn't alone.

Once EMS and Fire Rescue arrived, they stepped aside as the paramedics worked to stabilize him and the fire department prepared the jaws of life.

As Pete studied the hive of activity something caught his eye and he headed toward the rear of the car, Fish beside him. "Do you see what I'm seeing?" he asked.

He pulled several branches out of the way so they could get a closer look. "Paint transfer on the quarter panel."

Lisa took pictures with her phone, expression grim. "This was no accident. Someone forced him off the road."

He nodded, jaw hard. "On his way to meet you with information."

"We need to search the car, see if we can figure out what he wanted to tell me." She pulled out her phone, hesitated, then called Byte, apologizing for waking him, and asked him to get a search warrant started.

"You'll have to step aside, ma'am," a fireman said as he pulled the cord and fired up the powerful chainsaw.

They watched in silence as the jaws of life screeched through metal. Then the paramedics slowly, carefully, maneuvered Wells out of the mangled car and onto a stretcher.

Once the ambulance raced away, they told Patrol Officer Tompkins what they suspected.

"Do you have any idea who might have done this?" he asked.

"Not yet, but Wells had just called me, said he had information about an ongoing investigation," Lisa said. "We were headed to meet him."

Tompkins glanced at the car, then back at her. "Looks like somebody wanted to make sure he didn't get there."

"That's what we're thinking," Bulldog added. "Before the wrecker takes off with it, we need to see if there's anything inside that can help us."

"You have a warrant?"

"Waiting on it as we speak," Lisa responded.

Byte came through in record time and they went to work. Twenty minutes later, Lisa huffed out a breath and wiped her forehead with the back of her arm. "There's nothing useful here. You have any luck?"

They had emptied Wells' battered leather messenger bag and had gone through all the scribbles and notes on the legal pad inside, but none of it seemed to have a thing to do with Brad Larsen. There was no laptop or tablet in the car, and nothing hidden in the glove box, change drawer, or cup holder.

Bulldog checked one last side pocket and sighed. "Nothing. Either he hadn't written down whatever he wanted to tell you— "

"Or whoever ran him off the road took it."

Lisa pulled out her phone as all the ramifications ran through her mind. "I'll send the pics to Byte. Maybe he can figure out what kind of car the paint comes from."

"I'll tell Tompkins we're done here." When he returned, he said, "I'm going to check Shelley and Brad's place again, see if there's anything we missed the first time. Did you see an outbuilding or shed of some kind?"

"I wasn't looking for one. Should have been."

"I didn't either. Let's head back there."

Her cell phone buzzed. Medical examiner's office. "Hey Doc. What do you have?"

"Hello, Officer Bass. I wanted to give you my preliminary findings on your drowning victim."

"Thanks for getting to him so quickly. I appreciate that."

"It was a slow day at the office, so to speak. I found some things I didn't expect, like alcohol far above the legal limit in the victim's system. But the most unexpected finding didn't show up until I scanned the body. The head trauma was fairly mild, but I found subcutaneal bruising around the neck, indicating strangulation."

Lisa's whole body stiffened. "Are you absolutely sure?"

"Yes, Officer, I am absolutely sure." She sounded affronted.

"Sorry, Doc, I meant no disrespect. I'm just surprised."

"I also found fluid in his lungs consistent with drowning. Lake water."

Lisa took a second to process what Dr. Ward was telling her. "You're saying someone held him down in the water?"

"That's entirely possible, yes. Likely, even."

"Would the perpetrator have to have had substantial strength to pull that off?"

"Not necessarily. Given the amount of alcohol in his system— "

"That could have kept him from fighting back."

"Correct."

"Just to be clear, there is no way he hit his head and then fell out of the boat and drowned?"

"None, in my opinion." She paused. "Based on the bruising pattern, someone held his head under water." She shuffled some papers. "Since this is now considered a homicide, I was going to call Detective Tanner next. He'll be taking the lead on the investigation, correct?"

Lisa wanted to protest, but couldn't. "Yes, he will." It galled her to give up her case, especially her first as Acting Lieutenant, but she knew protocol as well as Tanner did. The sheriff's office handled homicide investigations. "Actually, he's right here. Would you like to speak with him?"

"I would, thank you."

"Thanks for the info, Doc. Here's Bulldog. I mean, Detective Tanner." She handed the phone to him. "Medical examiner needs to speak to you."

Lisa paced while she processed this new development. Not only had Brad been murdered, someone had run Casey Wells off the road before he could give them information to do with Brad. Wells' comment about something big suddenly seemed much more ominous.

Bulldog hung up, turned to her. "That was unexpected."

She nodded. "I hadn't even considered it, not the way we found him."

"But it does open up a whole new line of questioning." He paused. "Like whether or not Shelley killed him and is on the run."

Lisa stiffened, as every protective instinct shot to the forefront. "I know spouses and significant others are always the primary suspects, but I won't let you railroad her without a thorough investigation."

He leaned closer until they were nose to nose. "I don't railroad people, Fish. I follow the evidence. Which means we need to find Shelley, ASAP, get her version of events."

He turned toward his car. "I'm heading back to Brad's."

Chapter Ten

As she followed Bulldog back to the Larsens,' Lisa deep-sixed her frustration and then updated her captain on the M.E.'s call and transfer of the case. Then she checked in with Byte and the rest of the squad to update them, as well. She'd planned to schedule a meeting this afternoon, but now that wasn't up to her. Neither was the press conference. She wanted to blame Bulldog for taking over as lead, but her frustration had nothing to do with him. He was following protocol, same as she was.

But she'd been unfair to him, and he didn't deserve that. He'd proven himself a good man and a good cop.

"You go left, I'll go right," he said when they arrived at the Larsen house, hand on his weapon.

Lisa nodded, took two steps and stopped, looked at him over her shoulder. "I apologize for making unfounded accusations." She paused. "I'll follow your lead."

A beat passed before his eyes widened and he realized she meant more than right here, right now.

"I appreciate it. And I'll try not to do anything stupid." There came that lopsided grin again, the one she couldn't seem to resist. She smiled back, then shook her head and started around the opposite side of the house, hand also on her weapon. Several minutes later they found a shed tucked deep in the woods, barely visible, with a jagged hole in the rusted metal roof and a door that gaped open on rusted hinges.

They shined flashlights around the dirt floor, over the rusted lawnmower and scattered garden tools. Given the thick cobwebs, none of it appeared to have been touched in years. If Brad had been doing taxidermy, it wasn't in here.

They retraced their steps to the house, assessing everything with new eyes.

Once the warrant was issued, they went inside. Lisa searched Shelley and Brad's room again, opening dresser drawers, riffling through the meager contents. She found typical stuff, like a drawer filled with tee shirts from local establishments.

She straightened and almost ran into Pete, who appeared in the doorway, waving several sheets of paper. "Why didn't you tell me Shelley had a separate bank account at another bank?"

His tone made her stiffen. "Because I didn't know. We looked into his financials and their joint accounts. Where did you find that?"

"Taped under a drawer in her nightstand. I get that she's in your self-defense class and that Brad was acting like a jackass, but you can't protect her. Not in a murder investigation."

"What the heck, Bulldog? I wasn't withholding information. Geez. Weren't you protecting him when you said I overreacted the other night? Just because he's dead, doesn't mean she killed him. For all we know, she and Remy are dead too, and we just haven't found their bodies yet."

Tension crackled in the sudden silence and when their eyes met, Lisa was shocked at the storm clouds churning in his expression. He was clearly furious, but there was something else there, too. Something a little hesitant, which stopped her in her tracks. Bulldog charged in like Thor on a mission. He was never unsure.

"So much fire," he muttered and suddenly, he was standing much too close, his hand raised as though to touch her, some unnamed emotion crackling between them.

She glanced at his lips, then unconsciously licked her own. His eyes tracked the movement and his hand dropped to his side. Time slowed and a delicious lethargy slid through her. The intensity in his gaze had her taking a single step in his direction, almost, but not quite bridging the gap that would ignite the attraction simmering between them.

Inches before she reached him, reality hit, hard. This was Bull-dog, he was a detective, and they were in the middle of a case.

And he'd just accused Shelley of murder.

She eased away, cleared her throat, not meeting his eyes.

He scrubbed a hand over the back of his neck, took a deep breath. Then another before he spoke. "If we leave Shelley out of the equation for the moment, who else had a motive to kill Brad?"

"Nothing unusual turned up in his background. But it was common knowledge that his behavior had changed recently, and not for the better. What if Wells stumbled onto the reason for that change?"

"Or maybe it was a crime of opportunity," he said. "Jason Holberg was there and killed him to protect Shelley." He paused. "Or maybe, Shelley acted in self-defense to protect Remy."

Lisa's gaze shot to his as she considered. Shelley wasn't a fitness junkie, by any means. She was hoping the self-defense class would make her stronger. "Is she strong enough to have done it?"

"Physically? If he was drunk, yeah, I think so," Pete said. "But more than that, I think mothers will go to impossible lengths if they feel their children are in danger."

The gentle tone and absolute conviction made her pause. "You know a mother like that, Tanner?"

One corner of his mouth curled up. "Absolutely. My mother could control us with just a look. But if someone dared say something ugly to one of her kids, she'd be all up in their faces. Quick, too."

Lisa pictured the changes in his mother since her stroke and sadness filled her, for all of them. She compared her lonely childhood with his for just a moment, then yanked her thoughts sharply back to the case.

Could Shelley have killed Brad? She was forced to agree with Bulldog. If he'd threatened Remy, no question.

Which meant she had to find Shelley before Pete did. If she'd killed him, Lisa would do whatever it took to help. She'd empty her meager savings in a heartbeat to make sure Shelley had the best defense lawyer money could buy. Shelley would not go to jail if she'd been protecting herself and her daughter. Not if Lisa could help it.

Maybe Shelley already had another ally? Lisa grabbed her phone and called Gran again, left another message when she wouldn't pick up. "Gran, please let me know you and Remy are all right. Shelley is in trouble and she needs our help."

By the time she pulled into the driveway of her cottage later that night, Lisa was bone weary, frustrated, and worried. As usual, she turned her truck around so it faced the road, ready to leave in a hurry if needed.

She'd stopped by Gran's again, but there was no evidence that she'd returned. If Gran had helped Shelley leave town, why hadn't she come home?

Replaying her conversation with Bulldog didn't help, either. In truth, she could argue it both ways. If Brad had gone after Remy, Shelley would have done whatever she had to do to protect her daughter. She'd seen the extremes mothers would go to for their children time and again in her years in law enforcement, though she had no personal experience with that kind of maternal devotion.

Perhaps that wasn't entirely true. In her own crazy way, she supposed, her mother had tried to protect her by keeping her existence a secret. Memories of hiding in the armoire in their dingy living room with her hands over her ears while Dazzle had her men friends over churned inside her. Lisa had vowed then she'd never put a child through that. Ever.

She climbed out of her truck, automatically scanning the area as she did.

Her gaze sharpened as the hairs on the back of her neck stood up. Just as when she and Bulldog arrived at Brad's place earlier, the feeling that someone was watching persisted. Her hand went to her weapon, and she kept her truck between her and the surrounding forest.

"Shelley? You out there?" She kept her tone casual, friendly. Nothing. She tried again. "Gran, is that you?"

There was no response, no rustle in the trees to give her a clue as to where they were. But there was definitely someone there. Bulldog would call it gut instinct. She called it training. Do this kind of work long enough, and you knew. The trick was to realize it in time to keep something bad from happening.

"If you want to talk, I'm here. Come on out. I can help." She waited, watched.

Nothing moved. No shadows shifted, but they were still there.

After several minutes, she eased around the tailgate of the truck and hurried up the walk. She kept her weapon in one hand and unlocked the door with the other.

"If you change your mind, come knock on the door. We'll figure things out, okay?"

This time, she didn't wait for a response, not out in the open like this. She locked the heavy oak door behind her and tossed her keys in the basket on the small console table.

Then she stopped.

Someone had been inside her house.

She could smell them. Some kind of expensive, sickly-sweet cologne still lingered in the air. Just a trace, but enough to make her stomach clench. She raised her weapon and walked into the living room, careful to avoid the squeaky floorboard by the fireplace, then eased into the kitchen. It too, was empty.

No one hid behind the shower curtain, or under her bed or in her closet.

She swept into her workout room. Also empty.

Once she was satisfied she was alone, she went back through every room, trying to figure out what, if anything, had been taken.

On the end table in the living room, a candle stood beside two framed photos. One was of her as a six-year-old, standing between Mama and Gran, taken just before Mama took her to California. Gran had leaned close and whispered Lisa's favorite Winnie the Pooh quote in her ear: *"You're braver than you believe, stronger than you seem, and smarter than you think."*

Lisa swallowed hard and studied the other photo, of her with Captain Jim Barrett, the man who encouraged her to become a cop, taken the day she became a SWAT team member. Neither photo was in its original spot, the coating of dust confirming where they'd been before.

Her hand tightened on her weapon. What had they been looking for?

She returned to the kitchen. The junk drawer hadn't been closed all the way, and the pad by her landline phone had been moved. Was there a page missing? She thought back. What was the last thing she'd written down?

She'd have to let that simmer a while. Her subconscious would pull it up eventually.

In the small dining room off the kitchen, an old desk she'd picked up at a yard sale stood in the corner. The chair hadn't been tucked all the way in, and one of the drawers wasn't completely closed. It stuck, so you had to give it a good shove.

She pulled gloves on before she powered up her laptop. She checked the recent searches, then did the same for her documents. Byte would be able to tell more, but it didn't look like they had figured out her password. She'd have to thank him for nagging her about cyber security.

The haphazard disarray of her file drawers indicated someone had gone through them, especially files containing pay stubs and bank statements. Why? For a potential bribe?

They'd searched her bedroom too and revulsion shot through her at the thought of someone riffling her underwear drawer. The photo on her nightstand of her and her mother after Mama's last stint in drug rehab two years ago had also been moved. For once, her lack of housekeeping fervor worked to her advantage.

But it still didn't answer the question of why. What were they looking for? And had they found it?

Thoroughly annoyed, she picked up her phone and dialed Bulldog, then instantly regretted it. He answered before she could hang up. "Someone searched my house."

"Don't touch anything. I'll be right there."

She didn't know exactly how far away he lived, but he showed up in full detective mode before she'd finished checking for fingerprints.

Feeling suddenly foolish, she crossed her arms over her chest, chin up. "You didn't have to come. There's nothing you can do here. I didn't find any obvious prints, so whomever it was wore gloves."

His jaw was tight, expression shuttered. "It's a murder investigation, Fish. And you're law enforcement. Of course, I came. I've got a crime scene tech on the way. Show me what you've got."

He pulled on gloves and took notes, asking questions as she showed him the evidence, confirming everything she said.

In the doorway to her bedroom, she pointed to the nightstand. "The photo was moved, as you can see by the dust trail."

He cocked an eyebrow. "Good thing you hadn't dusted today."

"Or this year," she quipped, hoping to dispel the awkwardness of having him in her bedroom. She cleared her throat. "He also dug around in my underwear drawer, but didn't take anything." She stepped in front of the dresser. No way was he double-checking.

"You keep saying he. You sure it was a man?"

"Based on the heavy cologne I smelled when I opened the door, yes."

Anger and something else rippled under his carefully modulated questions, but she couldn't tell what.

"He take anything?"

"Not that I can tell."

"I don't like this at all," he muttered, scanning the room. He turned and studied her. "You okay?"

She nodded. "I'm fine."

"Doesn't feel good to have your sanctuary breached and searched."

His insight caught her off guard. Reminded her, again, that there may be more to him than his overbearing exterior.

"No, not fun. But I'll be fine. Thanks for coming over so quickly."

The silence stretched as they looked at each other. Part of her wanted to wrap her arms around him and just breathe him in, feel his body next to hers, push the loneliness aside for a little while. The practical side of her reminded her of all the reasons that was a terrible idea.

They heard a car turn into her driveway. He broke eye contact first. "That should be the tech."

Introductions were made and Bulldog walked the tech into the cottage.

"I'll wait out here," Lisa said. She didn't want to watch another person go through her things. She knew it was necessary, but it still made her feel small and vulnerable. She hated that.

It wasn't long before the tech finished up and left. Bulldog appeared in the doorway, leaned against the jam. "I should go."

She nodded, trying to keep the unwelcome stew of emotions churning through her from spewing out. The sudden temptation to cry on his shoulder came out of nowhere, unsettling her. She cleared her throat. "It's late. Thanks again for coming."

"Lock up behind me."

Once she heard his vehicle drive away, she changed into workout gear and took out her frustration on her punching bag. Tonight, it would take a whole lot more than crocheting to calm her racing mind.

Her brain churned with questions about the case, and she tried to pound out her confusing feelings for Bulldog along with her absolute fury that someone had searched her house. She didn't stop until her arms gave out from exhaustion.

Too keyed up to sleep, Pete sat on the covered front porch of his log cabin, a beer in one hand, his sketch pad in the other. Just beyond the railing, his bug zapper kept all but the most persistent insects away. Even if they snuck by, mosquitos didn't gnaw on him like they did Charlee and Josh, which annoyed his siblings no end.

Every cop needed a way to decompress and this nightly ritual was his. With the sounds of the forest around him and a small lamp beside him, he gave his mind free rein to process and pick through the details, looking for patterns and context, thinking ahead to the next day's questions. Tonight, though, as memories flashed through his mind, Fish's face appeared under his pencil. He drew the flames flashing in her pretty green eyes when she told him someone dared to dig through her underwear drawer. Was it any wonder he'd wanted to taste some of that fire?

Thankfully, he hadn't been stupid enough to act on it. They were working a case together.

Fish had never said much about her life before FWC and he'd never asked. But now, suddenly, he wanted to know.

What made her teach self-defense classes at the community center? He got the obvious—to help women—but he sensed there was more to it than that, something related to the black hole where any information about her past lived.

She was shifting in front of him, becoming someone he didn't know. Or maybe, he was just seeing her clearly for the first time. His pencil kept moving, adding texture and details, shading in the blonde hair she hid under a ball cap, defining that strong jaw and determined chin, trying to make sense of a woman he'd known for several years, but who he didn't really know at all.

He totally got her worry for Shelley and Remy and believed it entirely possible that Shelley'd killed Brad and taken her daughter and run. He believed it was equally possible Brad had suspected Shelley was going to leave him and killed them both, though there wasn't a shred of evidence, and he sincerely hoped he was wrong. He could also see Jason getting fed up with the abuse and killing him, especially since he'd then have Shelley for himself. Pete knew men had killed for less. If that was the case, was Jason hiding them somewhere? And if he was, had he shown up at Shelley's house earlier to throw them off the trail?

His pencil kept moving as thoughts whirled in his head, looking for patterns and connections that weren't clear yet.

Chapter Eleven

Lisa gulped coffee the next morning, still hacked off that someone had dared to sneak into her home and touch her things. There were no signs of forced entry, so they must have picked the locks, which she should have replaced when she moved in. Given how remote it was, she'd never expected a problem, which was really dumb, especially for someone in law enforcement. Hindsight only made her more annoyed with herself.

She'd made a careful circuit of her cottage and the surrounding woods at three a.m., but there was no sign of anyone. A quick rain shower about one a.m. had not only woken her, but erased any footprints.

When the local big box store opened this morning, she'd been first in line. Lucky for the hapless clerk, they had what she needed in stock. She stepped back to check the location of the trail cameras she had installed. Though they were motion activated, she didn't hold out hope her watcher would pass directly under them. Still, having them there, along with the ability to check in remotely, made her feel better.

Installing new deadbolts had taken longer than she had time for, but she got it done.

She felt marginally less feral now that everything was in place. She climbed into her FWC truck and called Byte.

"Any activity on Gran's or Shelley's credit cards?"

"Nothing on either one, but it looks like neither one uses them much, anyway."

"Nothing on either of their vehicles, either?"

"Sorry, no hits. Yet."

"Thanks, Byte."

She told her captain her plans on her way back to Gran's. Brad's death had been all over the news, so if Gran was anywhere in Central Florida, she knew he was dead. Lisa was betting Gran had helped Shelley and Remy get out of town. But then why not come back and pretend ignorance to cover for them? It wasn't like Gran didn't know how to stonewall. She did it to Lisa all the time.

Unless Gran couldn't come back for some reason.

That's the thought that was gnawing a hole in Lisa's gut. And she wouldn't, couldn't, ignore it. Not after Mama.

She grabbed the key from under the fake rock again and took a closer look around inside. What if all those small things she'd noticed – partially open drawers, pictures moved, just like at her house – weren't signs of haphazard housekeeping, but of a lackluster search of the premises. She checked all the obvious places, but didn't find anything to tell her what someone was looking for.

Could it be connected to whatever Wells had wanted to tell them?

If Bulldog were here, he'd tell her it was a stretch. And maybe it was. But those random pieces were often what finally made the puzzle fall into place.

After she'd gone through the house, she went back to the garage. She flipped on the overhead light and looked around. As she stepped inside, something caught her eye. A muddy footprint. And another. They weren't heading into the garage, but out through this door. She followed the path and noticed the prints started where Gran's Harley was usually parked, led out the overhead door, then another set came back to the door where Lisa stood.

As though someone rolled the bike out, came back in and closed both doors before leaving.

Which made sense if Gran was planning to leave on her Harley.

It didn't make sense when you considered the size of the footprints.

They were big. Much larger than Gran's.

They hadn't been here the last time Lisa was here.

Gooseflesh rippled over her arms.

She'd just pulled out her phone to call her captain when he called her. Before she could fill him in on what she'd found at Gran's, he said, "I'm guessing you still haven't located Shelley or Remy Larsen?"

"No, sir, but we're doing everything we can to find them."

"And we don't have any hard evidence that Shelley killed her husband."

"No, sir," Lisa said again.

He sighed. "You know the family, Fish. If the little girl is with her mother, is she in danger?"

"No," Lisa said emphatically. "Even if Shelley was somehow involved in Brad's death, there is no way she would hurt that child."

Ed sighed again. "Then we can't issue an Amber Alert on Remy." Lisa heard a thump, as though he'd pounded his desk in frustration. "Have you tracked down your grandmother yet?"

"I'm at her place now." She told him about the footprints and the missing Harley.

"I've met your gran a few times and she seems sharp as a tack. No cognitive issues like dementia?"

Lisa knew where he was going with this. Silver Alerts were issued if a missing senior had degenerative cognitive issues that would prevent them from making decisions in their best interest. "She can run circles around me, Sir."

"Do you believe Remy Larsen is with her?"

Lisa paused, considering.

"What does your gut say, Fish?"

"My gut says Gran wouldn't put that child on the back of her Harley if she didn't have to. But I can see her helping Shelley and Remy get out of town." She took a deep breath. "Brad's death has been all over the news, so if she could, I think she'd be here stonewalling us."

"But you're not sure."

"No, I'm not sure." She knew Gran would be furious about what she was going to do next, but she'd run out of options. "I need to file a missing person's report."

She heard his fingers drumming on his desk. "Agreed. We'll also expand the area of the BOLO for both women, Shelley's car and Sunny's Harley and see if that nets us anything. We'll get their pictures and Remy's on the news, too. I'm joining the sheriff's office for a press conference at noon. Keep me updated."

He hung up before she could respond.

Lisa swallowed hard, the "if she could" circling in her head. Had she waited too long to act? Again?

She couldn't go down that path. The best way to help Gran, and Shelley and Remy, was to find out who murdered Brad.

Lisa filed a missing person's report on Gran, then drove toward the hospital to check on Wells. She sent pictures of the muddy boot prints from Gran's to Byte, with a request to get a tech out there to make a cast so they'd have it. She also asked Sanchez to question any of the Larsens' neighbors they hadn't talked to yet. She hoped Casey Wells had woken up, though Bulldog would have called if that were the case. Or maybe not. He'd just made detective, so he had as much to prove as she did as acting lieutenant.

She had the windows down on her truck when she rounded a bend and almost rear-ended a slow-moving semi towing a heavily loaded trailer. As that was the second time this had happened recently, she decided to see where it went.

When the driver spotted her in his side mirror, his expression seemed to freeze. Interesting.

She sent him a friendly smile and stayed behind him for the next twenty minutes, until the end of a long narrow strip of blacktop ended and he came to a stop in front of an automatic gate with a keypad. She debated following him through, but let it swing shut before she pulled up and pressed the "o" key. She eyed the camera mounted above a sign that read, "Castile Animal Rescue," while she debated what to say. This wasn't the section of the county she regularly patrolled, so she hadn't realized Castile's property had an entrance way out here.

A tinny voice sounded from the box. "Please state your business."

Lisa held up her badge. "Officer Bass, Fish and Wildlife Commission. I'd like to speak with whoever is in charge."

"Someone will be with you shortly."

The gate did not open, so she pulled out her binoculars and watched. The truck hadn't gone far down the dirt road. A man on a golf cart intercepted it, glanced her way, and then waved the driver forward.

Lisa hid her surprise when none other than Jason Holberg approached in the golf cart. She stepped out of the truck, but kept the door between her and him.

He was dressed in his usual jeans, but this time he sported a polo shirt with the organization's name embroidered on it. Hope flared in his eyes before it was tempered with dread. "What's happened? Have you found Shelley and Remy? Are they okay?"

He was either a really good actor or he had no idea where they were. "No, we haven't. I'm sorry."

His shoulders slumped, but then he straightened, as though something just occurred to him. "Then why are you bothering me at work?" He glanced over his shoulder. "I have things to do."

She took a careful look at the barns in the distance, the scattering of outbuildings barely visible through the thick forest. "What do you do here?"

"I take care of the animals. Why?"

Bulldog's research had confirmed that he used to be a vet, and Byte was digging deeper to uncover why he wasn't one now. "Did Brad work here, too?"

Jason sighed. "Sometimes. He made deliveries for us and also did odd jobs, when we needed extra hands and he needed extra cash."

"What about taxidermy? Did he do any of that?"

Jason stiffened as though he'd been poked. "This is an animal rescue. We don't stuff them. Jeez. What kind of a question is that?"

"Does Brad do taxidermy?"

"How would I know?"

"You said you were friends, didn't you?"

"I said we've known each other a long time. Or, I guess, we knew each other a long time."

"Is there anything you can tell me, anything at all, that would help us figure out why he died?"

Jason froze and the way his eyes narrowed gave Lisa the sense there was a very sharp mind under his generally affable demeanor. "I thought he drowned. What are you asking?"

Lisa hesitated, then plunged in. Sometimes, opportunities landed in your lap and you had to follow up right then or the moment was gone. "He may have had help."

There was a stunned moment, then his eyes widened. "You're saying he was murdered? What does that have to do with me?" Another beat while he connected the dots. "You have a lot of nerve coming here— "

Lisa held up both hands. "Easy. Just asking if you have any info that can help us, or know anyone with something against the man."

"We hadn't spent much time together lately, so I have no idea. I can't help you. Sorry."

At that moment, a late-model luxury SUV pulling an enclosed trailer arrived at the gate. It drove around Lisa and toward an enclosure not far from the road. An older sedan and a local news van followed right behind them.

"I have to go. We're unloading our newest resident." He stopped, sent her a long, considering glance. "Why don't you come along and see for yourself what we do here, Officer Bass."

He opened the gate and told her to follow him. When she got out of her truck, she saw that Martin Castile, well-known local veterinarian, had been driving the SUV. He was in his fifties, his black hair starting to gray at the temples, but he moved with an old-world grace. With Jason's help, he was transferring a fairly young bear into a large enclosure.

Once the bear was safely inside, Castile looked up and annoyance flickered over his face. "What's going on, Jason? Why is FWC here?"

Lisa strode over to him and held out a hand, not about to be ignored. "Good morning, Dr. Castile. I'm Officer Bass."

Jason hitched his thumb in her direction. "She's asking about Brad. Apparently, he was murdered. I told her he'd done some odd jobs here, but that's all."

Castile straightened and turned in her direction, eyes hidden by the dark glasses. "If you have questions for my employees, kindly go through my office and they'll refer you to our lawyer. Now if you'll excuse me." He walked over to the camera crew and his demeanor completely changed as he shook hands, smiling, working them like a politician at a fundraiser.

Lisa stood back and listened to his pompous speech about Castile Animal Rescue and their passion for rehabilitating local wildlife. Then he expounded on the benefits of his newest venture: plans for a drive-through safari to let people experience the wonders of Africa without leaving the country. At the end of it, he swept a hand over the compound and gave the media their soundbite. "This is why we're here. To make a difference."

Bulldog wouldn't be happy that she'd let her curiosity get Castile's defenses up. Jason's body language said he knew more than he was saying, and given his feelings for Shelley, she'd bet whatever he was hiding had something to do with her. But was Castile's Rescue involved as well?

By the time she reached the trauma hospital in Ocala, it was lunchtime. She stepped off the elevator and almost collided with Bulldog.

"Where have you been?" he growled by way of greeting.

"What bee got up your bonnet, as Gran would say? We didn't have a meeting scheduled."

"I sent you a text. Two, actually."

Lisa looked down just as her phone chirped. One text. Then two. She sighed as she held up her phone. "I was out of range. They just came in."

Cell service in parts of the forest was iffy at best, and so far, no amount of complaining by the community had changed a thing.

"What did you want to tell me?" she asked.

He hitched a chin toward the double doors behind him. "Wells is in a coma and they don't know if he'll wake up. It's touch and go."

Except the deputy stationed outside his door, she didn't see anyone by Wells' bedside or in the waiting area. She didn't like the man, but that still made her sad. "Does he have any family?"

"Paramedics didn't find anything in his wallet. We're checking."

She eyed Bulldog, noting the way his brownish hair stood up like he'd been running his hands through it, and then his wrinkled shirt, the sleeves rolled up. "How long have you been here?"

He shrugged, took another sip of the coffee he held. "About four this morning, I guess."

When she looked at him steadily, he shrugged. "Couldn't sleep."

She understood. An ailment common to law enforcement the world over.

Then he straightened. "Where have you been all morning?" That sounded a lot like an accusation, but given his short night, she let it slide.

"I had a few things to take care of at home, stopped by Gran's, learned our bosses are holding a press conference, and then I spoke to Jason Holberg."

His gaze sharpened, exhaustion gone. "My captain says they're expanding the BOLOs and showing Shelley, Remy and your gran's photos, too."

Lisa filled him in on the footprints in Gran's garage.

"You thinking someone took her bike?"

"Maybe. I don't know." She sighed.

"None of it makes sense. Yet." He paused. "What did Holberg have to say for himself?"

"Not a whole lot. He works at the animal rescue place owned by Martin Castile. Holberg said he hired Brad to do odd jobs. Nothing major."

He studied her a moment. "What else?"

She looked away. "What do you mean, what else?"

He sighed. "Don't do this, Fish. We're on the same side. What else happened?"

"Castile showed up with a rescued bear and did a PR stint for the cameras, promoting his upcoming safari drive-through."

"And?"

"And he said if we had any other questions, or wanted to speak to any of his employees, we should call the office and talk to his lawyer."

The explosion she'd expected didn't take long. "Crap on a cracker, Fish. Castile was next on my list to interview."

"And maybe when you show up—though you might want to clean up a little before you do—he might be more willing to talk to you." She propped her hands on her hips. "Besides, I didn't go looking for him."

"What were you doing at the sanctuary in the first place? Especially without telling me you were going?"

Her eyes narrowed. "I wasn't aware I had to report in every time I left my house."

"Don't be an idiot, Fish. We need to work together."

He was right. She was suddenly embarrassed, realizing she was behaving like a recalcitrant child. "You're right. I followed a fully-loaded semi out there."

That got his attention. "What was it loaded with?"

"No idea, but it was sitting pretty low and since you don't usually see trucks that size on those roads, I followed."

"You still should have told me."

"I'm telling you now."

His phone chirped. He glanced at it, then said, "I have to go."

"What's going on?" When he speared her with a look, she added, "You know, in the spirit of cooperation and everything?"

"I have a lunch date."

The urge to demand to know with whom was strong, but she bit the words back before they escaped. It was none of her business. And it didn't bother her. Why should it? They were professional colleagues.

His smile curved up at the corners, eyes twinkling. "With my mother."

And didn't the love in that smile smack her right in the heart? What woman could resist a man who took his mother to lunch? Especially when said mother was recovering from a stroke. Her insides got all gooey just picturing the two of them, but she shoved all that aside. She didn't have time to feel anything for Bulldog Tanner, gooey or otherwise. Her smile was genuine and she hoped it concealed the mix of conflicting emotions the man had started churning inside her. "Have a wonderful time. Please give her my regards."

He grinned, winked. "Will do." Then he scrubbed a hand over the stubble on his chin, grimaced. "I'll touch base with you later."

The woman was going to make him crazy. She had a comeback for everything and damn, if he didn't find that sexy as all hell. He wiped the goofy grin off his face as he rode the elevator down to the first floor.

The look in her eyes when he said he had a lunch date with his mother had nearly scrambled his brain. It was the same punch to the gut he felt every time he said things to get her riled up. When her eyes sparked with temper and she stood straighter, the electricity that crackled in the air between them always tempted him to move closer, to reach out and run his hands over the curves hidden under all that khaki.

He had to quit thinking like that or their working together would not go well. She was a professional colleague. "Keep your distance, Bulldog," he muttered, but his libido didn't seem to want to hear it. All it kept yammering about was how good she smelled, and how soft her skin looked, and how much he wanted to touch her.

He was still berating himself for acting like a horny teenager when he climbed into his sedan and decided he had time for one quick stop before he cleaned up for his lunch date.

The man was going to make her crazy, Fish decided. Just when she thought she'd figured him out, he said or did the next dumb thing and made her want to smack him. Or kiss him. And that's the part that kept freaking her out. She didn't want to kiss Bulldog.

Right.

The heart wants what the heart wants, or so the old saying went. Well, the heck with old sayings. And it wasn't her heart she worried about. Her lady parts seemed to have chosen this inconvenient time to wake up and take notice. Of Bulldog. Out of all the possible men in the world, her body decided it wanted him? Made no sense. She had to work with him and if he had any idea she was attracted to him, even a teensy bit, he'd be insufferable to live with, never mind work with. He had an ego the size of Canada.

She decided to treat her attraction to him like she would a cold. If she ignored it long enough, it would go away. Eventually. Hormones, for that's what she decided lay at the root of this sudden awareness, would run their course and then she'd stop staring at his mouth when he wasn't looking and wondering if he wanted to kiss her too. These absurd feelings would go away and they could get back to annoying each other like normal people.

That decided, she felt much better. She just had to quit sneaking peeks at him, that was all.

She used her badge to get past the locked doors into the trauma unit, and stepped over to Casey Wells' bedside. Bandages covered most of his head and bruises stained the rest. Several machines beeped and all sorts of wires ran under the sheets that covered him.

"Hey, Casey. Can you hear me? It's Officer Bass. You said you had information for me, but you never showed up to our meeting. I'm sorry you were in an accident. But you're in the hospital, in case no one told you that, and they're taking really good care of you." She'd been told people in a coma could hear, so she wanted to put his mind at ease, at least a little. "I need you to wake up and tell me what you found out, okay? What was so urgent we had to meet right away? Can you do that?"

She waited, but he didn't so much as twitch. Just to be sure, she stayed another twenty minutes before she rode the elevator back down.

As she approached her truck, she slowed. She never left her window down. To do so was completely unprofessional. Anyone could walk off with her laptop or mess with her equipment. To say nothing of the rifle locked in a compartment behind her seat.

She thought back to when she'd arrived. Her mind had clearly not been on what she was doing. So, yeah, it was possible. *Crap.*

Completely annoyed with herself, she flung the door open, tossed the spare uniform shirt lying there into the back and slid up onto the seat.

The moment her butt hit the upholstery, she heard the rattle and realized her mistake, but she wasn't quick enough to scramble out of the way.

The rattler slammed into her right butt cheek and she gasped in pain at the strike. She lost her balance and fell backwards onto the pavement, unable to stop the hiss of agony. Those fangs hurt. *Crap.*

She groaned again as the blistering hot asphalt seared the backs of her legs and burned the back of her arms where she'd tried to brace herself. She automatically scrambled up to escape the heat and then muttered a string of curses at her own stupidity. "Stop, you idiot. Think. Damn."

Her breath heaved in and out. Not good. First rule of snakebite: stay calm. Don't panic. She didn't want the venom pumping through her system. She forced air in through her nose, willing her heart rate to slow. *Think past the pain.*

She looked at her truck, saw the snake eyeing her from the seat, her phone on the floorboards right below him. There was no way she was reaching back in there. Now what?

Her truck was parked in the back corner of the parking lot. It would be stupid to walk that far. The venom would travel too fast. But man, she'd rather do that than have to explain what just happened to everyone on the squad. Resigned, she keyed her mic. "Dispatch, this is 565-Ocala. I'm in the parking lot of Ocala Regional Hospital and I need you to ask them to send a gurney outside, stat."

"You okay?" the dispatcher asked.

"Will be. Had an unexpected encounter with a rattler."

"Don't move. I'll send someone right out. Stay calm. Is the snake still there?"

"Affirmative."

"I'll send someone to come get him, too."

"Appreciate it. Ten-four. Thank you."

But staying calm proved easier said than done. Her heart raced with leftover adrenaline, which was the worst possible thing. She needed to get horizontal, so she carefully lay down in the shadow of the truck to wait for help. The pavement here was still hot, but not bad enough to burn.

She'd kept her eyes on the snake for what felt like four years before two members of the ER staff rushed into view with a gurney.

"Officer Bass?" the woman asked.

"Stop. The snake is still in the truck," she warned as they approached.

They eyed the open door of the truck and then disappeared. She heard the gurney clattering over the pavement as they came around from the opposite side.

They locked the wheels and then turned to her. "Snake bite?"

"Yes. Right butt cheek. Hurts like a bugger."

The man smiled. "No doubt. Let's get you inside, get some anti-venom going."

Together, they maneuvered her onto the gurney and rushed back into the hospital.

All she could think about as everything got a little fuzzy was, how had the snake gotten into her truck?

When she woke some time later, she knew she was being watched, so she didn't open her eyes right away. Where was she? It took a few minutes for the sounds and smells to fall into place and make sense. Right. Snake bite. Hospital.

"Quit playing possum. I know you're awake," Bulldog growled in her ear.

Her eyes flew open and before she could form words to argue, his worried expression registered. She'd seen him in many situations over the past two years, but she'd never seen him look quite this frantic before. Ever. It threw her completely.

"Thank God you're okay," he muttered.

He lowered his head and as she watched his lips move towards hers, she froze in shock. Was he going to kiss her?

Her surprise must have registered because his eyes widened and he stopped, then jerked away like he'd been burned and started pacing the room.

Long seconds passed while she tried to process what had almost happened. "I'm fine," she managed, wondering when she'd stepped into some alternate universe, where Bulldog worried about her and wanted to kiss her, for crying out loud. And where she was fighting the urge to pull him close and kiss him back.

"How the hell did you get bit by a freaking snake in the hospital parking lot of all places?"

And just like that, her unwelcome attraction morphed into her usual irritation. "It's not like I planned it."

He stopped, stared at her like she'd switched to a foreign language. "Of course, you didn't plan it. But what was a snake doing in your truck? Sanchez said it wasn't that big, but big enough to cause some damage. Did you not see him?"

Right. Think logically. She attempted to corral her slippery thoughts, picture the scene. "I noticed the window of my truck was down as I got closer." When he opened his mouth to say something, she held up a hand to stop him. "I always leave it closed and locked, standard operating procedure, which is why it caught my eye. I thought maybe I'd been distracted earlier, so I climbed in and basically sat on the snake."

His eyes narrowed as he studied her. All cop. "I know you, Fish. How did you not see him?"

She squeezed her eyes shut, thought back, but her brain still felt murky, and that annoyed her no end. Her eyes popped open. "Wait. One of my uniform shirts was on the seat. I tossed it in the back as I slid in."

"Someone deliberately planted the snake and tried to hide it."

He kept pacing, which made her dizzy, so she studied the ceiling instead, scrolling through possibilities.

"What do you know that someone doesn't want you to tell?"

"Or what does someone think I know?"

"Right. For the sake of argument, let's assume Shelley killed Brad. What reason would she have for planting a snake?"

"Even if she killed him in self-defense, which I have a hard time believing, I can't see her doing something like this. Someone had to get the rattler from somewhere—either buy it or trap it—then get it here, follow me, and plant it without anyone seeing it. That shows serious planning and motivation."

She stopped, tried to think. "What if someone thinks I did meet with Wells?"

"They would have to know about the meeting."

"Or they saw us at the crash site."

"Agreed. But we were both there and the snake was in your vehicle, not mine."

"My head feels stuffed with cotton, but I'll keep thinking about it."

One corner of his mouth quirked up. "Can't imagine why, Fish. Don't you deal with snake bite every day?"

She couldn't help smiling back.

He set her cell phone on the bedside table. "You'll be happy to know Sanchez retrieved your phone after he removed the snake. And I've got a crime scene tech processing your vehicle as we speak. In the meantime, I'm going to check the hospital security cameras. Stay put."

Before she could protest, he was gone.

Chapter Twelve

Pete left the room, his worry carefully hidden. Lisa had enough to worry about without him adding to it. Something about the deliberateness of this gnawed at him. Someone was following Fish and had some as-yet-unknown agenda.

Which meant he was going to keep a much closer eye on her.

No hardship, that, he admitted. But then he shook his head at his own idiocy. What had possessed him earlier? They were colleagues, even rivals if you got right down to it. But all he could think was that she'd almost been killed and man, was he glad she hadn't been. He had to keep his lips to himself and quit thinking of her as a woman. She was Fish, his annoying co-worker. He had to remember that, no matter how much the call from Sanchez about the snake had paralyzed him with fear for just a moment.

"Head in the game, Bulldog," he muttered. "Figure out who did this."

He walked into the hospital's small security office. "Hey, Dooey. How's that honey-do list coming?"

Frank Dooey looked up from the monitor he was watching and his blue eyes twinkled behind his glasses. "Slowly. Can't get too much done, you know, since I'm working here." He grinned as he said it. He attended the same church as Pete's family and three months after he retired from his CPA firm a few years ago, he became the daytime hospital security guard to escape his wife's endless to-do lists.

"You're a smart man, Dooey, no matter what Gladys says."

"What can I do for you, Bulldog? I'm guessing it's not a social call."

"You heard about Officer Bass getting bit by that snake, right?"

"Of course. Terrible thing. Is she going to be okay?"

"She will be. Thankfully, she was right here when it happened." Which was pretty ballsy of whoever did it.

"Do you know how the snake got in her truck?"

"I'm working on that. But in the meantime, can you pull up the security tapes from this morning?"

Dooey turned back to his keyboard. "Sure. How early do you want to start?" He looked over his shoulder. "You're thinking someone put the snake in there?"

"Right now, I'm just gathering information."

"Here you go." Dooey pointed to one of the screens that faced the parking lot, but it didn't show the area where Lisa's truck had been parked.

"Do you have cameras that reach all the way to the back of the lot?"

"Never needed to. We just keep an eye on the doors, see who's coming and going."

Pete asked him to speed up the recording and they both studied the steady stream of people who passed through the door.

They watched the footage twice, but nothing jumped out at Pete. No one looked suspicious or furtive in any way. "Stop. Play that back again." He spotted Cal, one of the boys on the basketball team he helped Josh coach at the Forest Community Center. As they watched, Cal came outside and sat on the curb, looking like he was bored and killing time. But then he stood, straightened, and seemed to be intently staring at the area where Lisa's truck would have been.

Shortly after that, a truck stopped at the curb, and Cal climbed inside and it drove away. Once the tape played through to the end, Pete said, "Can you make me a copy of this?"

"Sure. I'll put it on a CD for you." Dooey handed him the CD a few minutes later. "Hope you find whoever did this."

Pete shook his hand. "Thanks for the help, Dooey. Give my best to Gladys."

Pete rushed home to clean up, then took his mother to lunch at the Corner Café, where she was greeted like a local celebrity. He'd offered to take her wherever she wanted, but she said she liked seeing all her friends at the Café.

She was starting to tire by the time they finished lunch, so he took her home and tucked her into her recliner for a nap before he got back in his car. Then he called the community center's director and got an address for Cal. He drove out to where the youth lived with his mother in an aging mobile home off a dirt road in the forest. The minute Pete pulled up, two pit bulls launched themselves from under the only shade tree and raced to his car, snapping and snarling. He waited, hoping someone would come to the door and call them off.

Sure enough, Cal stepped outside and whistled sharply. Both dogs ran to him, tails wagging, tongues hanging out. "It's okay, Detective Tanner," Cal called.

Pete eyed the dogs, and Cal grinned as he clipped a leash to their collars and hooked them to a lead by the tree. "You can come out now. They won't bite."

Chagrined that the young man was making fun of him, Pete walked over to the house and sat beside Cal on the narrow steps. "They only bite on your command?" he teased.

Cal grinned. "Depends on who it is." He looked Pete up and down, noting the suit jacket and dress pants. "You look all fancy today. Are you working a case?"

"Actually, I am and I thought maybe you could help me with something."

The boy's eyes widened. "Me? Sure."

"You were at the hospital earlier? Is someone in your family sick?"

Cal's face fell. "My grandma. She fell and broke her hip. Mom's pretty upset."

"I can understand that. Scary stuff, when someone we care about gets hurt and we can't fix it or make it better."

Cal nodded solemnly. "Mom wants Grandma to come live with us, but Grandma always says no. Says she likes her old place. She's lived there like, forever."

Pete thought of his folks, of his mother's love of her porch swing overlooking the river. And about how he and his siblings worried about her going up and down the few steps into the house since her stroke. He sighed. "It's hard when you want to take care of someone, and they want to take care of themselves. But I know you and your mom and grandma will work something out. That's not why I'm here. Did you hear about Officer Bass?"

Cal's head snapped up. "Did something happen to her?"

"Somebody put a snake in her truck while it was parked at the hospital today. You wouldn't know anything about that, would you?"

Cal leaped up from the steps. "I'd never do anything to Officer Bass. She's a real nice lady." His ears reddened a bit. "Real pretty, too."

Has a crush on Fish, does he? Pete grinned. "Yes, she is. And I'm not saying you did anything to her. But I know you were sitting outside the hospital for a while this morning. Did you maybe see anyone near her truck?"

Worry replaced Cal's indignation and he sat back down. "The snake didn't hurt her, did it? What kind was it?"

"Actually, it was a rattler and it bit her."

"Oh, man. Is she okay?"

Pete ruffled his hair. "She will be. She's tough." And hot enough to make him stupid, but he refused to think about that.

Cal looked away and then back at Pete. "I did see a guy near her truck and it seemed kind of weird."

"Weird, how?"

"Well, he pulled up in a brand-new silver Ford F-250, King Ranch edition, with a full crew cab and fancy bed liner and tool box in the back." Pete's eyes widened at Cal's detailed, earnest description. "It's a really sweet ride and those don't come cheap. He pulled in right next to Officer Bass's truck, which seemed weird, since there were plenty of other parking spaces. He was trying to look like he worked on a ranch, but his clothes were way too new. His jeans were so stiff he walked like he had a stick up his butt."

Pete hid a grin. "That's good police work, Cal. You trying to take my job?"

"No, sir. But I didn't have nothing else to do, so I was just watching."

"Most people wouldn't have noticed all that. Anything else seem odd to you? Did you get a good look at his face? Or see anything that might help us figure out who he was?" Maybe he could get a good enough description from Cal to do a sketch.

"Nah, he was wearing a fancy cowboy hat that covered his face." Then he brightened. "He was wearing a dark blue tee shirt and it looked like he had a tattoo around his left arm. Looked kinda like a picture of a rope." Cal shrugged. "Lots of people have tattoos, though, but I noticed it when he moved."

"You've been a huge help, Cal. Thanks." He stood. "Do me a favor, except for your mom, let's keep this between us, all right? Don't tell anyone about the guy you saw."

Cal's face paled slightly. "You think he put a snake in her truck to try to hurt her?"

"Too soon to tell for sure, but I'll be checking into all of it. You've been a really big help. Thank you."

Cal stood, his skinny chest puffed out a little. "Happy to help."

"I'll see you at basketball practice." Pete opened the door. "And remember, nobody but your mom."

Cal gave him a thumbs-up and then watched as he drove away.

By the time Lisa ran the paperwork gauntlet required to get discharged, she was exhausted. And cranky. All she wanted was to go home and recover from the embarrassment.

Because the snake wasn't very big and they thought she'd gotten a dry bite, which meant no venom, the doctor was letting her go home. They'd given her a shot of anti-venom, just in case, with orders to monitor the site and check for a host of possible reactions and side effects.

She tucked the bottle of pain meds the doctor insisted on in her pocket, but she hadn't taken any because they made her sleepy. Dumb idea, actually, since her backside throbbed like a bass drum in a marching band. Which meant her temper was a hairsbreadth from blowing. She really wasn't fit company for man or beast, but she couldn't go home. Not yet.

She checked in with her captain and ignored his offer to take the rest of the day off, then checked in with the squad, but nobody had any new information to offer. They were combing through leads from the press conference, but there was nothing solid. She hadn't heard from the dive captain, either, which meant they'd found nothing. Patty and Delilah had nothing to add, gossip or otherwise.

She pulled into the parking lot at the Forest Community Center. Thankfully, nurse Kimberly Gaines's antique VW Beetle sat in the lot. Lisa hobbled into Kimberly's office, teeth gritted against the pain she tried to will away. The other woman eyed her over the top of her reading glasses. "What happened to you?"

Lisa bypassed the chair and leaned against the wall instead. "Sat on a rattler by mistake. He wasn't happy about it."

Kimberly narrowed her eyes. "I know you're not originally from around here, but even you know better than that. I'm thinking there's more to that story."

"There is, but I'm not inclined to tell it right now." She smiled to soften the words. "But I do need to know everything you can tell me about Shelley Larsen and her daughter, Remy."

Kimberly shook her head. "I never want to speak ill of the dead, but something was going on with Brad. He changed after his last tour in Afghanistan, was quieter, but it was more recent than that. He'd been acting very strange lately. I know Shelley was worried."

"Anything you can tell me about Remy's health?"

Kimberly raised an eyebrow at her.

"Let me put it this way. You heard she and Shelley are missing, right?"

"Yes. The sooner they can find that sweet girl, the better."

Lisa's focus sharpened. "Is there some urgent reason behind that statement?"

"You know I can't divulge confidential information. Remy is... fragile. Anything that disrupts her life is hard on her, physically."

Lisa nodded. "Then we'll have to keep praying she and Shelley are found ASAP."

"Amen to that."

"Will you let me know if you hear anything at all that might help me find them?" At Kimberly's nod she added, "You know we can't seem to locate my gran, either, right?"

"I heard. I go to Sunny's quilting class and this doesn't seem like her at all. She blew off the class last night, which has us all worried."

"She hadn't mentioned any plans to take a trip or anything like that?"

Kimberly raised an eyebrow. "You know your gran does what and when she pleases, right?"

"Right. I'm grasping at straws. Let me know if you hear anything, okay?"

"You know I will."

Lisa started to leave, then turned back. "You've lived here a long time. You know anyone who does taxidermy?"

"Only name that comes to mind is Redd. He been doing that for folks for years and years."

"Is that the same Redd as Redd's Rescue?"

"Mmhmm. He does love those animals."

"Thanks, Kimberly." She'd swing by his place, ask a few questions. She'd met him a time or two, pictured a rough, wild-looking mountain man.

As she limped back to her truck, she couldn't ignore the menacing sound of time ticking away. It throbbed through her veins, each thump, each heartbeat, like the footfall of an approaching monster that couldn't be defeated or stopped.

And she had no idea where to look next.

Chapter Thirteen

Pete headed to Castile's Animal Rescue on the off-chance that Jason would talk to him, man to man, provided Castile wasn't there. He didn't doubt that Jason was worried about Shelley. But how deeply he was involved with what happened to Brad was another story. And how much he would say to a cop was something else again.

When he arrived at the gate, he looked down the drive and saw a semi-truck backed up to what appeared to be a storage shed. He rolled down the window, looking for an intercom box, but there was only a key pad.

He sat in his car and waited. In his unmarked sedan, he didn't exactly scream official business, so maybe no one would bother to inquire as to why he was there.

After a few minutes, Jason rode up on a golf cart and opened the gate. When Pete drove through, the other man stopped beside him. "What brings you out here, Detective Tanner? I already spoke with Officer Bass this morning."

Since Jason didn't mention Castile's comment about lawyers, Pete didn't either. He looked through the windshield, where a fork lift unloaded bales of barbed wire and pallets of fence posts. "That is a whole lot of fencing right there. What are fence posts going for these days, anyway?"

Jason eyed him from under the brim of his cowboy hat. "I'm pretty sure you didn't drive all this way to ask me that, Detective. So why are you here?"

"Just following up on a few things. You don't happen to have any snakes on the property, do you?"

"This is Florida. What do you think?"

Pete laughed. "No, I mean, do you keep snakes as part of whatever you do here?"

"Not usually, no. Why?"

He kept his eyes on Jason as he said, "Someone left a rattlesnake in Officer Bass's truck this morning."

"Left it? Or it crawled in on its own."

"We're thinking it was deliberate. Know anyone who might have done something like that, maybe as a prank?"

"Rattlers are no prank. It's risky. Just getting a snake into the truck would be a gamble, if you didn't know what you were doing."

"And do you know what you're doing with snakes?"

Jason's eyes widened, then narrowed suspiciously. "Now hold on a minute. You think I had something to do with it? You can't just show up here making unfounded accusations. Officer Bass tried that this morning and Martin told her to go through his lawyers next time."

"I haven't made a single accusation. Yet." Pete added.

"You are barking up the wrong tree, Detective, and wasting time you could be out looking for Shelley and Remy."

"You haven't heard from Shelley?" He studied the other man's arms, but there were no tattoos, of rope or anything else.

"No. And I'm worried. I've been calling her cell phone nonstop and I've got nothing. I'd think if they were okay, they'd let someone know so we don't worry."

Pete was thinking the same thing. "Is it possible that Brad hurt them?"

Jason paled under his cowboy hat. "You mean, did he kill them?" He scrubbed a shaking hand over his face. "I keep thinking that can't be true. Brad could be unpredictable, especially when he drank, but to kill those two?" He clenched his jaw and swallowed hard. "I can't see it." He shook his head, then stopped, eyes wide. "Wait a minute. Are you thinking he, ah, hurt Shelley and Remy and then I killed him?"

Pete didn't blink. "Did you?"

"No. Brad was a friend. And Shelley...oh, God." His Adam's apple bobbed up and down as he swallowed, but he wouldn't make eye contact. "I had nothing to do with any of it. I just want to know they're all right. Even if they're far away from here."

"Where were you Wednesday night? Did you see Brad after he left the community center?"

Jason looked off in the distance as he answered. "No. If I'd known what happened, I would have checked on Shelley right then." He paused. "I worked late and then I was home, alone, pathetic though it is."

Which gave him the opportunity to off Brad. Add his feelings for Shelley and Remy, and that equaled motive, in Pete's mind. "Anyone who can vouch for you?"

"Nobody but the animals I work with. Didn't know I'd need an alibi for my boring life." He smiled, but it was obviously forced.

"You used to be a vet, lost your license due to missing drugs."

Jason scrubbed a hand over the back of his neck. "I was young and stupid and paid for my sins. I'm grateful to Martin for giving me another chance."

"Do you administer medications to the animals here?"

"Of course. It's part of my job. Why?"

Pete didn't answer, just hitched his chin toward the scrapes on Jason's hands. "How did you get all cut up?"

"Like you said, lots of barbed wire. Easy to get cut."

"Why does an animal sanctuary need barbed wire to begin with? Don't you rehab the animals and then release them into the wild?"

"When we can. Some can't go back, so they'll stay here forever." He paused. "The barbed wire is to keep people out. There's a local group that has a problem with what Dr. Castile is doing here, and we've had some issues with sabotage. Somebody has been sneaking in and opening cages, setting animals free that weren't ready for release. Just last week, one of the injured cranes was killed by a predator before we found her."

"Do you know who's behind it?"

"Not yet. But we're trying to find out."

"What about the proposed safari drive-through? Any opposition there?"

Jason narrowed his eyes. "You know the answer to that as well as I do. Though I really don't get it. It's a win-win all around."

"Different opinions, I guess," Pete said. "Keep me posted and let me know if there's any more sabotage."

He turned his car around and headed back the way he'd come. But at the first wooded area, he pulled over and took out his camera, snapping photos of whatever was being unloaded from the semi. Some of the boxes weren't marked, but maybe one of the techs, or Byte, could blow up the pics and find something useful.

He called the hospital, annoyed to learn Fish had been discharged. He set up a meeting with her at the Café, then checked in with his people, but no one had any new information. As he drove, he replayed his conversation with Jason. Could he have killed Brad? Yes. So could Shelley. But there wasn't a single shred of hard evidence either way.

Concerned that Byte's loyalty to Fish, and therefore Shelley, might bias him, Pete called one of the sheriff's office techs and asked her to dig deep into both Shelley's and Jason's backgrounds. Then he asked Byte to do the same with Brad's, not really surprised to learn that Fish had already asked him to do the same thing.

Lisa drove down the dirt road, following the hand-lettered signs to Redd's Rescue. Shelley had had one of his tee shirts in her drawer, so maybe he knew something that could help.

She pulled through the gate and stepped out in a compound about a quarter the size of Castile's operation. She'd only taken two steps before she heard the ratchet of a shotgun.

She held her hands out at her sides, but still in reach of her weapon. "Mr. Redd. It's Officer Bass, Fish and Wildlife. I'd like to ask you a couple of questions."

Redd appeared from behind a sagging outbuilding, rifle thankfully held at his side, barrel down. He had a wad of chewing tobacco in one cheek and his white beard hung to his chest, obscuring his Redd's tee shirt.

"What does FWC want with me this time? Don't you people have more important things to do?"

FWC had been called to investigate numerous complaints about the condition of the animals being rehabilitated here, but they'd never found any evidence of neglect. The animals were always well-fed and their enclosures clean, even if the facility showed obvious signs that money was tight.

"Sir, do you know a man named Brad Larsen?"

Redd stopped stroking his beard, surprised by the question. "You mean that guy what drowned? Shame, that. Read about it in the paper. What's it got to do with me?"

"We found taxidermy tools in his truck and I hear you've been doing that kind of work for a lot of years." She glanced around, couldn't help adding, "Even though you run an animal rescue."

He stiffened as though she'd slapped him. "Don't you be taking that tone with me, Missy, like I done something wrong. You sound like one of them num-nuts that accuse me of stuffing the animals in my care. I love animals. Last I heard, that ain't illegal. Yet."

Lisa raised both hands in a stop gesture. "I meant no disrespect. I just wondered if you knew Mr. Larsen, and whether he ever did any taxidermy work for you."

"Not recently, though I hired some work out to him several years back. He's good at it. Last time I called him a couple months ago, he said he didn't have time, was too busy doing other things."

"He happen to mention what those other things were?"

Redd tugged on his beard and all but rolled his eyes at her. "He didn't say, but it don't take a fancy uniform and a badge to figure it out."

"Give it to me straight, Redd. What do you think he was doing? And who do you think he was doing it for?"

Redd turned his head and spit tobacco juice into the sand, inches from her feet. "If it was me, I'd be taking a closer look at Dr. High-and-Mighty Castile and his operation." He straightened, hitched his chin toward her truck. "And now it's time for you to leave, girly. I got things to do."

"One more question. Do you know Shelley Larsen, his wife? She ever come out here?"

"Why do you want to know?"

Interesting reaction. "Because we can't seem to locate her or her daughter."

"I hope she finally up and left that worthless son-of-a-gun." He paused. "She did a bit of office work for me, but she was always worried Larsen might find out." He turned and walked away, looked over his shoulder and added, "I hope you find them."

Lisa mulled over their conversation on the drive to the Café. Redd's concern for Shelley came as a surprise, though law enforcement was well aware there was no love lost between him and Castile. Redd was a retired local construction worker who had been running his small operation for almost twenty years, always teetering on the verge of bankruptcy, surviving on local donations to keep the doors open. When long-time local vet Martin Castile opened his sanctuary a few years ago, everything inside it was big and shiny and new. She couldn't blame Redd for some jealousy.

But was there more to it? Did Redd know something about Castile's operation and Brad's connection to it?

When she hobbled into the Corner Café, Patty gasped and hurried from behind the counter. "What the heck happened? Why are you limping?"

"I got bit by a snake, believe it or not."

Patty cocked her head to one side. "Seriously? That doesn't sound like you at all. You're always hyper-aware of what's going on around you."

Lisa smiled. "It's certainly what I teach you ladies. Apparently, it's more 'do as I say, not as I do.'"

Patty didn't laugh. "So, what really happened?"

"I really got bit by a rattlesnake. In the hospital parking lot. Someone put it in my truck."

Liz, who owned the Café, joined them in time to catch the last bit. The Café was empty this late in the afternoon, and they were getting ready to close up for the day. "How would someone get it into your FWC vehicle? You're a stickler about keeping it locked."

While it flattered her that they knew her so well, she didn't like being quite that predictable, either. Routines gave stability, order, and provided a sense of calm, but also made her sound like an uptight bore. "Apparently, I left a window open and someone put one in there."

"And you didn't see it?" Liz asked.

"Not until I sat on him. He didn't like it, in case you were wondering."

Both women cringed. Then Liz waggled a brow and asked, "So how are things with you and Detective Bulldog?"

Lisa felt the blush crawl over her cheeks and tried to brazen it out. "Since I'm acting FWC lieutenant and he's a detective, we're working together. He's leading the murder investigation and I'm focusing on the search for Shelley and Remy. And Gran." She eyed both women. "Have either of you heard from her or know where she might have gone?"

Both shook their heads no.

"She does take off every now and again, though," Patty added.

"That's what everybody I ask tells me. Do you know where she goes?"

"No idea. She just disappears, then shows up again."

"But she missed her quilt class," Liz added, "which really surprised everyone. Do you think something happened to her? I saw her picture on the news."

Lisa's stomach clenched. "I hope she's just off on a little jaunt." *Please, God.*

Patty met her gaze. "You know if that's all it is, she'll be really ticked off when she gets back, right?

"Yep. I'll take my chances." Gran could rant all she wanted, as long as she – and Remy - were found alive. "If you hear anything, call me right away, okay?"

"Of course," Liz said, then turned the conversation back to the beginning. "I think Bulldog's gotten cuter since he became a detective." She fanned herself. "He looked good in uniform, don't get me wrong, but in a suit jacket? Be still my heart."

"I hear he's single," Lisa drawled. "I can put in a good word for you." As the words left her mouth, she wanted to call them back. She didn't want him looking elsewhere. But she wasn't sure she wanted him looking at her, either. *Crap.* She was being ridiculous.

"Is he going to the fundraiser at the community center? Maybe he'll bid on your basket," Patty suggested.

Lisa's entire body cringed at the thought. The picnic basket auction and fundraiser was a huge community event, one she wholeheartedly believed in. She just wished she didn't feel obligated to participate. Not only would Liz's basket be a homemade delight while her own would be a sad and pitiful store-bought offering, the idea of Bulldog spending the evening at Liz's side grated like a rock in her shoe. She turned to Patty. "You still haven't heard a word from Shelley, right?"

Worry made the lines on Patty's face stand out in sharp relief. "Nothing. And I've been leaving messages several times a day. I feel like she would have called." She paused. "If she could have."

Lisa shoved that thought aside. "Think back. Has Shelley ever mentioned somewhere she used to go? A favorite place? Or someplace her family owned or used to visit? Anything?"

"You think they're hiding out somewhere."

"I hope so. But I need to find them."

Patty stiffened as though she'd been slapped and crossed her arms. "Why? So you can arrest her for Brad's murder?"

Lisa sighed. "You know we have to look closely at the spouse or significant other. I need her to tell me what happened, so I can rule her out as a suspect." When Patty opened her mouth to interrupt, Lisa held up a hand. "And if she did kill him in self-defense, I'll do everything I can to see she never spends a day in jail. But my biggest concern right now is finding them."

Patty's posture didn't change, but she suddenly wouldn't meet Lisa's eyes. "If I hear from her, I'll tell her you want to talk to her."

Lisa's cop radar twitched. When Patty glanced her way, she caught a flicker of doubt in her expression before it disappeared between one blink and the next.

"If you know something, Patty..."

"I won't let you arrest her."

Bulldog slid in beside Lisa. "No one's getting arrested. Not right now, anyway."

The scent of his cologne filled Lisa's nostrils and tempted her to lean closer. He looked good in that suit jacket, too. Dang Liz for making her notice.

"I'm guessing there's still no word on Shelley and Remy?"

Both women shook their heads no.

Bulldog sighed as he ran a hand over the back of his neck. "Have either of you ladies seen a man with a rope tattoo on his left arm? At the Café? Or anywhere else?"

The women exchanged glances, then Liz said, "You know those are pretty common, right? But I haven't noticed anyone in particular with one." She looked at Patty.

"Me neither. Why?"

"Just something somebody said, that's all. Now, if you ladies don't mind, I really need to touch base with Fish..." He let the words trail off.

Liz stood. "Right. Patty, let's get the place shut down." She winked at Lisa before she walked behind the counter, Patty on her heels.

Bulldog looked from Liz to her and back again. "What was that all about?"

"I have no idea." She hoped her cheeks weren't flaming, but his quizzical look said they were. "What's this about a rope tattoo?"

He filled her in on his conversation with young Cal.

"Cal saw this guy park next to my truck?"

"Yes. He has no reason to lie."

"The truck doesn't sound familiar. But why a snake? What's the endgame?"

"That's what we need to figure out. You learn anything else?"

"I went out to Redd's, asked him about Brad." Lisa sat back, waited.

He went still. "He pull a shotgun on you?"

"He did. And then we had an enlightening conversation. Though I don't get how he can be so passionate about animals and also do taxidermy."

Bulldog shrugged, some of the tension ebbing away. "Not that far-fetched. I know people who have had him stuff their family pet, so they can keep them with them."

She couldn't imagine such a thing. It would completely creep her out. "He said Brad refused some taxidermy work recently, said he had other things to do. Redd thinks he was working for Castile."

"Which Jason already told us."

"Redd also admitted Shelley had done some office work for him." At Pete's raised eyebrow she added, "Saw a shirt with Redd's logo in Shelley's dresser."

He leaned closer, eyes on hers. "What are you thinking?"

"Same thing you are. Is there something in Brad's life that got him killed? Anyone have a beef with him? Maybe looking for revenge for something?"

"I've got people checking, but nothing has panned out." He paused. "From all the whispers and hints we're getting, Shelley's still our primary suspect. She had motive."

Her chin came up. "As did Jason."

He nodded. "I went to the animal sanctuary and had another chat with him. They were unloading a whole lot more fence posts and barbed wire than seems necessary."

"Barbed wire? For the proposed safari drive-through?"

"Maybe. But he said a group of locals don't like Castile and someone has been opening cages, letting the animals out."

"Redd's doing?"

"Possibly. He makes no secret of his animosity toward Castile."

Lisa thought about it, then met his gaze. "You're not buying it." She didn't either.

"Just feels hinky."

She smiled. "Is that a highly technical detective term?"

One corner of his mouth kicked up. "Damn straight. Never discount hunches or things that feel even slightly hinky." The smile disappeared. "Why aren't you home resting? I can't believe the hospital discharged you."

"They said it would just take time. I need to get the wound checked regularly, make sure no infection is setting in, but otherwise, there's nothing they can do."

"I'll be happy to check that wound anytime you need me to, Fish," he said, the wicked gleam in his eye belying the bland tone.

She rolled her eyes. "In your dreams, Tanner."

He laughed outright, then sobered. "Are you cleared to go back to work?"

"Light duty. No chasing anyone through the woods just yet." Her cell phone rang. The dive commander. "Hey Curt. Did you find anything?"

The man's voice was grim. "We can't find a single trace of either mother or daughter. You haven't been able to confirm that they definitely went into the lake, have you?"

"No. We haven't."

"We just got a call about a missing kayaker on another lake. I can keep two of my guys in the water the rest of the day, but then I'm going to have to call off the search. But if you can give me anything to go on, someplace to start looking..."

"I completely understand." Her shoulders sagged as defeat swamped her. "If I turn something up, I'll be in touch right away. Thanks for the help. Good luck with the kayaker."

"The divers get called elsewhere?" Bulldog asked after she hung up.

Lisa looked away, swallowed hard. "Yeah. They can't just keep searching the lake, not if we don't know for sure that they went in, and if they did, where they went in." She drummed her fingers on the table, picked up her phone again. "Let me call a couple of K-9 officers. See if the dogs can track their scent."

As she started to stand, he stopped her with a hand on her arm. "Go home and rest. I'll meet the team." It was an order, not a request.

She opened to her mouth to demand he stop trying to get rid of her, but then his expression registered. His concern was genuine. Even when he was issuing commands, his heart tended to be in the right place. Still, she couldn't stop searching, no matter how much her backside ached. She'd rest after Shelley and Remy were home safe.

"I appreciate the offer. But I need to be there. I'll meet you after I change into tracking clothes."

Lisa swallowed two ibuprofen dry on the way to Brad and Shelley's place. She couldn't ignore the pain another second, and she didn't want to hobble like an invalid when she got there.

It was nearing full dark, which meant they wouldn't have much time. To make matters worse, the weather was predicted to turn to crap shortly. Her competitive nature growled when she saw that Bulldog had beaten her there, wearing jeans and snake boots, and a tee shirt that showed off every inch of the hard planes beneath. He grinned as she parked and everything inside her shifted, again. Why did this annoying, frustrating, and to be fair, caring, hardworking cop have to look so good? And what was wrong with her that suddenly Bulldog Tanner was all she could think about? Flustered by her conflicting feelings, she focused on climbing out of the truck without wincing.

She approached the K-9 handler and stuck out her hand. "Hi. I'm Lisa Bass, Fish and Wildlife." She'd peg him as late twenties, solidly built, completely at ease in his own skin. He inspired confidence, and she figured the twinkle in his blue eyes didn't hurt either.

"Nate King. And this is Chief." He pointed to the beautiful German Shepherd lying at his feet, ears perked, taking it all in. "Bulldog just gave me the quick rundown on who we're looking for. If you can get me several pieces of the mother's clothing, each in its own zippered plastic bag, that would be great."

"What about the daughter?"

"I don't want to confuse Chief. Let's start with one and go from there."

Lisa went inside and came back with the tank top Shelley had been wearing at the community center. It had been lying on the closet floor, so she guessed it hadn't been washed yet. Based on the books on the nightstand, she removed Shelley's pillow case, and grabbed her hairbrush from the bathroom.

When she returned with the items, Nate thanked her and held the tank top to the dog's nose.

He gave the command to FIND and Chief took off at a trot, Nate behind him. Lisa and Bulldog fell into step behind them.

Chief ran around the carport, nose to the ground, then hurried to the shed in a straight line, and then turned and hurried back to the carport. Once he reached it, he did another circle around it, then walked several yards away and sat down, waiting.

They stopped behind the dog. "Why did he stop?" Lisa asked.

Nate sighed. "This is where he lost the trail."

"What? Can't you have him check again?" Lisa sked.

Bulldog studied the ground around them. "This is where Brad's truck would have been parked."

"This often happens. The dog will alert. And we'll realize it's where the trail went cold. Or in this case, where the person got into a vehicle."

Disappointment hit Lisa like a closed fist. She studied the scene, then turned to Pete.

"The boat ramp," they both said at the same moment.

But before they could get a new plan together, the sky opened up and rain poured down in buckets, soaking them to the skin. Lisa wanted to howl at the scents and evidence washing away.

But she wouldn't give up.

She gave instructions and sent everyone to the makeshift boat ramp, defeat nipping at her heels.

Chapter Fourteen

Florida squalls usually moved through in about fifteen minutes. Forty-five minutes, tops. But tonight, an hour went by, and it still wasn't over. Thunder boomed and lightning flashed. These conditions weren't safe for anyone to be out in.

She pulled on her rain slicker and ran over to the handler's truck and climbed in the passenger side.

"We won't accomplish anything tonight," Nate said. "And I won't risk Chief in this weather."

"I completely agree." If they had proof of any kind that this was where Shelley and Remy had gone, Lisa wouldn't let the weather stop her. But it was literally a shot in the dark. She couldn't risk more lives on a guess. "Will there be any scent left after the rain?"

He shook his head. "Truthfully? I doubt it. A light rain doesn't destroy it, but a storm like this?" He shrugged. "I doubt there's anything left. But scent is usually stronger in the morning, when it's damp. I'm happy to bring Chief and try again at first light. Maybe we'll get lucky."

"If there's any chance at all, we have to try."

"We'll be here. Sorry about tonight."

"Not your fault."

Lisa hurried over to Pete's car and climbed in, hissing when she landed harder than she'd planned. "Can't do anything more tonight. We'll try again at first light, though this rain may have washed all the scent away."

He leaned forward, arms wrapped over the steering wheel. "You want some company? I can stay on your couch."

Surprise flared through her. What an odd offer. "Pretty sure I can handle a thunderstorm by myself. But thanks."

"Why do you do that?" he asked.

She froze, hand on the knob. "Do what?"

"Shut people out. Refuse help."

She raised a brow. "Do you accept it easily or gracefully?"

He laughed. "Good point. But with you, it seems...I don't know, more defensive."

She didn't like the direction of this conversation, but surprised herself by answering anyway. "All my life, I've had one person to rely on: me. I'm used to doing for myself. If I can't do it, it doesn't get done. Keeps things simple."

"What about your family? Didn't anyone watch your back?"

She thought of Gran's whispered encouragement the day Lisa and Mama left, her mother hiding her in an armoire to keep her safe, and chose her words carefully. "My family taught me to be independent. The habit stuck."

He studied her, and Lisa looked away, fought the urge to squirm.

"You don't always have to be alone."

Her eyes flew to his, the want and need in his brown eyes igniting an answering longing deep inside her. What would he do if she reached over and pulled him to her for a kiss that would unleash all that banked heat?

She cleared her throat and reached for the door handle before she was dumb enough to act on the impulse. This was Bulldog, completely off limits because he was a cop. Worse, they were working a joint investigation. "Thanks. I'm good. See you in the morning."

She hurried back to her truck and drove home, her heart hammering to the beat of the windshield wipers. "No getting tangled up with a cop again. Ever." Lesson learned when she found out that Bill, the decorated cop who said he loved her, was using their relationship as cover for his drug operation.

The minute she stepped inside her cottage, water puddled under her feet. She mopped it up and then grabbed a hot shower to combat the chill from the air conditioner.

As she heated a microwave dinner, a pitiful meow sounded outside the kitchen door. Cat huddled under the overhang, wet and shivering, eyes pleading.

"Oh, so now you want inside?"

She grabbed another towel and leaned down, slowly opening the door. But Cat was quick. She slithered through the opening, slipped past Lisa's towel and raced around the corner, a trail of muddy paw prints in her wake.

Lisa followed the tracks, the pain in her backside reminding her it was time for more ibuprofen. She found Cat in the middle of her bed, grooming herself as she sprawled on one of Gran's quilts, which Lisa had bought at a fundraiser.

"Comfy?" Lisa asked, shaking her head.

Cat sent her an irritated look before she leaped off the bed and disappeared down the hall, trailing still more water.

"Fine. Be that way. I don't want a cat, anyway."

She set out food and water, and ate her own meal curled up on the sofa, smiling when she heard crunching from the kitchen.

More lightning flashed and thunder boomed. Lisa had to believe that Shelley, Remy, and Gran were somewhere safe and dry.

She just had to find them.

The sky was just beginning to lighten when Pete pulled up at the makeshift boat ramp. He had a change of clothes in the back of his car, but was dressed for search and rescue. He walked over to where Fish stood with Nate and Chief, a map of the area spread on the hood of her FWC truck.

He pulled one of the to-go cups from the cardboard carrier he held and offered it to Lisa. "Morning, Fish. Nate." He nodded to the other man. "Don't know how you take your coffee, so it's black, but I brought fixins'."

"Thanks, man."

She took a slug of hers and eyed him over the rim. "Thanks, Bull-dog. Café's not on your way, so I appreciate the detour."

He eyed her up and down, noting the dark circles under her eyes, the worry that pinched her face. "I didn't figure you got much more sleep than I did."

She saluted him with her cup, wouldn't meet his eyes. "Whatever the reason, thanks." She took another sip. "Let's get to work."

Cool professional distance this morning. Check. He'd go along.

Nate gave Chief Shelley's tank top to sniff. He immediately got excited and started tugging on his lead. Nate unclipped it and commanded, "FIND."

Chief circled the small area before he sat down at the top of the ramp and looked at Nate.

"That's where Brad's truck would have been if he launched a boat here," Lisa murmured.

Pete squatted on his haunches, gauging the distance. "Looks that way."

"What about the surrounding area?" Fish asked.

Nate scanned the area. "I can walk him around the perimeter, but I don't think he'll find anything."

"Humor me, will you?"

"Sure." He turned to the dog, gave him the tank top again, and commanded, "FIND." This time Nate kept the lead on. Though Chief seemed to pick up a whiff of something here and there, ulti-mately, he just went in circles until he sat down at the top of the ramp again.

"Looks like Shelley left here in a vehicle, Fish. Any tire tracks are long gone after the storm, so we don't know in whose vehicle, though."

"What's your take, Nate?" she asked.

"Despite less than ideal conditions, Chief found what he was looking for. I'd say she got into or out of a vehicle here."

"So it's probable she, and hopefully Remy, too, are still alive."

Pete's phone rang. "One of our tech guys. Morning, Chris. What have you got?" His eyes narrowed as he listened, then he thanked him and turned to Fish, who had been watching him.

"I had my guys dig a little deeper. When you went out to Redd's, did he mention that Shelley made two payments to him in the last month? Both for $1,000 each?"

Fish's eyes widened in shock, then narrowed. "No. He didn't. But I wouldn't have known to ask that, either. Your guys are the ones checking financials."

He propped his hands on his hips, squinted off into the distance. "Where does a woman who doesn't have a regular job get that kind of money? And what did she pay him for? To kill Brad?"

"Assumptions, Bulldog. Layered with nothing but speculation. You know better than that." She turned and marched to her truck. "I'll talk to Redd."

He kept pace. "We both will."

He sat in his truck, high-powered binoculars trained on the fish cop. He shook his head at her stubbornness. She just didn't quit. But that would work to his advantage. The fact she was still searching meant she thought Shelley was still alive.

He'd heard people talking about the kid and the way the mother went all mama bear around her, all the time. Logic said she would have to come back to town eventually. And who better to contact for help than her favorite fish cop.

Maybe it was a good thing the rattler hadn't killed the annoying female. He'd let his temper get the best of him and that wasn't a mistake he'd make again.

Breaking into her official vehicle had been surprisingly easy, but a quick search had proven the notebook wasn't there. Grabbing the snake from his own vehicle had been an impulse.

But it would work in his favor. Shelley was running out of options. She'd have to reach out. And when she did, he'd be ready.

Once he had the book, it would be child's play to bury both women's bodies out in the forest where no one would ever find them. Problem solved.

And he'd get his revenge on Officer Bass. Finally.

Chapter Fifteen

Only the threat of an obstructing justice charge had convinced Redd to admit that the money was a down payment on some property he owned in Georgia. Shelley was buying it from him, and had told him she planned to build a little weekend getaway on it. Bulldog had immediately called the local police. They'd sent a couple officers out there who had confirmed there was nothing and no one on the property. Another dead end.

Still nothing on the BOLOs on Shelley and Remy.

Nothing on the missing person search on Gran, either.

By late afternoon, Lisa was exhausted, frustrated, and dealing with an entirely different kind of stress.

She scowled at the basket on her kitchen table as butterflies swooped in her stomach. Why did events like this always make her feel like a failure in the Women's Olympics? And why on earth had she let herself get talked into it to begin with? She sighed. Because it was for a good cause. Tonight's fundraiser would bring much-needed cash to the Forest Community Center, and this year's basket auction was the highlight of the event. But still. The pressure was enormous. She knew the basics of cooking, learned mostly out of desperation, and she figured her potato salad wouldn't kill anyone. Since baking didn't interest her at all, she considered herself an expert at slice-and-bake cookies. But this...arranging stuff in the basket and making it look all Pinterest-worthy? Yeah, not in her wheelhouse.

The large tote bag was handmade in Uganda by women artisans, and its leather handle and bright colors drew the eye. It was what she was trying to arrange inside it that looked sad and pitiful. She'd stopped at the grocery store on the way home, purchased a nice bottle of sparkling grape juice, since this was a no-alcohol event, some chicken salad and croissants that she packed alongside the potato salad. She figured a guy would have to eat an entire box of the fancy-looking little crackers she bought, so she'd included a nice cheese, salami, grapes and sliced cheesecake to go along with the cookies. She'd have bribed Charlee to bake something, but she and Hunter weren't back from their honeymoon yet.

She stepped back to eye the whole thing, sighing at the ugly blue ice packs shoved in all around to keep everything cold. Maybe she could cover everything in more tissue paper to hide them. She added half a dozen more sheets, then worried they'd soak up the moisture and the whole thing would look like a discarded snot rag before the auction even began.

For the fifteenth time, she berated herself for letting Patty and Charlee talk her into this. Though if she were honest, it wasn't the auction that worried her most. It was the way Bulldog kept asking about her basket. He'd gone all intense with his questions and that's what had those dang butterflies doing summersaults in her gut. What if he bought her basket? She'd have to sit beside him and eat with him.

Just the two of them.

That felt way too much like a date. Her breath hitched and she worried she might hyperventilate if she didn't get a grip.

Beside her, Cat meowed.

"Yeah, I know. I'm acting like an idiot. Assuming facts not in evidence. I'm worried about something that hasn't happened and probably won't happen at all and..." she glanced at the clock, cursed. If she didn't get her butt in gear, she'd be late, which would make everything even more awkward. He probably wouldn't even bid on her basket, and she was behaving like a sixteen-year-old at her first dance for no reason.

She ran to her bedroom, yanked open the closet, and stopped. Dang. What the heck was she going to wear to this shindig? Why hadn't she thought this through? She should have asked Patty what she was wearing, but it never occurred to her, because that was a totally girly question and she wasn't a girly girl. But right then, she wished she were, and that she had the kind of friendships where questions like that could be easily asked and answered.

A glance at the bedside clock raised her panic another notch. She had about five minutes to decide and head for a quick shower. And even then, she was cutting it way too close.

In desperation, she yanked a colorful dress off the hanger and dashed to the shower. It probably wasn't the right outfit. No, she was pretty sure it was exactly the wrong outfit, but she didn't have anything else. Her former captain's wife, Claire Barrett, had sent it for Christmas last year and despite herself, Lisa had fallen in love with it. She'd tried it on a time or two, enjoying the way the soft fabric skimmed over her skin and swirled around her legs, but she'd never had the guts to wear it in public. It was sleeveless and rather low cut and made her feel too exposed. Too like a woman looking for attention, which she'd sworn she'd never be. Years of watching her mother attract nothing but misery had taught her that.

Her heart pounded as she studied the results in the mirror. She'd been right: it was the wrong dress. But she was out of time and options, so she snatched her comfortable black suit jacket and pulled it on, securing her weapon in the shoulder holster. It was fine. So what if she looked like an FBI agent trying to blend in at a garden party?

"Just go, already," she muttered.

She gave her lips a swipe with some lip gloss, also courtesy of

Claire, shook her head at her idiocy and hurried to the kitchen. At Cat's meow, she filled the water and food bowls and tried to pat her on the head—Cat darted away before she made contact--then grabbed the basket and headed out.

She couldn't believe she was doing this.

Pete knew the minute Fish walked in and damn if his heart didn't skip a beat. She'd never been one to primp and fluff, but with something shiny on her lips and a bold, form-fitting flash of color under the boxy jacket, she looked...incredibly hot. He almost choked on the ginger ale he was sipping.

Without conscious thought, he moved toward her, itching to run his hands through the shiny blonde hair she'd left loose and get another whiff of whatever perfume or body spray or whatever she wore that had started drawing his notice.

Stop. His job tonight was chatting up the locals, trying to figure out why someone wanted Brad dead, and where Shelley and Remy might be. He fervently hoped they were both alive, but Shelley had a lot of questions to answer. Today's information from Redd only made her look more guilty.

"Detective Tanner."

Pete stopped, surprised to see his captain approach. "Evening, sir. Glad you could make it."

"Always happy to support the community," Charles Hall said. He scanned the room, then turned back to Pete. "How's the Larsen investigation coming? Any new developments?"

"Not since I updated you a few hours ago, sir."

Hall slapped him on the back. "Keep me posted. And find Larsen's wife."

"Yes, sir," Pete said, but Hall had already turned away, talking to the mayor.

Pete was still wondering what that was all about as he strolled up beside Fish, who had just plopped a really nice-looking basket on the auction table. "Hey, Fish. Looks good."

She spun around and almost knocked the basket off the table. As he reached out to catch it, she crashed into him, and he suddenly found himself with her in his arms. She smelled as good as he had imagined.

She scrambled out of his grasp and busied herself straightening the contents of the basket. "Thanks. Sorry about that." She waved a hand to indicate them, the table.

He liked the sudden color in her cheeks, so he deliberately stepped closer, leaned over the basket, and studied the contents. "Hmmm. Nice. Is that chicken salad? My favorite. You must have bought it with me in mind."

Her eyes flew to his. "No. I—I mean— "

He laughed and let her off the hook, though something about her vulnerability brought out all his protective instincts. "I'm just jerking your chain, Fish. It looks great. You did good putting it all together. It'll earn quite a bit at the auction."

There was a screech as the director of the community center stepped to the microphone and cleared his throat.

"Looks like they're ready to get started. Good luck," Bulldog added, then winked and stepped over to talk to several people he knew.

But he kept his eyes on her as she walked away. He studied the confident sway of her hips, the long lean lines of her body emphasized by the flowy fabric, the severe suit jacket and shoulder holster she'd worn over the dress. Her outfit was as much a contradiction as Fish herself.

Suddenly, a working evening had the potential to be a whole lot more.

As Lisa hurried toward Patty, who was waving like she was cheering the home team at a football game, she wondered if she could still escape with her dignity intact. What had Bulldog been up to, teasing her like that? She had known him too long to miss the playful gleam in his eyes.

She felt completely out of sorts, and she didn't like it. Not one bit. She straightened her shoulders as she maneuvered through the crowd. She wouldn't think about Bulldog or the way he was starting to occupy far too much of her brain space. She'd just ignore him, keep her distance. Fellow cops were colleagues, she reminded herself. Possibly friends. Never spouses or parents.

"Oh, that basket is gorgeous. Is it yours?" Patty asked as she reached her.

Lisa found Kimberly Gaines holding her basket aloft for all to see, pivoting Vanna White-style. She groaned when Patty yelled, "Nice job, Officer Bass!"

Lisa elbowed her in the ribs as all eyes turned in their direction.

Director Bremerton grinned as he asked, "And what do I have as an opening bid for this lovely basket, donated by the most beautiful lady FWC Officer in town?"

"Since she's the only lady FWC Officer, I hope she's the only beautiful one," someone shouted, and everyone laughed.

"One hundred dollars," came the shaky voice of old Mr. Penrod, a Café regular who'd been a deacon at the Baptist Church since God was in short pants, as Gran would say.

Lisa's eyes widened and Patty grinned. "Nice start."

Delilah Atwood moved to stand beside them. "Hey, ladies."

With her short dark hair and compact figure, she looked sleek and elegant, as always, making Lisa feel like a gawky giant by comparison. "Josh not back yet?"

Delilah scanned the room. "Not yet, but he promised to bid on my basket, so he'd better show. Otherwise, I'm not sure anyone else will."

"They'll bid," Lisa said, but she understood Delilah's worry. Folks had strong opinions on the local feral monkey population, for and against, and as a monkey researcher, Delilah had dealt with her share of hostility over her desire to see the monkeys left alone. Others wanted to see them removed, as they weren't native. But since they'd lived in the Ocala National Forest since the 1930s, the whole thing was complicated.

"One fifty," Bulldog shouted, and a chorus of, "Ooohhhs," came from all the women present.

"Two hundred," Officer Sanchez said, and Lisa chuckled when his girlfriend, nurse Sara Dutton, sent him a steely-eyed glare. Sanchez didn't blink, just widened his grin.

She told herself not to glance at Bulldog, but her eyes found him nonetheless. Thankfully, he didn't notice, as he was busy glaring at Sanchez. Which, knowing Sanchez, was exactly the point.

Several other bids came in from local guys she didn't know, which was when a whole other worry occurred to her. What if she had to sit with a complete stranger?

"Two fifty," Gene Phillips yelled. Tall and ruggedly handsome, the long-time local owned one of the premier horse farms in the area. His wife was Gran's friend, Janet.

"Holy Moly," Lisa whispered. "That's a lot of money for chicken salad."

"All for a good cause," Patty reminded her.

"Three fifty," came a smooth voice from the back.

The crowd gasped as all eyes turned to look. A drop-dead gorgeous, thirty-something Latino man in a very expensive-looking suit smiled at Lisa.

"Who is that?" she whispered as a shiver of awareness slid over her skin.

"I have no idea," Delilah whispered. "Do you know?" she asked Patty, who shook her head.

Lisa's anxiety went up with every bid, especially when the field narrowed to him, Mr. Penrod, and Bulldog.

"Three seventy-five," Bulldog called.

Connie Mann

"Three ninety," Mr. Penrod shot back.

"Four hundred," Handsome called.

"Four fifty." Bulldog's tone was firm as he turned his back on the other man. He crossed his arms and raised a brow at Mr. Penrod.

Mr. Penrod shook his head, raised his fingers in salute. "Enjoy your picnic with Officer Bass. Too rich for my blood."

"Five hundred," Handsome called.

Heads swiveled back to Bulldog. He narrowed his eyes at the other man. "Five fifty."

Lisa watched the two men stare each other down. Finally, Handsome gave a slight nod and stepped back.

Bremerton banged his gavel on the podium. "Going once, going twice, Sold! to Detective Tanner for five hundred fifty dollars. We thank you for your service to our community—and for your generous donation to the community center."

"Nice," Delilah said as she applauded.

Patty squealed. "That's so cool. And he's oh, so hot," she whispered with a little sigh.

"Who, Handsome?"

Patty punched her arm. "No, Bulldog. You know he is. You just don't want to admit it." She leaned closer, "And in case you're wondering, the sparks that have started flying whenever you two are in the same room are hot enough to blister paint."

Lisa's jaw dropped. "You're imagining things." She had to be, because...was it that obvious?

The man in question appeared, extended his arm. "Good evening, Madam. Allow me to escort you to our table." He nodded toward the ring of small linen-covered tables lining the perimeter of the room. Each table was set for two, so the basket winners could sit with the person who donated it. Together.

She swallowed hard and linked arms with him, feeling like every single eye in the whole place watched as they wended their way across the room. Behind them, bidding for the next basket had begun,

146

but all Lisa could think about was the feel of Bulldog's arm under hers and the way his jacket fit over his broad shoulders.

"What?" she snapped, when she couldn't stand the way he was studying her another second.

"You look beautiful tonight," he said.

She snorted. "Knock it off, Bulldog."

He raised a brow. "I can't pay a lady a compliment?"

She felt her cheeks heat. "Will you stop?"

He leaned closer and his cologne teased her nostrils. "Relax, Fish. Enjoy the moment. I know I am."

She wanted to, but it was impossible. Acknowledging their attraction in private was one thing. But acting like this was a date, in front of the whole community, no less? They worked together.

They reached the table and he pulled out her chair, then set the basket down at an angle that shielded them from prying eyes. He pulled out all the items, wiping off the soggy bits of tissue paper before he set them down.

He pulled his chair closer and Lisa fought the urge to move hers farther away.

"Looks good. Thanks for packing all my favorite stuff." He held up the cheesecake. "Not as good as Charlee's, but still really good."

"Why are you doing this?" she blurted.

He opened the chicken salad, forked some onto a croissant. "Because I'm hungry."

"You know what I mean," she hissed.

He met her eyes then, his own serious. "It's for a good cause." He shrugged. "Besides, since we're working the case together, no one will think it's weird if we're seen together."

She rolled her eyes. "Except everyone in the whole freaking place is currently placing bets on whether our wedding will be in April or May."

"I think we should definitely go with April. Getting too hot by May." He took a big bite and opened the sparkling grape juice while he chewed. He poured them each a glass, then raised his. "To new adventures."

Somehow those words raised gooseflesh on her arms and sent the earlier butterflies swooping like demented birds. She raised her own plastic wineglass and tapped it to his, determined to keep her hand from shaking. "And to old friends," she added.

The smile he sent her seemed to come all the way from his soul and pulled her in. The crowd disappeared and she found herself grinning back like an idiot.

"Thank you for your generous donation to the Community Center."

"My pleasure."

They ate in silence for a while, the act of swallowing seeming to take all her energy. She tried and failed to find something witty or casual to say and apparently, so did he.

Lisa angled her chair slightly so she could watch the rest of the auction, cheering for the winners and getting a kick out of who paired up with whom. When Delilah's basket came up, she breathed a sigh of relief when she heard Josh's voice. She sent Hollywood a thumbs-up, glad he'd gotten back in time. Lisa and Bulldog cheered with enthusiasm to boost the rather tepid applause.

Next up was Liz and Lisa grinned at how flustered she was. She'd been in the kitchen, helping with the food, but was now wringing her hands as the bidding started. She met her friend's gaze and mouthed, "Relax. You've got this."

Liz's smile was tremulous and Fish turned to see what had the other woman so on edge. When K-9 handler Nate King called out his bid in a low, sexy rumble, Fish had her answer. "Well, isn't that interesting," she murmured.

"It's about time," Bulldog said, licking chicken salad off one finger. "He's had the hots for her for so long, he's going to go bankrupt eating at the Café twice a day."

"Really? How did I miss all that?" They did look cute together and the way they kept stealing glances at each other was hard to miss.

"Pay attention, Fish. There's a lot you've been missing."

His voice was low, intimate, and raised gooseflesh on her arms. But before she could demand to know what that meant, exactly, Nate won the basket and he and Liz headed off together.

By the time Pete polished off the cheesecake, Lisa was ready to bolt from the room. Every time he looked at her, her heart did this stupid little hop-skip that totally unnerved her, and she fought the urge to reach out and touch, to push his suit jacket aside and feel that hard chest under her hands, run her fingers through his hair where it curled just above his shirt collar. She cleared her throat. She had to get them back on familiar ground.

"Have you found any more information as to who wanted Brad dead?"

Pete looked at her oddly as he stood and gathered their trash. "You know as much as I do. I'm not keeping things from you."

She met his gaze squarely. "If we find out she killed him, it was self-defense. And I'll move heaven and earth to make sure she doesn't spend a day in jail."

"Don't get ahead of yourself, Fish. First we have to find her and figure out what happened." He paused. "Provided she's still alive."

Her heart squeezed, but before she could protest, the director's voice came through the sound system again. "All right, folks. It's time to really get this party started. We're square dancing tonight."

Hoots and hollers met this announcement as the fiddle player started a toe-tapping tune. The crowd started clapping to the music as the rest of the band joined in.

Pete stood, held out a hand. "Let's do this, Fish."

She looked up. "Oh, no. I, um, I don't, ah, square dance."

He pulled her up and headed for the dance floor without waiting for a response. "You do tonight," he said over his shoulder.

And dance they did, until Lisa desperately wanted to shed her jacket due to the heat. But with her gun in its holster, she couldn't. She was ready to cry uncle when the band leader stepped to the microphone.

"Whohee! Wasn't that fun? We'll play a couple slow numbers next, so grab your favorite lady and cuddle up."

That was definitely her cue to escape. Lisa took two steps forward, only to have Pete grab her hand and twirl her back into his arms. She bounced off his chest and he tightened his arm behind her back, keeping her against him. "Dance with me," he murmured, eyes suddenly serious.

How had she never noticed how deep and sexy his voice sounded, or how his brown eyes looked like the most decadent dark chocolate, warm and welcoming and slightly sinful? Her heart pounded as he took her right hand and placed her left on his shoulder. Then he slipped his arm around her lower back and expertly guided her across the floor.

"You've done this before."

He smiled down at her. "Mama made Josh and me take lessons, so we wouldn't embarrass ourselves, or her, she said."

"Seems to have worked." She, on the other hand, held herself stiffly, afraid she'd miss a step and fall flat on her face.

His smile distracted her and she stumbled over his foot. She would have fallen if he hadn't been holding her.

"Relax, okay? Let me lead, just this once," he whispered in her ear.

His low murmur coaxed her to lower her defenses enough to let him tuck her head under his chin. His hand made slow, soothing motions on her back, taking what was left of the starch out of her spine. She let herself melt against him, just a little, truly shocked by how nice it felt to be held against his rock-hard chest.

For once, she let herself stop thinking and simply enjoyed the moment. No looking ahead, no planning, no analyzing, no wondering. It was freeing.

It was terrifying.

When the song ended, Pete surprised her by leading her off the dance floor and back to their table. "Excuse me a minute," he said.

His sudden departure knocked her off balance, but then she realized where he was headed.

His parents sat at a table beside the dance floor, his mother in her wheelchair. Lisa knew she generally used a walker these days, but for long evenings, they would have brought the chair she loathed.

He bent down and whispered something in his mother's ear that made her throw her head back and laugh. She patted his cheek and shook her head no. He ignored her protest and pulled her to her feet and into his arms in one smooth motion.

Tears gathered in Lisa' eyes as he carefully lifted his mom's feet until they rested atop his, and then he slowly, carefully, danced with her, smiling all the while. His mother's grin could have lit up the room, such was her pride in her son. The other dancers gave them plenty of room and when Pete turned so that he was facing Lisa over his mother's shoulder, he sent her a grin and a wink that hit her square in the heart.

For all his bluster and teasing and overprotectiveness, Pete Tanner was one of the good guys.

She swallowed the lump in her throat and trotted over to where Pete's father sat at the table, watching. "May I have this dance?" she asked.

When he stood and smiled, she realized where Pete had gotten his smile—along with the twinkle in his eyes. "If you don't mind being seen with an old man," he said.

"The honor is mine, but be warned, I'm a notorious toe-stomper," she said as they moved onto the floor.

When the dance ended, Pete transferred his mother to his father's arms and pulled Lisa back into his own so smoothly she didn't have a chance to protest.

She leaned back and sent him a saucy grin. "You do know that they're all betting on how many children we'll have, now, right?"

"Three sounds like a nice round number, don't you think?" He guided them around another couple. "Though I could be persuaded to go for four, if you ask nicely and we get to work on it for a while."

She swallowed hard as the teasing in his gaze slowly changed into something else entirely. Promise whispered through her, a hint of what might be, wrapped in a dazzling smile that made heat curl in her belly and her heart start to pound like a runaway train.

They stared at each other, lost in their own little world as the dancers ebbed and flowed around them. When the song ended and the band leader announced a break, Lisa blinked, the spell broken.

Pete kept a hand at the small of her back as they wended their way back to their table. The heat from his touch warmed her back and made her want to shout, "What just happened here?" How could every encounter, every touch from this man, make him appeal to her all the more? It felt like her world had shifted on its axis and none of the pieces fit together the way they had before.

"Excuse me another minute," Pete said as they reached the table.

He walked away again, leaving Lisa even more confused. Where was he going this time?

She watched him cross the room, then a shadow blocked him from view. She looked up to see Gene Phillips standing beside the table.

He tipped his cowboy hat. "Evening, Officer Bass." He was wearing crisp blue jeans and a western style jacket, string tie at the collar of his white shirt.

"Mr. Phillips, thank you for coming tonight. And for bidding on my basket."

"I'm always happy to support worthy organizations, especially local ones that help our community." He pulled out Bulldog's chair. "Mind if I sit a minute?"

Interesting. "Please. What can I do for you?"

He sat and leaned forward, too far into her personal space. She didn't back up. "I saw the press conference and my wife said you called her looking for Sunny."

"Yes. Do you know anything that would help me find her?" She kept her eyes on his.

He looked uncomfortable, glanced down at his feet. Lisa followed his gaze and stilled as she spotted his boots. Big boots. Not cowboy boots, as she would have expected, but black biker-type boots, similar in size to the tracks she'd found in Gran's garage.

He cleared his throat. "The thing is, I've gotten to know your grandmother over the years, and she, well, she likes to be independent, coming and going as the mood strikes. Doesn't like being tied down or accountable to anyone."

Does that include you? "What are you trying to tell me, Mr. Phillips?"

He finally looked up again. "I also heard you're trying to get back into her good graces, as it were. I don't think it'll help if you try to find her when she doesn't want to be found."

"Do you know where she is?"

"No, ma'am. I'm just saying, this won't earn you any points with her, is all." He stood, tipped his hat. "Have a good evening."

Lisa watched him go, trying to figure out what that was all about.

Pete threaded his way across the crowded room where he'd seen Calvin and a couple of the other boys from the center basketball team hanging out. He'd been desperate to escape Lisa's pull for a few minutes. Otherwise, he would have thrown caution to the wind and kissed her soundly, right there, in front of his parents and the entire community. Only the possibility that she'd pull her gun on him if he attempted such idiocy had kept him from doing it.

Thankfully, Calvin had provided a much-needed distraction.

He walked slowly, trying to clear Lisa's scent from his head, greeting people he knew, forcing his mind back to the case at hand. He had a murder to solve.

"Hey there, Calvin," he said when he reached the group. He ruffled the boy's hair, eyeing his crisp shirt and tie and slightly too-short dress pants. "Don't you clean up nice."

Calvin blushed to the roots of his curly hair. "I look like a dork.

Mom got me new clothes from the center's clothes closet and made me dress up."

Pete looked him up and down. "I think you look very handsome. I also know the ladies go gaga for a man in a tie." He scanned the room. "Are you having a nice time despite the dorky clothes?"

Calvin's glance darted to a pretty girl with freckles and red hair wearing a yellow sundress.

"Who's that? She's pretty."

"Nobody. She's just a girl from my class."

"She's looking at you," Pete teased.

Calvin blushed again. Shrugged. "She's nice." Then he turned to Pete. "Have you found the guy who put the snake in Officer Bass's truck yet?"

"Not yet. But we're working on it. You haven't told anyone about him, have you?"

Calvin straightened. "No. Just my mom. I told you I wouldn't."

Pete nodded. "Thank you. It's good to know you're a man of your word. I was wondering if maybe you've seen the man again anywhere."

Calvin looked down, fiddled with his clip-on tie. "Maybe."

"Calvin? Talk to me, buddy."

The boy shrugged. "So I was maybe out riding my bike and I think I saw him."

Pete tried to figure out what the boy wasn't saying. "Did he see you? Where were you?"

"It might not have been him, and anyways, I was— "

"Calvin. Just spit it out. Were you somewhere you weren't supposed to be?"

His head shot up. "How did you know?"

Pete grinned. "Because I've worn that same look, when I was worried about getting busted for going somewhere I shouldn't."

Even the tips of Calvin's ears turned red. "Even though I'm almost twelve, Mom says I can't go too far from our house." He shrugged. "Sometimes I get bored and just start riding my bike."

"What did you see?"

"The guy with the tattoo was there with another guy, and they had shovels and were burying something."

Pete's heart gave a loud thud. "Could you see what it was?"

"Nah. I was too far away, but it was big, I know that."

"Can you take me there?"

"Maybe. But not at night." He shrugged again. "It was kind of hidden."

"How about I pick you up after school tomorrow and we take a ride out there? Is that okay? I'll make sure I ask your mom."

Calvin shot him a worried glance. "You won't tell her how far away it is?"

"I won't lie to her, Calvin, and neither should you. But I will tell her I need your help, which is true."

"Better bring your pickup, not that wussie cop car, or we'll never get through the sand."

"Good to know. I'll see you tomorrow afternoon."

Calvin nodded, but he still looked worried.

As Pete went to find the boy's mother, he made a mental list of legit items besides a body someone could have buried in the forest. It wasn't a very long list.

"What?" Lisa asked when he got back to the table and sat down.

So much for his poker face. "Calvin thinks he saw the guy with the tattoo bury something out in the forest. He's going to show me where it is tomorrow after school."

"I'm coming with you." Her chin came up, daring him to argue.

"Of course. But I'll tell you the same thing I've been telling myself: keep an open mind."

Lisa nodded absently. "I just had an odd conversation with Gene Phillips." She related the man's comments.

"Interesting. Why would he feel compelled to tell you that? Does he know where she is?"

"He said he didn't. Do you know anything about a relationship between those two?"

"Nothing, but I'm often in the dark on gossip."

"I'll see what I can find out." She glanced across the room. "Who did Jason work for before he took the job with Castile?"

Pete looked over his shoulder to where the man in question stood, looking a little too suave in an expensive suit, deep in conversation with Kimberly Gaines. "I'll double-check, but it seemed like nothing more than a series of odd jobs after he lost his veterinary license. They could never prove he was stealing drugs, so he didn't go to jail, but it still ruined his career."

As they watched, Kimberly patted his cheek and Jason walked over to talk with Sanchez who was standing by the Florida panther they'd brought along this evening. Kids were lined up three deep, listening to the FWC officer talk about the animal, its habitats, why it was important. The kids were rapt, watching the big cat.

"I don't believe I've had the pleasure," a smooth voice said.

Lisa looked up to see the handsome, dark-haired newcomer standing beside their table, hand extended. "I'm Julio Castile."

When she stuck hers out to shake, he smiled and slowly kissed the back of her hand instead, a decidedly old-world gesture. Behind him, Pete scowled.

Lisa smiled. "Hello, Julio. I'm Fish and Wildlife Commission Officer Lisa Bass. And this is Detective Pete Tanner with the sheriff's office."

The two men assessed each other as they shook hands, both trying to hide a wince at the other's grip. Lisa barely refrained from rolling her eyes.

"Any relation to Dr. Martin Castile?" Pete asked.

"Yes, I'm his nephew, up from Miami for a little while." He turned to study the crowd. "I spent summers in this area as a child, visiting my uncle. Haven't spent enough time here in the past few years. It's good to be back. My uncle's veterinary practice has grown, just like the whole area, but it's good to see the generosity and community spirit are still strong. This is an important center."

"It is. They do good work." Pete's tone dared the other man to argue.

The band struck up another slow song and Julio extended his hand, palm up. "May I have the pleasure of this dance?"

She was about to decline, but then she caught Pete's dark look and smiled at Julio instead. Wouldn't do to let Bulldog get too territorial. "Thank you. I'd love to."

Julio led her onto the dance floor, and she realized he was as good a dancer as Pete, who stood at the edge of the dance floor with his arms crossed, face like a thundercloud. She ignored him as Julio spun her around the small dance floor.

A sudden commotion on the other side of the room caught her attention. At the raised voices, she looked over Julio's shoulder at Bulldog, who nodded in that direction.

"Excuse me, please." She slipped out of Julio's arms and fell into step with Bulldog. "What's going on?"

"Let's find out."

They elbowed their way through the crowd in time to see Redd poke a finger in the direction of Dr. Martin Castile's crisp white shirt. "If I wanted to damage your fancy place, do you really think I'd be dumb enough to leave a trail?"

Castile leaned in until they were nose to nose. "That hawk's wing wasn't healed. It couldn't fly, so it died because of somebody's misguided attempt to set it free."

Redd clenched his jaw and stood to his full height. "You got a lot of nerve, making accusations like that. I wouldn't endanger an animal, no matter how much I dislike you."

Bulldog stepped between the two men. "Gentlemen, this is not the place."

Redd stepped back, jabbed another finger in Castile's direction. "You'd better stay out of my way, fancy man." He turned and disappeared into the crowd.

Castile tugged his jacket back into place, expression thoughtful. "I was convinced he's been sabotaging my animal sanctuary, but now I'm not so sure."

"What happened?" Lisa asked.

"Someone climbed the fence last night, released a hawk."

"Do you have security cameras?" Bulldog asked.

"I had several at the exits. I'll be installing some around the animal enclosures now, too."

"I can come by in the morning and fill out a report," Lisa began.

"Thank you, but that won't be necessary." His tone was clipped.

She paused, nodded. "All right. Please keep us posted." She spotted Julio approaching with a wide smile and decided it was time to go.

She excused herself and headed back to their table, Bulldog right behind her. As she picked up her purse and slung it over her shoulder, she caught a glimpse of Gene Phillips's cowboy hat as he went out the door. "Text me when you know what time we're heading to Cal's tomorrow."

Bulldog followed her outside, watched her crouch down in the dirt and take pictures with her cell phone camera. He looked across the parking lot and saw Phillips climb into a shiny white pickup. "You thinking he's the one who left the prints at your gran's place?"

"Can't hurt to check." She snapped a few more pictures, then tucked her phone back into her purse and started for her truck.

"That was one great picnic spread, Fish," he said, stepping up behind her. "I enjoyed all of it."

She glanced over her shoulder, and a soft blush raced over her cheeks. It hit him like a punch to the gut. "You're welcome. It was for a good cause."

When she reached her official vehicle, he leaned around her to open the door.

Her eyes widened. "What are you doing?"

He quirked a smile in her direction. "Trying to be a gentleman. Keep up, Fish."

"I don't like it. We work together. Don't blur the lines."

Their eyes met and he couldn't resist taking her hand, brushing a thumb over the soft skin, charmed by her determination to keep her distance. "Too late, Fish. They're already blurred and you know it."

She swallowed hard and then slipped from his grasp and climbed into the truck. She winced slightly when her backside hit the seat and he realized that rattlesnake bite must still hurt, though she didn't let on by so much as a flicker of an eyelash.

"See you tomorrow, Bulldog," she said, closed the truck door, and started the engine.

He was grinning as he climbed into his car.

Chapter Sixteen

Lisa checked the rearview mirror again. Seriously? Was he really going to follow her home as though this was some kind of date or something? Apparently he was, because when they reached her driveway, he waited while she turned her vehicle around and backed in. He did the same. By the time she stepped onto her little porch, he was right beside her.

"You didn't have to come all this way. We'd already said good night."

In the yellow light of her front porch, his smile widened, and the look he shot her could have melted rock.

"No, we didn't. We're going to do it right this time, and without an audience."

And with that, he pulled her into his arms, his hands at her waist, her breasts crushed against his hard chest. She braced for the kind of hard, possessive kiss she'd gotten over the years from idiots who got a thrill out of kissing a woman who could shoot.

Instead, Pete moved in slowly, hands running up and down her arms, eyes hot. The way he was looking at her made heat curl in her belly. "If you have a problem with me kissing you," he added, "now's the time to say so." His voice was a low rumble that raised gooseflesh on her arms.

Her mind raced, reminding her this was Bulldog. Tough cop. Pain in the butt.

He was also a boys' basketball coach and the guy who took his mother to lunch and danced with her at a fundraiser.

Her heart won out and she decided to stop thinking and enjoy the moment. "Just come here, already," she whispered, and leaned in to meet him halfway.

"I do love a woman who knows what she wants." One hand reached out to cup her cheek and angle her mouth just right, while the other wrapped around her back and pulled her closer still.

He brushed one quick kiss over her lips, then nibbled along her jaw before he moved to the sensitive spot right behind her ear. She turned her head into another kiss, but he chuckled as he scattered butterfly kisses along her cheekbones and over the bridge of her nose.

"Kiss me already," she grumbled.

"Don't rush me, Fish. I'm enjoying the appetizer." He leaned back slightly so he could see her face. "Aren't you?" He raised a brow, his wicked grin sending heat all the way to her toes.

She found she had no words, the look in his eyes and the feel of him wrapped around her, short-circuiting her brain and pushing all rational thought aside. She grabbed his tie and pulled him close. "Let's talk later," she murmured and watched heat flare in his brown eyes before their lips met in a searing kiss that turned her world upside down.

It went on and on, lips and tongues, teeth and hands, touching, stroking, learning.

"Inside," he murmured and she gripped his hand and fumbled with the lock with the other.

Lisa stepped inside to turn on the light and almost tripped over the blur that raced past her into the house.

Meow!

They both blinked against the sudden light and the moment shattered.

Cat hissed at Pete, who grinned in response. He bent down and petted her and wouldn't you know it, the little traitor actually stood still and let him.

"I didn't know you had a cat." He stroked a hand between Cat's ears and she purred. Actually purred. Unbelievable.

"I don't. She just showed up." When Lisa reached down to pet her, Cat hissed and raced for the kitchen.

Pete, the louse, didn't even try to hide his grin. "I don't think she likes you, Fish."

"Nope. She doesn't. But she likes my food well enough." She met his eyes. "Thanks for a nice evening. But you should probably go."

His playful expression vanished as he stood, and shutters came down over his normally expressive eyes. "You have a kitty door?"

"I do. But I lock it when I leave."

He reached for the doorknob. "We still don't know who put that snake in your truck. Or why."

"I'll be careful."

He sent her that lopsided grin. "I have no doubt." He paused. "I could sleep on the couch."

Temptation whispered in her ear. "Thanks, but I'm fine."

"Good to know. I have to be in court in the morning, but I'll pick you up later on to head to Cal's." He leaned in and gave her a kiss that made her wish she wasn't sending him away. "Sleep well, Lisa."

She listened to his car drive away, the taste of him still on her tongue. Her little cottage felt big and lonely all of a sudden, which annoyed her. Not only was he a cop, she'd sworn she'd never depend on a man, ever. Not after what she'd seen in her mother's life. She'd never let anyone use her feelings to control her, either, as Bill had done in the name of love. And that included Pete Tanner, no matter how much her heart whispered that she could trust him.

She went into her home gym and attacked her punching bag, determined to exorcise these strange and unsettling feelings.

Afterwards, she called Gran's cell and home numbers again, then uploaded the photos of Phillips's boot prints and compared them to the ones from Gran's place. The size was about right, but the tread didn't match. Didn't mean he hadn't been there, wearing different boots. Just in case, she sent them to Byte, but she figured he'd say the same thing.

Why had Phillips sought her out?

Unsettled, she plopped on the couch with a legal pad and her crochet hooks. She crocheted a row or two, then jotted down more questions, crocheted some more, scribbled more ideas, on and on as the hour grew late.

Somehow, the answers were here. She just had to find them.

As Pete drove home, the memory of Lisa in his arms taunted him, urging him to turn around and go back, explore more of whatever was growing between them. But he wouldn't. Not when she'd told him to go.

She'd snuck under all his defenses when he wasn't looking, and it scared the crap out of him. Maybe she was right. A little distance wouldn't be a bad thing right now. They were colleagues, working a case together. Best to keep their relationship separate.

He snorted. As though it was that easy.

He sat on his porch late into the night, sketching Fish's various and ever-changing expressions, one after another, page after page, trying to make some sense of the different components that made up this complex, tantalizing woman.

Then he turned his mind to the case. He wrote down everything he knew about Brad and Shelley and drew circles around each fact. Then he added Jason, the Castiles and Redd, Cal's mystery man with the tattoo, and whoever left a snake in Lisa's truck. And because he didn't know if she was part of this or not, he added Lisa's gran. And Gene Phillips.

When he finally stopped scribbling and looked at the page, he froze. He still didn't know who killed Brad. But one thing had become crystal clear.

Lisa was the single connection between all the pieces of the puzzle.

The sound of breaking glass woke Lisa with a start. She froze, heart pounding, trying to figure out if what she'd heard had been part of the nightmare she'd been caught in, or was part of the real world.

She raised up on her elbows. It sounded like the wind. She eased her weapon from the bedside table where she'd stowed it earlier, then tiptoed to the partly open bedroom door. Clouds covered the moon, leaving everything in shadow.

Without a sound, she stepped into her office, gun first, then cleared the bathroom before venturing down the short hallway and doing a sweep of the kitchen. When she turned into the living room, she gasped as her foot landed on broken glass. Her eyes shot to the big picture window, but it was intact. She turned in a slow circle, realizing the sound of glass shattering in the smaller dining room window was what woke her.

Careful of the shards littering the floor, she walked into the room, stunned to find a rock the size of her fist lying there, something wrapped around it with rubber bands.

Are you kidding me? Irritation spiked at such an amateurish threat. But then logic kicked in. She backed into her bedroom, brushed the glass off the soles of her feet and grabbed a pair of flip-flops. She'd bandage the cuts later. Whoever had thrown the rock had a good enough arm to break the window.

She wanted to study the rock immediately, but first she'd make sure no one was hiding in the woods, watching. Gun at her side, she turned off the motion-activated light above her kitchen door and eased around the back of the cottage. She used a large Live Oak tree as cover to slip into the surrounding woods.

Senses tuned to the night, she stopped and listened. The nocturnal animals rustled in the underbrush, but there were no human sounds she could discern. Slowly, carefully, she made a complete circuit around the house, but whoever it had been, was long gone.

She went back inside and pulled on a pair of gloves before she unwrapped the rock. A chill passed over her skin as she popped off the rubber bands and unfolded the note.

Someone had taken her picture while she was at the Chapel Lake boat ramp and had drawn a great big red x through it with what looked like permanent marker. Even though she knew it was pretty paltry, as threats went, it was still unsettling. She tucked everything into a plastic bag so Byte could do a full workup. Prints, type of marker, anything he could find.

A ripple of excitement fizzed along her nerve endings. This was the first real clue they'd found.

She called it in and dispatch had the sheriff's office send a patrol car to check out the area, but they didn't find any unfamiliar vehicles. She started a pot of coffee and then fired up her computer to check the feed on her trail cameras. "Come on, come on, where are you, coward?" She scrolled through all the footage, twice, but found no sign of anyone coming or going.

Which meant they knew where the cameras were and had deliberately avoided them. *Dang.*

Cat jumped up on the desk and startled a curse out of her. Heart pounding, she studied the annoyed feline. "How did you get in here?"

Of course. The dining room window. Cat walked across her desktop and Lisa's heart softened at the bloody paw print. "Poor baby. You got cut on the glass." Without giving Cat a vote, she scooped her up and headed for the bathroom, where a fierce battle of wills ensued over Lisa examining her paw. She finally settled for rinsing it off and letting her go. After Cat dashed out of the room, she wiped eight pounds of cat hair off her skin.

When she returned to the kitchen, she found Cat there, diligently licking her injured paw. "You'll be just fine." Lisa reached out to pet the top of her head and Cat hissed, but only once this time.

After she rummaged around in the shed for a sheet of plywood from her hurricane stash and covered the window, it was almost dawn, so she went outside with her flashlight, searching for evidence. By seven, she'd already talked to Byte and arranged to give him everything she'd found.

After Phillips's strange comments last night, followed by this threat, she was more convinced than ever that her gran was somehow tied into events surrounding Brad's death. The urge to find her, right now, had never been stronger.

She wouldn't make the mistake of ignoring her gut. Never again.

Chapter Seventeen

By the time Pete pulled up in front of her cottage in the early afternoon, Lisa was fighting physical exhaustion held at bay with too much caffeine. After she'd met with Byte, she'd also updated her captain, and then, search warrant in hand, she, Sanchez, and Josh had gone over Gran's house with a fine-toothed comb. Afterward, they sat down and went over every fact, clue, or guess they had, and it still added up to almost nothing. She'd followed that with a few hours of patrolling Chapel Lake, just in case. Now her nerves were buzzing and she simultaneously wanted to do nothing but sleep.

But a little shot of adrenaline hit her system when Pete showed up. Dressed in a tee shirt and jeans, gun tucked in his waistband, he looked good enough to eat. Memories of their fiery kiss sent a little shiver down her back, and she couldn't help admiring the way the denim cupped his backside when he reached into his truck. He caught her looking and winked.

"We'll take my truck," he said, and tucked her shovel into the back seat along with his own supplies. Her official vehicle would draw too much attention, as would seeing his sedan out on the dirt roads.

His scent filled the cab of his vehicle, sending more memories of last night washing over her, but she ignored them as she climbed in. When she reached for the coffee mug she'd brought along, he said, "No offense, Fish, but you look like a druggie coming off a high. Might want to skip the coffee."

She eyed his rumpled hair and tired eyes, raised a brow. "You are such a romantic, Bulldog." But she couldn't help grinning as she said it.

His smile kicked up at the corners, but then he sobered. "Don't expect me to apologize for last night."

The words sent a fluttery shiver all the way to her toes. She cleared her throat, looked out the window. "Not asking you to. But we need to keep things professional."

There was a pause, then he nodded. "You're right. For now. You make any progress this morning?"

"Josh, Sanchez, and I went over Gran's place again and I found one interesting thing. Those two payments Shelley made to Redd for the property? My gran gave her the money."

"Now that's interesting. Didn't realize they were that close."

Lisa ignored the jab of hurt that Gran had readily helped Shelley but barely spared Lisa the time of day. "Afterward, I spent more time searching Chapel Lake, but didn't find anything new." She paused. "But I am making someone nervous. I got a rock through my dining room window last night."

Pete shot her a glance, hands tightening on the wheel as they turned down the sandy driveway to Calvin's home. "Any luck finding out who did it?"

"Nope. I checked my trail cameras and the whole area and got nothing."

"Whoever it was knows where they are and avoided them."

"That's my take, too."

"But why throw a rock? Seems childish."

"The rock had my picture wrapped around it, rubber bands securing it. And a big red X over my face."

Pete's jaw tightened. "You should have told me."

"You were in court, remember? My captain knows and I gave everything I have, including photos of footprints I found near my house, to Byte. Which, by the way, do not match the ones in Gran's garage or Gene Phillips's."

"Somebody is trying to warn you away. But is it to stay away from Brad's case? Or to stop trying to find Shelley? Or even your gran?"

Lisa rolled her eyes. "And that, Bulldog, is the million-dollar question."

"You need to be careful."

"As opposed to how careless I've been until now?" she asked sweetly.

He frowned. "Don't twist my words. You know what I mean. You've obviously made someone nervous."

"Agreed. We just don't know who. I repositioned the trail cameras this morning, so maybe they'll come back and we'll get lucky."

He pulled up in front of Calvin's house and stopped her with a hand on her arm. "Let's make sure the dogs are inside before you open your door."

They scanned the empty yard, then followed a narrow path through the weedy lawn to the front door. A curtain twitched in one of the windows and dogs started barking from somewhere inside. "Somebody's home."

"I saw," Pete said as he knocked. "Calvin? It's Detective Tanner."

They waited, but no one came to the door. Pete knocked again. "Calvin? I know you're home. Open up, buddy."

Eventually, the door eased open a few inches and Calvin's anxious face peered out. "I can't come with you today. Sorry. I have too much homework." He tried to close the door, but Pete stuck his foot in the opening.

"What's going on? What happened?"

Calvin wouldn't meet his eyes. "Nothing. I just have homework."

"This won't take long. Promise. And if you want, I can try to help you with it later."

His eyes darted past them and he swallowed hard. "I can't help you. Please don't make me."

His voice shook and Lisa exchanged looks with Pete over the boy's head.

"Why don't you let us in real quick so you can tell us what's going on. It looks like you're worried someone will see us."

Calvin's face paled even more and he shot another frantic look around before he opened the door wider and yanked Pete's sleeve to pull him inside.

The minute they cleared the doorway, Calvin closed and locked the door, his eyes wide with panic.

Pete leaned down and laid a hand on the boy's shoulder. "Easy there, my man. Take a breath and tell me what happened. What has you so worried?"

The boy looked up and Lisa's heart clenched at the fear she saw.

"When I left school with my sister today, the guy was there, across from the school, watching me. When he saw me, he nodded to my sister and then shook his head. I don't know what he meant, but it scared me. As soon as we got off the bus we ran home, and I told her to stay in her room."

"Can you describe what he looks like?"

Calvin shrugged. "Pretty tall, dark hair." He shrugged again. "I don't know.

Pete took the boy's arm and led him to the sofa. "Can you get me some blank paper?"

The boy raced off and returned with several sheets of drawing paper clutched in his fist.

Pete smiled, then motioned him to sit beside him. "I'm going to have you help me draw a picture of this guy, okay? I'll start drawing and then I'll ask you some questions and between the two of us, we'll see if we can figure it out, all right?"

Lisa sat in a chair across the room and watched, amazed at Pete's gentle way with the boy. He made him laugh and slowly, his shoulders relaxed. Question by question with lots of erasing along the way, a face began to emerge.

Wow. How had she not known Bulldog could draw?

It took a while, but finally, Calvin whispered, "That's him."

Pete set his pencil down and turned the page so she could see. With the sunglasses and ball cap pulled low, he didn't ring any bells. She gave a small shake of her head.

"You've been a huge help, Calvin. We'll find out who he is and make sure he doesn't scare you again, okay?"

"What about my sister?"

"We'll notify the school to keep an eye out for him, too." He took a picture of the sketch with his phone. "Have you told your mom what happened?"

"Not yet. I didn't want to bother her at work."

"I'll call her right now." He spent a few minutes filling her in on what Calvin had said and assuring her they'd notify the school and were working to identify the man. He also confirmed she was still okay with them taking Calvin for a quick ride out in the forest. He hung up, then said to Calvin, "We'll figure this out, okay?" He stood. "You've been really brave, but now I need you to do one more thing."

Calvin hung his head. "You want me to show you where I saw the man bury stuff."

"We do. It's important."

"What if the man sees me helping you?"

The kid was smart. Lisa met Pete's eyes, then said, "That's why we're not dressed like law enforcement officers today. Officer Tanner will give you his ball cap and we'll disguise you, so no one will know it's you."

"Okay, but can we take my sister to her friend's house first?"

Lisa swallowed the knot of emotion in her throat. What a kid. "You are thinking smart, Calvin. We'll absolutely do that."

It didn't take long to put their plan into motion. After they called Calvin's mom and dropped his sister off, Pete put a ratty ball cap on

Calvin's head, then Lisa tucked him into her armored vest, slipped a jacket over that and zipped it up.

"Is somebody going to shoot me?" Calvin's voice shook as he asked the question.

Lisa grinned. "Nope. This is just part of the disguise. It'll make you look bigger, sitting in the truck. Up you go, champ," she added, patting the middle of the front seat. She'd cleared space for him and had put a duffle bag on the seat as a booster.

Once Calvin was in the middle, Pete climbed behind the wheel. "Good thinking, Fish. No one will suspect it's you, Calvin." Then he lightly socked the boy in the arm. "You're a natural at this undercover stuff. You ready? Lead the way."

For an almost-twelve-year-old, Calvin was surprisingly good with directions. With only a couple of false turns, he led the truck down dirt paths and through thick scrub, until they found their way to a small clearing.

The whole time, Lisa and Pete alternated watching the side mirrors, but there had been no sign that anyone had followed them. "Stay in the truck," Pete warned Calvin.

They scanned the area before they circled the clearing, searching for any signs the ground had been disturbed. When they found what they were looking for, they snapped a few pictures, then hurried back to the truck.

When Pete started the engine, Calvin looked from one to the other. "You're not going to dig?"

"We are," Pete said. "But first, we're taking you to where your sister is. Your mom will pick you both up there."

Calvin finally seemed to relax. "I guess you guys aren't too bad, for old people."

Pete clutched his chest. "Old? Who are you calling old? Just wait until basketball practice."

He reached over and tickled the boy and Calvin let out a squeal, the first real laugh Lisa had ever heard from the much-too-somber boy. He needed to be a child. And didn't it make her heart feel all melty to realize it was none other than Bulldog who had realized that instinctively.

Pete tossed another shovelful of dirt on the growing pile and used his forearm to wipe the sweat off his forehead. Even though the clearing was partially shaded, the heat and humidity were making this slow, sweaty work. Mosquitos and flies buzzed around them, while cicadas chirped in the background.

They hadn't found anything and she could feel Pete's frustration growing. Hers was, too.

"There's nothing here," she said, tossing another shovelful.

"Maybe whoever it was came back and moved it."

"Or, we're digging in the wrong—" She stopped midsentence as her shovel struck something hard.

They exchanged glances as Pete hurried over. She squatted in the dirt and pulled on a pair of gloves before she brushed the dirt away. He went to dig his shovel in to help, but she stopped him. "Hold on. Hand me that little trowel."

She used it to clear away some more of the dirt, then brushed the rest of it away with her hands.

"Oh, dear God," Lisa whispered as they uncovered a bone.

Pete crouched beside her and they slowly removed more dirt. A second bone appeared. He had his phone to his ear. "I'm calling the medical examiner."

Careful not to disturb anything, she studied what they'd uncovered. "Do we know for sure these are, ah, human bones?"

He paused, tucked the phone back in its holster. "No. Not yet. But if it were Shelley and Remy, or your gran, we'd be looking at bodies, not bones."

Right. She let out a slow, relieved breath. "Let's make sure we didn't stumble on some hunter's burial ground before we call anybody."

"Agreed."

Working quickly but carefully, they uncovered several more bones.

When Lisa found several pieces that looked like part of a human skull, they both froze. She swallowed hard, whispered. "It's too small to be an adult."

"Now I'm calling the medical examiner," Pete said as he dialed.

She stood and studied everything they'd uncovered, measuring, analyzing. She'd thought she left this sort of investigation behind when she left Los Angeles, but she knew that had been a pipe dream. Suspicious deaths were not confined to big cities.

"Once we know about how long the, ah, remains, have been out here, we can start figuring out what happened."

"Agreed." Pete took pictures of the scene with his phone and she did the same.

In short order, the medical examiner arrived, along with several more sheriff's deputies and FWC Officers. They secured the perimeter and she and Pete stepped back as the M.E. went to work.

Dr. Ward had brought along two helpers and they set about carefully excavating the scene. About twenty minutes in, they exposed a bone that was too big and long to be human.

"What in the world?" Fish whispered.

"You might want to get your biologist out here," the M.E. said, glancing up at them. "From the look of things, I'd say that bone belonged to an elephant."

"What?" Fish and Pete asked in unison.

"That's what it looks like. There appear to be several large animals buried here."

"Any other human remains?" Pete asked.

"Based on how fragmented the skull is, I'm not completely sure it's human, either. It could be a primate. But I won't know until I start putting the pieces together back at the morgue."

The biologist arrived and both teams kept digging, unearthing more and more bones, most of them animal, as far as Lisa could tell.

It was almost full dark before Dr. Ward climbed out of the hole. "I think that's everything, but you might want someone with ground penetrating radar to go over this area, just to be sure. I'll call when I know more," she added to Pete. After she'd supervised the loading of the remains, she got in her car and followed the van back to the road.

Meanwhile, the biologist packed all the animal bones they'd found into his van. "Same goes. I'll call you when I know more about what we have here."

"Best guess, based on what you've seen?" Lisa asked.

"The fact someone buried animals here is obvious. The elephant bones make me think it died at an animal park, and they didn't want a necropsy done for some reason. Or they're hiding evidence of some kind of poaching or illegal hunts." He frowned. "I'll leave you to figure out motive, while I focus on figuring out exactly what we have." He touched a finger to his hat and drove off.

Before long, she and Pete were the only ones left.

They leaned against his truck, sipping water. They were dirty, sweaty and tired.

"You hungry?" He glanced at his watch, wincing when he noticed the time.

"Yes, but I can't decide which I want more: a shower or food."

"I vote shower, then food. But we're not going to find either one out here."

She sent him a tired smile. "What, no magic fairies at your command?"

He snorted. "I don't see food dropping from the sky for you, either, smarty pants."

Fish sobered. "If the remains are human, I wonder how long they've been out here. And who they were."

"Given how many people disappear in the forest every year, we may never know. I have people standing by to start digging through missing persons' reports as soon as the M.E. gives me a timeframe. Otherwise, we're just wasting time."

"But an elephant? Out here?" She shook her head in disbelief. "I'll start calling zoos and animal parks in this part of the state."

"And I'll have another talk with our friend, Jason," Pete said.

"Did you see any elephants when you were at the sanctuary?"

"No, did you?"

She shook her head, but something beyond the clearing had caught her attention. She slid her weapon from the holster, entirely focused on a clump of trees.

Beside her, Pete pulled his gun, too, scanning the area. "What do you see?"

"Not sure, exactly. But something just moved out there."

"This time of night, probably a deer."

"Maybe. Maybe not." The prickle of awareness that slid down her spine said not. She raised her weapon as a shadow separated from the trees.

"Gun! Get down!" She shoved Pete to the ground, then spun toward the shooter.

Something slammed into her upper arm and sent her gun flying. She stumbled and fell, pain shooting through her as she landed on her right arm. She clutched it, surprised at the amount of blood pouring from it.

"Fish! What the hell!" Pete shouted as he crawled over to her. Bullets continued to spit up dirt all around them. "We need to take cover." He half dragged, half carried her behind a large tree and she sank to the ground, her back against the trunk. Her heart pounded, her wound throbbing in tandem. She realized the shooting hadn't stopped and scrambled to her feet. "Where's my gun?" She scanned the area, frantic, clutching her injured arm.

"Just stay down, dammit," Pete growled as he leaned around the tree and returned fire. "I've got this."

"They were aiming at you," she cried.

Pete didn't respond, which made her furious and cleared the fog in her brain.

She finally spotted her weapon several feet away and inched

toward it, but every time she tried to leave the cover of the tree, more shots hit the dirt at her feet. She ducked back again. "Cover me while I retrieve my weapon. We can't stay pinned down."

"Stay put, Fish. I've got this," he repeated.

Sudden silence filled the clearing.

He pulled a bandana from his hip pocket and deftly tied it around her upper arm. "Keep pressure on that. I'm going to see if I can track him." He retrieved her gun and handed it to her. "Be right back. Call for backup and EMS."

Frustration that he'd taken over warred with worry for his safety. What if this was exactly what the shooter wanted? She pushed to her feet and braced her weapon against the tree, working to hold it steady. Pete was counting on her to have his back.

She called it in, then peeked around the tree trunk. Where was Bulldog?

Another gunshot sounded, then silence.

Pete! Oh, God, not Pete!

She sprinted in the direction he'd gone, zigzagging from tree trunk to tree trunk.

Where was he?

Dizziness made her nauseous and her arm throbbed in time to her heartbeat.

Didn't matter. She had to find him.

She set out again, gritting her teeth. Every step felt like she was slogging through quicksand. She slumped to her knees and then everything went black.

When Pete barreled into the clearing, he saw Lisa face down and his heart stopped. "Fish!" He dropped down beside her and checked for a pulse. When he found it, he hung his head and heaved out a relieved breath. *Thank God.*

Had she been shot again? He made a quick check of her back

before he rolled her over. Besides some dirt and twigs, there were no additional wounds, but the bandana on her arm was soaked with blood.

He brushed the hair from her face, then patted her cheeks. "Wake up, Fish. Come on. Now's not a good time to play possum."

She batted his hand away. "Stop."

He kept patting. She shook her head against his hand, and then her eyes popped open. She tentatively touched the wound, hissed out a breath. Her fingers came away red. He pulled off his tee shirt and tied it over the bandana, then applied more pressure, silently apologizing when she moaned again.

After what felt like three years, the EMTs arrived, Josh and Sanchez right behind them.

"How is she?" Josh asked as Pete stepped away to let the EMTs work.

"What happened?" Sanchez asked, joining them. "The scene seemed fine when we left."

"Whoever had been watching started shooting once it got dark."

"But why wait until then? All the evidence had already been collected," Josh said.

"Good point. I have no idea."

"Did you see the shooter?" Sanchez wanted to know.

"I think Fish did. She said she saw movement, pulled her gun, and then the idiot leaped in front of me and got hit."

Josh's eyebrows climbed to his hairline. "They were aiming at you?"

"Again, I don't know. I didn't see anyone. I wrapped her arm and took off after them.

"I take it they got away."

Pete huffed out a frustrated breath. "Yeah. I couldn't find anything besides tire tracks in the dark. But I heard an ATV. It's not supposed to rain tonight, so I'll get an evidence team out here right away."

As the EMTs prepared to load Lisa in the back of the bus, he walked over, drew in a relieved breath when she scowled at him.

"What the hell, Bulldog. You could have been killed."

"Right back at you, Fish."

They glared at each other, then he turned to one of the EMTs. "Don't let anyone but medical personnel near her, understood? No one. I'll have an officer meet you."

The EMT's eyed widened, but he nodded. "Ten-four, Detective."

He leaned over the gurney, met Lisa's furious expression. "Later, you and I are going to chat about that stupid stunt you just pulled." He turned to the EMT. "Take good care of her."

"This is spiraling out of control fast," Sanchez said, once the bus pulled away.

"Agreed. You heard someone threw a rock through her window last night, wrapped in her picture with a big X over her face?"

Josh's jaw hardened. "We did. But how are the two connected? The rock seems like something a kid would do. Shooting at you is something else."

Pete shoved a hand through his hair. "None of it makes sense. Yet. Once we hear from the M.E. and the biologist, we can start figuring out how any of this relates to Brad's death. Or if it does." He blew out a breath, walked over to his truck and grabbed his Maglite. "Let's see what we can find. Then I'm going to the hospital."

Chapter Eighteen

A feeling of déjà vu swept over Lisa as she woke up. Someone was watching her. Again.

"Finally. Quit hiding, Fish," Pete growled by her ear.

Her eyes opened slowly, and for a moment, the room swam in and out of focus. Then everything settled as she looked around, orienting herself. Equipment, beeping, antiseptic smells. Hospital. Again. *Crap.*

She gave Bulldog a onceover as she hit the bedside control that brought her to a sitting position. "You look terrible." His hair stood up in tufts and he was wearing a scrub shirt with his jeans. "What time is it? How long have you been here?"

"It's a little after three." He sent her the lopsided grin that did funny things to her insides. "I've been here long enough to know that chair is not very comfortable."

"You didn't have to come. I'm fine."

"Someone painted a target on your back, Fish. Of course, I'm here."

Memories rushed back. As did her frustration with the mule-headed detective. "They were shooting at you, not me."

She watched him fight for control, fists clenched as hard as his jaw. "What in the name of all that's holy were you thinking, to step in front of a bullet? You know better than that."

Her throat closed. "You could have died tonight. And that would have seriously pissed me off."

His fury vanished, replaced by such a tender look it took her breath away. He leaned over and brushed the back of his hand down her cheek. "Same goes, Fish. Don't do something that stupid again. I have no desire to watch you bleed out in my arms. Last night was scary enough."

The low rumble of his words unfurled something deep inside her, touched her in ways she'd never been touched before. "How about we both stay safe?" She tried to smile, then winced when she accidentally moved her arm. She looked down. "How bad is it?"

"The bullet went straight through your upper arm, but they want to keep an eye on you for a while, just in case. You'll be fine, but you're not going to be using it for a couple days."

She swung her legs over the side of the bed and reached for the sling. "I need to go. We need to process that scene and figure out what the heck is going on. Still no word on Shelley, Remy, and Gran, I take it?"

"Slow down, Fish. No news on our missing persons, or I'd have told you right away. We already have a team in the woods. We should hear from the medical examiner later this morning. She'll try to reassemble the skull first thing."

"How did you get to the front of her line?"

He grinned. "Bribed her with Charlee's cupcakes."

"And since your sister is still on her honeymoon, did you inform her how many dozen she's baking when she gets back?"

"I sent her a text. We made a trade."

"Really? What did you offer in return?"

An embarrassed flush raced over his skin. Interesting. She'd have to ask Charlee what that was all about.

A nurse walked in just as Lisa opened the closet to retrieve her clothes. "Good to see you up and around. I have your discharge papers, Officer Bass."

"Great, thanks."

The nurse held up a hand. "Before you get too excited, you should know the doctor wants you to take it easy for a few days."

Lisa didn't ask what that meant, because it didn't matter. She aimed a glance at Pete. "If you don't mind, I could use a ride home."

"Sure. Take your time." But she heard the steel under the words. He was going to try to sideline her.

Not happening. The sense of time running out got more insistent by the minute.

She absolutely refused to believe it was already too late, that they were buried somewhere. Until she found proof that said otherwise, she was assuming they were alive and needed help.

Within twenty minutes, she was dressed, papers signed, and sitting in the passenger seat of Pete's truck. As soon as he dropped her off at home, she'd take her own truck and head back to the scene.

Pete watched Lisa's head bob like one of those dashboard dogs and heaved a sigh of relief when she finally fell asleep. She was one tough, stubborn lady. Even getting shot hadn't been enough to convince her to rest. She did so now only because her body overruled her mind.

He still couldn't wrap his head around the fact she'd stepped in front of a bullet for him. Without hesitation or giving it a single thought.

What was he going to do with that?

When he pulled into her driveway, he backed in and went around to open her door. He fished around in her jeans pocket for her keys and scooped her into his arms and carried her up the steps. He shifted her while he unlocked the door and she murmured, "You smell sweaty," against his neck before she drifted off again.

He grinned as he swung the door open, then almost tripped when a streak of orange fur flew past him into the house.

He walked into the living room and looked around, surprised at the bold colors and homey space, the hardwood floors. Somehow, he'd have pictured her going for a sleek, modern look. It suited her, though. Comfortable. Welcoming. He hadn't noticed a bit of it last time he was here, as all his focus had been on her and the fire blazing between them.

He walked down the short hallway, past a workout room, and found her bedroom. The walls were a rich blue, and he pulled the covers back and eased her down on green and blue swirly-looking sheets that reminded him of the ocean. But when he tried to loosen her grip from around his neck, she surprised him by tightening her hold and spearing him with a look, suddenly wide awake. "I need to get back to the site."

"There's nothing more we can do tonight, Fish. I've already got a team out there, remember? You need to rest."

"So do you."

Long seconds passed while they studied each other.

"Fine," she said. "Stay here, then, so I can make sure you don't go back without me."

He almost smiled at her commanding tone, but he caught a flicker of something else in her eyes, a quick flash of loneliness that matched his own.

"All right. We'll grab a few hours shut-eye and then head back together. I'll just shower first."

When he stepped into her claw-foot tub, he laughed. The showerhead hit him mid-chest, so he figured she had to duck pretty far to get her hair wet, too. Which made him picture her naked, but he shoved the images away. He couldn't think about her that way. Not now.

When he stepped out of the bathroom, he almost tripped over her cat again. She sent him an icy glare and an indignant meow, so he detoured to the kitchen and filled her water bowl, then rooted around until he found cat food. He bent down to pat her head and got a hiss in return. Guess she didn't like him today. The cat regarded him haughtily for a moment before she sashayed over to the bowl and started eating. He shook his head. Even Fish's cat had attitude.

Lisa was sound asleep when he returned. He stood for a moment and studied her, then climbed under the covers and pulled her into the curve of his body, careful of her injured arm.

Her scent surrounded him and he tightened his hold, drifting off almost immediately.

He woke several hours later to her murmuring and thrashing beside him.

"Mama! Oh, God, Mama! No! What have you done to her?" Her voice was hoarse, anguished.

His touch was gentle as he whispered, "You're okay. I've got you. You're safe."

She gradually stopped crying out and settled back into his arms, calmed by the soothing nonsense he whispered in her ear. After a while, she turned and tucked her head under his chin before she slid back into a deep sleep.

He stroked her back, glad his voice comforted her and made her feel safe. But he also wondered whether Fish would ever trust him enough to tell him about her past.

The smell of coffee and bacon woke her and the ache in in her arm brought last night back in a rush. She looked over her shoulder. The other side of the bed was empty. Had she imagined Pete beside her? She grabbed the other pillow and breathed in his scent. Nope, he'd been there, all right. And if she remembered correctly, she'd snuggled in and held on for dear life. A flush raced over her skin and she sighed. How should she play this? She decided to ignore it and hope he didn't push. She had to think about these new and confusing feelings he stirred in her—and the middle of a case wasn't the time to do it.

At least that's what she told herself.

She eased out of bed, glad for the sling cradling her arm, and padded into the kitchen. Pete sat at the kitchen table, Cat purring contentedly on his lap while he worked on his laptop.

When he saw her, his smile lit up the whole room. "Morning. Coffee's ready. So is breakfast."

She gaped. "She's letting you pet her."

The sight of that big strong hand rubbing the cat's back sent an answering tingle down her own. "She likes me. At least today." His grin turned cocky. "What can I say? I'm a likable guy."

Lisa went to the cupboard and pulled out a mug. "Cat doesn't let anyone pet her."

"Anyone but me, obviously."

She smiled at the teasing tone. But she didn't turn around, focused on filling her mug and adding milk and sugar without spilling everything. She'd never been very good left handed.

"How's the arm this morning?"

She opened another cabinet, rooted around for ibuprofen. "Better." She washed it down with coffee before she turned.

"That good, huh?" He eyed the sling. "Maneuvering is going to be a pain."

"Tell me something I don't know." She lifted her mug and confidently took a big sip, then ruined the effect by sloshing coffee onto the front of her wrinkled uniform shirt.

"You haven't even had time to recover from that snakebite yet. Need help getting dressed? Showered?" He waggled his eyebrows like a cartoon villain and made her laugh. Then he sobered. "Seriously, I won't peek. But I can help."

"Maybe I'd want you to peek." She sloshed more coffee when she realized she'd spoken aloud.

How was this keeping her distance? Keeping things casual?

He grinned, then his eyes darkened and flames fairly leaped from them. "Just say the word, Officer Bass." He stood, nudged her aside with his hip, suddenly all business. "Have a seat. I'll bring the food and then help you get ready. We have work to do."

Lisa blinked at the lightning-fast switch from bossy to flirty and back again. It was enough to make her head spin. But knowing he was as affected by whatever this...thing was between them, settled her nerves like nothing else.

Within the hour, Pete had gotten an update from the crime scene techs, telling him they'd made casts of all the tire treads and footprints they could find. One footprint in particular had a flaw in the tread pattern. If they could find the boot it came from, it would tell them who'd been out there.

And if they could find the guy with the rope tattoo Calvin had mentioned, they could check his boots.

Fish emerged from the bathroom, hair wet and tangled, uniform shirt half tucked, frustration stamped on her features. He hid a grin.

She'd refused his help, but he'd heard some colorful language and thumps coming from the bathroom while she struggled to get ready.

He stood and plucked the wide-toothed comb from her hand. "Sit." He led her to a chair at the table, pressed her into it. "Let me help."

"I'll get it. It'll just take a minute."

"It'll take all morning," he corrected. "We need to get going."

He stepped behind her and gently took a handful of her hair in his hands, then carefully combed out the tangles. He did one section at a time, enjoying the feel of the strands sliding through his grip, the way her shoulders finally relaxed.

"Where did you learn to do this?" she asked. "I can't see Charlee trusting you enough to get near her hair."

He laughed. "You'd be right. When we were kids, I'd have

knotted it up on purpose, given half a chance." He paused. "I've done it for my mom a few times since her stroke. I know not to yank the tangles."

Lisa looked up at him. "Your mother is lucky to have a son like you."

To cover the effect of those words, he shot her a cheeky grin. "Be sure you tell Josh that next time you see him."

"Always the comedian."

He tugged on a strand of hair.

"Hey! I thought you knew not to pull the tangles."

"I do know. Doesn't mean I won't."

They both laughed. He pulled her to her feet and tucked in her shirt before she realized what he was doing. "All set, Fish. Let's go."

"I need to go to the elementary school, talk with Remy's teacher and classmates. Maybe someone knows something about where they might have gone. Can you drop me off?"

"I'll go with you," he said as they walked out to his personal truck.

"Don't you have other things to do?"

"Nothing we can't do together."

She narrowed her eyes at him over the hood of the truck. "Did the captain tell you to babysit me today?"

He laughed. "No one in their right mind would ever imply you needed babysitting. But he did suggest teamwork might be the right move today. Interagency cooperation and all that."

Her annoyed expression never wavered. "I'm not buying a word of this, but I'll play along, since this wing is pretty useless." She climbed in, waited until he started the truck. "But don't make this a habit."

He shot her a wink as he headed toward the elementary school. She ignored his teasing, her mind on Remy.

Pete had reluctantly agreed to wait in the hallway while Lisa talked to Remy's class. She figured it would be less intimidating if there was only one cop, especially since she was a woman. Many of the children knew both of them from the community center, but still. This was an official visit.

"Hi class. For those who don't know me, I'm Officer Lisa Bass with Fish and Wildlife. Most of you know Remy hasn't been in class for a few days. She's not at home with her mom, either, so we're trying to figure out where she is, just to make sure everything's okay. Has anyone talked to her lately? Or seen her anywhere?"

One little girl with dark curly hair asked, "Is she hurt? Like her daddy? My mama said he died."

Lisa's heart clenched. "It's very sad that her daddy died. But Remy's just fine, as far as we know. We want to be absolutely sure, so that's why we're trying to find her and her mom. Does anyone know anything that might help us?"

The students exchanged glances and shrugs, but no one had anything to offer.

The teacher lifted her hands, palms up. "Think hard, class. It's important."

"When was the last time any of you saw Remy?" Lisa asked.

No one had seen her since last Wednesday at school, so that wouldn't help. "Did any of you see her outside of school? Maybe get together to play somewhere?"

More shrugs, but Lisa noticed one little girl twisting her hands in her lap. She exchanged glances with the teacher, who had also noticed.

The other woman crouched beside the girl's desk, voice quiet. "Kailey, why don't you go to the back of the room and talk with Officer Bass while we do our math. Whatever you remember, it's okay to tell."

Kailey looked between her teacher and Lisa and finally swallowed hard and eased out of her chair. She ran to the row of hooks along the back wall and reached into a Little Mermaid backpack and pulled something furry out.

Lisa folded herself into one of the small chairs and tried to figure out what to say that wouldn't scare her. "Thank you for sitting with me, Kailey. Remy is your friend?"

The little girl nodded, pigtails flying. "We're best friends."

"That's great. Best friends are important." She nodded at something clenched between Kailey's hands. "What's that you're holding? It looks pretty. May I see it?"

Kailey hesitated, then unwrapped a square of fur. Lisa swallowed a surprised gasp. Unless she missed her guess, this came from a snow leopard, a gorgeous, elusive, endangered cat from the Himalayas. "That's beautiful! Where did you get it?"

"It's Remy's. She said it's from a really pretty cat that lives far away from here. Remy let me borrow it. I was scared about going to visit my daddy and his new girlfriend, but she said petting it would help me not be scared."

Lisa smiled. "Did it work?"

Kailey shrugged. "A little. I was supposed to give it back right away, but Remy hasn't come to school. Are you sure she's okay?"

Lisa didn't want to lie to those innocent eyes, so she said, "That's what we're trying to figure out. Do you know where Remy got the pretty pelt?" Lisa was betting on Brad, but wanted confirmation.

"From her daddy." Kailey leaned closer. "He was mean to her sometimes, but she said it wasn't that bad, because he gave her pretty things."

A wave of fury and sadness rushed through her. Fathers should never be mean to their children. But she couldn't focus on that until she found Remy and Shelley. She held a hand out. "Is it okay if I take this? I'll make sure Remy gets it back."

Kailey looked uncertain, but then gave a shaky nod and handed it over. "She probably needs it, since her daddy died. She might be afraid." Her eyes filled with tears and Lisa's heart broke. She gently squeezed both Kailey's little hands. "I'm going to do everything I can to find Remy and make sure she's not afraid anymore, okay?"

"Promise?"

"I promise."

The little girl scampered back to her seat and Lisa thanked the class and teacher before she hurried out to the hallway where Pete waited. She relayed her conversation with Kailey and then showed him the pelt, watched his eyes widen.

"What kind of cat is that?" They started walking toward the exit.

Lisa had her phone out, tapping quickly. "I think it's a snow leopard, but I want to be sure." Her phone rang as she was scrolling through a list of images. "Hi Kimberly. What's up?"

"I've been following the news, but wanted to ask you directly to be sure. Has your gran come home yet?"

Lisa stopped walking. "Not yet. Why? Have you talked to her?"

"No. Nothing like that, though I've been trying to call her."

"What's wrong, Kimberly?"

"Like everyone else, I figured your gran just took off for a few days, like she does sometimes. But she usually comes by to pick up her monthly prescription by now."

"And she hasn't come in yet."

"No, and I'm getting worried."

Lisa's mind raced. "What's the prescription for?"

There was a pause. "You know I can't tell you that. I'm sorry. You're not on her list."

But I should be. "How about if I ask a general question. If someone who took this particular medication didn't have it for a while, would their life be in danger?"

"If they went without it for too long, definitely."

Lisa thought of a few offhand heart comments Gran had made. "Would it mainly affect say, the person's heart?"

Another pause. "Yes. The person's heart might start beating much too fast."

Lisa's own heart sped up. "How long before the prescription runs out?"

"Two days."

Not much time. "Thank you, Kimberly. If I hear from her, I'll have her get in touch with you right away."

"Okay. I'll do the same. I hope you find her."

I won't stop until I do.

Pete's eyes reflected her worry. "Your gran needs her heart meds?"

"You know she takes them?"

He looked away. "I picked that up somewhere, yeah."

Great. Another reminder that everyone knew her gran better than she did, even after living here for two years.

Come on, Gran. Where are you??

They reached his truck. "You find pictures of that cat?"

Lisa mentally switched gears. "Yes, it's a snow leopard. Check it out." She held the phone so he could compare the photos to the pelt.

"They live in the Himalayas, right?"

"Yes, they do."

"So how does a guy in Ocala, Florida, get hold of the hide of an exotic, protected cat?"

Their eyes met. "Good question. And given the taxidermy tools we found in his truck, did he do the work himself? Or did he just do the delivery? Also, given how small this pelt is, where's the rest of it?"

"Maybe it came from a much larger piece. That could account for the deposits in his bank account." Their research had turned up several cash deposits, all under $10,000, with no record of where they came from.

"It doesn't explain where he got the pelt to begin with," Lisa said.

Pete paced a few feet away, turned back. "What if this is the missing piece we've been looking for? Maybe someone is importing exotic hides and Brad was killed because he knew too much. Or was involved."

"What about Shelley and Remy? How do they fit into it? Or Gran's disappearance?"

He scrubbed a hand over the back of his neck. "Maybe they aren't related at all, and Brad's death boils down to a simple, though sad, domestic dispute."

"I don't know. I believe Shelley planned to leave Brad and the self-defense classes were step one. But even if she did kill Brad to protect Remy, I don't think she'd want to spend her life on the run. I think she'd contact me. Or you. Or maybe Gran."

Pete considered as he opened the truck's door and helped her inside. "You think someone is holding them prisoner? For what purpose? If so, do they have your gran then, too?"

"I don't know. Let's go back to Redd's and show him the pelt, see what he says."

"Then we'll swing by Castile's and ask Jason the same questions."

They got the same shotgun reception at Redd's that Lisa had gotten the last time.

His eyes widened when he saw the pelt, and he ran a hand lightly over the fur. "That there is one of God's most beautiful creatures. Where did you get such a thing?"

"It's part of an ongoing investigation," Lisa said. "You wouldn't happen to know who did the tanning work on it, would you?"

Redd spit tobacco juice inches from her boots. The man was nothing if not predictable. "You got something to say, you say it straight out, girly." He straightened and stepped closer. "But I will tell you I had nothing to do with that animal. I've never seen that pelt before in my life."

"Do you know who did the work?" Pete asked.

"Nope."

Lisa propped her hands on her hips. "Would you tell us if you knew?"

He narrowed his eyes at both of them. "You people aren't hearing me. I love animals. And I follow the rules. I don't do trophy taxidermy and I certainly don't contract to tan the skins of endangered animals like a snow leopard. Whoever did that," he pointed to the pelt, "was either sure they wouldn't get caught--or they didn't care."

They thanked the man and headed for Castile's, where they showed the pelt to Jason.

He whistled. "That is one beautiful animal. Where did you get it?"

"We were hoping you might be able to tell us."

Before he could respond, they heard Martin's voice from the other room. "Get in here, Holberg."

"Excuse me," Jason muttered, then hurried from the room. Lisa and Pete followed him down the hall, stopping short of the open doorway, where they wouldn't be seen.

"Where are the tranquilizers I ordered?"

"They haven't come in yet. But they should be here any day now."

"And yet I got a notification on my phone that they'd been delivered. Where are they?"

"I-I don't know. Let me look." They heard cabinets opening and closing. "By the way, FWC and MSO are here, asking about a pelt."

"And you're only now telling me?"

Pete and Lisa sprinted halfway down the hall, then turned back as though they were just arriving.

Dr. Castile did not look happy. "What are you two doing here again?"

"Hello Dr. Castile." Lisa held out the fur. "We're trying to figure out who did the tanning on this."

Was she imagining it, or was that a flash of unease she saw before he wiped all expression from his face.

"I have no idea. This is an animal sanctuary, not a taxidermist's workroom. You're wasting my time and my associates' with this nonsense. I have things to do. Good day."

"Redd knew what kind of animal it was and Castile looked nervous when we asked about it," Lisa said, once they were back in Pete's truck.

"I noticed that, too."

"And Castile basically accused Holberg of stealing tranquilizers."

"Which could simply be a shipping delay," Pete warned.

"Except that Jason Holberg lost his veterinary license over the same accusations." Her mind raced. "We need to get everyone together." She set up a meeting with Josh, Byte and Sanchez at the Outpost, and they swung by the Café to pick up sandwiches on the way.

Their timing was perfect, catching the lull between the morning rush and the beginning of the lunch crowd.

"Hey, Liz," Lisa said.

The other woman scanned her from top to bottom before she stepped from behind the counter and wrapped her in a big hug, making Fish wince.

"I know you're tough and all that, but could you please stop almost dying? My nerves can't take it."

Liz's concern warmed her down to her toes. This feeling of being part of something, of having friends who cared about you? She hadn't had it since she left LA. Truthfully, she hadn't allowed it since then, except with Gran, who'd rebuffed her every overture. She'd kept her distance, but Liz, Patty, Charlee, and the Ocala Scrub Squad wouldn't let her hide. They'd pulled her out of the shadows and into their circle. She hadn't realized how much that meant until now.

The other woman gave Pete the same thorough once-over. "That goes for you too, Bulldog. What is it with you people lately? This is a quiet town. Why do you keep stirring up trouble?"

"Actually, trouble keeps finding us," Pete said, then nodded to Fish. "And this one stepped in front of a bullet meant for me."

All the color drained from Liz's face. "Seriously?" She looked from one to the other. "I'm so glad you're both okay." Then she lifted her chin, determination shining from her eyes. "Tell me how I can help you catch whatever scumbag did this."

"How about dishing some local gossip," Lisa said. "Have you picked up anything about exotic animals? Any whispers about hunts in the area, anything like that? Or anything else that struck you as unusual?"

Her eyes widened. "Not really, no. But people have been talking about how many semis they've seen on the back roads lately. Truckers cruising down SR-40 often stop in for coffee, but they don't usually veer off the main roads. At least, not that I've ever noticed."

Lisa and Pete exchanged a look.

"Did anyone happen to mention any company names or markings on these trucks?" It was a long shot, but she had to ask.

Liz shook her head. "No. Sorry. But I'll keep my ears open."

The bell over the door jingled and Liz's whole demeanor changed. "Good morning, handsome. What can I get you?"

"Good morning, Liz."

Lisa turned and saw Nate King, the dog handler, striding in, sunglasses covering his eyes. "Your coffee is just too good. Almost as tempting as your smile. I needed both this morning."

Liz's flirty grin could have lit up the county. "Then you've come to the right place, sugar. Let me get you set up."

As she and Pete left with their order, Lisa couldn't help envying Liz's ease with men. Why couldn't she be more like that, comfortable in her own skin, secure in herself as a woman? Except for her almost deadly involvement with Bill, she'd only dated casually, and it usually ended by the third date, when the jerk would admit it was her ability with a gun, not her, that really turned him on.

She eyed Pete, who'd just donned his sunglasses and was scanning the parking lot, looking like a cover model for an outdoor magazine. A model with a tender heart he didn't think anyone saw.

She remembered the feel of his arms around her, the way he saw her—for her. Maybe she did want to figure out how to turn him on with just a look.

But that would have to wait.

Right now, the pelt and animal bones offered a new line of investigation, but she couldn't see how it brought them a single step closer to finding Shelley and Remy.

Or getting Gran home so she could get her heart medicine in time.

Chapter Nineteen

By the time Lisa and Pete arrived at the Outpost, Josh and Sanchez were already in the office, chatting with the elder Tanners. Pete walked directly to his mother, who was using her cane this morning instead of the dreaded wheelchair, and kissed her cheek. He whispered something in her ear that made her laugh like a young girl. When Mrs. Tanner patted his cheek and then self-consciously patted her hair, Lisa felt that familiar tug on her heart. There was just something about a man who cared for his mother.

"Good morning, Mrs. Tanner. Pretty top," she said as she approached.

Mrs. Tanner sent Pete another beaming smile. "Got it from this rascal for my birthday, though I told him I didn't need or want anything."

He shrugged. "You say that every year. So we ignore you every year."

"Go talk to your brother. I want a word with this young lady."

Wariness crept over Lisa's skin. Pete looked between her and his mother, winked, then walked over to the men without a backward glance.

Mrs. Tanner chuckled. "This isn't a firing squad, young lady, so don't look so worried. I just wanted to know how you're really doing. I figured my chances of getting the truth went up if Peter wasn't hanging over your shoulder."

At her surprise, Mrs. Tanner grinned. "What? You don't think I know my children? Bulldog got his nickname honestly, but there's a huge heart underneath all the bluster."

"I figure you know your children quite well. And I'm feeling much better, thank you. It wasn't too bad."

"A gunshot is always bad. And when a cop gets hurt, it's hard on the people they love." She glanced at her husband and her obvious love for him lit up the room. "For thirty years, every time he put on that uniform, I knew there was a chance he wouldn't come home. It takes a special kind of woman—or man—to love a law enforcement officer. Same goes for soldiers." She sent Lisa a piercing glance. "I figure you're strong enough to love one. And be loved by one."

Lisa wanted to laugh off the idea, but the words stuck in her throat. She cared about Pete. No question. The mule-headed, stubborn, gorgeous man had gotten under her skin in ways no one ever had. But love? That was a horse of a different color, as the locals said, the dividing line between for now and forever. She heard him laughing at something Josh said, and her heart inched a little closer to that line.

She backpedaled onto safer ground. "You raised good men, Mrs. Tanner. And a wonderful daughter. They all deserve nothing but the best."

"Fish! You ready?" Pete called.

She leaned over and kissed the other woman's cheek. "It's good to see you on your feet, Mrs. Tanner."

"Thank you. I'm finally getting stronger and it feels good. Now I think it's high time you started calling me Alice."

"All right then, Alice. Take care." She still couldn't fathom why the Tanners and their friends were slowly pulling her into their circle, but she couldn't deny she liked it. She hurried to the pavilion, where the rest of the squad milled around, fairly vibrating with anger.

"What's going on?"

"The hospital just called," Pete said. "The Ocala Police officer I had posted outside Wells' room went to take a leak and when he came back, he saw someone leaving the room. He yelled for the nurses to check on Wells and gave chase, but the suspect got away in a white van."

"Security cameras?" she asked.

"They're checking. We already have a BOLO on the van."

Lisa looked from one to the other, noting the clenched jaws and fisted hands. "And Wells?"

Pete shook his head. "He was already dead when the nurses got to him. Doctor thinks he was suffocated. Medical examiner will try to tell us more."

Shock rippled through her. "I didn't like the guy. But he didn't deserve to die."

"It does tell us he knew something worth killing for. Maybe had information that could incriminate someone," Josh said.

Lisa and Pete exchanged glances.

She straightened, her brain clicking through a list of next steps. "We need to search his car again." She also had to take control, quick, before Pete stepped in and tried to sideline her. "Sanchez, you and Byte find out where his car ended up and turn it inside out. Josh, you and I will search Wells' house."

Pete stood in front of her, hands on his hips. "It's a good plan, but don't get ahead of yourself, Officer Bass. You know the sheriff's office takes lead in murder investigations."

His officious tone grated like a burr under her saddle, but she waved that away like it was no big deal. "Right. But since he got run off the road headed to a meeting with me, we work together. We need to figure out what he knew that got him killed." She raised a brow. "Interagency cooperation, remember?"

He huffed out a breath, rolled his eyes. "I remember. But you're also on light duty, Officer Bass, and shouldn't overdo." His cheeky grin said he was onto her. "I'm heading to the hospital. I already have a couple officers there to interview staff and a tech team on the way to gather evidence."

As they turned to leave, Lisa's cell phone buzzed. "Officer Bass, FWC."

"Good morning, Lisa," the medical examiner said. "I just ran some tests on the remains we uncovered. You'll want to get your biologist over here to pick them up."

"You're already finished?"

There was a pause, then a gruff, "I couldn't sleep. Anyway, when I put all the pieces together I confirmed my suspicion that it's not a human skull. Near as I can tell it came from a chimpanzee. He'll know more."

This case just kept getting stranger and stranger. "Thanks, Dr. Ward. Have you gotten a call about Casey Wells yet?"

"Yes. I just left for the hospital. Is Pete Tanner taking lead on this one, too?"

Lisa hid her irritation. "Yes, he is. Please keep us both posted. Thanks."

She turned to the expectant faces. "Medical examiner says the skull isn't human. She thinks it's a chimpanzee."

There was a moment of stunned silence.

"So this is what, someone running an off-the-books sanctuary?" Sanchez asked.

"Or canned hunts of some kind," Josh ground out.

She muttered a curse. Like the rest of the squad, she abhorred the practice, where animals were staked out or baited or even shot in cages so some so-called hunter could bag his exotic trophy without leaving the country. It made her sick. "Pete, while your team works on Wells' murder, Byte, keep tracking down all the zoos or parks in the area that have, or have had, chimps and elephants in their facility.

See if any have died in the past couple of years. Once I hear from the biologist I may have more animals to check on."

"What about Castile and his animal sanctuary?" Josh said.

"Or Redd's Rescue?" Sanchez asked.

"We need to dig into both. It's also possible that if someone is running hunts, they're then selling the pelts. Or just importing pelts for sale. Regardless, we need to figure out what Wells uncovered that got him killed. And how that links to Brad's murder and in turn, whether that can lead us to Shelley and Remy and my gran."

When she turned around, Pete stood right behind her, arms crossed over his chest. Admiration shone in his eyes. "Your captain knew what he was doing, making you acting lieutenant." He leaned closer. "And personally, I find it sexy as hell. But when it comes to your safety, you need to quit taking chances."

The warm fuzzy feeling his pride inspired morphed into the familiar frustration. "Right back at you, Bulldog. On all of it. Right now, let's catch whoever is trying to cover their tracks before someone else dies."

By the time Josh drove Lisa home that afternoon, she was exhausted, frustrated and her arm ached. When they'd arrived at Wells' Ocala home with a search warrant, it was obvious someone had beaten them there and trashed the place in their rush to search it. Every cushion had been sliced open, every cupboard, shelf, and closet emptied onto the floor. Wells' laptop was gone, the charging cord still plugged in under the cluttered desk. Given the dates on the receipts and statements in his filing cabinet, he kept all the important stuff on his laptop. She hoped whoever was behind this had gotten sloppy and left a print--or something—behind for the techs to find.

But there was a bit of good news, too. Sanchez investigated a call from someone who lived on Chapel Lake. The guy said he'd been out of town and just learned of Brad's death. He didn't know if it would help, but he'd seen an airboat on the lake at two a.m. with two guys in it. He recognized Brad Larsen as being the driver, but didn't know the man beside him. He knew the time because he'd been annoyed they were making noise so late.

His account confirmed what the other eyewitness had said and helped establish Brad's time of death.

After she called her captain with an update, she swallowed a pain pill and collapsed on her bed, fully clothed. When someone pounded on her door a while later, she jolted awake.

She stumbled to the door and sighed when she spotted Pete through the peephole. She wasn't up to sparring with him. She turned and was halfway down the hall when his voice stopped her.

"Open up, Fish. I know you're in there. It's important."

Oh, no. Shelley. Gran. She reversed her steps and yanked the door open several inches. "Did something else happen? Why didn't you call me?"

He held up a grease-stained bag and the smell of French fries wafted out. "Figured we both need to eat and with that wing, you wouldn't be doing any cooking." He took a step closer, his grin daring her to refuse him entry.

She met his gaze, worried the last of her defenses would crumble if she let him in. Suddenly, her stomach rumbled loud enough for him to hear. When he threw his head back and laughed, she couldn't keep her own grin from escaping. He was invading her space and being his usual brash, bossy self but somehow, the caring behind it made it impossible to turn him away. She swung the door open and Cat immediately appeared, winding around his ankles.

"Your cat likes me." He looked far too pleased with himself. "Today, anyway."

"She's a stray. What does she know?"

"Have you named her something besides Cat yet?"

She walked toward the kitchen, Pete behind her. "She's not staying. I just feed her now and then.

He snorted as he bent down and stroked Cat's back. "You have food and water bowls, a litter box. You have a cat, Fish."

"All that stuff was already here. It came with the house."

"Except you installed a cat door."

She ignored that as Pete set the food on the counter and scooped up Cat, who snuggled against his chest and started purring like mad, the traitor. He scratched between her ears and cocked his head at Lisa. "I think she looks like a Henrietta."

"What kind of name is that?"

"You have a better idea?"

She opened her mouth, closed it, avoiding the trap just in time. "She's a cat. Therefore, that's what I call her." She turned to the fridge. "You want a beer?"

He nodded. They clinked bottles and drank in silence for a while before she said, "Someone had already searched Well's house by the time Josh and I got there. His laptop is missing. But Byte and Sanchez searched his car and found a flash drive tucked under the driver's seat." She eyed him over her bottle. "I'm wondering if he realized someone was trying to run him off the road and stashed it there, planning to retrieve it later."

"I'm betting that's why he wanted to meet. And it's what got him killed. Any word yet from Byte?"

"Too soon. I've learned to give him time to work his magic."

Pete eyed her kitchen, then sent her an approving glance. "I like what you've done with the place. Very bright and bold." He paused. "Like you."

A little thrill slid over her at his words. "It's home."

"Nice workout room, too." He looked her up and down, waggled his brows.

She rolled her eyes, snorted. "I hate dealing with crowds at the gym."

He wandered to the newly installed French doors and stepped onto the covered porch. Four previously rusted, yard sale chairs now sported crisp blue paint and comfy cushions. She'd painted the old porch swing white, but it still sat on the floor. He walked over to it, ran a hand over the wooden slats. "Nothing beats a porch swing on a nice evening." He lifted one end, grabbed the chain. "Are the brackets secure?"

"They are. I just haven't had a chance to hang it yet."

In one smooth move, he slipped the chains onto the hooks in the ceiling beams. Then he sat down, started it swinging. "Perfect. Let's eat here."

They brought their picnic outside and Lisa added a colorful cushion to the swing. Pete sighed as he pushed off with his foot, looked around. She eased down at the opposite end, suddenly unsure what to say, how to behave. She knew how to spar with him at work, but this was different. He was a guest in her home, her very first official guest, and that felt like another leap toward intimacy when she'd told herself to keep things casual.

Pete finished his burger and stuck the wrapper in the bag. "Tell me how you got from being on a SWAT team in LA to living in a cottage in the Ocala National Forest?"

Lisa nearly choked on a French fry. Talk about leaping toward intimacy. Should she gloss over the question, or let him further into her life? She swallowed, took a sip of her beer for courage, and waded into uncharted territory. She'd never told anyone about her past, except in the most general of terms. But Pete had served in the military before becoming a cop, so she figured he would understand.

"I lived with my mother in Gran's house. Back then, Gran and I were close. I felt safe with her. My mother was always restless, flitting from job to job and boyfriend to boyfriend and I worried Mama might take me away. That day came when I was seven. Mama told me to say goodbye to Gran, that we were heading west. She had a lead on a part in a movie and was going to be an actress."

She looked up. "You know how the rest of this story goes. She didn't get the part. Or the next one. She started waitressing, which led to bartending and later to drugs to deal with the disappointment of her nonexistent acting career. The drugs got her fired and eventually led to prostitution to keep a roof over our heads." She paused. "Still, she tried to protect me. She built a little fort inside a wardrobe and she'd tuck me in there whenever any of her gentlemen friends came over." Lisa crumbled her napkin, then shredded the edge. "The drug use got worse and food was scarce. I was ten the day I accidentally picked a cop's pocket, looking for cash for food. Mama went to rehab and I went to foster care."

Pete slid over and wrapped an arm around her shoulders. She hesitated for only a moment before she tucked her head in the curve of his neck and absorbed his wordless support.

"They didn't send you back here to Gran?"

"I begged them to, but Gran had been in a motorcycle accident and was in rehab."

"Did you end up with a nice foster family?"

She snorted. "I was small for my age, too skinny, and got beat up a lot--by the boys because they could, and by the girls to get my stuff. Either way, I was lonely, miserable and scared. I was shuffled around for several years, getting more and more angry but unable to channel that anger. Eventually, I ended up in a group home."

"No child should ever have to go through all that." He paused. "So how did you get from angry teenager to competent cop?"

She smiled. "The cop's name was Jim Barrett and he stayed in touch, even when I was a mouthy, defensive teenager. When I was a senior in high school, he asked me if I wanted to go to a self-defense class he taught. Later, he taught me to shoot. Jim's the reason I went to the police academy. He and his wife, Claire, made me part of their family."

"I'm glad there were people who took an interest in angry young Lisa."

She smiled. "I didn't make it easy on them, but they didn't give up on me." She pulled a small Leatherman multi-function tool out of her pocket. "Jim gave me this the night I tried to rob him, said I should always be prepared, and I've carried it ever since. I decided I wanted to make a difference, like he did." She gave the swing another push, lulled by the feel of his arm around her, the beer, and the motion of the swing in the quiet evening. She felt lighter somehow, for having told her story. "What about you? I know you and Hunter served together. Was that always the plan?"

The swing stopped. The silence lengthened, then he pushed it back into motion. "Not always. My dad was a sheriff's deputy his whole career, so I'd always planned to follow in his footsteps. Thought that was what the oldest son should do."

When the silence lengthened again, she prompted, "But?"

"But by the time I got into high school, Dad and his rules and expectations for my behavior started to chafe." He grinned. "In other words, I was your typical smart-ass, self-centered teenager who thought he was all that and a bag of chips." He resumed stroking her arm and she settled close again. "I decided to see the world, get away from this little town, carve my own path." He paused, shrugged. "That didn't turn out quite the way I planned."

She waited, but he didn't say anything else. "War never does, I imagine."

"I still have nightmares sometimes." His breath came out on a sigh. "What happened to your mama?"

The question was so unexpected, she stiffened and tried to move away. He tightened his hold, kept her in place. "Just asking, Fish. No obligation to tell me anything, but I'm willing to listen."

Her heart skittered. "I had a nightmare last night?" She felt his nod against the top of her head. She'd never talked about the night Mama died. Not even with Jim and Claire. She couldn't force the words past the guilt clogging her throat.

But instinct said Pete would understand and would never use it against her. Maybe it was time to let the ghosts out. "After I graduated from the academy, I got a job in Los Angeles, at a different police department than Jim's. Like you, I was trying to carve my own path, I guess. It wasn't long before I was tapped for Metro and their SWAT team. I loved the comradery and the idea that my skills could make a difference for good. Of course, I got crap from some of the guys for being a woman— "

Pete interrupted with a snort. "I've seen you on the firing range. They were lucky to have you."

More of the walls around her heart crumbled at his words. She smiled. "Yeah, they settled down after they saw me shoot. Anyway, Mama had been in and out of rehab over the years. I'd finally accepted the very harsh reality that until and unless she wanted to change, it would never happen."

"Tough thing to accept."

"Yeah. But I didn't want to cut her out of my life, either. She seemed to be doing well after her last stint in rehab, and was going to AA meetings regularly. I went with her when I could. For the first time in years, I was cautiously optimistic. But I was also feeling a little overwhelmed. She was calling me multiple times a day to ask silly questions."

"She was lonely, I'm guessing."

"Yes. I helped her get an apartment away from her druggie friends and she was really trying hard. About that time, I was put in charge of my first big case."

Lisa cleared her throat, swallowed hard. This was harder than she'd expected. She likened it to ripping off a bandage: best to get it done all at once.

"She called again one day and I was in the middle of a hostage situation, so I didn't answer. I meant to call her back later, but— "

"You got wrapped up in the case. We've all been there."

She couldn't let herself off the hook so easily. "Actually, my partner, Bill, whom I was dating, convinced me to focus on the case, let Mama manage her own life for a while. Twenty-four hours later, when I couldn't get hold of her, I went looking. By then, Gran had left several messages saying she couldn't reach Mama either. I finally found Dazzle in the dumpster behind her apartment, tossed away like so much garbage." She drew a ragged breath. "Her body was still warm. The M.E. said she died of an overdose. But she also had a gash across her throat that made me think the overdose was forced. There were definite signs of a struggle."

"I tracked down her dealer and he surprised me by insisting I talk to my boyfriend, instead. I finally listened to Mama's voicemails, which Bill had told me to delete for my own well-being, and on the last one, I heard Mama say, 'What are you doing here?' I checked the cameras of every business nearby and found Bill. And then I found a syringe behind the dumpster with Bill's prints on it. Using Mama's voicemails, my investigation uncovered the partnership between the dealer and Bill. The dealer is in jail, but Bill ate his gun before we could arrest him." She took a deep breath, suddenly exhausted. "Gran hasn't forgiven me. I haven't forgiven myself, either. I should have looked for her sooner."

"It wasn't your fault, Fish. You know that."

She shrugged. Intellectually, yes, she knew that. But her heart couldn't accept it.

"We're going to find your gran."

"What if I'm too late. Again?"

Without a word, Pete hauled her onto his lap and crushed her against his chest, arms tight around her, murmuring in her ear. It wasn't till her tears dampened his shirt that she realized she was crying. She never cried. Didn't think she'd shed a single tear since the day she'd found Mama's body. But now, here, with Pete wrapped around her like a warm blanket, the grief poured out, along with deep, gulping ugly sobs.

"It's not your fault," he kept saying, over and over and over.

"I should have saved her. I should have gone looking for her sooner."

He just rocked her back and forth. Finally, when the tears ran dry, he reached into his back pocket and handed her his handkerchief.

"I didn't know guys still carried these." She sent him a watery smile as she mopped her face.

"Dad always said a man wasn't fully dressed without one. I use

bandanas. No fancy monograms. Works the same."

He brushed the last of her tears away with his thumbs, eyes steady on hers. "This is not on you, Fish. The fault lies with the guy who pumped her full of drugs."

Down to the marrow of her bones, she wanted to believe him. Wanted to imagine she could somehow escape the guilt and shame of failing to protect her mother. But the past couldn't be changed, or rewritten, or wished away. Mama was still dead. "If I hadn't waited. If I'd gone looking for her sooner— "

"Woulda, shoulda, coulda, Fish," Pete said bluntly. "You couldn't have known. You have to let it go."

She shot him a look. "You make it sound so simple. But it isn't. You haven't told me about your nightmares. Have you let it go?"

He sighed. "Not really, but I'm trying to."

"You going to tell me about it? Fair's fair and all that." It was more than just a dare. She wanted him to trust her with his past, to let her in.

He studied her a moment, then nodded. "You're dead on your feet. Why don't you grab a shower, and after I clean up, too, I'll tuck you in and tell you a bedtime story. Fair warning: This one doesn't have a happy ending."

Their eyes met, held. She let the implications sink in. He was not only going to tell her about his past; he planned to stay. Again.

"I'll even brush the tangles out of your hair." He cocked a brow, grinned.

She laughed. "Who could refuse an offer like that?"

The look in his eyes started an answering heat shimmering in her belly.

"Just so we're clear, I'll gladly sleep on the sofa, but I'm not leaving you alone. Not until we figure out what's going on." His chin came up and jaw hardened in a stance that was pure Bulldog.

A week ago, she would have sputtered and spit at such a bold statement. Call her crazy, but she liked his tough protectiveness, especially when all that intensity was focused on her. His blunt honesty didn't hurt his case, either.

"That sofa is way too short for you. The bed will be much more comfortable." Her mouth went dry at the wicked grin he sent her. Then she hurried into the house.

Chapter Twenty

Pete hurried through his shower, worried suddenly that some crazy would break in while he couldn't hear past the running water. When he reached the bedroom, barely dry, he stopped in the doorway, not surprised to find Fish sound asleep. Between the snake and getting shot, plus dredging up all that emotion tonight, she was exhausted.

He slid under the covers and tucked her against him again, enjoying the feel of her smooth skin and unexpected curves. His body instantly reacted, but he forced his mind to the case, instead. No way would he take advantage.

An hour later, he was still wide awake, theories and possibilities careening through his mind like billiard balls. When she murmured and cried out, he whispered soothing nonsense in her ear until she drifted back to sleep. His heart ached for the young girl she'd been, and for the guilt she carried still. He knew all about that.

He finally gave up on sleep and sat on the porch swing with his phone and sketch pad. He turned on a small lamp and looked off into the darkness beyond, his fingers flying over the paper. He wasn't surprised when Lisa's face appeared under his pencil again, her eyes shadowed and sad. He sketched her as he'd seen her the other day.

The tough FWC officer, hair tucked under her official ball cap, chin set, eyes serious as she stood at the helm of her patrol boat.

He flipped the page and started another, this one as she'd looked earlier. Curled up on the swing, her feet tucked under her, still in uniform but clearly off duty, the top two buttons undone to reveal just a hint of cleavage, eyes tired and sad.

"What are you doing?" she asked.

He glanced up to see her leaning against the door frame, cradling her injured arm. She'd blush if she knew how the backlight showed off the body under her tee shirt and shorts. He swallowed hard, kept his eyes on her face. "Couldn't sleep."

They studied each other for a long moment, then she sat beside him on the swing. "You owe me a bedtime story."

He curled her into his side as before. "You sure you want to hear it? It's not pretty."

"I'm sure it's not. But maybe you need to tell it."

He sighed, rubbed a hand over the back of his neck. Tried to decide where to begin. "Hunter and I were working in Afghanistan. We had a local translator, Ahmed, who agreed to work for the U.S. military because he needed the money to survive. He told me once that if he'd had a choice, he'd never work for us. It was too dangerous, but his wife was pregnant with their third child and he was desperate to provide for them. He'd been a carpenter, but a mine had blown off his arm and he couldn't find work after that. Who wants a one-handed carpenter? But he was afraid. If the local warlord found out, he and his family would die.

"I'd seen some kids hanging around the camp and kept an eye on them, because children were often forced to do the warlords' dirty work. Then I realized they were just hungry and scavenging for scraps of food. I started saving little bits here and there and would leave them outside the camp for one little boy in particular, hoping I wasn't making a mistake.

"One day, Ahmed showed up, terrified. Someone had reported him. He warned us about an upcoming ambush and said he was taking his family and getting the hell out of town. I didn't think there was a single safe place in the whole damn country, but I understood. I wished him Godspeed and sent him on his way.

"Ahmed's intel led us right into an ambush. Whether he'd known it, or if he'd been fed false information?" Pete shrugged. "We'll never know. But we'd definitely been set up. We got out alive, but Ahmed, his pregnant wife, and both children had not only been killed, they'd been displayed publicly—a warning about what happened to traitors." He paused, took a deep breath, trying to force the images back. "That's when I discovered that the boy I'd been feeding was Ahmed's son.

Lisa's quick indrawn breath and the way her grip tightened on his shirt helped him get the rest out. "I swore I was going to track down whoever did this and wipe them off the face of the earth. Hunter forced me to calm down enough to think, to formulate a strategic plan, so I didn't get our whole team killed, too."

He squeezed his eyes shut to block out the faces of Ahmed's family, but they wouldn't leave. Lisa didn't say anything, just rubbed a gentle hand up and down his chest, over his pounding heart and waited for him to continue. Finally, she asked, "And did you get them?"

"Yeah. We tracked them to a cave in the hills, with only one way in or out. We thought this would be easy." He snorted. "Nothing is ever easy over there. We were ready to move in when they sent a boy out, couldn't have been more than nine or ten, with explosives strapped to his chest.

Lisa froze, tension humming under her skin. He could feel it. His heartrate speeded up, too. "I tried to save him, though I knew it was impossible. Hunter tried to keep me from running out into the open, but I had to try." Behind his closed eyelids, the flash of the explosion turned night into day, the memory burned like a brand. He rubbed a hand over his chest. "Hunter came after me, dragged me back to cover, saved my life."

"Did you get the warlord and his men?"

"Hell, yeah. We didn't stop until they were all dead." He sighed. "But it didn't make a difference. It was like playing whack-a-mole at Chuckie Cheese pizza as a kid. Every time you whack one, another pops up somewhere else."

Lisa shifted beside him and cupped his cheeks in her warm palms. "My turn to say the same thing you said before. You did what you could. You and I both know you couldn't have saved that boy. You did not cause his death, or Ahmed and his family's either." Her voice was gentle as she repeated his own words back at him. "Woulda, coulda, shoulda, Bulldog. Don't do that to yourself."

Her caring undid him, ground like salt into raw wounds. He stood and strode into the house without a word. In the bathroom, he tossed cold water on his face and braced his arms against the tile, trying to get himself under control.

Telling her had been a mistake. He should have followed his first instinct and kissed her instead.

Lisa let him go, surprised by the urge to go after him, hold him tight and rock him like a baby. She'd never been the cuddling kind. She'd always been afraid if she let a hint of softness in, she'd become a marshmallow, someone weak and unable to care for herself. "Caring doesn't make you weak, Lisa," Jim's wife Claire had said, more than once. "It makes you strong enough to risk being hurt."

The words echoed in the quiet night as she pushed the swing. Because of her envy of the Tanner family's closeness, she hadn't considered that Pete battled his own demons, had dark memories that haunted him, too.

She picked up the pad he'd set on the antique trunk and her jaw dropped open in shock. He'd captured her likeness perfectly. Her features, the sadness in her eyes. But he'd seen other things, too. Did she really look at him like that, all sultry and wanting? Did her eyes really sparkle with invitation? She wasn't sure if she was sending him unconscious signals, or if this was wishful sketching on his part.

Unsettled by his careful scrutiny, she turned the page, stunned to find five more sketches of her, all with different expressions, all hauntingly beautiful. He was incredibly talented.

She flipped to another page and her heart stopped for a beat. He'd drawn the scenes from his nightmares, the little boy with explosives around his chest and absolute terror in his eyes. There were Ahmed and his family, full of life on one page. The horror of their deaths depicted on the next. When tears clouded her eyes, she brushed them away, needing, somehow, to see it all, to know the battle he fought.

"That's the bastard who had them killed," Pete said. He was propped in the doorway, arms folded over his impressive chest, a pair of worn jeans clinging to his hips.

She forced herself to look away and focused on the drawing instead. The pencil marks were hard slashes and you could feel the anger seething from the paper. "He can't hurt anyone else, thanks to you and your team."

"Doesn't make up for all the ones he killed before we got there." He sat down beside her, tried to slip the book from her hands, but she held fast.

"Why the pictures of me?"

Time stretched as she waited for his answer. He scrubbed a hand over the back of his neck, which she'd noticed he did whenever he was debating how much to say. "It's how I process. Good. Bad. And...confusing."

She raised an eyebrow. "And how do I confuse you, Detective Tanner?"

He shook his head as he huffed out a breath. "That, right there, is how you do it. One minute you're playful and teasing, and the next I worry you'll kill me in my sleep."

A surprised laugh burst out. "I keep you on your toes? How is that any different than what you do?"

"Me? I'm an open book."

She snorted. "You have more layers than an onion." She reached out and laid a hand on his arm, needing to touch him, to say the words. "But under all the bluster and bossiness, there's a big heart, Bulldog. I like it."

Flames lit his eyes as he leaned closer, a little smile playing at the corners of his mouth. "Do you now? Well it just so happens I like you too, Fish."

Lisa wasn't sure who moved first, but suddenly, his mouth was on hers and her hands were cupping his jaw to keep him in place. She sank into the kiss, stroking his cheeks, enjoying the feel of the bristles under her palms.

Without breaking the kiss, he picked her up and settled her on his lap. Better, but still not close enough. When his hands gripped her waist and pulled her up until she was plastered against his chest she thought, *yes. This.* He opened his mouth and their tongues danced and played as the heat between them grew.

Time faded away as they explored each other, hands and lips stroking and touching, hearts beating in unison.

When the chains supporting the swing let out an ominous groan, they both froze. "We should get some sleep," Pete said and scooped her into his arms.

After he set her down on the bed, she climbed under the covers and turned her back to him, trying to slow her heartbeat, to keep from grabbing him and finishing what they'd started.

Professional distance, remember? She snorted. *At least, don't let this go any further. Protect your heart.*

He tucked her against his side and his warmth surrounded her. As she drifted off to sleep, she thought, "Too late. I love him."

Pete stiffened and she froze in horror as she realized she'd said the words aloud. She wanted to snatch them back, but knew she couldn't. She lay still, barely breathing, trying to decide what to do, what to say.

He kissed the top of her head. "Get some sleep, Fish."

She was going to have to take some risks.

Sunny's heart raced, and no matter how many slow breaths she took, she couldn't get it to slow down. This wasn't good. But at least the dizziness had faded, so there weren't three of everything anymore.

She sat on the bed and leaned back against the cabin wall as she tried to re-read her notes, but that brought the headache roaring back.

Eyes closed, she tried to think. After she'd come to in the woods, she'd walked for what seemed like miles before she found this abandoned cabin. She wasn't sure exactly how much time had passed since then, but she knew she couldn't hide here forever. She needed more food. A cell phone.

Mostly, she needed someone she could trust. Lisa's face popped into her mind, but she discarded the thought. She couldn't involve her. Not any more than she already had. Besides, she didn't trust her. Not for this.

Her hand shook slightly, despite her best efforts to control it, as she reached into her bra and pulled out her emergency fifty-dollar bill and the phone number she'd scrawled down so she wouldn't forget it. She'd been carrying emergency money since her mother had handed her her first bra along with a twenty-dollar bill. "Never get caught without resources, girl," her mother had said. "If you do, there's no end to the trouble you could find yourself in." All these years later, the habit stuck.

She waited until it was almost dawn before she ventured out. The moon offered enough light to see the faint game trail through the woods and then the man-made trail that led to the convenience store on SR-40 outside of Ocala.

She felt like she glowed neon orange, like everyone would know who she was just by looking at her. She'd taken the ratty pillowcase from the bed and used it to cover her hair. It wasn't much as disguises went, but it would have to do.

Approaching from the rear, she scanned the pitted parking lot, relieved there weren't any security cameras on the exterior of the building. *Thank you, Jesus.*

She kept her chin up as she walked toward the door, knowing furtive behavior would look suspicious.

Inside the store, she nodded to the clerk, who barely looked up from his phone as she entered. She grabbed several cans of food and some toilet paper. She found a prepaid phone on the other side of the store, and set everything down on the counter.

"Going camping?" the twenty-something clerk asked as he rang her up.

"Love it out in the woods. Nothing like it."

His eyes widened for a split second and she clamped her mouth shut. Had he recognized her?

She hurried around the side of the building and set up the phone in the parking lot, squinting to make out the instructions under the hazy streetlight. Then she walked behind the building, into the shadows, before she pulled out the scrap of paper and dialed. She didn't want to wait in case she didn't have a signal at the cabin.

The phone rang four times before a sleepy voice answered. "Hello?"

"Shelley? It's Sunny."

"Oh, thank God. Are you okay? I saw the press conference."

"I should be asking you that. Are you and Remy all right?"

"Yes, we're fine. Safe. But the police are still looking for me." She paused. "You don't sound so good. Are you all right?"

Sunny realized her racing heart was making her pant like she'd run a marathon. She tried to slow it down, but couldn't. Taking a slow deep breath, she tried to keep her voice even. "I'll be fine. I'm more concerned about you. I've read through the book, several times. If it means what I think it means, Brad was holding a ticking bomb. You and Remy won't be safe until we're able to stop whoever is behind this."

"That's what I thought, too. We should give it to Lisa. She'll figure out how to stop them."

Sunny instantly rejected the idea. "She has enough on her plate." Besides, when she'd needed her granddaughter, Lisa had let her down. She wouldn't make the mistake of depending on her now, not when Shelley's and Remy's lives were at stake.

Suddenly, two sheriff's vehicles raced past her, lights flashing, and skidded to a stop in front of the convenience store. The officers raced inside.

The clerk had recognized her.

"I have to go. Stay put until I call you back."

She hung up and then melted into the woods behind the store.

Chapter Twenty-One

When Pete's phone buzzed with an incoming call just after six a.m., Lisa and Pete had jolted awake, thrown on clothes, and rushed to the convenience store in separate vehicles. Pete had stayed a sedate distance behind her the whole way, which made her laugh. She thought he'd fly around her the first chance he got. She kept thinking she had him all figured out and he just kept surprising her.

The clerk rewound the tape from the register camera, and Lisa gripped the counter as she sagged in relief. Gran was alive! She looked tired and she was moving stiffly, but it was definitely her. She nodded to the young man. "Thank you for paying attention and calling it in."

The clerk had printed them a copy of the receipt, which showed that she'd paid cash and purchased a burner phone. Who had she called? Lisa checked her phone again, just in case, but there were no missed calls. She stashed her disappointment.

Who else would Gran call?

She left a message on Shelley's phone and then dialed nurse Kimberly Gaines. Her phone also went to voicemail.

"Hey, Kimberly, it's Lisa Bass. Do me a favor. If you hear from my gran, would you call me right away? I think she got another phone, but I don't have the number. Thanks."

Maybe she'd gotten a ride home. Since she knew Gran would have a good reason for hiding out until now, Lisa thought it was a long shot. Still worth checking, though.

Pete was on the phone, so she let him know where she was headed. On the way to Gran's, she stopped at the Corner Café for coffee, and hopefully, information. She walked in and headed straight for the counter. "Morning, Patty. Coffee and an English muffin, please."

"Good morning, Fish. Looks like you got dressed in a hurry." Patty grinned then sent a quick glance at Pete, who'd walked in behind her.

Lisa glanced down, mortified when she realized she'd missed one of the buttons on her uniform shirt and had been giving Pete an up-close view of her lacy bra. No wonder the young clerk had been staring, too.

She fumbled for the button as Pete reached them. "Don't fix that on my account," he murmured, low enough that only she could hear. Then he had the audacity to wink.

A laugh escaped. He was outrageous.

"Morning, Detective Tanner," Patty said, eyes darting back and forth between them like this was a ping pong match.

"Morning, Patty. I'll have whatever she's having,"

"Coming right up."

"Still no word from Shelley, right? Or my gran, either?"

Patty had her back to them and froze. Then she turned, studied both of them. "No. I told you that. Why? What's happened?" Her eyes went wide and she set the coffee pot down with a thump.

"Gran was spotted at a nearby convenience store, buying a burner phone," Lisa said.

"Oh, thank you, Jesus. Was Shelley with her?"

"Sadly, no. And Gran has disappeared again. Did either of them call you? Or maybe Mama T?" Lisa asked.

Patty's gaze sharpened at the mention of her mother. "I already told you no." She looked from one to the other. "Why would I lie?"

"Because Shelley's a person of interest in a murder investigation, so maybe you're protecting her," Pete said.

Patty planted both fists on her hips and Lisa felt a surge of pride at the way the other woman stood up to him. She would not have had the guts to do that three months ago. "Don't play tough cop with me, Bulldog. Because it won't work." She spun away and slammed things on the wooden counter as she worked.

When she set their cups of coffee down with more force than necessary, Lisa tilted her head at Bulldog. He nodded, paid for their food and sat down at a table at the back.

Lisa studied Patty, leaned closer. "Last time I was here, I got the feeling you might know where they might hide. I need to find them, Patty." She took a deep breath. "Gran needs her heart meds. Please."

Patty sucked in a breath, then studied her for a long moment. "If it turns out Shelley killed Brad, you'll help her?"

"I meant what I said before. Whatever the circumstances turn out to be, I'll do absolutely everything in my power to help her. You have my word on that."

Patty nodded, grabbed a napkin and drew a sketch. "There are two places out in the forest a-ways, both abandoned, that me and Mama T and Shelley talked about using as an escape hatch if we ever needed one. But," she warned, "I've already checked them. Twice. There's no evidence anyone has been there in a long time."

"When was the last time you checked?"

"Yesterday."

The bell above the door jangled and a couple of old-timers came in, arguing over last night's ball game.

"You'll let me know if either one calls you?"

Patty nodded and Lisa signaled Pete, who headed outside with their food. "Thanks, Patty."

She updated Pete but her gut churned with worry as they rushed to Gran's place.

Chapter Twenty-Two

Lisa had known it was unlikely, but she'd still had this fantasy that she'd find Gran at home, puttering around in her flower beds, floppy straw hat on her head and gardening gloves over her hands. But the house was as empty as the last time she'd been there. She made a careful search, but there was no sign that anyone had come or gone.

From there she and Pete headed into the Ocala National Forest. By the time they found the second location Patty had sketched, the sun was high enough to determine this was another dead end. Just as Patty had said, there was no evidence anyone had been here in a while. No recent tracks, no disturbed grasses, nothing. By unspoken agreement, they crossed the clearing and into the shade of a Live Oak to escape the heat.

"We knew this was a long shot, but I hoped." No sooner had she said the words than both cell phones started pinging with incoming texts and emails. "Wonder of wonders. Cell service." They both scrolled through their lists. "I've got something from our biologist." She looked at Pete. "He confirmed Remy's pelt is definitely from a snow leopard and the skull is from a chimpanzee."

"Then the question is, did Brad get the pelt from someone?" Pete asked, "Or did he get it directly from the animal? And if so, how did he come in contact with a snow leopard in Florida?"

"I'll call the biologist. See if he has any ideas."

Pete looked down and scrolled some more. "Byte just sent a text." He checked his watch. "Actually, he sent it to both of us an hour ago. He found some interesting things on Wells' flash drive. Says we should meet him."

"You go and fill me in later. I have to swing by the doctor's office in Ocala to get officially cleared. I'll call the biologist on the way."

She expected some protest. Instead, Pete studied her a moment, then said, "Call me when you're done and we'll meet up to compare notes."

Just that quick, he was gone.

She hadn't gone six miles before her cell phone rang, with a call from the Forest Community Center. "Officer Bass."

"Lisa?" There was a pause. "It's Kimberly Gaines. I, uh, just heard from your gran."

Relief flooded her, but she stayed calm. "Great. Give me the number." She fumbled for a piece of paper and pulled a pen from the cup holder.

"I told her you were trying to reach her. But she, ah, didn't want me to give you her number."

"What? Why not?"

A pause. "She wouldn't say. Just asked me to get her meds and meet her."

The idea that Gran trusted an acquaintance above her grand-daughter cut deep. But that wasn't Kimberly's fault. "Give me the address. I'll deliver the meds."

Kimberly's breath came out in a rush. "Are you sure? I'm slammed with patients today, but I don't want her angry with me."

"I'm sure. I need to see her, find out why she feels she can't go home."

"Okay. I'll have her meds ready when you get here."

Lisa squealed the tires as she spun the truck around in the middle of SR-40 and rushed back toward the clinic. She rescheduled her doctor's appointment, then called Pete. His phone went straight to voicemail, so she left a message.

Twenty minutes later, she turned into the clinic parking lot and a frantic Kimberly handed the medicine and a hand-drawn map through the window and hugged Lisa. "Let me know how everything goes, okay? And you be safe."

"Will do. Thanks, Kimberly."

Lisa was touched. First the Tanners and the ladies at the Corner Café, now Kimberly. This whole community thing, people caring about her? It was strange. Unsettling.

It felt really nice.

But she didn't have time to indulge in mushy-gushy feelings.

She'd just rolled up the window when Kimberly spun back. "Wait. I almost forgot. I don't know if it has anything to do with why your Gran can't go home, but Sunny mentioned she wanted me to get a notebook from her, said she needed me to hang onto it for her for a while."

"Did she say what kind of notebook? Never mind. I'll ask her about it. Thanks." Lisa's mind raced with possibilities as she sped down the highway.

She kept one eye on the rearview mirror, the other on Kimberly's messy scribbles. The road stretched out behind her in a straight black ribbon, so a tail would have been easy to spot.

"Take a left at the burned-out tree," Lisa muttered, leaning over the steering wheel. Even after two years, this driving-by-landmarks stuff still made her crazy. Give her a nice tidy grid any day.

"Ha! Gotcha!" She spun into the turn and headed down the dirt road, careful of soft spots. She'd heard plenty of horror stories and had a few of her own now, too. She didn't have time to get stuck in the sand.

As she slowed to approach the clearing, she cast quick glances behind and in front of her. The tiny cabin looked more like a large shed, and was tucked way back in the trees. Without directions, she would have driven right by and never seen it. Someone had gone to a lot of trouble to make it invisible.

She pulled off to the side and sat for a moment, scanning the area. There were two small, grimy windows on either side of the rickety door, but the place had an empty feel. Still, she took out her weapon and eased out of the truck, keeping it between her and the cabin. "Gran, it's Lisa. I have your medicine."

No response, no telltale shift of a shadow behind either of the windows, either.

"Gran? You here?"

Still nothing

She walked around the perimeter of the building, the path through the high weeds indicating someone had walked this way. Recently.

Maybe Gran was just running a bit late.

A shiver slid over her skin as she walked into the woods surrounding the cabin, using the trees as protection as she searched the area. The unmistakable feeling of being watched made the hair on the back of her neck stand out.

"Gran," she called. "Please come out. I need to talk to you."

She checked her watch again, and her worry grew. Gran should have been here twenty minutes ago.

Lisa made her way from tree to tree and then ran across the open area and up the two front steps. When she reached for the door handle and the door swung open under her hand, her concern morphed into something deeper.

"Gran?"

Lisa crossed the threshold and gaped. The small one-room cabin had been completely trashed inside. Just like Brad and Shelley's place. Just like Wells' place. Someone was desperately looking for something. The mysterious notebook Kimberly mentioned?

Her heart clenched. What would they have done to Gran to get it?

"Florida Fish and Wildlife Commission. If anyone is here, identify yourself. Now." Lisa kept a tight grip on her weapon as she scanned the room. She stepped over several cans of soup that rolled across the sagging wood floor. A hand-crank emergency radio lay shattered next to a rickety wooden table. The sagging mattress had been yanked off the bed and ripped to shreds.

Where was she? Had she seen whoever trashed the place and hidden in the woods?

A horse's whinny sounded from outside.

Lisa spun and ran for the door, weapon drawn. "Stop! FWC!"

A man dressed all in black sat atop a huge black stallion, trying to hold onto a flailing Gran. He had an arm banded around her waist to keep her in front of him, but she was fighting with all her might to break free.

Atta girl. Lisa ran down the porch steps and tracked them with her weapon, desperately seeking an opening, all too aware that if she missed, she could hit Gran instead. The horse whinnied and started bucking, clearly unhappy about the squirming humans on its back.

She could shoot the horse, but it might land on Gran. It was huge. She'd be crushed.

Gran suddenly reared backwards. The man jerked sideways to avoid getting hit in the nose with her head. Lisa saw her opportunity and pulled the trigger. The shot grazed his shoulder and he roared with fury. He pulled out a gun and fired in Lisa's direction.

Lisa crouched as she raced across the weedy grass. "Let her go. Now!"

He jerked the reins hard before he spun the big animal around and spurred it into a gallop. Lisa ran after them, tracking them with her gun as they flew over the woodpile and raced toward the deep woods.

Gran's face was sheet-white, her eyes terrified as she looked over her shoulder and screamed, "Lisa!"

Lisa hopped into her truck and took off in pursuit, careening between trees, trying to avoid the sandy spots, desperate to catch them, but within two minutes, they were gone, swallowed up by the dense forest.

Heart pounding, she stopped to listen, but the pine needles that carpeted the forest floor muffled the hoof beats. Frantic and frustrated beyond words, she kept driving, trying to pick up their path, but those same pine needles thwarted her there, too.

She finally turned off her truck, straining to hear. *Come on, come on.*

She heard nothing but the sounds of the forest.

Gran was gone.

And just like with Mama, Lisa hadn't shown up until it was much too late.

Oh, God, Gran. I'm sorry.

Defeat wanted to paralyze her, but she shoved it aside. She had to think.

She was dialing Officer King to ask him to bring Chief for a K-9 search, when a sudden gust of wind spit sand through her open truck window. A quick glance at the black clouds confirmed a squall was moving in, fast. A minute later the sky opened up and a torrential downpour instantly obliterated every hoof print, scent, or trace of evidence the man may have left behind.

Gran's terrified scream as she was taken away was louder in Lisa's head than the storm raging outside her truck.

Chapter Twenty-Three

Pete had never been to Byte's place, so when the other man led him to a bedroom-turned-office that looked like command central for a space shuttle launch, he let out a low whistle. "Wow. I did not know you had all this."

The other man shrugged. "It's something of a hobby of mine." He sat down in a comfy-looking leather chair and motioned Pete into the one beside him. His fingers flew over the keyboard and he nodded to one of the screens with his chin.

"I've been going through that flash drive, and it seems Wells had been doing some serious digging into our friend Dr. Castile and his associates."

"He mentioned him before and obviously didn't like the man. Wasn't sure if his claims of shady activity were personal or verifiable fact."

"From what I've gathered so far, I'm thinking fact. Check this out." He pointed to a spreadsheet that showed huge quantities of animal feed and meat being delivered to Castile's animal sanctuary.

Pete looked at the screen, then at Byte. "Call me stupid, but isn't that expected if you run an animal sanctuary?"

"Yes. But." Byte grinned behind his glasses. "I spoke to a friend who works at a zoo, and he gave me some food purchase comparisons. These are way too high, given the animals Castile lists on his website and Facebook page as being in his care."

"So maybe he has more animals he's caring for than he publicizes? Or maybe he's getting ready for his proposed safari rides? The vote is next week."

"Or maybe he's smuggling exotic animals through there or something."

Pete drummed his fingers on the desk, trying to sort it out. "Brad did odd jobs for Castile. Jason is a frustrated former vet. Brad was a delivery man and did taxidermy and his daughter had an exotic animal pelt. But it still doesn't explain why he was killed."

"You don't think it was a domestic dispute? I heard he had PTSD and when he drank, he was rough on his wife."

"I've heard the same." And it made him furious with Brad and angry with himself for not taking action. "That's still a theory we're pursuing. But so far, we don't have any hard evidence." He turned to Byte. "Have you checked the social media accounts for Brad, Jason, and Castile?"

"Yes, but we can check again." They went through each one, but nothing new jumped out at them.

"The biologist says that hide came from a snow leopard."

Byte grinned. "I'm right there with you." More clacking, then, "Here. I did an image search of that particular cat."

They leaned closer and Byte enlarged the image of a snow leopard draped over some hunter's neck. The animal had obviously been shot.

Pete shook his head. "Infuriates me to see these gorgeous animals destroyed for so-called sport. Especially endangered ones like these." He paused to think. "See if you can track down anything from Wells' flash drive or anywhere else that will give us enough for a search warrant for Castile's sanctuary. No judge will sign off without something more solid than that he's buying too much animal feed."

Byte scrolled through several more pages of online images until Pete drew a sharp breath and said, "Stop. Go back. There."

While the fast-moving storm raged outside her truck, guilt pummeled Lisa with both fists.

If Gran died, it was all her fault.

Just like with Mama, her efforts were too little, too late.

She should have expected something like this. There was a reason Gran had been hiding. It was Lisa's job to expect the unexpected. Logic said it was about this mysterious notebook.

The heart meds sat on the seat beside her, mocking her. How was she going to track Gran down?

By the time she found her way back to the cabin, the storm had passed. She hopped out of her truck and instantly sank into the mud. She searched the area around the cabin, desperate to find some identifying thing the man had left behind, but there was nothing.

Frustrated, she walked up the porch steps. But as she scanned the destruction inside something broke, deep down inside her. Her vow to protect Gran mocked her, tearing strips off her heart.

She'd let someone take her and now she had no way to track them.

The terror on Gran's face as the man whisked her away was an exact replica of the expression on Mama's face when Lisa found her, dead.

She leaned over the porch railing and threw up, so disgusted with herself she could barely breathe.

All she'd ever wanted to do was protect people, but that skill was obviously beyond her.

Yet despite the soul-crushing guilt, she couldn't abandon her. Gran needed help. With shaky fingers, she dialed Pete's cell. "Gran's gone, Pete." She took a deep breath and forced out the rest. "He took her...I don't know where. You need to find her, please."

"Where are you, right now?" Pete demanded.

She gave him the GPS coordinates.

"Don't go anywhere. I'll be there in twenty minutes."

She climbed back in her truck and laid her head on the steering wheel.

I'm so sorry, Gran.

Worry churned in Pete's gut as he raced through the forest. Fish didn't sound right, at all.

He let out a sigh of relief when he found the clearing and spotted her truck off to the side. He pulled his weapon and scanned the area as he slogged through the mud.

She was slumped over the steering wheel, unmoving, and his heart kicked into overdrive. "Fish." He jiggled her shoulder, then checked for a pulse, relieved to find it. "Hey, talk to me. Where's your gran?"

Her green eyes slowly blinked open and the anguish in her expression hit him like a fist. "They're gone. He grabbed her and rode away. I didn't shoot. I just...let them go." She swallowed hard. "It's all my fault. I didn't stop him."

"Start at the beginning." He opened the door and pulled her out of the truck, then reached in and grabbed a water bottle from the small cooler on the passenger seat. "Drink this and then tell me what happened."

Once she emptied the bottle, her voice was steadier. "Gran called Kimberly at the Forest Clinic and asked her to bring her heart meds. Kimberly called me and I said I'd bring them. When I got here, I couldn't find Gran. Next thing I know, some guy on horseback gallops by with her. I tried to follow in my truck, but I lost them. Then the downpour started and obliterated their tracks."

She slumped back against the truck and her eyes filled with tears. What the hell?

"You have to find them. They need you." She tried to edge past him, wouldn't meet his eyes. "I have to go."

"The hell you say." He grabbed her arms, hard. He'd seen this before, more than once. Soldiers could get so overwhelmed they went numb, couldn't think straight. Hell, it had happened to him and Hunter had forced him out of it.

Pete got right in her face, determined to tick her off enough to make her fight back. "You're not doing anything until we find her, you hear me? You think he's just going to let her go? You are not that stupid." He shook her. "Snap out of this, Fish, or you're really going to have things to regret."

Her head came up at that.

That's my girl.

"I can't do it anymore. I can't keep letting people die because I can't save them. I just...can't."

"You've been fighting for Shelley, Remy, and your gran this whole time. You were sure they were still alive against all odds. And you were right. Your gran still needs her medicine, and we need to find her. And Shelley and Remy."

"It's never enough. No matter what I do, it's never— "

He clapped a hand over her mouth, relieved when she glared and shook off his hold. *That's it, Fish. Fight back.*

He led her to his car, pushed her into the passenger seat, and reached for his sketch pad. "Tell me what this guy looks like. Any distinguishing marks?"

She cocked her head, thought for a moment, then her eyes widened. "I think he had a rope tattoo around his bicep. I saw it when he wrapped his arm around Gran."

"So, it may have been the same person Cal saw. Now we're getting somewhere. Okay, how tall was he?" Pete kept firing questions and then showed her the sketch. "Close?"

Her eyes widened. "Wow, you're good. Yes, that's what I saw." Then she sighed. "But he was wearing a hat pulled low, sunglasses, and a bandana over the bottom of his face, so we still can't identify him."

"Tell me about the horse."

She gaped at him. "It was a horse. Big. Black."

"Any distinguishing marks on it? White streaks anywhere?"

She squinted, then shook her head. "No, solid black. But it was huge."

He nodded. "We'll see if Castile has an animal that matches that description." He snapped a picture of the sketch of the guy. "I'll have Byte run this through facial recognition, too, just in case."

She climbed out of his car. "Good luck. I'm going to the office to fill out a report and turn in my badge."

Crap. He eyed her over the roof. "Not until we search the cabin." He stepped to her truck, pulled out the prescription bag and held it in front of her. "You can't quit until we figure out how to get this to your gran."

All the color leached out of her face as she narrowed her eyes at him. He saw the debate raging. Then she snatched the bag from his grasp and spun back toward the cabin.

He let out a careful breath and followed her.

Chapter Twenty-Four

Lisa slogged back to the cabin, furious with Bulldog's high-handedness. But mostly with herself. He was right. She wasn't a quitter.

Gran's long-ago words came back to her, a quote from Winnie the Pooh: *You're braver than you believe, stronger than you seem, and smarter than you think.*

She snorted. Whether that was true or not, Gran still didn't have her meds. She had to find her, and also make sure Shelley and Remy were okay.

She and Pete stood on the threshold of the cabin, eyeing the mess. Based on the convenience store video of her purchases, this is where Gran had been staying.

"Kimberly said Gran asked her to get a notebook for her."

Pete's eyes shot to hers. "What notebook?"

"Kimberly didn't know and Gran didn't say. But it might explain why her place was searched. Maybe even why Brad and Shelley's place was trashed, along with Casey Wells' place."

Pete narrowed his eyes. "It's possible this notebook is the thread that connects it all. But to what?"

"I don't know. But it might be the reason she felt she couldn't go home." Lisa crouched and looked under the bed. "Maybe she hid it here and whoever it was didn't find it."

They walked the perimeter of the room, checking for loose floorboards. Lisa rooted around in the small cabinet under the sink and checked the small closet, while Pete searched the other side of the room.

Outside, they heard a car door slam, then running footsteps.

Lisa exchanged glances with Pete as both pulled their weapons and trained them on the doorway.

Shelley burst through the door. "Sunny!"

Shock froze Lisa for a split second. "Oh, thank God you're alive. Where's Remy?"

Shelley skidded to a stop when she spotted Lisa and Pete, then turned to race back the way she'd come.

"Stop right there," Lisa ordered, holstering her weapon with one hand and reaching for Shelley with the other.

She wasn't quite fast enough, and Shelley slipped past, leaped down the steps and took off running.

Lisa raced after her, Pete right beside her. "Stop, Shelley. Do not make this harder on yourself."

Shelley glanced over her shoulder but didn't slow down.

With an internal sigh, Lisa put on a burst of speed but Pete was faster. He tackled the other woman, hooking an arm around her waist and taking them both to the muddy ground.

"Let me go," Shelley pleaded, struggling to free herself.

"No can do." Pete pulled both of Shelley's hands behind her and hauled her to her feet.

Lisa reached them, zip ties in hand. "Do we need to put these on?" she asked Shelley.

When Shelley shook her head, Pete kept one hand on her arm and led her back inside the cabin. He pushed her into a rickety chair. "Sit."

Shelley's eyes darted from Lisa to Pete. "Where's Sunny? Did she get her meds? She didn't sound right on the phone."

Lisa took the other chair, across the table from Shelley. "I brought them, but before I could give them to her, someone took off with her on horseback."

Shelley dropped her face in her hands. "This is all my fault. I never should have given it to her."

"Given what to her?" Lisa asked. "A notebook?"

Shelley clamped her lips shut, shook her head.

Pete leaned against the table, arms folded over his chest. "We'll get to that in a minute." His tone brooked no argument as he looked from Lisa to Shelley. "You need to tell me what happened the night Brad died." He pulled a small notebook from his shirt pocket. "But first, I need to read you your rights."

After he'd mirandized her, Shelley asked, "Am I under arrest?" Her voice trembled.

"Not at the moment, but I need a timeline of events. Start with after you left the community center."

Shelley took a deep breath, sat on her trembling hands. "Brad was really upset, but he wouldn't tell me what about. I pretended to be asleep, and then he woke me and said we were going frog gigging." She shuddered.

"What time was that?"

"It was after midnight, close to one a.m."

"Did you go out on the boat?"

Shelley looked away. "No. At the boat ramp, he, uh, he got mad at me and I used some of the moves Lisa taught us to get away."

"Which moves?" Lisa asked.

"I spun around and kicked him and he fell backwards."

"Did he get back up?" Pete asked.

Shelley glanced at Lisa, then buried her face in her hands again. "No. I didn't know what to do, so I took the truck, and—and I left.

"Was he alive when you took off? Did you check for a pulse?" Pete's voice was hard.

"Of course I checked." Her voice faded to a mere whisper of sound. "But I couldn't find one."

"And you didn't think to call 911?" Pete demanded. "Get him some help?"

"I didn't know what to do. I had to protect Remy." She took a deep breath and the words came out in a rush. "But I didn't kill him. I called Sunny and she went by the boat ramp, ready to call 911, but he was gone. I figured he was okay."

She and Pete exchanged glances.

"Remy was with Gran, right?" Lisa asked.

"Yes, I picked her up and we left town."

"What time was that?"

"It was late. When we passed the bank, the digital clock said two a.m."

"Where did you go?"

"I planned to head to Georgia, but then when I didn't hear from Sunny, I decided I shouldn't go too far in case she needed me." She met Lisa's eyes. "She's become like a mother to me. You are so lucky to have her."

Lisa gamely smiled past the longing clogging her throat.

"Is that the property you're buying from Redd?" Pete asked.

Shelley's face paled. "You know about that?"

"We do," Lisa said, then followed a hunch. "Was this fight with Brad about a notebook?"

Shelley's eyes widened in surprise, before she carefully blanked her expression. "What do you mean?"

"Do not start lying now, Shelley," Pete warned.

She sighed, resigned. "Okay, yes, Brad kept ranting about a notebook, so I went looking for it. When I found it, I hid it. I wanted to see what it said, why he'd been acting so strange."

"Did you give it to Gran for safekeeping when you picked up Remy?"

She nodded miserably.

"Where is Remy now?"

Shelley's head snapped up. "She's safe."

"And you don't know where this notebook is or what it's about?" Pete demanded.

"It was in some kind of code with numbers and letters. I couldn't figure it out, but I was hoping Sunny could." She turned to Lisa. "She's really smart."

"Yes, she is." Lisa's mind ran through possibilities. "Do you have the clothes you wore that night with you?"

"I do, but why?"

"Did you go into the lake that night?"

"No. We were just getting ready to leave the ramp when Brad, ah, got angry."

"Have you washed them since that night?"

"No.

"Which bank did you pass at two a.m.?"

Shelley named the institution and Lisa called Byte, asked him to see if he could find Shelley's car on a security camera at that time.

"Officer Bass, let's step outside," Pete said. He nodded at Shelley. "Stay here."

They walked far enough away so they couldn't be overhead.

"She could have held Brad under the water without getting her clothes wet," Pete said.

Lisa crossed her arms, met his hard stare. "That's one explanation. His head wound is consistent with her story, which the M.E. says isn't what killed him. So, if she was in her car in Ocala at two a.m., and Brad was seen on Chapel Lake, alive on his airboat with another man at two a.m., then she couldn't have killed him."

"I agree. But let's make sure Byte can confirm her story."

"We need to call this in," Lisa said, but worry nagged at her. She paced back and forth, mind racing. Neither one was safe, not yet.

"I think we need to stash her and Remy somewhere safe until we figure out exactly what's going on," Pete said.

Lisa stopped pacing, surprised at his response. "We are definitely thinking the same thing, Bulldog."

After they called to update their respective captains, they went back inside, where Shelley sat on the bed, arms wrapped around her waist, rocking back and forth. She looked at Lisa, eyes wet. "I need to get Remy. Please. You can take me to jail after that, but will you take care of my girl? She's all I have." She buried her face in her hands and sobbed.

They drove to Mama T's where Shelley had left Remy that morning. The little girl leaped into her mother's arms and then chatted with Bulldog like nothing unusual had happened. Mama T didn't say a word, just lifted her chin at Lisa's accusing look.

Byte confirmed that Shelley had indeed been in Ocala headed out of town at the same time Brad had been seen alive on Chapel Lake. Shelley had not killed him during their fight at the makeshift boat ramp.

Shelley had wanted to stay at Mama T's, but Pete vetoed that and arranged for mother and daughter to stay in a furnished rental house that belonged to one of his co-workers. Lisa agreed with Pete that there were still too many unknowns for them to return home safely.

Outside the nondescript house in a nondescript neighborhood, Lisa turned to Pete. "We need to search Gran's house again. See if she hid the notebook there. I can't think of any other way to try to find her."

"One of my tech guys is searching online photos of local horses, but he hasn't found that big black one yet," he said, and climbed into his truck to follow her.

They went over every square inch of the house once more, moving throw rugs looking for trap doors, checking behind the fridge and washing machine, all to no avail.

He found her in Gran's sewing room, holding a ratty-looking stuffed elephant under her arm.

"Gran gave me this when I was a kid. When Mama took us to

California, I left it here, hoping it would mean we'd come back." She set it down, then picked it back up. "I think I'll keep it with me."

"Remy has one, too. Did your gran give it to her, do you think?"

Lisa smiled sadly. "Wouldn't surprise me." She took one last look around the room, then headed toward the front door. "Let's try Gran's neighbors again on the off chance they saw someone coming down the street."

It hadn't netted them anything before, but Pete didn't argue.

His admiration for Lisa's instincts grew when Gran's elderly neighbor reported that a man had indeed stopped by, twice, claiming to be a friend of Sunny's. The neighbor sniffed and assured them she'd told the stranger nothing. She also confirmed the man had a rope tattoo around his bicep.

It was close to nine p.m. and they were back in Ocala, parked outside a local restaurant to grab a bite before they called it a night.

Lisa climbed out of her truck and the minute those worried eyes locked with his, he yanked her into his arms and dropped a quick kiss on her lips.

A couple of teens walked by and whistled. He slowly let her go. Right. Public place.

"What was that all about?" she asked.

"You are amazing, you know that?"

Surprise, then disbelief crossed her expression. "Amazingly stupid, you mean."

He gripped her shoulders, tempted to shake her until her teeth rattled. "You don't get it, do you?" He'd never been prouder of anyone in his life. Except maybe his mother, as she fought back against the stroke that tried to take her down. He'd seen Lisa do the same thing: She'd dug deep and found the warrior inside her. "It takes guts to keep going and keep fighting when the odds are stacked against you. But you've done it. And you're going to keep doing it, until we find Gran and bring her home and then catch the scumbag behind all this."

She studied him, as though judging the truth of his words. Then her chin came up. "Some annoying detective told me I'm not a quitter."

He grinned. "Damn straight. I have your back, Fish. Every step." He brushed a hand over her cheek. "You can count on that." He tilted his head toward the restaurant. "Let's grab some grub and then figure out what's next."

Once they'd ordered, he reached for his cell phone, pulled up his email, and then handed her the phone. "Check out this message from Byte and look at the photo. He said he found something interesting."

Fish opened the photo of the hunter and the snow leopard and frowned. "Where was this taken?"

He shot her a quick grin. "I knew there was a sharp brain under that extremely hot bod."

His voice was way too loud and she glanced around, saw a couple at a nearby table grin. A flush slid over her skin. "Quit. You're embarrassing me, Bulldog."

"But it's so much fun." He slanted her another glance, then sobered. "Byte checked the vegetation in the background and it's not what should be there in the leopard's natural habitat."

Her eyes narrowed. "It wasn't hunted in the Himalayas?"

"That's what he's thinking."

She enlarged the picture, then huffed in frustration. "There's something in the background, but I can't make out what it is."

He went out to his car and came back with his laptop. Once he'd enlarged the photo, he turned it so they could both see.

"What is that?" Lisa asked, leaning closer.

He got momentarily distracted by the citrusy scent of her hair, then sent her a bland look when she caught him at it.

"Focus, Bulldog."

He squinted. "Isn't that...? Wait. I think I know where that is. I've driven past it before." He took the laptop and pulled up the map function, then switched to satellite view. He pointed as he enlarged an area. "There. See that old barn? It has an odd shape." He flipped back to the photo, then back to the map.

"Holy smokes. You're right. Do we know who owns the property?"

He ran a quick check on the address. "No, but we can find out in the morning."

"Let's drive out there and check it out."

"Probably won't be much to see in the dark."

"Maybe there will be lights on in buildings and there will be quite a bit to see."

He closed the laptop just as the waitress delivered their food. "I like the way you think."

They left his car at her place and rode in her truck, since the location wasn't too far away. After a few wrong turns, they managed to find the property, located just off County Road 315. She pulled off the dirt road and they studied the shadowed barn and outbuildings. Unfortunately, those convenient lights they'd been hoping for did not materialize.

"Is this property connected to Castile in some way?" Lisa asked, peering through the windshield.

"I've been wondering the same thing. But if he's orchestrating illegal hunts of exotic game, wouldn't he try to cover his tracks better?" Pete indicated the farm. "The place looks like it's been abandoned for years." He yawned, then glanced at his watch. "We'll use the photo to get a warrant to search the place. But for now, we need a few hours' sleep so we can function."

Lisa tapped a finger on the steering wheel as she shuffled the pieces in her mind. "Maybe this book is a record of whatever is going on. Maybe Brad was killed for it and now someone thinks Gran has it."

"Which, according to what both Shelley and Kimberly Gaines told you, is true."

She nodded, rubbed a hand over her heart where anxiety pounded under her skin.

"As long as whoever it is doesn't get their hands on this mysterious book, he'll keep her alive."

It wasn't much, but it was all they had. Lisa let out a shaky breath, put the truck in gear. "Where to next?"

"Your place. We're going to get a few hours' sleep and be back at it at first light."

She opened her mouth to argue, then closed it again. Much as she hated it, he was right. Both her snakebite and her injured arm throbbed like crazy and her vision was starting to blur from exhaustion.

She didn't think either of them would be able to sleep for the worry and ugly scenarios running through their heads, but when Pete climbed in next to her and pulled her close, she wrapped her arms around him and immediately dropped into sleep.

Neither was aware of the watcher who stomped through the trees behind her cottage, seething with fury.

Where was the damn book?

Chapter Twenty-Five

"Wake up, Bulldog, time to go." Lisa had been up for almost an hour, laptop in hand, studying the terrain of the abandoned farm they'd discovered the night before. Now, the sky was finally starting to lighten. She sat beside him on the bed and allowed herself a minute to admire his sleek back before she gave his shoulder another shake. "Up, or I'm going without you." That should get his attention.

Sure enough, he instantly rolled over. But rather than spout some male nonsense, he took hold of her uninjured arm and pulled her on top of him as though she weighed nothing. Before she registered that she was sprawled across his body, he'd cupped her jaw and claimed her mouth in a kiss designed to make every nerve ending in her body wake up and take notice.

"Morning, beautiful."

She slowly pulled back, no doubt looking as dazed as he did. "Um, good morning. But we need to go."

Rather than the disappointment she expected, he grinned as he squeezed her butt, then froze when she winced in pain.

"Dang, I forgot about the snakebite. Sorry." Then one side of his mouth kicked up. "But I'm happy to check that wound for you, make sure there's no sign of infection. Or maybe I can just kiss it and make it better?"

She rolled her eyes as she tried to hide a smile. "While I appreciate the concern, Detective, it's really not necessary."

"Pity," he said, then gave her another lingering kiss before he slid out from under her. "That should give us both something to look forward to. For later."

He grabbed his go-bag and disappeared into the bathroom with a wink while she chuckled at his arrogance. Then she allowed herself a private smile. It *was* something to look forward to. But if she let him know that, he'd be insufferable all day long.

Enough. They had far more important things to focus on today. When he reached the kitchen, she had coffee going and had plunked a few English muffins in the toaster, thrown a bunch of grapes in a bowl. He eyed the spread.

She shrugged. "Take it or leave it. No time for fancy." She spun the laptop toward him. "Come see what I found."

He leaned closer and she told herself to ignore his woodsy, clean scent and the urge to run her fingers through his still-damp hair. Instead, she pointed out the access roads to the farm. "I think our best bet is to go in from this side."

Her cell phone rang. Dispatch. "Officer Bass." She listened for a moment, then said, "Say that again? The caller said they heard an elephant?" She met Pete's surprised look with her own. "Where, exactly, did the caller hear this?" She typed in the address and glanced at Pete, who had both eyebrows raised over his coffee mug. "I'm, ah, with Detective Tanner. We'll head that way right away. Thank you."

She ignored the flush heating her cheeks and called Byte. "Do we have that search warrant yet?"

He yawned in her ear. "We will, just as soon as the judge wakes up. Cool your jets a bit, Fish. I'll get it and call you ASAP. Don't I always?"

"Right. Sorry."

She hung up and turned to Pete, who was peering at her laptop. "We were right. I think someone is conducting illegal hunts out here."

"Looks like it, but how do you sneak an elephant into the area without anyone seeing it?"

Pete took another sip of coffee. "Airplane. Or," he paused, "those semis we've been seeing."

Lisa grabbed her muffin and wrapped it in a paper towel, poured coffee into a travel mug. "We need to get out there. If Brad – or this notebook – is the connection, maybe this is where Gran is being held."

Pete stood, grabbed his gear, too. "Maybe. But let's not stop thinking because we have a working theory."

She slipped her weapon into her holster. "I'll meet you there."

Pete followed Lisa's cloud of dust, thinking. The good news was that she was her old self this morning, all that self-doubt quieted by some much-needed sleep. He yawned. Not nearly enough sleep, but enough to keep functioning. He understood her need to rush in, guns blazing. He was fighting the same sense that time was running out.

She pulled up at a tidy, newer mobile home and he pulled in behind her. She'd barely cleared her truck when the front door opened and a tiny white-haired woman waved them in, gnarled hands gripping a crisp white apron.

"Good morning, ma'am. I'm Officer Bass with Fish and Wildlife. This is Detective Tanner with the sheriff's office." They showed their badges. "Are you the one who called us?"

"I did. I'm Myrtle Hanes. Come in, come in. Coffee's hot and fresh."

They followed her through an immaculate living room into an equally pristine kitchen, filled with tchotchkes. The fridge was papered with drawings for Memaw made by tiny hands. She poured them both coffee and then sat at the table. "I know what I heard. I'm not crazy." Her jaw firmed and she eyed them both sternly.

"No, ma'am. No one thinks you're crazy. Can you tell us exactly what you heard?" Lisa asked.

"Well, it was about an hour ago, now. I couldn't sleep. Curse of the elderly, you know. When I was younger and craved sleep, I didn't have time. Now I have time, but can't sleep. Anyway, I got up to make the coffee and heard it. It was an elephant's trumpeting. Clear as a bell."

"Is it possible you heard something else and just thought it was an elephant?"

Pete's question earned him an indignant sniff. "I know what I heard. What other animal in all of God's creation sounds like an elephant?"

"Do you have many neighbors out here, Mrs. Hanes?" Lisa asked.

"Not many and none have any hooligan teenagers who might resort to such a prank." She shook a finger at Lisa. "I taught school for twenty years. I'm not easily tricked."

Lisa and Pete exchanged quick smiles.

"Could you tell the direction the, ah, trumpet came from?" Lisa sipped her coffee. "This is excellent, by the way. Thank you."

Mrs. Hanes pointed out the kitchen window. "It came from over that way."

"How can you be so sure?" Pete asked.

She looked from one to the other as though they were idiots. "Because that's where I heard the truck engine. I'm guessing someone was either loading or unloading that poor creature and he—or she—wasn't happy about it."

"What truck?" Lisa asked.

"There's a road on the other side of those woods. And now that I think on it, I have been hearing more trucks than usual."

"What's out there? Why are there trucks?" Pete asked.

Mrs. Hanes took a sip of her coffee and patted her lips with a napkin. "I'm sure I wouldn't know. I'm not given to gossip," she said primly.

Lisa leaned forward. "Mrs. Hanes, I appreciate that. Discretion is a valuable trait in a neighbor. But we're looking for a missing woman. A grandmother."

"Oh, my stars. But what would that have to do with an elephant?"

"That's what we're trying to find out. Can you tell us how often you've seen—or heard—trucks on that road in the last couple of days?"

She looked from one to the other, then pushed her chair back. "I can do one better than that." She marched to the drawer next to the sink and pulled out a flowered journal, opened to a page filled with dates and times. "As I said, I haven't been sleeping well since my Willard passed, so I jotted down what I saw, just to pass the time."

Pete exchanged a quick look with Lisa as their hostess set the book in front of them.

Lisa ran her fingers down page after page, her excitement matching his own.

"Did you ever hear any other, ah, animals?" Pete asked.

She thought back. "Now that you mention it, I thought I heard a very large cat several days ago. But I could be mistaken."

Pete looked from the journal to Mrs. Haines. "May we borrow this for a few days?"

She hesitated, uncertain, but then her chin came up and she nodded. "Yes, of course, if you think it would help."

Lisa set her coffee cup in the sink and touched the older woman's shoulder. "Thank you, Mrs. Hanes. You just might have saved a life."

The older woman grabbed a Ziploc bag and tucked the journal inside before handing it to Lisa. "I'll pray you find her, safe and sound."

"Thank you for your help," Pete added as they hurried out.

Once out of earshot, Lisa muttered, "Let's check out that road."

"We'll take my unmarked car," Pete added.

They called dispatch and requested backup, then hid her truck just beyond Mrs. Hanes's property and slowly cruised the dirt road. The deep grooves in the sand indicated a heavy vehicle had passed that way, but except for birdcalls, there was no sound of life, elephant or otherwise.

When Lisa eyed the fence surrounding the property, Pete warned, "Don't even think about it. If we want to stop whatever is going on here, we need to do it by the book. Let's head to the Café and wait for the warrant. Once we get it, we'll come right back."

"I'm not leaving."

"Fine, but we don't go in until we have the warrant. And backup."

They stared each other down, but she finally nodded, though she wasn't happy about it. He understood the urge to root out the bastard who'd taken her grandmother, no matter the cost. He felt that same buzzing under his skin that demanded immediate action, but he wouldn't let her do anything stupid that might get her killed.

By the time they got word that two deputies were headed their way with the search warrant, too much caffeine sloshed in Lisa's stomach, making her slightly queasy. She paced outside her truck, praying and shaking out her hands, trying to burn off the buzz. "Please, God, let Gran be okay. Please."

She shoved the voices that called her a miserable failure to the back of her mind, at least for now. Pete was right. As long as there was a chance Gran was alive, she couldn't give up. It wasn't in her.

By the look of things, the farm had been abandoned a long time ago. There was no evidence that anyone had walked up the weed-covered path in quite some time. The windows were dirty, though none of them were broken.

The two sheriff's vehicles pulled up outside. She and Pete approached the weathered farmhouse together, both with weapons drawn. They carefully stepped onto the sagging wraparound porch and stood on opposite sides of the door as Pete pounded on it. "Sheriff's department. Open up. We have a search warrant."

No sounds from inside disturbed the morning quiet. The other officers stood behind their vehicles, watching and waiting. No curtains twitched. Pete pounded again, announced himself again, and then used his shoulder to open the door. It swung open so fast he almost fell into the room.

"It wasn't locked," Lisa said, studying the handle.

They split up and searched room by room, yelling, "Clear" each time, but found nothing that suggested anyone had been here recently.

Lisa pointed to the dust coating the wood floor. "Ours are the only footprints."

"We need to check the barn."

Once outside, they greeted Sanchez and Josh, who had just arrived, and asked them and the two deputies to search the outbuildings.

She and Pete hurried toward the weathered barn, walking on either side of the sand and gravel track that led up to it. Lisa crouched down for a closer look and her heart rate sped up. "These tire tracks are fresh. And deep."

Pete had also bent down. Their eyes met across the sandy track. "I'll take the front. You go around back."

They split up and approached the massive old building, guns drawn as before. The huge sliding door was padlocked and Pete called for a pair of bolt cutters to remove it. Lisa walked around the left side of the building, striding through the tall grass, out of view of the others. There were rusting pieces of old farm equipment leaning up against the wall. She studied them for a moment, then scaled an old hay baler to peer through one of the high windows. She couldn't see much through the grime, except that it appeared as abandoned as the house.

But the tire tracks leading up to it were fresh.

She hopped down and kept walking, studying the matching roll-away door on the back of the building. It looked just like the one in front, padlocked. She studied the ground around it. Nothing here had been disturbed in a long time.

More farm implements leaned against the wall, weeds growing around them. She walked all the way around and joined Pete, who stood, hands on hips, studying the interior of the aging structure. Was there anything more tempting than a guy in a black tee shirt and faded blue jeans? *Not now. Geez.* But their gazes met and the heat that flared in his eyes said he was thinking about their kiss this morning, too. And about his promise of more later.

She shook off her wayward thoughts before she reached him. "Nothing around back, just old rusty equipment." She scanned the interior just as he was doing. Hay bales were neatly stacked in the hayloft above them, with more bales stacked off to one side on this level. Empty stalls ran down the other. Loose hay covered the area where they were standing, but beyond that, the place was completely empty.

Pete eyed the loft. "You going up, or am I?"

She waved a hand. "After you."

They scrambled up the rickety ladder and found a few old trunks filled with clothes an antique shop would love, but that was it. She turned and crashed into Pete. He automatically caught her by the shoulders and that same tension buzzed between them. He leaned forward as though he was going to kiss her, but stopped and stepped back. "Dang, you tempt me," he muttered, then pointed to the ladder. "Nothing here. Let's go."

She hid a smile as they hurried back down and met Sanchez and Josh outside.

"I didn't find a thing. Hollywood, either," Sanchez said.

"There's nothing here," Josh agreed.

The two deputies said the same.

"What are we missing?" Pete asked.

"Based on the tire tracks and the neighbor's description of trucks coming and going, someone is delivering stuff here. But what? And where is it?" she asked.

They studied the area again.

"The only thing that makes sense," Josh said, "is that one truck drops it off—whatever it is—and another comes and takes it away."

"But if you were doing that, why not use the truck stop outside town and just switch trailers? Or switch the signage and registration numbers?"

They all knew thousands of dollars' worth of stolen and illegal goods traveled through Marion County every year on the Interstate. The truck stops off the highway were regularly used to swap trailers and slip contraband through undetected.

"We need to watch this place for a few days. See what's going on."

"Gran doesn't have a few days," Lisa growled.

Pete turned to her. "You have a better idea? I'm all ears."

She sighed, shook her head. "No, dammit."

"We don't know that she's anywhere near here."

He was right. She couldn't let desperation cloud her judgment. Gran's life depended on clear thinking. As her mind scrambled for other options, dispatch radioed with a report of a bear in someone's yard. She sent Sanchez and Josh to go check it out, then turned back to Pete. "Why don't I head to the animal sanctuary and pay our friend Jason another visit. He might be more willing to talk to me, since I'm a woman."

"Worth a shot. I'll head over to Castile's office in town."

"What, exactly are you going to ask him? Whether he's importing elephants for illegal hunts?"

"I just might. Shake him up a bit. See how he reacts."

"I don't have any better ideas." She huffed out a frustrated breath. "We've got nothing, Bulldog. How are we going to find her?"

"We keep following the breadcrumbs." He raised her chin. "It is way too soon to give up."

She swiped his hand away and stepped back, propped her hands on her hips. "Who said I was giving up?" What kind of wimp did he think she was?

He raised a brow and sent her a little half smile and she realized she'd been had. Again.

"Keep me posted," she muttered, as they hurried back to their vehicles.

He pushed her, always. But not to keep her behind him. He forced her to push herself.

She couldn't help smiling. How could you not love a man like that?

Wait? What? No. She didn't love Bulldog, despite what she'd foolishly blurted out the other night.

She couldn't. Maybe if she told herself that enough times, she'd actually believe it.

"I don't know who you are, but you need to let me go. Now." Sunny kept her voice firm, chin up. She sat on the floor where he'd tossed her earlier, her back against the wall of what looked like a dark, dank cellar. Her head pounded along with her heart. She tried to ignore both. She had to stay strong. Lisa would find her. Wouldn't she?

The man looked down at her and said nothing. He hadn't uttered a single word since he'd taken her and dumped her here. She'd tried to get a look at his face, but he stayed in the shadows, always wearing sunglasses and a ball cap. She prayed this meant he'd eventually let her go, since she couldn't identify him. But she wasn't that naive.

He turned and opened a small cooler he'd brought with him, set a sandwich and a bottle of water in front of her.

"What is it you want from me? Why am I here?" She figured she knew, but she wouldn't make it easy on this scumbag.

"Where's the book?"

Sunny held herself still, determined not to give herself away. "Book? What book? I have no idea what you're talking about."

He struck like a snake. His gloved hand slapped her hard enough that her head banged against the stone wall. She tried to bite back the scream, but a whimper escaped. She swallowed hard. She would not cower. Not ever.

Her chin came up, despite her blurred vision. "Tell me where this book is or what it looks like and if I have it, I'll give it to you. I'll do whatever it takes for you to let me go."

He raised his hand and Sunny braced herself, certain he was going to hit her again. "If you want your granddaughter to stay alive, you may want to rethink your answer. My patience wears thin." He pulled out his phone and held it toward her. It was a photo of Lisa and Pete Tanner walking into her house.

Lisa was looking for her. Relief shuddered through Sunny and she blinked back tears. Even though she'd been so ugly to her granddaughter, Lisa was still looking for her.

She'd been so heartbroken by Dazzle's death, she'd blamed Lisa for it. Here, in this dank prison, she could admit how wrong she had been. It had never been Lisa's fault. Dazzle had made her own decisions since the day she'd decided she wouldn't answer to Donna any longer. No one had ever been able to make her daughter do a single thing she didn't want to do. Not Sunny. And certainly not Lisa, though she could well imagine her granddaughter had done everything she could to save Dazzle from herself.

Sunny knew that. Deep in her heart, she'd always known that, yet she'd pushed Lisa away for the past two years, punishing her for something she hadn't done.

It was easier than accepting her own failures as a mother.

Her captor walked to the stairs, looked back over his shoulder. "You have until I get back to tell me what I want to know."

Sunny swallowed hard. It was time to step up, take care of her granddaughter.

She just had to figure out how.

Castile's business office occupied a renovated Victorian mansion on Fort King Street in Ocala, separate from his veterinary clinic and animal sanctuary.

Before he exited his vehicle, Pete tossed a suit jacket over his tee shirt to conceal his shoulder holster. He wiped his feet on the mat and stepped into an immaculately restored foyer with a curving staircase and stained glass windows. A twenty-something blonde in a severe navy suit sat behind an antique desk, long fingernails clacking on a state-of-the-art computer keyboard. She looked up as he approached. "May I help you?"

"I'm here to see Dr. Castile. Is he in?"

"Do you have an appointment?"

Pete pulled out his gold shield. "I believe I do."

The woman paled slightly and picked up the phone. "Dr. Castile. There's a detective here to see you. Yes, sir." She hung up. "Come with me."

She led him down a short hall of closed doors and into what must have once been the library. Gleaming floor-to-ceiling shelves filled with books lined the walls. Castile waved a hand to indicate one of the two leather chairs before his massive desk.

Pete reached over the desk, hand extended. "Thanks for seeing me."

Castile studied him a moment before reluctantly shaking his hand and Pete hid a grin. "Did I have a choice?"

"Not really, no." He sat down, crossed an ankle over the opposite knee, ignoring Castile's disapproving look. "I came to ask what you know about elephants." He watched Castile, looking for a reaction, but got nothing, not so much as a flicker of an eyelash.

The older man slid a hand over his black hair, adjusted his cuff links, diamond-studded, unless Pete missed his guess. "What are you talking about? What would I know about elephants?"

"Do you have any at your animal sanctuary? Maybe preparing for the safari rides you hope to implement after the commissioners' vote?"

Castile narrowed his eyes. "If I did, I'm sure you would have checked that already, detective. Again, why are you here?"

"Somebody heard an elephant trumpet near your sanctuary. Since you don't have a permit for elephants—yes, I checked—I'm trying to figure out why you have one."

That got to him. Castile's eyes narrowed. "Someone claims to hear an imaginary elephant and you decide I'm what, hiding one?" He pushed a button on his desk. "Julio, please show the detective out. He's wasting my time."

The thirty-something man who'd shown up at the fundraiser with Castile—and who'd held Fish much too closely when they'd danced—appeared from a side door, also wearing an expertly cut suit tailored to hide his weapon. Both men had the same olive complexion, dark hair and eyes that bespoke their Latin American heritage. Byte's research said the younger man was not only Castile's nephew, but they had invested in several business ventures together. He also fit Fish's description of the height and build of the man who'd taken Gran.

"This way please." He indicated for Pete to precede him out the door.

Pete looked from one man to the other. "Do either of you own or ride a large black horse?"

The two men's expressions remained carefully neutral as they shook their heads no, giving away nothing.

Once they were out of the elder Castile's earshot, Pete asked, "What do you know about an elephant?"

"Elephant? What are you talking about?"

"Somebody heard an elephant near the animal sanctuary."

"Since we aren't permitted for elephants and have no elephants, someone was clearly mistaken and heard something that sounded like an elephant."

"What would that be, exactly, do you think?"

Julio held open the front door. "I wouldn't know. Have a nice day, detective."

Pete smiled and glanced over the other man's shoulder just in time to see the secretary blanch and duck her head. He'd have to find out what she knew.

Later.

Chapter Twenty-Six

Lisa pulled up at Castile's animal sanctuary outside of town, frustration gnawing at her gut. She glanced at the heart medication on the seat beside her. Gran needed those pills.

She pushed the intercom button and looked past the gate to the nearby outbuildings, but this time, there were no signs of movement. After several minutes, she pushed the button again and held her badge in front of the camera.

A disembodied young male voice said, "Can I help you, officer?"

"I'm here to speak with Jason Holberg."

"He's not in today. Sorry. Something I can help you with?"

"Was he scheduled to work today?"

"Um. Yes. But he could be running late."

"What time did you get in this morning?"

"Early. Just before seven to feed up."

"No sign of his vehicle, or that he'd been here?"

"No, ma'am. What's going on? Is he in some kind of trouble?"

"I'm not sure yet. But if he comes in, please call me right away. Do you have a pen?" She repeated her number, twice, and had him read it back to her. "One more question. Do you all have a really big black horse here?"

"Um, no. No horses. Sorry."

"Okay, let me know if you hear from Jason." She executed a U-turn and headed back the way she'd come.

Was the kid lying? Didn't seem like he'd have a reason to.

She tried to picture Jason all in black, wearing a ball cap and sunglasses. The build was right. It was possible he was the one who'd taken Gran, though she wasn't sure why he would. Still, her gut said he was connected to this. She just couldn't figure out how.

To protect Shelley, she could see him choking Brad to death, but that didn't prove that's what happened. Dust billowed behind her truck as she raced toward his place.

She notified dispatch that she was doing a wellness check, but it was quickly apparent Jason wasn't home. The place had that empty feel, but she kept her weapon handy as she walked the property, peeking in windows, looking behind the shed. She wouldn't risk missing something obvious.

Discouraged, she called Pete, filled him in. "Jason never showed up for work. I'm at his place. He's not here, either."

"I spoke to Castile and his nephew, Julio. I asked about elephants. They had nothing to say, though Castile's secretary went pale when she heard the question. I'll have Hollywood chat her up, see if a bit of flirting will net us some answers. Both denied having a black horse."

"The guy at the animal sanctuary said the same. I think we should talk to everyone who lives near that abandoned farm. We passed a couple of other houses. Let's see if anyone else heard an elephant or diesel engines. Sound carries on a quiet night."

"I'll grab a couple sandwiches and meet you there."

Lisa parked in the shade and waited for Pete, the temps rising along with her anxiety. She felt like she was in a burlap sack, trying to fight her way out, unable to see the drawstring that was the key to her freedom. Her mind kept going back to the mysterious notebook everyone seemed to want to get their hands on. Where was it? And what, if anything, did it have to do with elephants?

Pete pulled up beside her and shed his suit jacket before he climbed into the passenger seat. He handed her a white bag and an iced tea.

"I still don't— "

"Let's eat first, Fish. I'm starving and we'll think better after food."

She sent him a side eye. "Are you trying to say I get hangry?"

He shrugged and grinned. "If the cliché fits." He finished his first sandwich in three bites and reached in for another, eyeing the untouched sandwich in her lap. "Keep up, or I'll start in on yours."

"We're still missing the connection— "

"Sandwich. Then strategy."

She huffed out a breath and took a bite. Her stomach immediately rumbled its appreciation and she conceded he was right. They made short work of the food and collected the trash.

"Canvass the neighbors?" Pete asked.

"Unless you have a better idea."

He shook his head. "No, and it's bugging the hell out of me. Whoever took your gran has to be after the notebook she mentioned. Nothing else makes sense."

Lisa cringed at the stark reality. "Gran is smart. If she has it with her, she'll find a way to buy us some time. Let's focus on the elephant angle, and hope that's the clue we need to find where she's being held."

There weren't many houses out here, but he and Fish knocked on every single door. No one was home at two of them and the other three ladies claimed to have heard nothing. Since one had a yapping dog and the other two crying children, Pete believed them.

There was only one house left, a small cottage two doors past the abandoned farmhouse. The house and yard were immaculately kept, with fresh yellow paint and white trim, a riot of color in the flowerbeds. They stepped onto the shaded front porch and Pete eyed the aging, though pristine, Buick under the carport. "I'm thinking retired folks."

Sure enough, an older woman in a polyester pantsuit and lacquered hair pushed the screen door open. "Good afternoon."

"Hello, I'm Officer Bass with Fish and Wildlife and this is Detective Tanner with the sheriff's office. We'd like to ask you a few questions."

From the other room a male voice yelled, "Who's at the door, Mildred? If that's the Jehovah's Witnesses again, tell them we're already saved."

"It's the police, Frank." She called over her shoulder.

"What do they want?"

"Why don't you get out of your easy chair and come find out?" She turned back to them. "How can I help? Is someone in trouble?"

Pete sent Lisa a 'go ahead' nod.

"Ma'am, we're trying to find an older woman." She held up her phone and showed Mildred a photo of Gran. "Have you seen her anywhere?"

"Can't say as I have. Has something happened to her?"

Frank stepped up behind his wife. He was a huge man, tall and thick. "What's going on?"

Lisa repeated what she'd told Mildred and when she showed him the photo, his response matched his wife's.

"We got a report from one of your neighbors that they'd heard what sounded like an elephant in this area. Have either of you heard anything like that?"

"An elephant?" Mildred asked. "Heavens, no. Why would there be an elephant around here?"

"We've also heard about semi-trucks, diesels, in the area. Have you heard those?"

The husband and wife exchanged glances.

"I know what I heard, Mildred."

"You'd been drinking—" she began.

"Not that much," he insisted.

"Sir. What did you hear?" Pete asked, interrupting the squabble.

"It's happened a couple times here lately. Middle of the night, here comes some diesel truck, grinding his gears, coming down this here gravel road. It ain't designed for that, mind you, but they're doing it anyway."

"Who's they?"

"No idea. But they keep waking me up. They got no business out here disturbing the peace."

"Frank—" Mildred warned, but he held up a hand to stop her.

"One night, I had enough. I got in my car to follow them, confront whoever it was, and tell them to knock it off. If they need to drive down our road, they ought to do it during the day like normal people." He narrowed his eyes, bushy eyebrows forming a straight line. "Made me think they were up to something fishy."

"What did you see?" Lisa asked.

Another exchanged look with his wife. "I followed one of them down to the old Jenkins' place and watched them pull up to the barn. They drove the truck right inside."

"Did you talk to the driver? See what company it was from?"

He scratched his head and glared at the look his wife gave him. "This is where it gets a little weird. They closed the barn door behind the truck, but when I went up and knocked, nobody answered. I walked around the barn, looking for another way in. The back door was locked, too, so I climbed up on some old equipment and looked in the window. Dang truck was gone."

"Gone?"

"Vanished. Like it went up in a puff of smoke."

His wife waved all that away. "Oh, Frank. Enough." She turned to Lisa. "He's just guessing, making up what he thinks happened. When he gets to drinking, well, his memory isn't so good."

"I only had one beer, Mildred. I was fine and I know what I saw. How many times do I have to tell you that?"

Pete stepped between them. "Can you describe the truck for me, sir? Any particular markings or logo on it that you remember?"

"Nothing. It was white. There was some kind of logo on the door, but it was pretty dark and I couldn't make it out. If I'd known it was going to disappear, I'd a paid more attention."

"What do you think happened to the truck, sir?" Lisa asked.

"Danged if I know. It was there. Drove right on in, plain as day, and then, *poof*, it was gone. Never seen anything like it."

Pete pulled out a card and handed it to him. "Thank you for your time. If you folks see another semi late at night, or hear an elephant," he grinned as he said that, "please give me a call right away, day or night. We appreciate your help."

"I hope you find that lady," Mildred added before she closed the door. As Pete and Lisa walked down the steps, they could hear them squabbling from inside.

Lisa swung the passenger door open, hopped in. "We need to check that barn again."

As he drove, Bulldog requested an updated search warrant and asked for backup. Lisa tapped a finger on the dashboard, anticipation humming under her skin. She believed the old guy. Why risk his wife thinking he was a drunk who made stuff up? She wasn't sure what he'd seen, but her money was on some kind of trap door or tunnel. Florida sat on a thick layer of limestone, so there were caves and caverns all over the place. Years ago, when the StuffMart was built in Ocala, construction was temporarily halted when they realized there was a cave system below the building site.

When Pete pulled up beside the barn, she grabbed her heavy

Maglite and waited while Pete retrieved his. Once the warrant came through, they approached together, weapons drawn, eyes scanning the area. The birds continued their chirping and showed no signs of being on guard.

Pete slid the heavy door all the way open and they spread out and studied the floor, looking for a telltale gap in the flooring.

Lisa grabbed one of two brooms conveniently leaning against the outer wall. She handed Pete the other and they started sweeping loose hay out of the way.

Her hands were getting red and about to blister when she spotted a thin line. Dropping to her knees, she used her hand to brush more straw out of the way. "I think I found it."

Pete was crouched beside her almost before the words were out, sweeping the area clean with quick swipes of his hand. Sure enough, there was a seam in the floor. Lisa stood and used her broom to follow the groove, clearing hay as she went. Pete headed in the opposite direction, doing the same thing. When they met up again, they'd outlined most of the barn floor.

"Holy crap," Pete muttered.

"How does it open?"

"Let's find out."

They ran their hands along the outline, but found no button or hidden mechanism.

Jumping up and down to try to weight activate it didn't help either.

Lisa hurried to one side of the building and ran her hand and her flashlight along the wall, searching for a switch or lever of some kind. She found nothing.

She turned and found Pete standing in the middle of the floor, looking up. There were several cables attached to the hayloft with giant hooks on them. His eyes followed the position of one of the hooks and he moved directly under it and kicked the hay aside.

"Found it!"

Sure enough, there was a ring attached to the floor. A quick search revealed three more rings at regular intervals. All of them lined up with the cables above.

"If it's some kind of trap door, there's got to be a switch some-where." She ran back to the wall, searching for the controls for what appeared to be an overhead crane.

She'd gone about halfway around the perimeter when Pete called, "Got it! It was hidden under a couple of old buckets."

There was the sound of gears turning and the overhead lines, weighted by the hooks, began to lower to the floor. When the cables reached the ground, she and Pete attached them to the four rings. He hurried back to the control box and hit a button.

Lisa stood beside him and they watched, open-mouthed as most of the barn floor slowly went vertical, revealing what amounted to a driveway down the middle of the barn. It disappeared into the dark-ness below.

"Frank wasn't drunk or imagining things. The truck disappeared."

Lisa started down the ramp but Pete grabbed her arm to hold her back. "Let's wait a minute or two and see if anyone underground pops up. They had to have heard us or the crane. I don't want to walk into an ambush. Backup should be here shortly."

She nodded and tried to keep her impatience at bay. Gran was down there. She felt it, all the way to her bones. But he was right. "Two minutes, and then I'm going down. Backup or no backup."

Weapons drawn, they walked down the ramp back to back, alert for trouble every step. The hard-packed dirt had one-by-twos set across it every few feet as a way to offer traction. Which meant trucks not only went down this steep grade. They came back up, too.

Once they descended beyond the ramp, they both stopped, stunned.

Lisa turned in a circle, head tilted back to see the ceiling. "This cave is huge."

She was still amazed by the geology of this area. Limestone is very porous, and made this part of the state prone to caves and sinkholes, but this cave was larger than any she'd seen. Since she'd been with FWC, she'd rescued more than one unwary hiker from a sinkhole when the limestone caved in, dumping the person into the cave below. Other times, water forced its way up from the Floridan aquifer and a sinkhole became a spring. Either way, they were unpredictable and she took them seriously.

As they walked, the tunnel leveled out and the temperature dropped. Lisa shivered as they turned on their flashlights. She was surprised to see electric lights attached to the cave walls at regular intervals. "Someone has done a lot of prep work down here. Which tells me this isn't a one-time thing."

Pete shined his light as far ahead as he could. "No visible switches. There must be one up top we missed."

A smaller cave veered off to their right. Lisa stepped inside and shone her light around, glanced back at Pete. "Empty. Not even a soda can." She stepped back into the main tunnel and they picked up the pace. She wanted to run full tilt, propelled by a gut-deep certainty that if she didn't, she'd lose all chance of finding Gran. Which logically made no sense, since they had no proof she had ever been here. But her instincts were screaming at her to hurry.

They heard a woman's muffled scream, then a door slamming.

She and Pete took off at a dead run.

Chapter Twenty-Seven

Lisa's heart pounded in time to her feet. *Please let us get there in time. Please let us get there in time.*

They rounded a slight bend and Lisa almost crashed smack into the cave wall. Beside her, Pete pulled up short, too and they looked at each other. The tunnel simply stopped.

"Where is that smell coming from?" Hand over her nose, Lisa turned in a circle, trying to find the source of the stench. It smelled like the back end of a zoo. Beside her, Pete did the same.

"What did we miss?" She moved closer to the rock wall, running her hands along it, looking for a hidden mechanism, something. The scream had definitely come from this direction.

Hang on, Gran.

She stepped into a shadowy corner and suddenly felt a cool breeze on her face. She leaned closer and realized what she thought was a section of the rock wall, was a cleverly painted tarp that looked like rock. "Pete!"

He was beside her in seconds. They slipped around the tarp and found themselves in yet another cave, this one larger than the first. As they shined their lights around, they discovered empty cages in every size and shape. Some were small, sized for a dog or cat. Others were huge, big enough to transport, say, an elephant.

"There has to be another way out." She'd think about the missing animals later. Right now, she was more worried about the scream they'd heard.

It took two sweeps around the cave before Pete whispered, "Found it."

As she ran toward him, Lisa almost tripped over something lying on the dirt floor. She bent down to scoop it up and froze. The certainty that she'd been right didn't help the fear. Not one bit. "Gran's been here." She held up the bright yellow hair tie. "She always ties her braid with these."

Pete nodded grimly. "There's another hidden door."

Which made no sense. You would think anyone down here had come on purpose. The camouflage should be to keep people on the surface from finding the entrance.

The door was locked and bolted from outside. Pete slammed his shoulder against it, again and again, until Lisa said, "Stop. It's no use."

She grabbed a length of wood from a pile and they combined their strength to try to force it open, but the wood didn't give.

Sweaty and panting, they stopped to catch their breath, and that's when they heard a feminine voice shout, "Let. Me. Go!"

"Gran!" Lisa leaped to her feet. They heard a cry of pain, then the sound of a car door slamming, then another. An engine started, then faded into the distance.

In unison, they attacked the door again.

That's when they heard it.

Tick. Tick. Tick.

Her eyes met Pete's.

"We have to get out of here."

"Go, go, go, before it explodes," Pete shouted.

They took off running.

Two steps out of the cave, a loud bang reverberated off the walls.

Half a second later, an ear-splitting explosion shook the cavern, the sound a deafening roar that rumbled up from the depths.

The ground shuddered and Lisa's feet flew out from under her. She was tossed through the air before she landed on the hard-packed dirt with a bone-jarring splat.

She lay there for a stunned moment, taking inventory. Everything hurt and she couldn't see past the roiling dust. "Pete." She tried to shout, but her voice was barely a squeak.

"Yeah! You okay?"

"Think so." Coughing against the rock dust, Lisa wobbled to her feet, trying to get her bearings. Her snake bite throbbed and her shoulder was in agony, but incredibly, her phone was still clutched in her hand.

Pete struggled to his feet, as well, scanning the smoky area with his flashlight, looking for an opening. "This way! Quick!"

Stumbling and still disoriented, they raced back the way they'd come, frighteningly aware of the ominous creaking above them.

Single file, they tore through the tarp-covered entrance and ran along the tunnel as though the hounds of hell were hot on their heels. Lisa chanced a glance over her shoulder and gasped at the cloud of dust billowing behind them, followed by the unmistakable thunder of crashing rock.

Her lungs heaved and she fought for breath, desperate to get back to the barn before everything caved in on itself.

Exhaustion pulled at them by the time they reached the ramp, and their steps were faltering. Pete grabbed her hand, tugged. "Keep going." He coughed. "Almost there."

She found another burst of speed and they galloped up the ramp and into the barn, then out onto the driveway and well away from the structure.

Lisa stumbled around, breath heaving, coughing against the rock dust, before she finally slowed to a stop. Nearby, Pete did the same, coughing and trying to catch his breath.

She leaned forward and braced her hands on her knees as she

tried to calm her racing heart. Slowly, gradually, the coughing lessened and she was able to draw a full breath. Then another. And another.

She straightened and listened. The rumbling had stopped. She looked around, surprised to realize it was full dark. They'd been down there longer than she thought.

She called dispatch and reported what happened, then asked about their back up. A pileup on SR 40 had delayed officers, but they were now enroute.

Pete jiggled his ear as though it were still ringing. He looked up. "You okay?"

Seeing him there, alive, covered in dust, tripped something in her heart. Without thinking it through for even a second, she launched herself at him. He caught her as she leaped into his arms and wrapped her legs around his waist. She anchored her good arm around his neck and kissed him like she never wanted to let him go, ever.

He froze in surprise for half a second before he tightened his hold and kissed her back with the same deep longing. He could have died in there. A couple seconds' hesitation or bad timing or whatever, and he could have been buried under tons of rock.

She didn't think she would have been able to bear losing this man.

The kiss went on and on until slowly, gradually, desperation turned to comfort, and reassurance slid into a need for more. Pete eased back to look at her, brown eyes smoldering. She lowered her shaky legs and he steadied her before gently cupping her cheeks, brushing at the dirt on her face. "We're okay. We're okay."

Lisa nodded, took a deep breath and let the words sink into her skin. Her heart.

Pete was alive. They were okay.

She took a deep breath, and then reality smacked her, hard. What about Gran? She raced back to the barn door. "Gran?" Lisa shouted. "Are you here? Gran?"

When she would have rushed inside, Pete stopped her with an arm around her waist. "Stay back. It's not safe."

She turned frantic eyes his way. "What if Gran's still down there?" She couldn't abandon her now.

"Think, Fish. We heard her being taken away. Whoever has her must have heard us and panicked." He looked her up and down. "Are you hurt anywhere?"

The question completely surprised her. "I'm fine. It's Gran I'm worried about."

"Then let's get to work."

They took photos as best they could in the dark while waiting for the teams. The moment they arrived, she and Pete handed out assignments.

She turned to Pete. "We need to find the opening, figure out where the tunnel came out. I'm going to get my truck."

He held up his phone, the GPS lighting the screen as he opened his car door. "I was thinking the same thing."

Within minutes, they were in her truck, scanning the GPS on her dashboard laptop, using satellite view to see the topography more clearly. There were several homes, barns, outbuildings and what looked like small hunting cabins dotting the area.

"The tunnel continued in a mostly straight line, so we were heading east."

Pete put his phone to his ear, dialed Byte. "Let's see if we can figure out who owns all the properties in that direction."

They crossed two dirt roads and several open fields and thick woods, but saw no billowing cloud of dust to indicate where the cave-in had been. "Somebody obviously didn't want us snooping around, but blowing up the cave seems extreme, given how much effort went into building it."

Pete shrugged. "Maybe not that much, given the natural cave and tunnel, but I see your point. Was the explosion set to go off when someone accidentally triggered the mechanism? Or did whoever we hear toss in the explosive after they hustled Sunny out, to keep us from following?"

Worry gnawed at her like a rabid dog. "I'm not sure it matters, since the result is the same. We weren't able to follow."

As the night lengthened, her worry deepened. She drove back and forth across the nearby farms in a tight grid pattern, but they found nothing. No hole in the ground, no depression, nothing to indicate where the tunnel emerged.

Byte called with the list of owners and they got a search warrant for another farm that didn't look like anyone had been there in years. Neither the sagging house, nor barns, nor outbuildings netted a single clue.

They finally sent the exhausted crews home just past midnight.

The only saving grace was that the teams had dug through the underground rubble and found no evidence of a body. It wasn't much, but it was the only thing that kept her panic at bay. She had to believe that they were right and Gran had been moved out of the tunnel before the explosion. It was the only thing that kept her from climbing out of her skin. Which meant whoever had her would keep her alive until they found this mysterious notebook.

She wanted to howl in frustration and turn over every rock and stone, dig under every bush, but they didn't know where to look. The clock was ticking and if they didn't search in the right place, they were just wasting time.

She took another step and her vision blurred, her body swaying from exhaustion. Every cell in her rebelled at the admission, but without some sleep, her body wouldn't keep going.

Pete sent one more text and looked up. "You look like I feel. We need a couple hours shut-eye, Fish, or we won't be able to function. I'll meet you back at the house."

Completely out of the energy needed to argue, she nodded and climbed in her truck, bleary-eyed and still frantic, but strangely warmed by the fact that he'd be right behind her. She wasn't alone.

As always, she slowed as she approached her cottage, making sure there were no cars or people around who didn't belong. Satisfied, she backed into her driveway and waited while Pete parked alongside her, so neither vehicle was blocked in.

She made a circuit of the interior, checking for unwelcome guests, and to make sure no one had been there while she was gone. Cat howled at Lisa's neglect so she fed and watered her, then sent Pete to shower while she headed outside to check the camera feeds. Afterwards, she stumbled down the hall for a hot shower of her own.

She wasn't surprised to find him sound asleep, so she climbed in beside him, sighing when he rolled over and tucked her against him. With all the worry and uncertainty of what tomorrow would bring, she didn't think sleep was possible, but somehow, with his arms locked around her waist and his breath against her neck in a soothing rhythm, she held tight and slid into oblivion.

Chapter Twenty-Eight

When she woke in the pre-dawn light wrapped in Pete's arms, her spontaneous jolt of happiness instantly vanished under the worry for Gran. If she didn't bring her home, she wouldn't be able to live with herself.

She automatically reached for the St. Michael medallion Dazzle had given her and stroked the warm metal, hoping it would help her think, offer up some guidance as to where to look next.

Pete's hand gently closed over hers, stroked the chain. "It's beautiful, like you," he rumbled, propping himself on an elbow so he could see her face. "Who gave it to you?"

She opened her mouth to brush the question aside as she usually did, but stopped herself. "Mama." She held it up. "St. Michael, patron saint of law enforcement. She gave it to me when I graduated from the academy. I've not taken it off since."

"She loved you. And if she were here, she'd tell you that."

Lisa squeezed her eyes shut, the words gliding over the raw places in her heart.

He leaned closer. "It wasn't your fault, you know that. You have to let the guilt go." His kiss was gentle, healing, and as she floated in the sense of security he inspired, her heart hoped that maybe, just maybe, she could believe him.

Someday.

A cell phone buzzed.

"Yours or mine?" Lisa asked.

"Mine."

They hurried to the kitchen.

"Hey, Byte. No, I was awake." He put the call on speaker. "What can you tell me?"

A few days ago, Lisa would have bristled at the fact that Byte, who worked for FWC, was calling Bulldog and not her, but somehow, they'd all become a team, working toward the same goal. And she trusted Bulldog. Completely.

Which she'd also have to think about. Later.

"You know the guy in the social media photo you sent me, with the snow leopard? Turns out he's co-owner of an architectural firm in Miami. The other owner is none other than the guy you brought in a couple days ago after that traffic stop, Santiani."

"The one who tried to bribe me."

"Right. And to make things even more interesting, I dug a little deeper and discovered their latest project is a big high-rise for none other than Miami developer Julio Castile.

Lisa and Pete exchanged glances. Another piece of the puzzle. Another connection. But still not enough to give them a clue to Gran's location.

"Can you get me contact info on this guy?"

"Texting it now."

"Thanks, Byte."

As Lisa started coffee, her phone rang. "Good morning, Captain. Yes, sir. I was just coming on duty. I'll head that way now." She hung up and turned to Pete. "Someone driving by the area where Brad launched his boat got passed by a guy in a pickup who raced down the road and cut off another guy headed to that same spot. The good citizen was nosy, so he stopped to listen, heard a lot of yelling and called it in."

Pete narrowed his eyes. "That sounds...odd, doesn't it?"

"The situation or the call?"

"Both. The caller leave a name?"

"No, but I'll check it out. Keep me posted on what you find, too."

As she stepped past him, Pete laid a hand on her arm. "Be safe out there, today, Fish. Don't do anything stupid, okay?"

"Not part of the plan, Bulldog, today or any day." She paused. "Same goes, you know."

"I know." He winked before he walked out.

Sunny woke to darkness, her back stiff from leaning against the rock wall. Her legs were numb, and she was shivering in the damp cold, but she was still alive. Her heart alternately thumped and fluttered like a crazy bird, anxiety crawled over her skin like ants, and her breath was coming in short bursts, but she wouldn't let her AFib distract her. She couldn't.

Right now she had to figure out how to get out of here.

But how? It looked like she was in another cave of some kind. After he'd blindfolded her and hauled her into a car what felt like days ago, he'd marched her down a bunch of stairs, shoved her in here and left.

She didn't know how much time had passed, but she supposed it really didn't matter.

All he wanted was the book.

If she couldn't escape, she had to buy time and pray that her wicked-smart granddaughter had figured out what was happening and had gotten Shelley and Remy tucked away somewhere safe. Even if Lisa couldn't save her, at least Sunny would die knowing those two were safe.

But she wanted to live. Badly. She wanted to apologize to Lisa, to make amends and repair the once-strong relationship she'd shared with her granddaughter. Lisa was everything Sunny could have asked or hoped for: She was strong and wise and kind. Tears dripped down Sunny's face. She wanted so much for that dear girl, but she'd acted the fool for so long. Had she squandered any chance to make it right?

The thick wooden door suddenly opened and the man strode in, boot heels ringing on the stone.

She studied his face in the gloom, searching for something to identify him, but he was again wearing a dark ball cap and sunglasses and all black clothing.

He took two angry steps toward her and glared, hands fisted at his sides. "Where's the notebook?"

Inspiration struck and she met his gaze. "Hidden someplace you'll never find it."

His gloved hand shot out and the smack slammed her head against the wall, same as last time. She cried out and then locked her jaw, keeping any other sounds inside.

"Tell me where it is. It wasn't in the house."

Her mind raced, but she sent him a casual shrug. "Then you weren't looking in the right place. Take me with you and I'll show you where it is."

He studied her, judging the truth of her words. Sunny prayed he couldn't see the fear behind her bravado. She had no idea what he'd do when she couldn't produce it, but maybe it would offer an opportunity for her to escape. Or for Lisa to find her. Step one was getting out of this cave.

Several minutes passed while he studied her, then paced the room. Finally, he reached into his pocket and pulled out a gun, aimed it at her. "Let's go, then."

Sunny stood and he yanked her hands behind her and secured them with a zip tie.

"Stay quiet and do exactly as I say." As he forced her up the steps, he hauled her close and whispered, "If I find out you're lying, I'll make you watch as I kill your granddaughter. And then I'll kill you."

Sunny nodded, her knees threatening to give out. She felt like Scheherazade, the king's wife in the ancient Arabian Nights story, who played a very dangerous game, spinning elaborate tales every night to buy time and save her life. Sunny would have to be equally clever, leading him on a wild goose chase long enough for Lisa to find her.

Lisa climbed into her truck and propped her childhood stuffed elephant on the passenger seat, right beside Gran's heart meds. Having it there made her feel closer to her grandmother and upped her determination. "I'm going to find you, Gran. Just stay strong until I get there."

When she arrived at the makeshift boat ramp on Chapel Lake, she wasn't surprised no one was there. But she drew her weapon before she climbed out of her car because everything about this call seemed off.

The caller hadn't completely manufactured the story, though. There were, in fact, skid marks in the dirt to indicate someone had driven through in a big hurry. She walked beside them until she reached the clearing, then spent a few minutes looking around. She found nothing—no trash, no cigarette butts, no signs of a struggle.

Still sitting on her haunches, she turned and examined the area. Actually, there were signs of a scuffle in the sand, but someone had used palm fronds to wipe away all traces. Why?

Whoever it was had gone to a lot of trouble to deliberately waste her time. What were they trying to keep her from?

Frustrated, she headed back to Jason's place, hoping to catch him still in bed and ask why he hadn't shown up for work yesterday. Her brain clicked through the facts of the case again as she drove, searching for patterns and connections. Jason was the link that connected Brad—and by extension, Shelley and Remy—to Castile. And the notebook linked Gran to Shelley.

Jason's truck wasn't at his house and they'd gotten no hits on the BOLO Pete had issued. Either he'd killed Brad and was hiding from the police, or—and Lisa thought this more likely—he was trying to find Shelley and Remy, too.

She knocked on the door and when it swung inward, all her senses went on alert. Someone was constantly one step ahead of them. She knew she should get a search warrant, but she didn't have time for all that. Gran didn't have time.

Weapon in front of her, she called, "Fish and Wildlife. Anyone home?" She methodically cleared each room before she holstered her weapon and pulled on a pair of gloves. This place had been carefully searched, too, everything put back almost perfectly, but not quite. A partially open drawer here, a cabinet there.

The only thing that made sense was that someone was still looking for the notebook.

But had they found it?

An hour later, she decided she wouldn't find the answers here. Maybe she'd missed something at Brad and Shelley's.

She drove too fast, ever aware that if Gran had been taken because of the notebook and she didn't have it—or couldn't produce it —her life wouldn't be worth spit.

Once she reached the Larsen place, she went through the same steps, ignoring the little voice again nagging her about a search warrant. Dang it, there wasn't time. She quickly searched the perimeter and the shed out back, then knocked on the front door. When there was no answer, she checked around under a couple flower pots, found the spare key, and hurried inside.

Fingerprint powder covered every flat surface, but she found nothing that looked like a log book or journal. She leafed through every fishing magazine and beat up paperbacks on the rickety bookshelf, then looked for hidey-holes, secret compartments in closets, false bottoms in drawers, anywhere someone might have hidden this mysterious notebook.

When footsteps sounded on the wooden floor, she grabbed her weapon and stepped through the open doorway into the living room.

"Fish and Wildlife!"

Jason stood in the doorway, his weapon drawn.

"Put the gun down," she said firmly.

"Whoa, sorry." He set it on the floor, raised his hands in the air. He was clearly nervous, eyes darting around, looking like he was searching for an escape route.

"Where have you been? We've been looking for you."

"I've been trying to find them, but they're gone. I don't know where else to look."

He met her eyes, and the fear in them struck her right in the heart. He spun away and started pawing through the bookshelves, grabbing a paperback, flipping through it, then tossing it on the floor. "We can't stop looking." His voice broke. "I have to find it."

Lisa stepped closer. "What do you have to find?"

"The notebook. I have to find the book. He'll kill them if I don't." His gaze darted around like pinballs, ricocheting off everything they touched.

She laid a hand on his arm, tried to calm him. "Let me help. Tell me what you know."

The scent of a man's heavy cologne reached her just as Jason's head snapped up.

"I—I." His face went white as he glanced over her shoulder.

Before she could turn to see who it was, an arm came around her neck and something was pulled over her head.

She felt a sharp prick in her neck and then nothing.

Chapter Twenty-Nine

Pete dialed as he drove. "C&S Architectural Design, how may I direct your call?"

"I'd like to speak to Mr. Santiani, please. It's urgent."

"I'm sorry. But Mr. Santiani is not in the office."

"When will he be back?"

"I'm not at liberty to say. Who's calling?"

"This is Detective Tanner with the Marion County Sheriff's Office. I need to know where he is. It's urgent that I speak with him."

"Oh, um, detective. He's on vacation for a few days."

"Where did he go?"

"I'm not sure I should give you that information."

"How will he react when he finds out you kept me from reaching him?" The truth was that Santiani would probably give her a raise, but Pete didn't say that. "Where is he?"

She cleared her throat. "Actually, I believe he's in Marion County. Said he planned to do a bit of hunting with a friend."

"Where is he staying?"

"Let me check." Pete heard keys clacking. "He's booked at the Ocala Hilton through the weekend. What's this about?"

"Do you have a cell number for him?"

Another hesitation, then she rattled off the number.

"Thank you. I appreciate the help." As Pete drove towards Ocala, he wondered how many seconds passed before she called Santiani to let him know. When Pete approached the front desk twenty minutes later and asked for Santiani's room, he was told—surprise, surprise—that the man had checked out. "How long ago was that?" he asked the young desk clerk.

"About fifteen minutes ago, sir."

Of course. "Did he happen to say where he was going?"

"No, sir."

"Was there anyone with him? Or did you see him with anyone while he was here?"

"No, sir. But I'm not always on duty."

"Where is your security footage?"

The clerk called the manager and they scrolled through the last few days, but the tape recording didn't show Santiani with anyone else. Pete slipped his sunglasses on as he walked back outside. Despite the heat, a chill slid down his back, a trickle of foreboding his military days taught him to never ignore. Time was running out.

And he was being watched. He scanned the area, and though he saw no one, he knew better.

On impulse, he called Fish to check in. There was something about being with her, about waking with her wrapped in his arms that he'd never experienced before. Josh would tease him no end if he realized it. Or maybe he wouldn't, since he and Delilah seemed to have found the same kind of connection that had Charlee and Hunter honeymooning in Hawaii. He grinned. If he played his cards right and didn't revert to his idiotic, overbearing ways, maybe he'd have a shot at forever, too. And a forever with Fish by his side suddenly looked bright and shiny and inviting.

But first, they had to find her gran. And figure out who killed Brad.

When her phone rang four times before going to voicemail, he hung up and dialed again. This wasn't like her, especially if she was on duty.

When the same thing happened, his chill got deeper. He sent a text: *You're not answering your phone. Let me know you're okay.*

He climbed into his car and called Josh. He didn't want to call her captain and undermine her acting lieutenant status in any way. "Hey, bro, have you talked to Fish today?"

"Earlier. She was headed out to check a call from where Brad's boat had been launched. Why? What's wrong?"

"She's not answering her cell."

"That's not like her. Let me check dispatch and see where she is." He heard keys clacking. Fish and Wildlife officers could see the location of their fellow officers at any time, and they checked in with dispatch at regular intervals. "System says she's at Brad's address. She hasn't missed a check-in yet, but I'll head that way, make sure everything's okay."

"I'll meet you there."

When Lisa woke, her hands were tied behind her back and a rock was digging into her shoulder blade. There was a foul-smelling rag shoved in her mouth and when she tried to move her legs she found them bound as well.

Her head cleared slowly and she bit back the nausea that threatened. She did not want to throw up while gagged. She squinted, trying to bring the room into focus. Incredible relief flooded her when she saw Gran leaning against the wall across from her, eyes closed. Thank God. She had a nasty bruise on her cheek, but appeared unhurt overall, though her breath was coming in short pants. Not good. Jason was slumped not far away. He was also bound and gagged, but wasn't moving.

Lisa tried to crawl toward Gran, hoping she could untie her, but she couldn't move forward more than two feet. As she tugged at the bindings, Gran opened her eyes, whispered, "Stop. You're tied to a hook in the wall." She tried to steady her breathing. "He told me he knows where Shelley and Remy are hiding and if I helped you, he'd kill them. I'm sorry." She coughed and flicked her eyes to a camera mounted on the wall.

Lisa nodded, to show she understood. "You don't sound good. I was trying to get your meds to you." Watching Gran struggle made Lisa's heart hurt.

"I'll. Be. Okay, long as I. Stay. Calm." She coughed again then leaned her head back, winced.

Lisa's worry amped up even more. The room still had a tendency to spin, so she closed her eyes to try to think. She had to get Gran out of here. Once she missed her check-in, her squad would be notified and they'd start looking.

But where were they? It looked like they were in another section of the cave system.

She glanced down at her uniform, not surprised her radio was gone. She'd bet her gun was, too, along with the knife she kept in her boot and the multi-purpose Leatherman tool in her pocket. Their kidnapper was no fool.

The door creaked open suddenly and the man strode in, scanning the room in one glance. Lisa recognized him instantly, despite the ball cap and sunglasses. Julio Castile, Martin Castile's nephew and the smooth talker she'd danced with at the fundraiser, aimed a gun at her heart.

"On your feet, Officer Bass."

The complete lack of inflection or emotion in his voice sent a chill skittering down her spine. She tried to get up, which wasn't easy with her hands and feet tied, to say nothing of her aching shoulder. But it was an opportunity to stall.

One eye on him, she flailed and struggled far more than was strictly necessary before she made it to her feet.

"Let them go," she demanded, trying to shout through her gag. She pushed with her tongue, rubbed her chin against her shoulder, and finally managed to spit out the nasty piece of fabric. "My gran has a heart condition and needs her medication! Let her go! Jason, too. They're not part of this."

He chuckled. "Seems you're not in a position to call the shots this time." He glanced at Gran and Jason. "Though I'm sure they appreciate the effort you've gone to on their behalf. Pity it won't matter."

She exchanged a quick glance with Gran, thought of Pete and the future they might never have, then straightened her spine. "Let them go and I'll give you the notebook."

His smile was chilling as he raised the gun, took aim. "Nice try, Officer Bass, but I don't believe you have it."

"Not on me, no. But I know where it is."

"She said the same thing." He pointed the gun in Gran's direction. "One of you is lying."

She scoffed. "Who are you going to believe? A trained cop or some old lady?" She cocked a brow, ignoring Gran's sharp intake of breath. "But if you kill the wrong person, then what are you gonna do? Are you willing to take that risk?"

His eyes narrowed, then he stepped closer, aimed the gun at her temple.

Chapter Thirty

Pete got to Brad's place before Josh did. He wanted to roar up the drive, lights and sirens, but he resisted the urge. If she were in trouble, making his presence known wouldn't help. He pulled off into the forest right before he reached Brad's driveway and sent Josh a quick text.

He was threading his way through the trees, approaching the house from the back, when Josh caught up to him.

"Told you to wait for me, Bulldog."

"No time." He hurried through the forest, gun at his side, keeping Brad's house in sight. "No sign of anyone else here. Hers is the only vehicle."

They searched the shed first, found it empty, then split up to circle the house. Pete stepped onto the front porch and bit back a curse. The front door stood ajar. He went in first, Josh right behind him. It didn't take long to confirm the place was empty.

"No sign of a struggle, at least," Pete said, eyeing the living room. "The only reason she'd go willingly is if she was trying to protect Sunny."

"Or someone pointed a gun at her," Josh said.

Pete wanted to snarl, but his brother was right. He looked around. "The place has been tossed since we searched it."

"Do we know what they were looking for?"

"Shelley said something to Lisa about a notebook, so we're thinking Brad compiled evidence of some kind, and that's what got him killed. The only reason to nab Sunny is if they think Shelley gave it to her."

Josh narrowed his eyes at him. "Okay, but how does Fish fit into it?"

Pete's mind raced, trying to hold his panic at bay. He quickly told Josh what they'd learned about Santiani and the Castiles. "Based on what Fish and I found in the tunnel, let's assume this is about illegal game hunts. Brad did some work for Castile, taxidermy, deliveries, or maybe other odd jobs, and figured out what's going on and kept a record. Maybe tried to blackmail them. And now they're thinking Shelley or Sunny gave the book to Fish."

"But we don't have anything concrete to connect Brad to either Castile. Or to connect Fish to what's happening."

"Someone has been watching her house."

"Martin or Julio Castile? Or one of their minions?"

Pete scrubbed a hand over the back of his neck. "Don't know yet. Could be Jason, too, because we think he's trying to find Shelley."

"Let's check Fish's laptop." Josh called dispatch as they headed outside, Pete hot on his heels. He told the dispatcher they'd found Lisa's truck, but there was no sign of her. Sanchez and Byte would be monitoring the frequency and would immediately join the search.

Pete grabbed Sunny's heart meds so he'd have them handy when they found her, then leaned over Josh's shoulder as they scrolled through Lisa's search history. "She's been digging further into both Castiles." He studied a picture of Julio, dressed in a tuxedo at an art gallery opening. "He fits Lisa's description of whoever took Sunny." His mind raced through possibilities. "We need to search the caves again. That's the only place I can think of where they'd be hidden."

"I thought the explosion destroyed them all." Josh said as they ran back to their vehicles.

"There may be more tunnels we didn't find. And we never found the opening at the other end. We need to find it. Now."

Lisa whispered a quick prayer as she stared down the gun barrel and braced for a bullet. How was she going to keep Gran and Jason alive? With her feet so tightly bound, it was hard to keep her balance. She considered dropping to the floor and trying to kick the gun away. But after a single glance at Gran's white face, she stayed still. She couldn't risk it.

Julio waved the gun at Gran. "Untie her feet. But if you do anything else, I'll shoot you where you stand."

Gran scrambled over, hands shaking as she struggled with the knots.

"Hurry up."

"I'm trying. I-I can't get the knots undone."

He pointed the gun at Jason. "Try harder."

"It's okay," Lisa murmured. "Take it slow. You're braver than you believe, stronger than you seem, and smarter than you think."

Gran's eyes shot to hers, clearly surprised to hear the familiar quote she'd said to Lisa so many times. She took a deep breath and visibly tried to slow her breathing, nodded, and then slowly, deliberately, worked the knots until the ropes finally dropped to the floor.

Before Lisa could yank her out of the way and grab Julio, the other man was beside her, the gun again held to her temple. "Move, Officer. Now."

He forced her out of the room and down another tunnel, dimly lit with overhead lights every few feet. As they passed a branch channel, Lisa glanced inside and saw the rubble piled high. This was the other side of the explosion. Would Pete have figured out where to look yet?

She didn't have time to wonder, because they came to a set of stone steps cut into the rock wall.

"Up."

As he prodded her with the gun, she considered kicking backwards and trying to disable him, but decided to get him farther away from Gran and Jason first. Their safety was priority one. Always.

Once they exited the tunnel, Lisa squinted against the light. The sun was going down, which meant more time had passed than she'd thought. She also realized he was leading her into an old barn at the back of Castile's Animal Sanctuary property. She'd seen the building on a satellite map, but hadn't given it much thought.

The inside reminded her of pictures of Noah's Ark she'd seen in Sunday School. Instead of horses, each of the barn's stalls held a caged exotic animal. There was an elephant, which must be what the neighbor had heard; a couple of antelope; a grizzly bear; and a Florida panther, who stared at her with angry eyes as he paced his cage. She couldn't blame him. She couldn't tell what animals were in the cages farther down the aisle.

Julio motioned to the empty cage next to the panther and waved her inside, then locked the door and grinned.

"This should hold you until the rest of our associates arrive. Then the fun will begin in earnest."

"What fun, exactly?"

The glee in his eyes made her stomach cramp. "The hunt, of course. We've been planning this for weeks, and our guests are very excited about the variety of species they'll be able to track and take down tonight."

He waved a hand to indicate the cages all around. "I hope you can run fast, Officer. That'll make things so much more fun."

Lisa stood stock still as the implications sank in. Her heart pounded, but her voice was calm, matter-of-fact. "I can't lead you to the notebook if I'm dead."

He appeared to consider, then shrugged. "If you're all dead, the notebook won't matter."

She glared until he stepped out of the barn and closed the door. Once she heard the lock click into place, she sank to the floor.

Dear God. They planned to hunt her.

Then they'd kill Gran and Jason.

Her stomach roiled but she ignored it. The longer they held her captive, the more time Pete and her co-workers had to find her.

Meanwhile, she certainly wouldn't make things easy for them. First, she twisted until she got her bound hands in front of her. She almost popped her shoulder out of its socket to make it work, but it was worth it. Then she used her teeth to loosen the binding on her hands. She left the ropes partially tied so she could slip her hands back into them later, to make Julio think she was still tied up.

Now all she needed was a plan.

Pete forced every worry from his mind as he climbed into his unmarked sedan and used his laptop to search for 'underground caves + Marion County'. Fish needed him focused. He flipped through the search results one by one, but nothing showed this section of the forest. Which might simply mean no one had mapped this area. Often, caves were discovered during a building project, and since there wasn't much construction out here, he found nothing.

When Josh pulled up, Pete climbed into his truck, frustration bubbling inside him. "There's no cave map of this area, so we'll have to search from above ground."

"Was the tunnel straight? Or did it wind around?"

"It was a pretty straight shot, if I remember right." He pointed. "Head this way and let's see if we get lucky."

Josh started driving across the pasture, bumping along. "Do you remember how far from the entrance you were at the time of the explosion?"

He considered. "I'm guessing about a hundred yards, at least."

"So they housed animals down there, but they were gone by the time you and Fish showed up."

"Right. There wasn't lots of feed, either, so we assumed this was some kind of holding area before the men moved them."

"And you didn't see how they got them out?"

"No. We were heading that way when the explosion caved everything in."

"Which tells me there were either cameras by the entrance, or someone followed you."

"We heard a car leaving, and a woman scream right before the explosion."

"Sunny?"

"That's what's we're hoping. Means she's still alive. Although the longer she's without her heart meds, the dicier things get." He held up the bottle. "I grabbed them out of Lisa's truck."

Josh drove slowly, both of them scanning the ground on either side, looking for something that might be the other cave entrance. "You said the tunnel wasn't tall enough for a semi to go that far back, so how were they transporting the animals?"

"It was big enough for a truck, or a golf cart, and we did see tire tracks."

"Then they must have taken them off the semi and transported them to the holding area. And then, what? Taken them out the other side? That seems like an awful lot of work. Why not just drive the trucks farther back on the property?"

Pete checked the compass on his phone. "I don't know. Unless you wanted to make sure no one heard any noise."

Josh reached a dirt crossroad. The property on the other side was surrounded by a tall fence, surprising way out here. "How far are we from Castile's animal sanctuary?"

Pete switched over to the map function, expanded the view. "There are another thirty acres between his place and here." He looked out the window, studied the fence. "Unless he owns this property, too, under another name." He dialed Byte.

"Hey Bulldog," Byte said. "Was just about to call you. I've been digging through Wells' flash drive and found two interesting things in some of his encrypted files."

"Hold that thought. I'm sending you my location. Can you check if Castile owns any more of the property around here, either under his name or a corporation?"

"On it. I'll let you know what I find."

*Great."

*Wait. Don't hang up. Wells mentioned Brad Larsen running his mouth at the bar the night before he died, talking about some kind of book that was going to change his life forever. Wells also said Brad went on and on about a date and time. It's tonight, at nine p.m."

Pete's blood ran cold as he checked his watch. It was already after seven. "Did you find anything that gave you a clue as to *where* it's happening tonight?"

"Sorry, no. But based on everything we've found, sounds like there's a hunt scheduled. You find Fish yet?"

"No."

Byte muttered a curse. "I'll keep digging."

"Thanks, man." After he hung up, Pete looked at Josh. "Get Sanchez to push Martin Castile, see if our local vet is behind the hunts or if this is his nephew, Julio."

Josh grabbed his radio and called him. "Sanchez, what's your 20? You in Ocala?"

"I am. Have you found Fish?"

"Not yet. Need you to track down Martin Castile. Try his office, his house, don't stop until you find him. Find out what he knows about a hunt tonight at nine and push for a reaction to a book. Wells said Brad bragged about it the night he was killed."

"Will do. I'll let you know. Let me know as soon as you find Fish."

"Roger that."

Pete clenched his fists as the emotion he'd shoved aside burst through. Fish was out there, somewhere, waiting for him to show up, while he was running around chasing his tail, with no damn idea how to find her.

He cursed and scrubbed a hand over the back of his neck.

Even more damning, idiot that he was, he hadn't told her how he felt about her.

He loved her, he realized, and if he didn't find her, fast, he'd never get the chance to tell her.

Chapter Thirty-One

It took every ounce of Sunny's strength to keep from giving in to despair. Despite the strong front she'd tried to project, her AFib was getting worse the longer she was without her medication. Dizziness, more heart fluttering, weakness, increasing fatigue. While Lisa was there, she felt they had hope. But they'd taken her away. Had they killed her? She swallowed hard and swiped her cheek against her shoulder to wipe away the tears. *Please, God. Keep her safe.*

Across the room, Jason moaned and she sighed in relief. As soon as Julio left with Lisa, she'd slipped over and checked his pulse. He was alive, but no amount of shaking or slapping his cheeks had brought him back to consciousness.

Until now.

He pushed himself to a sitting position, sagging against the rock wall. He winced and his eyes opened and he slowly looked around. When he saw her, he blinked, once, twice. "Sunny? What are you doing here? Do you know where Shelley is?"

"Safe, I hope." She prayed their captor was lying when he said he knew where they were.

Jason tried to stand, but swayed on his feet and slumped back down. "I've been trying to find her. I think Brad got mixed up on the wrong side of Castile. If they find her..."

Sunny pushed the fear aside. "I have to believe she and Remy are safely hidden. And that Lisa's co-workers are trying to find her. Don't you give up the faith now."

Jason took a deep breath as he looked around. "You're right. We need to get out of here. Come on."

"He has cameras," Sunny said, nodding in that direction.

"Doesn't matter. We can't just sit here and do nothing." He tried the door, but it was bolted from the outside.

Julio suddenly opened the door, weapon in hand. "Step out where I can see you, Jason, or she dies right here."

Jason stepped from behind the door, hands raised.

Julio pointed with the gun. "It's time to go. Come on. Move."

Sunny exchanged glances with Jason and climbed the steps.

Where the hell was it? Pete's patience was gone, as were the last flickers of daylight. It was creeping up on nine p.m. and they still hadn't found the entrance to the cave. There had to be another trap door of some kind, but it was cleverly hidden. He swept his flashlight around as he walked, covering the same ground one more time. It had to be here.

"Keep your eyes out for trail cameras," he told Josh.

"You think they'd put them way out here?"

"Unlikely, but let's not take chances."

"Agreed."

They retraced their steps several times, but there was nothing in the barn or outbuildings, no outcropping of rock, no hidden mechanism. Nothing.

Or was there?

He walked over to the rusted hulk of a 1950s Oldsmobile and studied it more closely. Weeds and grasses surrounded it. But the grass was trampled on one side. He stepped closer, then looked at Josh. "Come give me a hand."

They brushed the sand away and between them, the outline of a large flat piece of wood became visible. They swept more sand away and uncovered a metal ring. Pete's heartrate kicked into overdrive when they pulled it up and exposed the stone stairway.

Now they were getting somewhere.

Both men kept their weapons in one hand and their flashlights in the other as they slowly descended into the darkness. But hope dimmed the farther they walked.

"You aren't bringing a truckload of exotics out this tunnel, that's for sure," Josh said, eyeing the narrow passage and dim lighting.

Pete reined in his frustration. His brother didn't deserve his anger. "Let's see if it connects to the larger tunnel up ahead."

It was full dark by the time Lisa heard several vehicles pull up outside the barn. She rolled her neck and shoulder, then stretched her legs, trying to loosen her muscles to get ready to run. Her shoulder throbbed, but she'd maneuvered her hands behind her again so they wouldn't realize her bindings were loose.

She scooted closer to the front of the cage. She could distinguish at least three excited male voices, joking and teasing about their hunting prowess. They made her sick. It was illegal to import these majestic creatures, and wrong on every level to kill them for sport.

When the large barn door swung open, she pretended to be asleep, determined to pick up any tidbit of information she could use.

"Where is she?" a male voice demanded. She couldn't be sure, but it sounded like Martin Castile.

"Right this way," Julio said. Boot heels thumped on the wooden planks.

They stopped in front of her cage and a flashlight shone in her face. She held still. A gun rapped against the bars. "Wake up, fish cop. Time to go hunting."

She slowly blinked her eyes open, squinting against the light. She couldn't see faces, but there were two men staring at her, and several more behind them, based on the number of legs.

The cage door opened and a hand reached in and hauled her to her feet. She made sure she gripped the ropes around her wrists so they didn't fall off and give her away.

She'd expected to see Ocala's beloved veterinarian, Martin Castile. Instead, she caught a familiar whiff of male cologne and found herself looking at Gene Phillips, the long-time Ocala resident and local horse farmer whose wife was Gran's friend. She pushed her shock aside and studied his build. He's the one who drugged her. And searched her house. He could definitely have been the one who kidnapped Gran. The man certainly knew horses.

"Officer Bass. We're so glad you've decided to join our little hunt," Phillips said. He waved a hand. "After you."

Lisa straightened her spine, eyes hard. "My backup will be here any minute. Let all three of us go, right now, and things will go much easier on you in court."

"We'll talk about all that after the hunt," Phillips said, chuckling.

His condescending attitude poked her like a sharp stick. "The courts take a dim view of people who kill law enforcement officers."

"I'm not planning to kill you, Officer. Though it is a shame you went out hunting by yourself and got mistaken for a deer." He *tsked* and shook his head. "You should have worn a hunting vest."

"Nobody will believe that. It's not deer season." The moment the words were out, she wanted to call them back.

Phillips stopped, considered her. "I may have underestimated you." Then he shrugged. "But no matter."

Julio's grip tightened as he marched her outside. He stopped in front of the barn, then turned to stand beside Phillips. All eyes focused on Lisa.

The other five men were dressed like hunters in camouflage gear, orange hunting vests, weapons cradled in their arms. The clothes were stiff and obviously fresh off the shelves of the nearest sporting goods store. Several of the men held their weapons in an awkward grip. These were clearly not experienced outdoorsmen.

Phillips waved to indicate the now-empty cages behind them. "Gentlemen. Thank you all for coming this weekend. I'm delighted to offer this little show of appreciation for our partnership and the good work we're doing together. I promised you a once-in-a-lifetime experience and I guarantee you won't be disappointed." He puffed out his chest. "We have released an elephant, several antelopes, a couple of hogs, a grizzly bear, and of course, that rare cat, the Florida panther, for your hunting pleasure tonight. To make things even sweeter, we also have a two-legged species to offer. Officer Bass is with the Florida Fish and Wildlife Commission, and she has been trying diligently to uncover what we're doing here."

Lisa's mouth went dry at his rational tone. The man had clearly lost his grip on reality. She scanned the faces of the other hunters to gauge what she was up against. Two looked uncomfortable, glancing at each other uncertainly. That could work to her advantage. One studied the ground, which she also took as a positive sign. But the last two had an eager gleam in their eyes that made her stomach clench.

She raised her chin, put every bit of authority she could into her tone. "Let my grandmother and Jason go. They have nothing to do with this."

He smiled. "We already did. They're in the hunting cabin about half a mile east of here." He turned to the other hunters. "They are also available for hunting. The cabin is marked on your maps of the area."

Without thought, Lisa lunged toward Phillips. Two steps before she reached him, he pointed a handgun at her face. She skidded to a stop, remembering at the last second that her hands were supposed to be tied. She gripped the loosened ropes behind her and dropped her head as though defeated, refusing to make eye contact.

"Good choice, Officer, or the fun would be over before it started."

She remained silent, jaw clenched against her fury. Her focus had to be on finding Gran – and Jason - before the hunters did. She was positive she and Pete had seen the cabin on the satellite image. She just had to get her hands on one of the maps.

Phillips checked the watch strapped to his wrist. "You'll have a five-minute head start, Officer Bass. Starting now."

Lisa didn't hesitate. She took off running, sliding in the sand as she slipped behind the barn. She stuffed the rope that had been around her wrists into her pocket and raced into the forest, desperate to stay a step ahead of these deranged killers.

Pete and Josh hadn't walked very far before they found a side corridor. Once they stepped through, the tunnel widened significantly.

Josh studied the high ceiling. "This'll allow a truck, for sure."

They picked up the pace and Pete found a small room. "Here." He stepped inside and stopped in the center. Excitement built as he shone his light around. "This is it. The room Fish and I found."

Josh circled the perimeter, reached down and grabbed a barrette. He sent Pete a sharp look as he held it out. "Sunny's?"

Pete swallowed hard as he nodded. He tucked it into his pocket as he continued to scan the room. "That's my guess. Damn. Where is she?"

The words were barely out of his mouth when they heard gunfire from above.

They exchanged glances. Both said, "Fish," and took off running.

Chapter Thirty-Two

Lisa hid behind a fallen tree not far behind the barn, heart pounding, trying to think. She needed a weapon. And a map to the cabin. As her eyes adjusted to the darkness, she watched the hunters step out of the barn, consult their maps, and go their separate ways. She'd counted five, plus Julio and Phillips.

For the moment, she ignored the four who took off running and zeroed in on the last one, who seemed to be more deliberate, stopping regularly to turn on his phone's flashlight and check the map.

She followed him, ducking behind trees, until she was sure the others were far enough away not to interfere.

Her grip tightened on the rock in her hand.

Come on, you lousy—

As he stepped even with her, Lisa tossed the rock behind him. It hit a squat sabal palm and the clatter of palm fronds brought the man around, gun to his shoulder as he pulled the trigger, decimating the poor bush in a hail of bullets.

Lisa stepped behind him, grabbed the weapon and tossed it aside before he realized what was happening. She yanked his hands behind him, holding tight as he struggled to break free.

"Let go," he gritted, trying to shake her off.

"Not happening," she muttered. He was bigger than she was, but she had fitness and fury on her side. She quickly wrapped the length of rope around his hands like he was a heifer at a rodeo.

"Hey!" he shouted when she pulled the rope tighter. "What the hell?"

"Quiet."

He twisted and kicked and yelled some more.

"You're not listening." She didn't want him drawing attention to her location, so she swept his legs out from under him and shoved his face into the sand.

He coughed and spit, then gave a mighty heave and bucked her off. Hands still bound behind him, he threw himself at her. She lunged left and pulled her feet up, then kicked out at his abdomen and launched him several feet away.

Before he could get to his feet, she jumped onto his chest, knocking the wind out of him. She didn't have much time, since he was still making too much noise. Breath heaving, she rolled him over while she searched his pockets. She plucked out a stiff new bandana and gagged him.

He kept fighting as she grabbed the knife from the sheath at his waist, cut his pant leg into strips and secured his ankles.

Furious, he yelled even louder behind the gag and kept trying to buck her off him. Out of breath and out of patience, she finally used a pressure point in his neck to render him unconscious.

"I warned you," she said as she climbed to her feet and braced her hands on her knees. She checked the phone she'd taken from his belt and bit back her frustration. No signal. She sent Pete a quick text anyway, hoping he'd get it the moment she reached even a hint of cell service. Texts needed very little signal so they often went through when calls wouldn't.

She searched the man's pockets, pulled out his map and took a moment to get her bearings. She grabbed his rifle, tucked the phone into her pocket and started running toward the cabin, ever alert for the other hunters. She really didn't want to fight every one of them. But she would if she had to.

She ran deeper into the forest. "One down. Six to go," she muttered.

Pete, with Josh on his heels, burst out the trap door and stopped, trying to identify where the gunfire had originated. While Josh muttered about lack of cell service and sent a text requesting backup, Pete waited, straining to listen, though every instinct urged him to start running and not stop until he found her.

They spotted the outline of a barn in the distance and raced in that direction. They eased up to it and peered in through one of the windows, staying in the shadows. They found a double row of empty cages, all the doors hanging open. But from somewhere in the back of the building, they heard a whinny and then hooves beating against wood. "That could be the black stallion Fish saw," Pete whispered.

Josh nodded and indicated he'd check the other side. Pete leaned against the building and studied the forest around them. Thirty seconds later he saw a muzzle flash just before he heard gunshots. He took off in that direction. Son of a—were they hunting *her?*

Josh was behind him in seconds. "We stay together, Bulldog. I don't want to risk shooting you by mistake,"

Pete nodded, but didn't slow.

Somewhere in the distance, an elephant trumpeted in alarm. "Damn, what other exotics are they hunting tonight?"

The question was answered when they heard the distinctive roar of a panther, followed by a decidedly human scream.

"Serves the bastard right," Josh muttered.

When they reached the area where they'd seen the flash, they slowed their steps. Pete almost stumbled over the man lying on his stomach, trussed up and snoring softly. He crouched down for a better look, then shook his head in admiration. "Guess Fish already found this one."

He and Josh exchanged a grin, then Josh snapped the guy's picture. "Still barely any signal." But it was enough to send it to Byte, while Pete texted their backup and gave the man's location.

They kept going, moving fast.

As she raced toward the cabin, Lisa found the next hunter thrashing through the forest like a kindergartener, not even trying to quiet his footsteps. She employed the same rock trick as before and took him down, then undid the braided para-cord bracelet he'd been wearing and used its length to tied him up. Nice of him to provide his own rope.

She aimed his rifle at him and his eyes widened. Words gushed out. "Don't shoot. Please. I wouldn't have shot you, I promise. Hunting animals is one thing, but I didn't sign up for hunting people. Please, you have to believe me."

His quick surrender annoyed her. If he had the gall to be out here, he should at least give her a chance to get in a few punches. Which was ridiculous, but there you go.

She gagged him, removed the ammunition from his pockets and weapon, then tossed the unloaded rifle aside. She added his cell phone – still no signal – to the first and took off running toward the cabin once again.

If she let her fury about every bit of this whole deranged scenario into her mind, she wouldn't be able to think clearly. She pushed everything aside but the task at hand. It was the same mental trick she'd employed on the SWAT team. Her job was to neutralize the targets. Emotions of any kind would be dealt with later.

She kept to that, until she saw another hunter take aim at the elephant.

"Oh, hell no," she muttered, raising her rifle. Her training said to aim for center mass, but that would be too easy. She didn't want any of them dead. She wanted them to answer for what they were doing and spend years of their life in a jail cell regretting this exact moment.

She aimed for his shoulder and gave a satisfied nod when he screamed and fell, clutching the wound. She slipped up behind him and aimed the rifle in his face when he kept howling like a toddler. "Quiet, you imbecile, or I'll shoot you again."

He grabbed his shoulder and grimaced, looking surprised at the blood on his hand. Then his skinny face took on a sneer, visible even in the meager moonlight. "Too bad your aim isn't very good."

She refused the take the bait and tucked the barrel under his chin. "I hit what I'm aiming at. I want you alive and thinking, so you'll get to repent of your idiocy for a very long time."

He snorted. "Julio is gunning for you. It's personal for him. You won't leave here alive."

The smile she sent him should have scared him. "Hands at your sides."

He grabbed for the rifle barrel, so she pushed the end into his skin, near the wound. He cursed and panted, gripping his shoulder.

She stepped out of reach but kept the rifle aimed at him. Then she waited while he cursed some more, glared, cried, and finally complied. She patted him down, took his knife and hacked off the sleeve of his shirt to use as a gag.

"On your feet, back against the tree. Fight me and I'll put another hole in you."

He cursed, but nodded and climbed to his feet. She strapped him to the tree with a length of rope he had clipped to his belt.

She stepped back. "I recommend you use your hands to keep pressure on that wound. It's still bleeding quite a bit. Or you could work on getting out of the ropes. Your choice." She shrugged and melted back into the forest while he tried to shout through the gag.

When the dilapidated hunting cabin finally came into view, Lisa deliberately slowed her pace, even though every instinct urged her to rush right up to the door. She didn't want to walk into a trap. She paused behind a tree and listened. Nothing stirred and her gut said it was empty. But she had to make sure.

Rifle at her shoulder, she slipped up beside the building and peered through a broken window. She couldn't see in the dark, so she made her way to the door, wincing at the squeal of rusty hinges. Inside, she turned on the cell phone flashlight and cupped her hand around the beam as she scanned the interior. No footsteps had disturbed the dust on the wooden floor.

She doused the flashlight and muttered a stream of curses. Phillips had lied. Gran had never been here.

There was only one other place Gran and Jason could be.

She took off running.

Pete and Josh were following the sound of the elephant when they heard thundering hoof beats behind them. The huge beast was almost on top of them before Pete realized it was the horse, huge and black.

The animal slowed when Pete stepped in its path.

"What are you doing, Bulldog?" Josh muttered.

The animal was clearly agitated, blowing and dragging its reins in the sand behind it.

"Easy there, fella," Pete murmured, approaching the horse slowly. "This must be the stallion. Looks like he broke out of his stall."

The horse eyed him warily, but Pete kept talking in soothing tones.

"We need to find Fish, Bulldog. We don't have time for you to go all Doctor Doolittle right now."

"I don't want him caught in the crossfire. Or to be a handy means of escape for anyone." Pete had one hand on the horse's bridle when they heard a female scream. Without a second's hesitation, he gripped the mane and launched himself onto the horse's back. The animal whinnied as it reared on its hind legs. Pete held tight, then turned the horse in the direction of the scream, Josh's flurry of words nothing but background noise.

Hang on, Fish. I'm coming.

As she raced toward the barn, Lisa practically tripped over Idiot number four, which was a good thing, because she was exhausted. She was soaked with sweat, craving water and worn out from running through deep sand and over uneven ground. This guy had doused himself with so much insect repellent, all she had to do was follow the noxious fumes. He was aiming his rifle into the trees when she crept up behind him and used a pressure point to knock him unconscious.

She looked up and locked eyes with the panther crouched in the tree. Fury pushed her exhaustion aside when she spotted the bloody gash on his shoulder. They would not get away with this.

For one tense moment, she and the big cat studied each other. Then he twitched his tail and disappeared into the darkness, as though he knew she meant him no harm.

She searched the guy, but he didn't have anything on him she could use to tie him up, so she pulled out his belt and used it to tie his hands. She dragged him against a tree trunk, wrestled him upright, then looped the belt over a notch partway up the trunk. It forced him up on his toes and he'd have a devil of a time getting himself down.

Breath heaving, she slipped back into the forest and kept running, alert for any movement. There was only one hunter left, besides Phillips and Julio. She hoped the elder Castile wasn't involved too, popping up like some crazed slasher in a haunted house.

Lisa had the barn in sight when something heavy dropped out of a tree and took her down. She let out a yell as she landed, then instantly rolled to her feet, but she wasn't quite quick enough. The last hunter wrapped an arm around her neck and put his gun to her temple.

She froze, then dropped toward the ground, forcing him down with her. She tried to twist free, but he stayed with her, tightening his grip as he dragged her back to her feet. He grabbed her bad arm and she cried out in agony.

Determined to gain the upper hand, she curled her foot around his leg, but he blocked the move. *Dang.* This guy knew self-defense and thwarted her every move.

His arm tightened around her throat and she started seeing spots before her eyes. She twisted and bucked, but couldn't break free. Panic rose in her throat as she struggled for breath.

"I should shoot you right here and now, but that's no fun," he muttered.

Suddenly, he removed his arm from around her throat, grabbed her rifle and gave her a shove. "Run, cop. Run!"

Lisa didn't hesitate. She took off, zig-zagging around trees, bullets whizzing by her head. She headed away from the barn. No way would she lead him right to Gran.

The ground exploded by her feet as she ducked behind another tree.

She leaped over a fallen log, slid in some pine needles and skidded on her belly. She scrambled to her feet and looked over her shoulder.

He was gaining on her.

She spun and kept going, wincing as another bullet whistled past her head.

Several yards farther, she ducked behind a tree, ready to tackle him as he went past. As she peeked out from behind the trunk, she heard a gunshot and a muffled yell. She watched the hunter crumple to the ground.

Silently thanking whoever had taken the shot, she circled back, grabbed the hunter's gun and kept running. She picked up speed when another shot exploded through the night, followed by the panther's scream.

She cringed, but couldn't stop to help. She had to neutralize Julio and Phillips before she could rescue Gran and Jason.

Both men were dressed all in black, but these two were also smarter, wilier. They wouldn't make it easy. She stopped, sniffed the air, and listened.

She turned. There. A slight rustling in the underbrush.

Chapter Thirty-Three

Quiet as a shadow, she circled around behind Phillips and stuck the barrel of the gun into the back of his neck. She didn't know if any of them were wearing body armor, but she wasn't taking any chances. "Hands in the air."

Phillips froze and his hands slowly came up beside his head, exposing his rope tattoo.

"Where's my grandmother?" she demanded.

He spun and made a grab for her weapon, pulling her to the ground. She rolled away and kicked the weapon from his hand, then jumped to her feet. She lunged for the rifle and scooped it up just as he reached for it. She slammed it against his hand, then pointed it squarely at his face as he screamed in pain.

"Move. And answer the question."

They stared at each other.

She raised the gun until it was pointing at his head. "I won't ask again."

He started walking, but didn't answer. She shoved him with the rifle stock.

"Last I saw her she was in the cabin."

"You're lying. I checked."

He shrugged. "Believe what you want, fish cop."

She hesitated. Had she missed something? She took a gamble and prayed she was right. "I think she's been hidden in the barn all along. You're going to take me to her. If you make a sound or try to run, I'll shoot you in the head. Understood?"

He snorted.

As she prodded him along, Lisa scanned the forest. His cooperation came too easily, so there must be some other plan in play she didn't know about. They'd walked for several minutes before she asked, "Where is Julio?"

"I assume he is also part of the hunt. Magnificent creatures available tonight, are they not? I especially like the elephant. And the two-legged varieties."

Lisa's grip tightened on the gun, but she didn't respond.

"Is Martin Castile here, too?" she demanded.

Again, he didn't answer. Which told her nothing. When they reached the barn, she scanned the dimly-lit interior, but didn't see either Castile lurking anywhere. She stopped with her back against the wall, Phillips in front of her.

She raised her voice. "Get out here, Julio, and bring my grandmother and Jason with you if you want your friend to live. I'm willing to trade."

She waited, but there was no sound, no response. "Clock's ticking." She glanced at the luminous dial on her watch. "Five minutes, then I shoot him where he stands and tell the authorities I watched you shoot him."

Phillips stiffened at that, the only reaction he'd shown so far.

Lisa watched the barn, and the area just outside, alert for anyone approaching from either direction, but all remained quiet, except the wildlife. She heard running and assumed the antelopes were together, then the roar of the panther, which scared the elephant into trumpeting again.

But here, nothing stirred. Was Pete or her FWC squad here yet?

She shifted her grip on the rifle. "Looks like you're worth less to your associate than you thought."

He was getting nervous. She could feel it and smell it, even above his nauseating cologne.

Finally, she heard a noise from the other end of the building. Julio approached, shoving Gran ahead of him with his gun, while gripping Jason's bound wrists in his other hand. Blood dripped from Julio's nose while Gran's fury crackled like lightening. But it was her grandmother's pale skin and shaking hands that terrified Lisa. Was her heart giving out?

"Guess maybe he likes you after all, Phillips." She raised her voice. "Nice of you to join us, Julio. So let's make this easy. You send Gran and Jason to me and I give you Phillips. Provided," she added when he started to respond, "I have your word you'll leave Shelley and Remy in peace. They have nothing to do with any of this."

"Give me the notebook," Julio said.

She glanced at Gran, willing her not to argue. "As it happens, I don't have it."

"You're lying. I want that book, Officer Bass. Now. It does not belong to you."

"Or what? Your friend Phillips makes a handy shield."

"Make the trade, Julio." Phillips couldn't keep the command out of his voice. "I'll take care of this."

Julio suddenly focused on Phillips. "You'll take care of it? Like you've taken care of things till now? We wouldn't be in this mess if you'd taken care of things."

Lisa saw Julio's intent a split second too late. She tried to drag Phillips down, but she wasn't fast enough. Gran bit back a scream as the gun fired and Phillips fell forward, unmoving.

Rifle to her shoulder, Lisa stepped closer to Julio. "That wasn't very nice. Now let her go."

Julio took aim and Lisa ducked. The shot went wide. She stood up, steadily advancing.

He slung the rifle over his shoulder and pulled out a knife, then grabbed Gran and held it under her chin. "Don't come any closer, or I'll slit her throat."

In that moment, Lisa froze as déjà vu struck with a vengeance. Past and present melded and fused and Lisa froze, unable to draw breath. Mama's still face and the gash at her throat mixed with Gran's. She shook her head to clear it, then bit down on her lip. She had to stay grounded in the present. This was Gran and she was alive.

"Let her go and you can have me, instead. I'll go with you."

He laughed. "So generous." He looked her up and down in a way that made her skin crawl. "I'm going to have you regardless. Your self-defense classes and ridiculous talk of female power cost me the love of my life. You will pay for that. Later. Right now, I want the book."

A chill slid down Lisa's spine. "I said I didn't have it--with me--but I can get it for you. If...you let Sunny go."

Julio's eyes went wild and the suave businessman disappeared under a wave of fury. "I am done playing games, Officer Bass. You have until the count of five to tell me where it is, or I slit her throat. One."

Gran made a small sound of protest, but Lisa kept her eyes on Castile.

"Two."

The past tried to drop over her like a shroud, but Lisa shoved it away. She hadn't been there for Mama, but she was here now.

"Three."

She took aim, steadied her heartbeat. She could do this.

"Four."

She blocked out everything but her target, held her breath as she'd been taught. She flicked her eyes to Gran, then focused solely on Julio.

From outside, Lisa heard pounding hooves and a horse's whinny.

Gran tilted her head as far away from Castile as she could.

It was enough. In one smooth motion, Lisa started squeezing the trigger and braced for the rifle's recoil.

Everything seemed to happen in slow motion after that. The sound of a weapon firing. Julio's surprise at the neat hole in his forehead. Gran's silent scream as the knife cut her throat as Castile fell. Then the two of them slowly collapsing in each other's arms as if in some macabre dance.

Lisa was in motion before they hit the floor. "Gran!" she screamed, shoving Julio's body aside so she could get to her. Lisa tore off her uniform shirt, tried to stop the bleeding. She felt for a pulse, but couldn't feel or hear it for the roaring in her ears and her shaking hands.

"Gran, oh God, Gran, don't you die on me. Don't you dare die on me." Her heart thundered and tears swam in her eyes as she applied pressure, muttering prayers and pleas.

Pete suddenly appeared beside her, eased her hands away and replaced them with his. "I've got her. You did good, Fish. Help is on the way." He glanced at her out of the corner of his eye. "You okay?"

Relief that he was here flooded her. She nodded, eyes never leaving Gran's still face. "She can't die."

"We're going to make sure she doesn't." He lifted the makeshift bandage. "The cut doesn't appear to be too deep. And she's tough. Like someone else I know."

"She needs her heart meds."

"I've got them. Paramedics are on the way. They'll take good care of her."

Lisa took a deep, shuddering breath, swiped at the tears. She checked Julio's pulse, just in case, though she knew she wouldn't find one.

Pete repositioned the shirt, checked Gran's pulse. "The rest of your squad is enroute and trappers are headed out to gather up the exotics before they get too far."

"There's a Florida panther among them."

He nodded grimly. "We heard him. Nice job, trussing up those idiots the way you did." He sent her a quick grin, then his eyes widened as he glanced at her. She realized she was shivering in her lacy black bra.

"Keep the pressure on," he said and pulled off his shirt, then held it while she slipped her arms into it, one at a time, without letting up on the pressure on Gran's wound. The smell of him embedded in the fabric surrounded her, helped steady her pulse.

The sirens were getting louder.

He nudged her hands aside again and Lisa wiped her blood-stained palms on her pants before she gently took Gran's hand. "You stay strong, Gran, and you fight. I need you, now more than ever."

Gran gave a slight squeeze and whispered, "I need you, too. And I'm sorry." Each word came out like a pant, and Lisa's heart squeezed.

"We'll talk later. Just rest." Lisa clung to her hand, trying to give her courage, until the EMTs arrived and took over.

Lisa watched them do a quick evaluation and then her own heart started hammering when they pulled out the defibrillator and shocked Gran's heart.

"What's wrong? What are you doing?"

"We need to get her heart back in rhythm."

Once. Twice. Three times.

Come on, Gran.

"There we go," one of the paramedics said, sitting back on his heels. "Back in rhythm."

Lisa's own heart stuttered with relief and tears ran down her cheeks.

As they carefully loaded Gran on the gurney, Pete tugged Lisa to her feet and wrapped her in his arms. He pulled back, her cheeks cupped in his hands. "When I heard you offer yourself in trade, I didn't know whether to shoot Castile or you. What possessed you to make such an offer, woman?"

Her eyes met his, desperate for him to understand. "I meant it. I had to make it right." She glanced at her grandmother. "For Gran's sake." She looked back at him. "Are Shelley and Remy still ok?"

"They are both fine."

Lisa noticed the huge black stallion standing nearby, stomping his feet. She looked from the horse to Pete and everything suddenly fell into place.

"You made the shot."

He nodded. "I did."

"I could have done it."

"Of course you could have. But I didn't want you to have to live with it."

"But now you do," she whispered.

He nodded. "I had to protect you." His eyes went tender, voice soft. "Your debt is paid, Fish. None of it was your fault, then or now. Don't pick up that sack of mental crap again. Leave it all here, tonight. Start fresh with your grandmother."

She couldn't help smiling through the tears welling in her eyes. "You do have a way with words, Bulldog."

He brushed his knuckles down her cheek and the way his hand trembled almost brought her to her knees. "I have a few more you might like."

"Fish! He's still alive!" Sanchez called.

Lisa glanced over to where another team of paramedics were bent over Phillips body. "I need to go."

Pete kissed her forehead. "We'll finish this discussion later."

Worry hummed under Lisa's skin as they processed the scene. When they finally let her and Pete go, he drove her directly to the hospital. She rushed into Gran's room, shuddering to a stop at the sight of the other woman's still face, the swath of white bandages circling her throat. Only the doctor's assurance that the wound wasn't life threatening kept Lisa sane. There was an oxygen cannula in her nostrils and the heart monitor beeped out a steady rhythm.

Gran slowly opened her eyes and reached a hand out to her. "Thank you, Lisa. I'm so sorry," she whispered, over and over.

Lisa gripped her hand and sagged with relief. Had Pete not been standing beside her, arm around her waist, she would have fallen. "I'm so glad you're going to be okay."

When Gran tried to say more, Lisa pressed a kiss to her forehead. "You rest now. We'll be back in the morning."

Gran's eyes slid closed and she squeezed Lisa's hand before she drifted off to sleep.

She was going to be okay, Gran was going to be okay.

The refrain rang in Lisa's head the whole way home.

Once they reached her cottage, she headed for the shower, desperate to wash the horror of this night away. When she walked into the kitchen a few minutes later, the smell of bacon wafted in the air and Pete stood at the stove, scrambling eggs.

"I'd have grilled a steak, which is my only culinary specialty, but you don't have any steak. Or a grill. So I improvised. You keep forgetting to eat."

She raised a brow. "We were a little busy tonight."

He nodded. "True. But since I was starving, I didn't think you'd mind."

Cat finished eating and wrapped herself around Pete's ankles, purring like a lawnmower.

"I just fed her, the ungrateful wench." Her stomach rumbled. "Thank you." She smiled and reached past him for a glass, kissing his neck as she stepped behind him.

He looked over his shoulder and that one, smoldering glance pushed the events of the night aside and ignited the ever-present attraction between them. She shivered all the way to her toes.

"Eat. I'm going to grab a shower. And after that, you and I have a discussion to finish.

But by the time he came looking for her, Lisa was curled up under the covers, fast asleep.

Chapter Thirty-Four

Lisa was already dressed and sipping coffee when Pete entered the kitchen the next morning. "The hospital said Gran's awake."

"That's great news." He eyed the car keys on the counter. "I guess you want to head over right away."

"Soon." She smiled and pulled him close for a dreamy kiss that went on and on.

He slowly pulled back, then kissed her again. "Give me ten minutes to clean up."

Josh called while they were on the road. "In surprising news, Phillips just might pull through. He claims Julio killed Brad, but of course, he can't prove that. Admitted the whole thing was about money."

"Was Martin Castile involved at all?" she asked.

"Not according to Phillips. Castile seems broken up over the death of his nephew. When I told him Julio set you up as prey for his hunters, he cried, genuinely sorry."

Lisa tried to untangle the emotions that brought, but there were too many to sort out right then.

"Also," Josh continued, "Jason admitted to following you and throwing the rock through your window to distract you from the case. He says Julio threatened to hurt Shelley if he didn't do what he said. He started following you, hoping you'd lead him to Shelley, so he could keep her safe. Or lead him to the book, so he could get Julio off his back."

"So why was he locked up with Gran?"

"Jason claims Julio decided he'd been lying to him about the book, so he put him in the tunnel and said he'd deal with him after the hunt."

"I'll be interested in seeing what's inside this infamous book."

They hadn't asked Gran about it last night, figuring a couple hours wouldn't change anything. The other woman had needed rest more.

"Does the black stallion belong to Phillips?" Pete asked.

"Yes. He was going to use him to make a quick getaway if things went sideways. He owns the property with the cabin Gran stayed in, as well."

"Thanks for the update, Josh. Now please go get some sleep," Lisa said.

"That's the plan. Just wanted to fill you in before I did."

"We appreciate it," Pete said, as they hung up.

Gran was sitting up in bed, scowling at her tray of food, which made the last of Lisa's worry ease. She was going to be fine.

"Where's the stuffed elephant?" Gran demanded.

"Good morning to you, too," Lisa said, leaning over to kiss her cheek.

"Do you have it?" Gran demanded.

Lisa paused, surprised at her insistence. "You mean the one from my childhood?"

"Of course that one. Where is it?"

"In my truck."

"Well, go get it." Gran's voice brooked no argument. She made a shooing motion with her hands.

"Yes, ma'am," Lisa said and hurried to her truck.

When she came back into the room, Gran asked, "Did you figure it out?"

Lisa froze. "Wait. You mean...?" Lisa ran her fingers over the threadbare gray fur, once, then again. She froze when she felt something hard inside. She ran both hands over the lump, grinning. "Oh, that's brilliant, Gran."

Gran still looked bone tired, but her eyes twinkled. "I had to do something, quick. They were coming for me." She told Lisa about the knock on the door and her mad dash through the woods. Then the ensuing head injury.

Lisa studied her, chose her words with care. "When did Shelley give you the book? Do you remember the time? Did she come to your place?"

Gran suddenly stilled. "Why does it matter?"

"Just creating a timeline. Trying to tie up some loose ends."

"It was just after 1:30 a.m. I gave her some money and told her to get the heck out of town."

She and Pete exchanged glances.

"Works for me," he said.

Lisa nodded her agreement, then turned the elephant upside down and opened the Velcro seam. She pulled out a small, leather-bound journal. She flipped through the pages, her eyes widening in surprise and disbelief. "Oh, man." She turned more pages.

Pete leaned over her shoulder. "What?"

She looked at Gran. "Did you figure out the initials? The code?"

"I did." As Lisa read off initials, Gran supplied names, a veritable who's who of Marion County society.

Half an hour later, Lisa looked at Pete. "We need to think through how to handle this. Every animal, exactly how much they paid for their hunt is listed here."

"What's there to think about, Acting Lieutenant? We turn it in."

"Think about it, Pete. *Who* do we turn it in to?"

Pete scanned the list again, muttered a curse.

The door suddenly opened and Pete's boss, Captain Hall, walked into the room. Lisa and Pete exchanged a quick glance, and Lisa stepped closer to Gran, sliding the notebook under the blankets.

"Good morning, Detective Tanner, Officer Bass." He turned to Sunny. "Glad to see you feeling better, Miz Bass, though I do need to ask you a few questions, namely about this so-called book of Brad's you mentioned to my officers earlier. We need to have a look at it for our investigation. Do you have it with you?"

Gran's eyes widened in alarm and she looked past him to Pete and Lisa. "I, ah, no. I don't."

"Then where is it?" Captain Hall asked.

Lisa stepped between Gran and Hall, hand on her utility belt. "Someplace safe." She met Captain Hall's gaze squarely.

"Naturally. I would expect nothing less." He held out a hand. "I'll take charge of it from here."

"I don't think so," Lisa said.

Surprised flickered across his face, then his eyes narrowed. "What are you doing, Officer Bass? This is a Marion County Sheriff's Office investigation. You do not want to interfere."

When his hand moved toward his shoulder holster, Pete stepped up behind him, grabbed the weapon and clamped a hand around Hall's wrist. "You don't want to do that, Captain, trust me. We've read the book. You're quite a prominent part of the story. Do you own a white van, I wonder?"

While the man sputtered and made threats, Lisa said, "I'll call my boss, and we'll start sorting this out." Ed's name wasn't in the book, and he'd know what to do.

Pete hand-cuffed Hall and hustled him out of the room. Lisa spent a few minutes with Gran until Ed arrived. She showed him the book and then helped assign officers to round up the people named in it. It included law enforcement, county officials, prominent business-men. The list boggled her mind.

But throughout the eternally long day, one thought kept running through Lisa's mind, making her smile, every time.

Gran was safe. Finally.

Epilogue

One week later

Lisa stopped at the edge of the crowd gathered under the pavilion at Tanner's Outpost, taking a minute to survey the crowd before she dove in. The elder Tanners' RV sat off to one side, a huge "Bon Voyage" banner draped over it. The older couple were finally heading out on their first trip tomorrow. They were only going across the state line into Georgia, but it was a start.

Off to one side, Pete, Josh and Mr. Tanner manned the grill and the smell of chicken and burgers wafted over the crowd. Barely using her cane, Mrs. Tanner approached them and allowed her husband and both her sons to kiss her cheek. The tenderness in Pete's eyes made Lisa's throat close up.

On the opposite side of the pavilion, Liz and Patty had set up two long buffet tables and were bustling around. One table held the food while the other groaned under the weight of the desserts. Which was just how it should be, in Lisa's opinion.

"Lisa!" Charlee called. Before she could brace herself, she was enveloped in a hug tight enough to stop her breath. "Congratulations on the promotion, Lieutenant! Hunter is thrilled for you!"

"Congrats to him on making Captain, too." She looked Charlee up and down, from her dark tan to her sparkling eyes. "Looks like Hawaiian honeymooning agreed with you."

Charlee leaned close. "We had the best time." She glanced at Hunter, who must have felt his wife's eyes on him, for he turned, winked, and both Charlee and Lisa sighed. "I do adore that man," Charlee said. Then she wiggled her eyebrows. "He's also hot enough to melt steel, so there's that."

Lisa laughed and accepted a glass of punch from Delilah, who stepped over and the three clinked their glasses together. "Glad you're okay, Fish. Heard you showed the boys how it's done, too." The monkey researcher had officially finished her master's program in Tallahassee--and had taken a job locally. No more driving back and forth. "Did you hear Redd sweet-talked me into coming to work for him?"

"I didn't know Redd knew how to sweet talk." Lisa said and all three women laughed. "Did you make him promise not to point that rifle at you?"

Delilah grinned. "Yep, it's part of my contract." She waved to Josh, who smiled from behind the grill, his grin wide enough to encompass the whole county. "By the way, Josh is thrilled to be doing more search and rescue work, so don't you feel bad for one second about that promotion. He loves what he's doing and said he honestly doesn't want a promotion right now. Too much paperwork. He's happy for you."

Lisa glanced at Josh and he sent her a-thumbs up and a wink, quieting the last of her doubts.

"Officer Bass," a young voice called and Lisa found her legs wrapped tight in Remy's arms. She crouched down to give her a proper hug.

"Well hey, Miss Remy. How are you doing?"

"Good." She tucked her stuffed elephant under her arm, buried her face in it. "Sometimes I miss my daddy."

Lisa hugged her tighter, unsure what to say. "I know you do, sweet girl. It's hard."

She looked up and saw Shelley approaching, with Jason right behind her, his hand at her back. He was out on bond. Lisa had talked with the D.A., fighting for reduced charges and possibly just community service for his part in things, since they were done under duress.

Shelley hugged her, hard. "Thank you will never be enough. Pete told me how you wouldn't give up on finding us, and how you didn't believe I'd—" she glanced at Remy, "had anything to do with what happened to Brad. I can never thank you enough."

"I did what I hope someone would do for me in the same situation, that's all."

"It was so much more than that, but no matter what, thank you."

"She's right, you know," Gran said from behind her after Shelley and Jason walked away.

Lisa turned and smiled. Gran wore a flowered scarf over the bandage on her neck, paired with a white peasant blouse, colorful skirt and her favorite biker boots. "Words will never be enough thanks from me, either. I heard how you wouldn't give up on this foolish old woman, in spite of the way I've treated you."

"You had good reason. I should have gone looking for Mama sooner."

Gran stepped over and tugged the medallion out from under Lisa's blouse, held it in her palm. "Dazzle was so very proud of you. And so am I." Her eyes met Lisa's, wouldn't let her look away. "It was never your job to save your Mama from her choices. Deep in my heart I've always known that, but it was so much easier to blame you, when she wasn't there to blame. Or myself, when I should have tried harder. Will you forgive me?"

Lisa's throat closed and she hugged her Gran, hard. "Of course. Thank you."

Gran leaned back, kissed her forehead, love shining from her eyes. *"You're braver than you believe, stronger than you seem, and smarter than you think."*

Lisa was still grinning at the familiar quote from Winnie the Pooh as Gran moved away to chat with Janet, Gene Phillips's wife. Lisa's heart went out to the other woman, whose world had been turned upside down. Phillips would recover, but would spend a very long time in prison, possibly forever. He'd finally given up the burial location of the animals they'd hunted and more charges had been added. The DA was also planning to charge him with Wells' murder.

Lisa's phone pinged with an incoming email from Byte. He had found the source of the buried bones. According to a former employee, a small wildlife sanctuary had buried animals in the forest years ago, because they couldn't afford necropsies. The owner had died recently, but had been known for taking wonderful care of the animals. She thanked Byte and tucked her phone away.

"Officer Bass."

She turned at the cultured voice, surprised to see Martin Castile behind her, dressed in a white linen suit and panama hat. "How can I help you?" she asked.

His eyes were shadowed and he seemed to have aged years in the past few days. "I came to apologize on behalf of my nephew." He paused, swallowed hard. "I cannot fathom all the things he did, and I feel like a foolish old man that I didn't know what was happening right under my nose. Julio changed after his girlfriend left him. She'd taken one of your self-defense classes before she moved to Miami and I know he blamed you. But I had no idea of the hatred in his heart. To send you out to be hunted like an animal?" He shook his head. "I cannot wrap my head around it. I am so sorry you were put through that."

His genuine grief touched something inside her. "Dr. Castile, I have been learning that none of us are responsible for the choices others make. Especially when we are unaware of what they are doing."

He swallowed hard, then cupped her hand in both of his. "Thank you. You are most kind." He tipped his hat and then turned and left the gathering.

One shoulder propped against the post, she sipped her punch—which someone had liberally spiked with vodka—and watched him go. It would take a long time for him to heal.

She thought about her own grief and Gran's. That would take time, too.

A herd of screaming children raced by, laughing and chasing each other and she smiled, taking it all in. She'd never expected to truly feel like she belonged, ever again, and yet here, now, surrounded by Gran and the friends she'd made, she did.

It made her feel strong, confident in herself. Most of the women wore sundresses and cute sandals. Even though she had on jean shorts and flip flops, she'd paired them with a flowy sort of top the likes of which she'd never worn, but it had caught her eye the other day. Maybe it was time to leave old patterns and expectations behind, try some new things.

She sensed Pete step behind her just before his lips touched the back of her neck and made her shiver. "Nice blouse," he murmured, looking down the front of it. She turned toward him and swatted him playfully on the arm. "Stop. There are children present. Where did you disappear to?"

He stepped in front of her, tucked a strand of hair behind her ear. "Damn, Fish, if I'd known you were waiting for me, I'd have gotten here sooner."

Everything inside her stilled as their eyes met. Held. The intensity in his expression made her breath catch. They both knew he meant more than just this moment.

"Good things are worth waiting for."

"They certainly are." He cupped her cheeks. "I love you, Lisa. And I'm sorry I didn't say it sooner."

She raised an eyebrow, decided to make him grovel, just a little. "Kinda left me hanging, Bulldog."

He sighed. "Yeah, not my finest moment. I was scared to death of getting involved with you. You were a colleague." He paused, huffed out a breath. "Okay, fine, the truth is, I was a coward. You stirred up all these feelings I'd never had before, so I did the mature thing and ignored them. Figured they'd go away after a while. Like a cold."

Lisa laughed outright at that. "I tried that, too. Didn't work."

He grinned, then took her hand and led her away from the pavilion, to a secluded spot by the water.

"Where are we going?" she asked.

"Just wait."

When they finally stopped, she found a blanket spread on the ground, a bunch of bright gerbera daisies in a Mason jar, and a picnic basket beside it. Her gaze shot to his. "What's all this?"

In one smooth move, Pete went down on one knee and opened a little velvet box. Inside was a sparkling, filigreed antique engagement ring with a lovely diamond in the center.

"Lisa Bass, I love you and I will love you forever. Will you do me the honor of becoming my wife?"

For a moment, she simply gaped at him, unable to process what he was saying. But then she grinned and pulled him to his feet, wrapping her arms around his neck tight enough to choke him. "I love you too, you big lug! Yes, I'll marry you!" She pulled back far enough for a long satisfying kiss.

When they came up for air, he slid the ring on her finger. "Do you like it? It was my grandmother's. She and Granddad were married for sixty years. I'm hoping for at least that long with you."

The absolute sincerity in his eyes made her own tear up. She swallowed past the lump in her throat. "It's absolutely perfect. Especially knowing it's part of your family. But how did you know I'd like one this girly?"

His raised a brow. "I've seen what you hide under that uniform, Officer Bass."

She was laughing when she stepped over and grabbed him in a

choke hold. "But I can still take you down, Detective, and don't you forget it."

"Yes, ma'am," he croaked, grinning, as she let him go. "By the way, I think we should change Cat's name to Henrietta."

Lisa's eyes widened. "Henrietta? Really? You weren't kidding before?"

"Why not?" His eyes twinkled.

"Okay fine, but I get to name the children."

He went still, then that slow, sexy grin appeared. "Done."

She wrapped her arms around his neck and her legs around his waist and they kissed and laughed until they heard little Remy calling for them to come eat cake.

Acknowledgments

Though authors work alone when writing a book, getting it out into the world requires a whole team of people. I could not have done this without the support and encouragement of Leslie Santamaria, Lena Diaz, Jan Jackson, Jenna Kernan and Rebecca Heflin. Thank you for giving so generously of your time and expertise. You ladies rock! Huge thanks to Kim Killion of The Killion Group for the fabulous cover. As always, all my love to my hubby and family for their unwavering support and encouragement. And last, but never least, thank you dear readers, for letting me share my stories with you.

About the Author

Connie Mann is a licensed boat captain and loves writing romantic suspense stories set in Florida's small towns and unspoiled wilderness. She is the author of the *Florida Wildlife Warriors* series, the *Safe Harbor* series, as well as several stand-alone titles. When she's not dreaming up plotlines, you'll find "Captain Connie" exploring the beaches along the Florida coast and captaining eco tours on the Indian River Lagoon in New Smyrna Beach.

She is also passionate about helping women and children in developing countries break the poverty cycle and build a better future for themselves and their families.

She and her husband love hanging out with family and friends and heading off to explore new places. If those adventures include boating, so much the better.

Please visit Connie's website at www.conniemann.com to sign up for her newsletter, which always offers her latest news and contest information.